PΩP
APΩCALYPSE

POP
APOCALYPSE

A POSSIBLE SATIRE

LEE KONSTANTINOU

AN ecco BOOK

HARPER ⬤ PERENNIAL

NEW YORK • LONDON • TORONTO • SYDNEY • NEW DELHI • AUCKLAND

HARPER ● PERENNIAL

HarperCollins books may be purchased for educational, business, or sales promotional use. For information please write: Special Markets Department, HarperCollins Publishers, 10 East 53rd Street, New York, NY 10022.

FIRST EDITION

Designed by Claudia Martinez

Library of Congress Cataloging-in-Publication Data is available upon request.

ISBN 978-0-06-171537-2

09 10 11 12 13   OV/RRD   10 9 8 7 6 5 4 3 2 1

For my father, my mother, and Sabrina

WRITE THE THINGS WHICH THOU HAST SEEN, AND THE THINGS WHICH ARE, AND THE THINGS WHICH SHALL BE HEREAFTER.

REVELATION 1:19

PROLOGUE
CALL TO PRAYER

FROM THE NEWLY BUILT MINARET of the al-Aqsa Mosque, the mu'azzin shouts the noontime call to prayer, sponsored today by the Caliph Fred Entertainment Group.

Outside the wall of the Old City, Jerusalem's lunchtime crowds compete with electric mopeds for space on narrow lanes. Vans bring in Ethiopian and Filipino laborers from distant worker barracks to stations by the Lions' Gate. Eastward, smoke rises from Arab ghettos and from inside the heart of the Riot Zone, inside a Palestine gripped by a Fourth or, depending on which pundits you believe, Fifth Intifada.

Today's Terror Forecast has predicted a day of low-to-moderate unrest for East Jerusalem with mild political pressure moving inward from the west. Offprints of the *Jerusalem Post* jam defabricator bins and proclaim in three-inch headlines that some new atrocity has been committed somewhere against someone. Have no doubt: many someones are furious about this outrageous crime. Pundits across the global mediasphere are certain that the Situation could erupt into a veritable Crisis at any moment, if not a total Catastrophe. Everything is, in other words, more or less normal here.

The mu'azzin repeats his phrase, lengthens and elaborates it. His voice, amplified by loudspeakers, adds a spiritual humidity to the summer's drier, more disputative heat.

In Western Wall Plaza, Hasidim consult outmoded mobile phones, download news from the mediasphere, and loudly debate the Situation among themselves in Hebrew. American evangelicals dressed in Hawaiian shirts and khaki shorts, pretty blouses and flowery skirts, tour the courtyard of the mosque, recently reopened to non-Muslims after the previous Crisis resolved itself. The Christians, awed at the glimmering golden Dome of the Rock, take video with palmcams, documenting this climax to their Holy Land vacation package tour.

From the mu'azzin's vantage point atop the new minaret, a gift of the Caliph, the Christians are tiny and insignificant. Clustered together, they record everything, pointing cyclopean palmcam eyes at the sky, uploading images wirelessly onto their mediasphere travelogues for friends, family, and coreligionists. They seem, the mu'azzin notices, very interested in the sky.

A pale blue dot cuts a parabola across the sky's deeper blue. When the dot reaches the apex of its arc, it spreads what look like wings. The dot—which now looks like a man with wings, what an angel might look like if angels still visited the earth—is coming fast. Something is about to happen. There are a series of pops, explosions. The mu'azzin adjusts the brown skullcap on his hairless head. The Hasidim turn away from their debate. The evangelicals gasp and cheer, then pause expectantly.

And this is how the end begins.

PART I
THE TERROR FORECAST

ELIOT R. VANDERTHORPE, JR., HAS
a curious revelation.

It hits him like a cartoon anvil during a self-consciously hip, sincerely debauched party—raging now into its second week—in the executive suite of Barcelona's Hotel Internacional. Something doesn't sit right with Eliot as he watches his friend William Pearson, the British prime minister's son, take off his plaid boxer shorts and climb onto the king-sized bed. William is wearing a puffy white tuxedo shirt and is kneeling on the mattress, his lower body exposed, penis engorged. Two girls, a blonde and a brunette, lie on either side of him. They had until recently been wearing scanty party dresses. Now they're zoned out. You might say passed out.

A man with a palmcam records William and the girls while another man wearing mediashades orchestrates their action. These two, the videographer and the director, work for the show *That's So Fucked Up*, which streams every evening on the popular Sex, Lies, and Celebrities Channel. A curt wave of the director's hand indicates that the time has come for Eliot to strip off his tux and join in the fun.

At that moment some long-forgotten inner gear begins to move within Eliot.

"We're exploiting these girls," Eliot says. "We shouldn't have sex with them."

William turns to Eliot. "Wha? Have the drugs finally gotten to you, dude?"

True, hallucinogens, amphetamines, entactogens, and a number of other substances whose pharmacological effects have yet to be fully mapped have all taken turns blasting Eliot's brain over the last few weeks, so this strange feeling of ethical revulsion might be the by-product of an unforeseen drug interaction. And yet.

"No, man, I think I may have achieved a legitimate ethical realization."

"Does that mean I've gotta, like, fuck both these birds by myself?"

"We're on a tight schedule here," the director says. "We're streaming for the East Coast markets in two hours. So could you please take your ethical qualms outside? Just, well, out there."

The door to William's bedroom is open. A private bodyguard stands watch, smoking and waiting for the orgy to begin. Music pulses in from the main dance floor. Eliot feels the beat.

"Well, no," Eliot says. "I can't take my qualms outside." He deepens his voice to make it resonate and feels oddly noble as he speaks. "And I'm not going to participate in this."

"What the hell has gotten into you, Eliot?" William says.

"This is wrong. These girls don't even speak English."

"They spoke through their actions. Look, they're on the bed."

"They're *passed out* on the bed."

"We were making out before. And they signed release forms to appear on *That's So Fucked Up*."

"Man, William—that's, like, so totally beside the point."

William's erection slackens slightly at the labor of thought.

"They want this. We'll give their Reputations a huge boost on the market."

QED.

With every philosophical angle now satisfyingly covered, William turns back to the blonde girl, begins kissing her unresponsive lips in an effort to reinvigorate his deflated penis. The videographer moves in closer to the action.

In his hyperconscious state, Eliot becomes aware that he is holding a champagne bottle. I'm holding a giant bottle of Dom Pérignon, he thinks. The container of prestige cuvée seems suddenly more like a bludgeon than a bottle.

Eliot jumps on the bed. His vintage '00s-era Converse All Star high-tops sink into the mattress, but Eliot manages to keep his balance. William doesn't so much react to the bottle clocking him on the head as simply decide to give up on sex for the night and take a nap. The next blow breaks the videographer's palmcam into three pieces. The director, eyes wide, instinctively shouts "Cut!" and runs away.

The bodyguard approaches cautiously, probably convinced that Eliot has had an amphetamine-fueled psychotic break. Perhaps he has. The bodyguard calls for backup on his communications rig, which sprouts from his left ear like tiny calla lilies. The girls, Eliot thinks. I have to save the girls. But he can't carry both of them, so he has to choose. Eliot picks the blonde who'd been making out with him earlier, figuring that if she wakes up soon she might even consensually sleep with him. He thinks her name is Sonya.

Sonya is unexpectedly light. If not for his amphetamine high, Eliot imagines, he might not be able to simultaneously carry the blonde and fight the bodyguard. But he is and somehow he does. When the guard gets near the bed, Eliot kicks out his leg. The kick misses but the bodyguard takes a step back to dodge the blow, slips on a fragment of the videographer's palmcam, and falls on his ass. Holding Sonya in a fireman's carry, Eliot flees the bedroom.

Eliot shoves his way through dancing drugged-out revelers. The electronic backbeat of party music quickens his pulse. The bodyguard follows from William's bedroom and is joined by two others, all three dressed in matching black outfits featuring private security logos on red armbands. One fires his stun gun. Its projectile claw misses Eliot and instead sticks to a random dancer, a tall blond man. The blond man flies backward into other dancers, setting off a chain reaction of party panic.

Eliot lopes across the common area of the suite—littered with cracked champagne glasses, empty beer bottles, uneaten crab cakes, used and unused condoms, dried and drying bodily fluids, and a stratum of multicolored drug vials, among other things—toward the relative safety of his bedroom. He makes it to his room and kicks the door shut behind him. The door locks automatically. Within seconds, the bodyguards start pounding on it.

Sonya groans. Eliot screams when he sees his room.

Someone has thrown up on Eliot's bed, maybe the same guy who's masturbating on it now. The large print of *Guernica*, a gift from Sarah, has been ripped from the wall. "Give war a chance" is scrawled in black marker over one of the Cubist figures. Eliot's fancy new holographic tablet computer has been cut in half with garden shears, which are jammed into the wall. Partiers have ransacked the room's drawers and cabinets: clothes everywhere, empty bottles of wine, bookshelf tipped over, offprints of his philosophy books in shambles. Russell, Wittgenstein, Quine, Kripke, Davidson, Putnam. Someone has defiled his books with crayon-drawn picture stories that seem to involve lots of stick-figure men with hard penises and stick-figure women with their legs spread. Years of annotations, destroyed. The pounding on the door intensifies. Fuck. The door to his walk-in closet is open. Inside, two men are making out.

"Fuck!" he says.

"Sorry, dear, but we're married," says one of the guys, a beautiful

East Asian man with a British accent. He holds up his left hand and shows his ring. It's a nice ring.

"Glad to hear it," Eliot says. "Would you make sure no one, ah, manhandles this girl?"

"We don't manhandle girls in this closet," the Asian-British man says, arching an eyebrow. "Put her over there by the shoes and shut the door behind you."

"Super!" Eliot says. "Great! Thanks so much!"

Eliot lays Sonya down and closes the closet door. At exactly that moment, his bedroom door flies inward off its hinges. The three bodyguards, accompanied now by a few entrepreneurial partiers, who seem excited about the prospect of smashing in someone's head, have repurposed a heavy coatrack into a battering ram. Eliot still has his champagne bottle. I can fight them, he thinks, trying to talk himself into a posture of macho bravado. No you can't, another, more Eliot-like voice tells him. They'll break your bones into toothpicks and pick their teeth clean.

A window with a gaudy art deco frame is open nearby. Although completely panicked, Eliot does the only rational thing: he goes out the open window into Barcelona's August heat. As he shuffles his way along the narrow ledge outside, Eliot does his best not to look at the barrio below, fifteen stories down. The most nimble of the bodyguards follows Eliot onto the ledge. Eliot grips the champagne bottle—his only weapon if he's cornered—as if his life depends on it. A dozen feet along the ledge there is another window, open. Eliot climbs in, slams the window shut, and locks it.

A sound-canceling curtain dampens the outside music here in the executive suite's third bedroom. A different aural mood dominates this space: drums, sitars, electric guitar, Indo-Pakistani Pop. A dense sweet pot smell. This room has for the last few weeks been occupied by Sen. Jim Johnson's (R-KA) son Paul Johnson, the party's DJ. On Paul's king-sized bed sits a group of teenagers, Indians or

Pakistanis. They pass around a bong and play make-out games. The bodyguard on the ledge, meanwhile, squats outside the window and talks into his communications rig. Eliot can sort of read his lips. Get. Get the. Third bedroom. The bedroom's door, Eliot notices, cannot be closed. It has been ripped from its hinges.

"Shit," Eliot says.

"Are you troubled about something?" asks one of the boys.

"Troubled? You could say that."

"Might we be of assistance?" He offers a bong hit to Eliot.

"Who're you and how exactly might you assist me?"

The boy pulls opens his dress shirt, Supermanlike, to reveal his answer. Stenciled on the T-shirt underneath is a white logo against a green field: NATIONAL INDIAN TEENAGE COED JUJITSU TEAM.

"What are you doing in Barcelona?"

"What do you think we're doing? We participated in the International Teen Coed Jujitsu Championship."

"Of course, I should've guessed. And how did it go for you?"

"Poorly. We placed second."

"To answer your initial question then, ah, yeah, you can help me," Eliot says. "A bunch of guys who are somewhat angry at me and who are carrying tasers are about to come through that door. What can you do about that?"

"I suppose that depends on why they are angry at you."

"Because, well, I used this champagne bottle here to hit William Pearson."

"The prime minister's son?" asks a girl.

"I had my reasons. They were good reasons."

"Awesome!" say a few of the kids on the bed.

Without another word, the teammates, six boys and six girls, put their bong aside and position themselves strategically around the room. When the first bodyguard charges in, the kids engage in an amazing display of defensive offense, leveraging the bodyguard's own weight against him, knocking him into the door frame. The second guard, operating according to a sort of cartoon logic, trips over the first and falls on top of him. No one else tries to come through. Eliot runs toward the stacked bodyguards, turns and says, "Thanks a bunch, kids," and steps over the bodies. Eliot leaps off the back of the second guard and flies past the freelance goons.

Eliot finds himself near the suite's main entrance and pushes his way into the hall through a clot of fresh partiers. He runs past the elevator bank and into the building's stairwell. The stairs are packed with partiers sitting around, tripping and talking. The sound of heavy running echoes through the stairwell, rising upward from the lower floors. Two armbanded guards stomp up the stairs toward this floor. Out of his mind with drugged panic, unable to think where else to run, Eliot climbs up the stairs to the roof.

The roof of the hotel is full of people, maybe a hundred. Most are smoking cigarettes. Many dance to music synchronized across their earbuds. Some lie down flat on their backs and admire the stars. Large black cylinders with yellow crosshatching stand sentry on the far end of the roof. Eliot navigates around the partiers toward the edge of the building, hoping to find someplace to hide. Barcelona looks beautiful splayed out below; La Sagrada Familia is visible in the distance. When they figure out I'm up here, he wonders, will they beat the shit out of me or throw me off the top of the building? Probably both, he decides, and in that order.

On the canisters is stenciled the picture of a stick figure wearing a funny jumpsuit and leaping off a building. Emergency Building Escape System. Parachutes or ultralight kites. Thank God everyone's so paranoid about terrorism. Eliot opens one canister, finding an array of rectangular escape packages inside. Eliot picks one that claims it's designed for a six-foot-tall frame and breaks its seal.

The package unfurls into the form of a bulky red jumpsuit with yellow bulges. A small parachute-like bulge protrudes from the back. Additional bulges wrap around knees, elbows, shoulders, and around the midsection. Yellow gauntlets cover hands and booties cover feet. The suit even has a bulky yellow hood. Japanese and Korean instructions are inscribed everywhere.

The guards, now also on the roof, command the partygoers to get out of their way. One uses his stun gun to shut up an aggressive man, inspiring the rest to scatter. Eliot doesn't have any time to waste.

As he zips up the escape suit, Eliot finally notices, juxtaposed with one set of Japanese characters, the English-language suggestion that he "Please remember the string." Eliot assumes this means he's supposed to pull the thick red chord hanging off the bulge on the suit's chest—which is, by no reasonable definition, a string—after he jumps off the building.

Eliot climbs onto the roof's parapet, the toes of his yellow booties hanging over seventeen stories of empty space. He looks back over his shoulder. The guards have finally pushed their way through the partiers, and they look sort of agitated. Behind the guards some partiers have regrouped, forming a stoned insurgency. For about two seconds the guards seem uncertain about what to do. They must think he's trying to commit suicide. When they realize that he has put on a building escape jumpsuit, they charge, stun guns ready.

Stay calm. Eliot looks down. Seventeen stories. He would be crazy to jump. They're coming. He can't jump. Why does he still have the champagne bottle? One guard aims his stun gun. Jump, you idiot. He jumps. He pulls the chord. The partiers whoop with joy.

Two contradictory emotions shake his soul in quick succession. He feels at first very powerful and capable, practically omnipotent, James Bond on a mission to save the world. Then, when he realizes that no parachute will be opening for him, he feels ridiculous, shameful and pathetic, a loser driven by stupidity and lust, a bit more like Wile E. Coyote than James Bond.

This is what happens next: The jumpsuit stiffens Eliot into a cruciform position, a spinning spread-eagled human X. The yellow bulges pop in a preprogrammed sequence. Airbags rapidly inflate from these areas. In under three seconds Eliot R. Vanderthorpe, Jr., has transformed from a person into a gigantic inflated red and yellow beach ball. Beach Ball Eliot first bounces off the wall of the hotel and then off the plaza seventeen stories below.

Eliot bounces. Then bounces again. And again. Each bounce carries him a bit farther away from the hotel. Bounce, free-fall, bounce, free-fall, bounce, free-fall. Each bounce hurts a lot. Eliot loses count of the number of bounces at around thirty. The suit has become very hot. At some ambiguous moment Eliot's bouncing becomes rolling.

Rolling down an incline away from the Hotel Internacional, away from the drugged mania of the weeklong party, toward the beach, Eliot wonders whether he's going to stop rolling before he throws up and, more important, whether this feeling of shame will ever leave him.

$$\Omega$$

Shortly before dawn, Eliot wakes up in Plaça Catalunya, lying on his back in a shallow fountain, near the massive El Corte Inglés building. Beside him loiter families of homeless Turks who, too proud to be filthy, clean old-fashioned natural-fiber clothing. The men chain-smoke cigarettes and jabber in Turkish while their women scrub socks and underwear in fountain water. Kids huddle together nearby in sleeping bags. The sky is clear of clouds and the day is going to be hot. An absurdly large champagne bottle is wedged between Eliot's legs. Two rubber chickens float languidly beside him.

On the nearby steps, teenaged partiers play drums, work hard to seem soulful. You can tell they're not Americans. They've ignored the return of the '00s, so popular now in the States, and wear instead re-fashioned particolored West African robes and sandals, a fashion for brown-skinned sun worshippers from Barcelona to Buenos Aires.

A man dressed in a corduroy jacket and jeans pushes through the kids and approaches the fountain, heading straight for Eliot. He ignores the kids and they ignore him; they exist in parallel subcultural universes, unbreachable parapets of style standing between them. The Turks get out of the man's way. His wraparound mirrored mediashades mark him as an American.

The man makes it to the fountain. His mediashades glow darkly. His crew cut is very black. A bike messenger bag hangs limply at his side. Eliot pretends to be dazed, averts his eyes, and lolls his head. The man is wearing nice shoes, shiny and new.

"Eliot R. Vanderthorpe, Jr.," he says, his familiar voice penetrating in the manner of a corporate executive. "You're coming with me."

He squats and grabs for Eliot's wrist. Eliot weakly waves him away.

"Leave me alone. I'm so hungover."

Eliot looks up. The man has taken off his mediashades, revealing a familiar face. Tom Feldman, one of Eliot's best friends from his undergraduate days at Harvard. They met ten years ago through heavyweight crew and became fast friends shortly before uncontrolled partying had gotten Eliot kicked off the team. Tom is, as always, rugged and handsome. The crew cut is a new look.

"Dude!" Eliot says. "How'd you find me, man?"

"I used Omni, *man*. How else could I have found you?"

"No, I mean, how'd you, like, know to come looking for me in the first place?"

"A smarter question to ask, my friend, would be how I could have avoided knowing. Footage of your performance last night is all over the mediasphere. Your father's lawyers are billing crazy hours to put the genie back in its bottle. Mr. and Mrs. Vanderthorpe are less than happy with you right now. They've asked me to bring you home."

"My parents are such sweethearts."

"*That's So Fucked Up* looped this one shot of you striking the prime minister's son on the head with a champagne bottle, over and over."

"You're shitting me. They recovered that footage?"

"They also have footage of you attacking the videographer. You were practically foaming at the mouth."

Eliot grins. "That *is* fucked up!"

Tom smiles, teeth large and perfectly straight. His jaw juts squarely, green eyes reflecting the light of the rising sun.

"Funny, Eliot. That's just what your father said."

Eliot tries to remember everything that happened last night, to find among all the confusing episodes a fragment of memory that might justify his conduct.

"I was trying to do the right thing. I had, like, an ethical realization."

"Whoa, my apologies. Did your ethical realization involve discovering new things to do with bottles of Dom Pérignon? I think Moët et Chandon is suing the Vanderthorpe Family for brand degradation."

"I'm too hungover for your sarcasm, man."

Tom puts his mediashades back on, releasing Eliot's eyes from judgment, and extends a conciliatory hand. Eliot lets Tom help him up this time. His body burns with simultaneous hangovers from multiple drugs. On his feet again, still shaky, Eliot wipes his hair away from his eyes, adjusts his tux, and meditates on what to do with his oversized champagne bottle. He gives it to one of the homeless Turks in exchange for a cigarette; Tom lights the cigarette for him.

"So about the rubber chickens," Tom says.

"I honestly can't remember," Eliot says. "And really, I think I'd rather not know."

"Fair enough."

They walk together, abreast, slowly and in silence, toward the southern end of the plaza.

"So, man," Eliot says. "You're the business-guru-to-be. How's my Name doing post-party?"

Tom pulls out his tab. "It's a mixed picture. Analysts aren't sure how your shenanigans are going to impact your Name's value in the long run. Look here. Immediately after the footage aired, the price your Name could demand from the mediasphere skyrocketed. I'm talking a median of more than fifteen hundred dollars per minute. The illegal sites popped up shortly afterward, cutting into the official value, but you're still raking it in."

"Too bad Dad still owns the rights to my Name," Eliot says.

"The polling data, meanwhile, is pretty mixed." Tom opens the appropriate graphs. "Overall, your likability quotient has dipped slightly, most severely in heartland communities, but among certain global market segments you've shot up in a big way. It's the 'tweens: they're hungry for Eliot R. Vanderthorpe, Jr.,–branded merchandise: T-shirts, masks, toy robots, mediasphere avatars. You're a walking, talking counterculture. Sticking it to The Man in ways they can't. You speak for them. Karl ran some focus groups and—"

"Fuck Karl. Fuck his focus groups. I hate this shit. That's why I had to get away, Tom. I'm more than just a spur to consumption, man. I'm, like, a man."

"Yeah, I sympathize, Eliot. Truly, I do. But I'm telling you, look at this."

Tom navigates to Pricewaterhouse's Name Consultancy site. Eliot's Name, which was steadily declining in value during the years that he had attended grad school, has made up more than half of what it lost over those four years. The Discussion Board at *Eliot's Den*, the most popular "unofficial" fan site, lists eighty-five new topics and seven thousand text-original and transcripted postings. There are five thousand hours of voice chat archived. Fifty text-chat channels with subject names in a dozen languages are active right now. The Japanese and Simplified Chinese Rooms, filled by students posting from school, are running up the numbers fast. All this in less than seven hours.

"Wow."

"Wow is right. You've become unusually popular in India and Pakistan—historically not your strongest regions. From the perspective of the market, you're doing pretty well right now. The long run is a bit uncertain—but, c'mon, enough of this bullshit, Eliot. I've got to hear this. What was your so-called ethical realization?"

"That I've, like, been living a pretty fucked-up life these last couple months, Tom."

"I think Sarah, for one, might agree with you."

Eliot has been trying not to think about Sarah, about their fragile, ambiguous second attempt at a serious relationship. She had stopped trying to call a few weeks ago and the drugs had helped banish her almost entirely from his mental universe. The idea that Sarah has learned of his recent debauchery from the gossip sites nauseates him.

"Sarah. Oh, man. Fuck. Christ! Fucking Christ!"

"You shouldn't be blaspheming, Eliot. What would your dear parents say?"

"I'm in no mood for theological advice, Jew Boy."

"Careful with your rampant anti-Semitism," Tom says, seeming simultaneously amused, like the undergraduate version of himself, and pained, more like an adult than Eliot has seen him. "We live in geopolitically troubled times."

"Yeah, what else is new?"

"So you don't know."

Eliot's not exactly sure what he doesn't know. Before he can ask, Tom pulls out a bubble-wrapped tablet computer from his shoulder bag, unwraps it, turns it on, and hands it to him. "Take this, pal: your new tab." Eliot presses his thumb to the biometric reader on the tab's handgrip, looks into its camera, and says "Eliot Vanderthorpe." The tab imprints itself to him, and the persistent mediasphere site where Eliot does all his personal computing opens. All his files and apps are there, safe.

"Thanks, man," Eliot says. "I really do appreciate this. You're an awesome friend."

"I know," Tom says. "Seriously though, you ready to fly home?"

"Yeah, guess so, but I think I lost my passport and wallet and, like, everything I own."

"Your genomics and good Name will get you through passport control, no problem. You have a first-class cabin reserved on a Gooney out of Heathrow in twenty-four hours. Your father has one of his Jumper jets waiting at the Barcelona airport. He let me fly it in when he found out I was visiting friends in London. It's a terrific plane, Eliot, really first-rate. It's waiting for you. You'll be back in New York in no time."

"No way, man. I'm not ready yet. Let's walk to the sea. I need some coffee and we need to catch up."

"Sure, why not. The coffee will have to be on me, though."

As they pick up their pace, Eliot begins to feel horribly sore from last night's whole-body whiplash. His precipitous escape from the Hotel Internacional miraculously didn't break any bones, but he doesn't think he'll be walking normally anytime soon.

Ω

Eliot and Tom ramble past hundreds of tourist traps opening up on Las Ramblas, a world-historical boulevard that has managed over the course of the first third of this century to efface anything unique or particular about itself, to metastasize into just another filament of the growing multinational Brand Europe monoculture. Teenaged adventure-tourists—who consult guidebooks instead of tablet computers, openly smoke marijuana cigarettes, sit on overfull backpacks, and work as hard as possible to look like expatriates ready for authentic adventure—complete the cliché.

As they've been walking, Eliot's tuxedo's smartfibers have been drying themselves, squeezing all traces of moisture to the surface of the suit through peristaltic action, letting gravity take care of the rest. By the time they reach the Café George Orwell near Barceloneta, the sun's way up and Eliot has completely shed all but trace amounts of water from his tux. His hair and All Stars, however, remain soaked. Eliot orders a double espresso and plays around with his new tab. He browses through his mail and chats with Tom about old times. Though they have emailed each other and even occasionally talked in real time, Eliot hasn't seen Tom in more than a year. Last Eliot heard, Tom was about to enter B-School at Wharton.

Watching tourists on the boardwalk, Eliot toys with ideas of resistance. He doesn't *have* to go home. He still has cash in his account and he hasn't alienated all his friends. His social management app reports five friends have removed him from their friends list, and about a thousand people have requested that he add them. Most of the new requests come from kids between the ages of nine and thirteen. Creepy 'tween shit. When he accesses his financial management app, he finds that his accounts and credit lines have been frozen. He couldn't, if he wanted to, buy himself a pack of gum.

"Dad's frozen my accounts," he says, face flushing with embarrassment. He sounds, even to himself, like a whiny teenaged boy.

"Like I said, the coffee's on me."

The waiter brings them each another double espresso and Tom clears up the bill.

"Yeah, well, whatever." Eliot turns off his tab. "I guess the one good thing to come from all this shit is that we get to catch up. You coming back to New York or staying in London?"

"Neither."

"Why so ominous?"

"You probably haven't been following the news or watching the Holy Land Channel. There's a crisis, the possibility of war, Arabs versus Jews, maybe even the Caliphate versus the Freedom Coalition."

"Yeah, so what?" Eliot takes a sip of his espresso.

Tom may love this stuff, but geopolitics has always seemed to Eliot like so much science fiction, full of inscrutable jargon and complexities that have meant very little to his life. Eliot has something like an allergic reaction to even trace amounts of political discourse.

"So you really don't know," Tom says.

"I've been too busy, like, celebrating my premature departure from grad school to pay any attention to shit like that. That stuff's for you and Dad and Sarah. No offense, but who the fuck cares? It's all so silly and senseless."

"A lot of people care this time," Tom says. "These evangelicals posing as tourists attacked the Temple Mount. They launched a guy on a hand glider with a rocket launcher from inside East Jerusalem. The incident aired live on the Holy Land Channel.

Tom plays a clip on his tab. Pilgrims fleeing from the Western Wall. Holy Land Channel videographers jostling to catch every angle of the attack. The golden dome crumbling inward. IDF soldiers scaling the mosque walls. Columns of smoke exploding upward into the afternoon sky. The gunfire, which has served as a kind of soundtrack to the footage, suddenly goes silent and IDF soldiers reemerge from the mosque, unharmed, crisis over, just like that. When the footage loops back to the beginning, Tom pauses the scene.

"Sorry about those End Times fanatics," Eliot says. "I renounced them when I was like twelve."

"The nuts might just get what they want."

Eliot needs to lighten the mood. "Some of the more fundamentalist types, the ones that think we're in the middle of the seventh dispensation—like, our seventh contract with God—they argue that, well, global warming isn't a big deal, 'cause the world's going to end so soon anyway, so why bother doing anything about it? The end is nigh, man!"

"Nigh, indeed. Don't laugh. I saw this report on the BBC. Some more extreme rabbis in Israel are saying, well, half the dome's gone. They have some kind of red cow, ready to sacrifice."

"They have a red heifer?" Eliot wonders if it's from one of his father's breeding lines.

"Yeah, so they can build a new Temple if they want. The Caliphate isn't feeling so warm and fuzzy toward the Freedom Coalition anymore. Caliph Fred is using the attack to call for the formation of an 'Umma Alliance.'"

"What the hell's an Umma?"

Girls in ridiculously skimpy bikinis saunter past the café, chatting loudly among themselves in German and texting on palmtop computers, heading toward the beach. Eliot averts his eyes, looking toward the churning sea.

"You paying attention, Eliot? The 'Umma' is the whole community of Muslims. Like, not just the Caliphate and Imamates, but everyone. We're talking the United Nations here—Pakistan, Indonesia. Everyone's pretty scared of Caliph Fred, that he might turn his back on the West."

"Terrible, man."

"That's why I'm flying to Tel Aviv and signing up for the IDF. That's why I was in London, Eliot. I was visiting friends en route."

This gets Eliot's attention. "You're signing up for what? You can't be serious, man. The Israeli Defense Force? Your mother's going to kill you, Tom! Kill, kill, kill you."

Tom's face hardens into an expression that he must have had to make many times in the last few days. He speaks as if he's rehearsed his response.

"This is something I have to do. My mother doesn't like it, but she doesn't tell me how to live my life anymore. I'm twenty-seven years old. I'm a man. I make my own decisions."

"Your fiancée! Ah——"

"Rachel."

"Right, Rachel! Think about Rachel."

"She's not happy that I'm doing this either."

"You're not ideological, man. You don't want to build a Third Temple or claim Greater Israel or whatever. You want to make money, be successful, live the good life, all that stuff."

"My decision isn't about ideology," Tom says, his eyes narrowing, continuing with the script he must have developed to justify this decision. "It's about the survival of Israel. I've always believed that in all of our lives there comes a moment when you have to choose between what's easy and what's right."

"Man, Tom, you've never believed that," Eliot says. ' "A moment when you have to choose'? Where'd you come up with that bullshit slogan? Isn't that some kind of cheesy line from *Harry Potter*?"

"Yeah, it's kind of cheese-ball," Tom says. "But I'm serious. I want to do my part."

Eliot laughs nervously. "The real question, Tom, is who's laid claim to intellectual property rights for the al-Aqsa attack on the CRAP Database?"

Perhaps thinking about the economic consequences of the attack will lighten Tom's mood. Indeed, his face immediately reanimates.

"Some group no one's heard of. Horned Goat. Funny name."

"Yeah, funny." Eliot closes his eyes and sorts through the database of biblical references that he jammed into his brain during his days as a somewhat-more-devout young man. "That's a reference to the Book of Daniel, I think. Doesn't make any sense. Anyway, who-ever they are, if they've triggered anything remotely like the Apocalypse, they're going to be swimming in mediasphere royalties. *That* is going to be some mad money."

"There's some small hope we might avoid that. A Summit Telethon has been scheduled for early September. Caliph Fred is slated to be there. POTUS Friendly and other Freedom Coalition bigwigs, various Imams, even representatives from the UN. Big, big news. Sponsors are crawling all over this. The Nonlinear Television Corporation has accepted an application to form a new ad hoc channel to cover the Summit Telethon, the Apocalypse Channel. The Apocalypse is hot stuff."

"Exactly what I'm saying. Let's be serious. You're not going to be a hero. Israel doesn't need saving from destruction. They're part of the fucking Freedom Coalition. No one can beat the Foresight System. Forget about enlisting, man, hang out with me in New York for the rest of the summer, and go to B-School like you're supposed to. This whole Apocalypse thing is, like, just another media circus. It'll blow over."

Tom grows pale, his eyes hollow out. "I hope to God you're right—"

"Tom—"

"But I can't just assume—"

"Tom, don't do this. You're being crazy."

"I'm flying to Tel Aviv tonight. No one can stop me."

Eliot decides not to make this decision any harder for Tom than it probably already is. Further opposition would only strengthen his resolve. And anyway, Eliot would much rather not talk about evangelicals or the Holy Land or the possibility of some sort of apocalyptic war. Such things aren't pleasant to talk about. They aren't light or fun. After finishing his double espresso, Eliot is ready to go. Tom says he's going to stay behind and meet some friends before he flies out tonight.

They hug good-bye and Eliot hails a cab, which Tom has to pay for. During the ride to the airport, Eliot envisions his friend not in his normal business suit and khakis but rather in an IDF uniform, a rifle strapped to his shoulder, sand in his eyebrows, a dinged and dirty helmet capping his crew cut. Eliot can't decide whether to laugh or cry.

Ω

"Ideas matter," Reverend Hart Shining says to Jenny Raytrace, their faces on a screen illuminating Eliot's private cabin on the Heathrow-to-Newark supersonic Gooney. "And while we at Shining Ministries condemn terrorism—in all of its forms—we have to understand the context and history, not to mention the derision and discrimination, many in the End Times community have long faced. The secular humanists have been mocking and ridiculing us for almost half a century. Many of us have been waiting for the End Times for a long time, so it's understandable that some believers might become frustrated and, in their frustration, take extreme action."

"Reverend," replies Jenny Raytrace, the computer-generated hostess of this program, *CNN Livestream Live*. Jenny's facial movements are being mapped in real time from those of an actor, probably based in India. "Are you suggesting that those who blew up the Dome of the Rock ought to be forgiven?"

The screen splits into two segments. The right contains Reverend Shining standing in front of an image of Shining Tower in Manhattan, the international headquarters of Shining Ministries, Eliot's family's megachurch. On the left loops footage of the dome collapsing, leased from the Holy Land Channel. On the ticker at the bottom of the screen scrolls an ad for the Omni Science Corporation, sponsor of this *Livestream Live* segment.

"Don't put words in my mouth, Jenny. I never said 'forgive.' Only God has the power to 'forgive.' What I said is we have to bring some understanding and historical context to this situation. And we should remember, these poor misguided souls—they only blew up *half* of the Dome of the Rock. And no one died as a result of the attack. Terror implies terrorized people. Who, in this case, is terrified? And of what? It seems to me the only people who ought to be terrified are those who haven't yet been saved."

"Mr. Corefield, how do you respond to Reverend Shining's call for understanding?"

Christopher Corefield, a chubby reporter for the *Financial Times*, appears on the television screen, live from the Freedom Coalition's Benelux occupation headquarters in Brussels; there is an image of the Atomium behind him. Between ads, the ticker indicates that Mr. Corefield won a Murdoch Prize for his outstanding coverage of the Freedom Coalition's invasion of Belgium, Luxemburg, and the Netherlands (*Operation Muscles in Brussels*, all rights reserved).

Prior to the invasion, the International Criminal Court (ICC) had indicted an American soldier in absentia for war crimes allegedly committed during a minor African skirmish; the Coalition had responded by executing the terms of the 2002 American Servicemembers' Protection Act, aka the Hague Invasion Act. Occupation rights were subcontracted to French and German private military contractors. *Operation Muscles in Brussels* had become one of the Pentagon's hottest brands. Mr. Corefield, the ticker reports, courageously investigated the Pentagon's secret archipelago of merchandising and licensing deals: warfare apparel, games, toys, handsomely illustrated coffee table books, limited-edition tins of Belgian chocolates, not to mention the massive mediasphere residuals.

Mr. Corefield sneers. "Oh, yes, ideas do matter. Very much so. And that's why I have some serious reservations about Reverend Shining's assertions. We have to be very careful. The Reverend's statements are easy to interpret as an apology for terrorism. He seems to think that he can justify any actions by referring to Revelations."

"I never said—"

"Let me finish, Rev-er-end—"

"Revelations? It's Revelation—singular—or the Apocalypse of John, you secular-humanist ignoramus. You've probably never even read—"

"I didn't interrupt you, Reverend Shining. I didn't call you names. Let me finish."

"Let Mr. Corefield finish, Reverend Shining," Jenny says.

"Thank you, Jenny. As I was saying, Reverend Shining apparently thinks that it's acceptable for people to commit terrorist attacks if they're doing so in the name of Jesus, but we've got to apply the same standards across the board. Which isn't to say I don't fully support Israel's right to use force to protect itself, and I fully expect now that the Dome of the Rock's half blown up that the whole al-Aqsa complex might as well be bulldozed and let's get on with building the Third Temple, as has been proposed. We have to be realists and moderates. This is just what the facts on the ground happen to be. But we should have the courage to say, in a principled way, that the terrorist actions Horned Goat owns the intellectual property rights to are immoral. Horned Goat, whoever they are, are especially responsible because they can collect royalties on for-profit video replays of this attack. They own this act of terrorism in a very literal sense and need to speak up."

Reverend Shining's long, angular face takes on a patina of wrathfulness. "You are fully aware, Mr. Corefield, that under the Conceptual Rights and Patents Act the legal owner of a terrorist action isn't *necessarily* criminally responsible for that action. A terrorist who has hijacked a plane, for example, has already signed over his intellectual property rights to the carrier when he purchases his tickets. Horned Goat's *criminal* liability has yet to be determined in this case, as I'm sure its lawyers will be shortly letting you know."

"You're right, of course," Mr. Corefield says. "But, if you were paying the slightest bit of attention, you would have noticed I said nothing—"

Eliot stops the program, disgusted at the debate, and loads up a classic episode of *The Simpsons*, the one where the family, in therapy, viciously electrocute one another. But even *The Simpsons* fails to divert his attention, so he shuts off the show. In the last month, it has come to seem as if nothing can distract him anymore, as if the part of his brain that once took pleasure in frivolity has died from over-stimulation. His dangerously close encounter with ethical thought has made things even worse. He reclines in his chair and listens to the Gooney hum.

Ideas matter. This was the slogan Father had given him before he began grad school. And indeed, ideas had come to dominate Eliot's life. As an undergrad at Harvard, freshly released from the private school mill that had built him into a strikingly accomplished and perfectly boring applicant, Eliot had discovered that he had pretty much no interest—or talent—in any discipline except for the art of partying and the science of analytic philosophy. This latter endow-ment, however useless as fodder for conversation at parties, dovetailed naturally into Eliot Sr.'s plan for him. Eliot Sr. had suggested that Jr. might benefit from advancing his knowledge in mathematical phi-losophy if he ever hoped to have a fruitful career. Suggested that get-ting a PhD in applied philosophy might be a necessary—though not sufficient—condition for Jr.'s admission into the executive ranks of the company Sr. had founded, the Omni Science Corporation.

Unsure of what else he might do with his life, Eliot eventually applied to Harvard's applied philosophy PhD program, and he got in, which was not a surprise. He was, after all, a Harvard man all the way.

Graduate school had gone well enough while he was taking classes, but at the dissertation phase of the program—after he had imbibed hundreds of technical books on meaning, concepts, heaps, piles, things, ideas, possible worlds, naming, necessity, truth, symbolic systems, and representation—Eliot found himself disgusted with having to split already endlessly split philosophical hairs more finely still. He had joined the Elvis Lab, which ran off a generous grant from Elvis Presley Enterprises. His dissertation's working title was *Sorting Problems with Young vs. Old Elvis Impersonators,* and it would have dealt with the logical and conceptual problems of demarcating parameters to generate models of Elvis impersonators who found ways of fusing and remixing defined classes of Elvis in ways evocatively Elvis-like but technically outside the formal definition of Elvis Presley Enterprises' Elvis Brand Family. Millions in royalties lost every year.

Things got bad for Eliot when a now former friend, a psych resident at Harvard's McLean Hospital, began surreptitiously writing him prescriptions for Axion, a new drug created by Pfizer designed to help victims overcome Self Doubt Syndrome. Under its confidence-boosting influence Eliot had ended up callously hurting many people—his friends, family, and (most important) Sarah—but he had not cared much at the time, having managed through pharmaceutical means to repress the self-consciousness that normally crippled him with paralytic doubt and uncertainty.

Eliot would rather forget his final meltdown. The Gooney will land in two hours. Enough time for a nap. He closes his eyes and falls asleep and dreams he's bowling with young Elvis and the risen Jesus. Elvis proves to be the better bowler.

Ω

When the scanner matches Eliot's genetic code to the records on file in the Homeland Security database, the gate swings open. A federal guard with an XM8 strapped to his neck waves him through. A red, white, and blue sign comes into view: WELCOME TO AMERICA. Eliot steps through the gate and follows his fellow passengers down a long corridor. The people coming off the supersonic Gooneys are generally so well-to-do that they do not even ogle Eliot (a frankly minor celebrity) as he walks among them toward the baggage claim.

The PA system announces in a pleasant-sounding female voice:

"The Terror Forecast reports that Background Rioting Levels are high tonight. Please proceed with caution if you're traveling into New York City."

Yeah, welcome to America, Eliot thinks, doing his best to forget his anxiety, letting himself notice the architecture of the terminal. Even in his funk, the new Gooney Terminal at Newark Airport is an impressive sight, a unique work of evolutionary design, organic, smooth, very Swedish. Sarah says it's one of the most important architectural achievements of the last decade, a surprisingly successful fusing of technological and biological motifs.

Eliot doesn't stop at the claim area. He has no baggage, nothing to declare. In the pickup zone, amidst a cascade of loving hugs and kisses, Eliot expects to see Father, Mother, possibly Sarah, maybe even his Reputation Manager Karl. He has so much to tell them and so much to apologize for. But the only one here is Pedro Ortiz. Despite being only twenty-two, Pedro has become one of the Vanderthorpe Family's most trusted drivers. Pedro wears a nondescript blue suit that's too large for his very skinny frame and holds a sign on which "ELIOT VANDERTHORPE" is written. The sign is upside down.

"Why Mr. Vanderthorpe," Pedro says. "Imagine meeting you here!"

"Don't Mr. Vanderthorpe me, man," Eliot says. "I'm really exhausted. Let's just try to get home without getting blown up."

"It's only Background Rioting, guy. Nothing to worry about."

"What a relief."

The drive into Manhattan is mostly quiet. Pedro has to take a detour through Staten Island and Brooklyn to avoid a large swath of New Jersey that the Terror Forecast strongly suggests drivers circumvent. A few rifle shots bounce off the Humvee's bulletproof carapace, a tempting target for amateur snipers. At one point, in Staten Island, Pedro swerves to avoid a large incendiary something or other—it looks sort of like a cat, on fire—that comes running toward them from the side of the road. Their trip proves otherwise uneventful.

Soon enough, the Freedom Tower comes into view, looming monolithically—illuminated in red, white, and blue floodlights—a striking sentinel keeping guard over lower Manhattan. All at once, the machine-gun- and antiaircraft-missile-studded parapets of the Manhattan Island Wall appear. Two nearby machine guns, mounted on the Brooklyn Bridge, turn on servos toward the Humvee. After the Omni-powered security system decides that the Humvee doesn't pose any threat to the island of Manhattan, their electronic visa clears with the final security checkpoint, and the E-ZPass toll collection system takes its due, they're allowed to proceed across the Brooklyn Bridge. Inside the Wall, pockmarked roadways become suddenly smooth and clean. Home again, Eliot thinks. Safe.

Near the southeast corner of Central Park, the Omni Science Building becomes visible. The skyscraper looks something like the most aerodynamic wing ever designed stood upright on its side, two hundred stories tall. Just above the tower's slender top hovers an O-shaped ornament, an electric blue halo seemingly unattached to anything, home to the corporation's executive offices, the tethers and walkways linking it to the substructure below invisible. A decade ago, Father had torn down the Plaza Hotel to build Omni Science's international headquarters, announcing to the city that a new force had come to town.

"That halo still freaks me out every time I see it," Pedro says.

Eliot smiles. "Dad used to say Omni Science was eating its own dogfood. Building it was, like, a dare to terrorists. 'Beat Omni if you can.'"

"A big fucking bull's-eye."

"I used to get these panic attacks thinking about it. What might happen. How it could happen at any time."

"It's still standing, I guess."

"Still standing."

"Guess Daddy Vanderthorpe, he turned out to be right."

"Yeah."

Pedro drops Eliot off in the underground parking garage of the Transcontinental Building on the Upper East Side. As soon as he gets to his suite on the top floor, Eliot strips off his clothes and collapses onto the bed in his bedroom and sleeps for almost twenty hours straight.

Ω

Eliot wakes from a dreamless sleep to find himself in an alien space. Blearily, he studies the white walls that surround him. This is his room in only the most abstract sense, one node of the globally distributed network of apartments that he calls home. The room's minimalist décor feels strange to him, very unlike the book-filled slop pits he chose to live in as a grad student. The invisible army of servants that his father pays to maintain this suite have probably spent more time among these rooms than he ever will.

A smartwatch sits on his dresser, put there while he was sleeping in case he should need it. The media elements on its face and wristband have been well-disguised. The watch recognizes his touch, purrs, and turns itself on. The time is 4:42 a.m. The skies over New York are the color of a deep bruise. A perpetual twilight stalks Eliot across the globe. Even when he stayed in one place for longer than a few weeks, even during the most routine moments of his graduate career, he woke up while others slept, slept while they worked. Eliot knows he won't be able to get back to sleep now, so he decides to piss, shower, eat, and take something strong for his headache.

Eliot stumbles through his mediaroom on his way to the bathroom. This room consists of three mediawalls, one wall-sized window that can also become a screen, and a central terrain landscaped with two futons, a media pit, and a glass coffee table covered with controllers neatly arrayed in a fan pattern. On the table, a meal has been prepared for him: an omelet, some fruit, and a glass of juice. He thinks at first that a servant has made this for him until he sees Sarah come out of the bathroom.

She is naked, holding a towel with which she has just been drying herself. A Chinese character—de or "virtue"—is tattooed below her navel. Her body looks to Eliot like just another element of this room's total design philosophy: sleekly lined, toned, awkward in a sexy way, breasts beginning to sag here at the tail end of her twenties. Their eyes meet. Sarah's curly blonde-brown hair, still wet from the shower, sweeps away from her head like the strokes of a Jackson Pollack painting. Her blue eyes bulge a bit from an oval skull, absorbing and warmly empathetic in a way that makes Eliot feel regretful. She's so incredibly beautiful, he thinks. So smart, so committed to improving the world.

Eliot discovers a dilemma in need of philosophical intervention: on one side of the existential ledger, he feels the need to immediately justify himself to Sarah, to confess all his myriad sins, to beg her for forgiveness, and, on the other, his bladder, very near to exploding, demands attention. What to do?

"Don't move," he says.

Sarah says nothing as he jogs past her. In the bathroom, he bends his morning erection uncomfortably toward the toilet, pees and pees, and notices that Sarah's mood stabilizer bracelet is by the sink. Not a good thing. She's not supposed to take it off. She'll be mad at him if he asks her about it, so he decides to pretend he hasn't seen it.

For reasons he cannot fully articulate, Eliot decides to take off his boxers and go back out into the mediaroom naked. Sarah is leaning against a mediawall, crying. Eliot does what he always does at moments when Sarah feels stressed out or sad: he gently rubs her shoulders and locks his eyes onto hers. His penis, at half mast, accidentally pokes her in the belly.

Sarah lets him stand close. Eliot begins to swivel his hips and pokes Sarah repeatedly in the stomach. "Poke, poke, poke," he says, enunciating the word "poke" in time with his actual pokes. At first she does not react to the poking, but soon she's laughing and crying at the same time. He stops poking her to wipe tears from her cheeks.

"Hi there," he says. It seems like the right thing to say, something he thinks he once heard in a movie.

"Hi there?"

"I suppose I have some explaining to do."

Eliot grins stupidly, adopting the naughty boy persona that has over the years served him so well with women by transforming all his doubt, guilt, and shame into a scripted but charming routine. Sarah knows exactly what he's trying to do and indicates her displeasure by grabbing his pathetic boylike chest hair. Her eyebrows come close to meeting at the center of her face. Her mouth twists into a snarl.

"Some explaining to do! Don't give me that sitcom bullshit."

"Sarah!"

She rips out a handful of his chest hair.

"Fuck, that hurts. Are we even now?"

"Not even close, you jackass." She grabs another handful of hair.

"The bracelet. Put the bracelet on. You're losing your cool, Sarah."

"No, darling, I'm not losing anything. I'm off the bracelet. The bracelet is just a way of dealing with women with deviant thoughts and I've frankly come to like my deviant thoughts. I only use the bracelet when I get really crazy."

"And this isn't crazy? My chest hair isn't misogynistic. If anything it's—fuck!—more of a feminist than I am. And, me, you know me, I *love* women. Stop!"

She stops pulling on his chest hair and looks at his chest. "What the hell is this?" she says.

She jams her index finger hard below his left nipple. An animated "Jesus Saves!" fish tattoo wiggles to life on his chest.

"When did I get that?" Eliot taps the spot under his nipple and the tattoo winks off; another tap turns it back on. "Must have been some kind of joke, I guess. Probably seemed funny when I was drugged."

"Ha ha," Sarah says.

She decides to rip another handful of hair from his chest. This hurts, but Eliot does not stop her. Then he finds that he's kissing Sarah and—much to his surprise—that she's kissing him back. Eliot goes with it, acting as if he knows exactly what he's doing. They haven't had sex in almost two months, but their bodies respond with familiarity and routine. We were so perfect for each other, he thinks as they move, wrapped in each other's arms, kissing frantically, toward the larger futon, before remembering that he had been the one to break up with her. Slightly drunk at the time, he had suggested that she was an idiot for ever wanting to be with someone as completely useless and fucked up as him; he had made it his mission in Europe to prove just how useless and fucked up he was.

After destroying his second chance with her, Eliot hadn't expected that he would have a third. They wordlessly have sex, amidst a small landscape of designer pillows, a Li'l El dancing doll, and stuffed animal robots—a bear, a bunny, and a kitten—which sit on the edge of the futon watching them, purring softly.

$$\Omega$$

Is Eliot a sexist jerk?

This question has often shot across the earth's girdle of satel-

lites and fiber-optic cable, pumping the mediasphere with a juicy
controversy that competes ferociously with Middle Eastern skir-
mishes and threats to the future of the species for a share of the collective attention of the viewing world. The mediasphere's consensus
goes something like this: "Sure he's a sexist jerk, but we sure love
that Eliot!" Professional analysts have tended to ask more serious
questions, such as: "How will Eliot's behavior affect the value of his
Name?" The market's answer has been complex.

After meeting her at a MOMA summer fund-raising event, Eliot
had pursued Sarah Glickman for most of the fall semester of their
sophomore year as undergrads at Harvard. She was an art history
major with a special interest in contemporary Chinese art. She had an
intense passion for politics and was drawn above all to driven men,
men of action. She was the kind of girl for whom you either mattered
or meant nearly nothing. Eliot found himself in the latter category.
Sarah wanted to date a man and Eliot was a boy.

At the time, she was involved with a senior political science major
named Chas Rockwell, who was passionately fighting for the rights
of some indigenous group or other in some backward part of the
world, and she spent most of her free time vigorously protesting the
Freedom Coalition's creeping global hegemony. She did this by writing articles about abstract artworks with politically subversive themes
and by organizing, on campus and around the Greater Boston Area,
"Art-Ins Against Empire." Her emotional intensity intrigued Eliot,
even if he didn't particularly care for any empire outside the radius of
his own dick.

Eliot was used to being around women who were eager to sleep
with him, women "whose sense of self-worth was proportional to the
value of the Name of the man they fucked," in the words of Vanessa
P. Trill, an amateur fan-scholar. But the value of Eliot's Name and
his middling celebrity status didn't impress Sarah at all. If anything,
she was anti-impressed.

Faced with these obstacles, Eliot did all the romantic things a guy in his position ought to do: he dogged her around campus, sent her thousand-dollar flower arrangements, and cornered her at parties to read kitschy love poetry. Creepy? Maybe, but Eliot was among other things ferociously smart and charming. As Sarah admitted later in an interview with *Vogue*, she "hadn't expected that." She had thought he would turn out to be some kind of legacy kid—Eliot's mother, maternal grandfather, and great grandfather had all gone to Harvard—a fool, a party boy, a jerk. She had dated enough jerks and had vowed to herself to never make that mistake again. Eliot ultimately did turn out to be a jerk, but he was a charming jerk, egotistical but self-effacing, amoral but self-conscious, and he could make her laugh. That—and not the flowers or the lavish gifts or his celebrity status—won her over.

They kissed for the first time after a February blizzard that had transformed Cambridge into a winter-themed amusement park. Eliot had recently sent an email to Sarah explaining how very much he admired her commitment to political activism and how he had himself recently become an avid fan of experimental art and how he had written a villanelle he thought she might like to hear him recite and so on. Sarah decided that she was sick of his buffoonish courtship—smart and funny were fine things for a friend, but she was committed to Chas—so she went to Eliot's house to confront him.

The blizzard, which started softly that afternoon, trapped her at his house. They stayed up all night talking. Why did she find these self-obsessed boys attractive? She and her therapist had been working for years, with little success, on finding an answer to this question. Some overcompassionate part of her, her therapist speculated, took pity on those who couldn't support themselves. By morning, she had fallen into the same trap.

As the sun began to rise, Sarah and Eliot walked together through the snow-packed streets of Cambridge. Trying to wade through a deep bank of snow, Sarah fell over into Eliot's arms. They stood there that way for exactly fifteen seconds, and then the sexual tension that had been building between them all night released itself: they kissed. After a kiss that lasted seven seconds, Eliot and Sarah fell over and were buried together under a foot of snow. To this day, there is no consensus on whether or not this fall was an intentional move on Eliot's part.

Footage of The Kiss, as it soon came to be known, hit the mediasphere in less than twenty minutes. A paparazzo hanging around in a tree ten blocks away, wielding a palmcam with a telescopic lens, had recorded the whole thing. Upset at his public humiliation, Chas broke into Eliot's house that night and beat him bloody. Eliot, a pacifist at heart, didn't stop him. Chas found himself newly single and charged with battery, his very long-term hopes for the White House more or less scuttled at the age of twenty.

Eliot's Name took a devastating hit as lovesick girls around the world started abandoning *Eliot's Den*. For their part, the evangelical gossip magazines—*Good Girl, Miss Magazine*, etc.—weren't entirely pleased that Eliot was dating someone Jewish or that he might actually, God forbid, be having premarital sex. Sarah, meanwhile, became the center of her own fan industry. Mediasphere sites were erected in her honor from Hong Kong to Stockholm. Searches for her Name on Omni spiked. At its peak, the median price her Name could earn hit $500 per minute of video.

Eliot and Sarah dated for three and a half years. It was a prickly relationship, subject to volatility and panic, mostly Eliot's, sometimes Sarah's. When the Freedom Coalition invaded Iceland (*Operation Icelandic Saga*, all rights reserved), Sarah's activist rage, coupled with Eliot's indifference to the political situation, almost led them to break up, but in the end they overcame the crisis and they decided to stay together. These were, all told, probably the happiest years of Eliot's life, the years during which he felt most fully human. Eliot knew his happiness couldn't last.

After graduation, Sarah went overseas for the year on a Fulbright to do research on emerging art markets in rural China. Eliot stayed behind in the States and burned through his father's endless supply of money, doing nothing much, always promising but never finding the time to visit her. With Sarah gone, the amateur fan-scholar Brad Alton speculates, Eliot must have begun to wonder "if it was Sarah he loved or the idea of Sarah, if she, in all her textual specificity, made him feel more fully human or if she was just giving him a taste of that condition of personhood toward which he so desperately aspired. The one way for him to find out would be to try dating other people."

Eliot loved Sarah—no one has ever doubted that—but he had never been particularly good at controlling his lustful impulses. On reflection, his three-and-a-half years of fidelity must have been some sort of freak statistical anomaly, "an outlier rather than a data point," in the words of one commentator. Women constantly hit on Eliot, angling for their fleeting chance for that share of the mediasphere's spotlight his presence could afford them, not to mention his money. After almost a year of celibacy in Sarah's absence, and only a month before she was going to return permanently to the East Coast, Eliot finally transgressed with Harvard junior Julie Soon, daughter of Reverend Daniel Soon, a family friend.

They had been at a party at his house in Cambridge, where Eliot had remained after graduation. Julie came to the party wearing only a designer bra and panties under her bathrobe, rebelling against the restrictive piety of her family. Wanting to help her in her rebellion, Eliot brought her to his room to help her remove even these. What Eliot had not anticipated was that his indiscretion would be recorded by one of his housemates and distributed onto the mediasphere. Within twenty-four hours the value of Eliot's Name shot up to a median of $1,000 per minute, and he became the talk of all the scandal sites. Sarah sent him a long, nearly incoherent email from Gansu province. She would be taking the first Gooney back to the US as soon as she could get to Beijing. When she sobered up, Julie blamed her actions on the booze. Eliot offered no excuses for himself.

It has been noted, in the amateur pop-histories of the Eliot-Sarah relationship available on the mediasphere, that even after Eliot's infidelity Sarah didn't want to break up; she blamed herself for being away so long, for failing to detect the warning signs that their relationship might be in trouble. It was Eliot who broke up with her when she finally came to Cambridge. The alcohol and drugs, Eliot later said in a *GQ* interview, had not really impaired his judgment.

Eliot knew exactly what he was doing when he slept with Julie Soon and his actions had helped him realize that he could no longer commit to Sarah. He had decided that the cult of monogamy was "a sham designed to make people feel ashamed of themselves." His and Sarah's tragic mistake had been to think that buying into this institution had any value whatsoever. Monogamy wasn't the only game in town. It wasn't the only route to personal fulfillment. Sure, Sarah was still attached to him, but she would move on, and their friendship would end up being that much more valuable to her because it was predicated not on any artificial set of expectations, conservative cultural symbols, or idealized standards of sexual behavior, but rather on a pure and loving free association.

In the mediasphere, different philosophical schools had developed among Eliot R. Vanderthorpe, Jr., fan-scholars on the ethics of Eliot's argument. A panel at a recent Amateur Celebrity Studies League conference in Cleveland, Ohio, ended inconclusively when Background Rioting overwhelmed the Cleveland Convention Center, catapult-propelled Molotov cocktails crashing through its second-story windows. The latest word on the subject has been offered by Dominick McWillis, an accountant who moonlights as a Marxist fan-scholar specializing in Celebrity Studies. He concludes in a recent article that:

> An examination of the historiography of the Eliot-Sarah breakup reveals an interesting division into three stages of the so-called Anarchist Argument controversy.... The final, current, and third stage of materialist inquiry has moved beyond the formal aporias of the "Anarchist Argument" into the fundamentally political—that is to say, always material—underpinnings of the dialectic of desire and boredom that has produced the chiasmic exchange of positions in which Eliot's putatively unfaithful act structurally inverts the justification of the breakup as, *inter alia*, institutional critique *as such*, thus marking Sarah into the negatively interpellated subject position of antifeminist traditionalist, revealing, in the barest trace of an outline, a kind of allegory of multinational space itself as the site within which institutional critique dialectically inverts all agency-based frameworks by unearthing the absent trace known as Utopia. We cannot overstress the importance of this development.

This is the consensus of the technical fan-scholarship, but Pat Singer—a barista based in Austin, Texas—perhaps put it best when he wrote, in a post on the *Celebrity Life* forum, that "Eliot's a self-satisfied jerk. Sure, Sarah might be a little unstable, and okay, she has a track record of dating some pretty terrible guys, but she is really a saint of a girl, and Eliot messed up big-time."

Eliot agrees with this statement and has always felt terrible about breaking up with Sarah but concludes that it was the best course of action, because he has always known that if he were ever to marry anyone it would have to be Sarah, but has also always known that Sarah deserves better than a bastard with a cheating heart, and has decided therefore that it's better that he cheated because actually cheating proved beyond any atom of doubt that he should never have been with Sarah in the first place, and so what else could he have done but fuck Julie Soon?

Ω

Dawn's first light gently shakes Eliot awake from a postcoital haze, coaxing him to shower and dress, as if he had plans for the coming day. Through his mediaroom's window Manhattan sprawls before and below him like an electrified coral reef, an ecosystem of steel and plastic and newer, more composite materials and a mass of small fleshy bug-sized humans going about their business before the morning rush hour. Near the horizon, past Central Park, a flash pops from inside the Riot Zone in New Jersey. Something has exploded. Eliot wonders where Sarah has run off to. He had promptly fallen back asleep after they had had sex and when he woke up, she was gone, the food she had prepared cold. Another column of flame erupts in the distance. Lights in the sky, helicopters, veer toward the place where the explosions went off.

His smartwatch rings—Father's ringtone. Eliot routes the call to his voice mail, which has accrued fifty-seven messages, all from handlers and assistants. This is, so far, the only call from a member of his family.

Eliot takes a step back from the window wall, makes a hand gesture to turn it reflective, and checks himself out. He's prepared himself in case Sarah should come back. The reflection that greets him wears a brilliant red T-shirt emblazoned with a Rorschach-fuzzy black Che Guevara image, corduroy pants, and a pair of bowling shoes, size twelve. A black five-point star is tattooed on the inside of his left forearm. He's wearing a silver thumb ring etched with a tribal

pattern. His facial hair has gotten out of hand and his eyes are ringed
with puffy flesh. The body before him appears to be in major-league
withdrawal from something.

Eliot gestures the mirror from reflective to opaque and wanders
over to a futon to watch television. Eliot browses through a batch of
news channels, but everywhere he looks he finds the same shit, tensions in the Middle East, markets on uncertain footing, devastating
weapons systems deploying here or there, Temple Mount this, nuclear
Armageddon that. Sick of all this End of the World bullshit, Eliot
waves away the news feeds and shuffles through various entertainment
channels—Pimp My Bitch, the Fluffy Bunny Network, the Gangland
Warfare Channel, and Toothpaste Central, among others—finally
settling on the VH3 livestream of *I Love the '00s*.

Second-tier celebrities reminisce about the year 2003 and recall
the "Shock and Awe" campaign against Iraq, back when the country was run by Saddam Hussein, before it was broken up and had
its sundry parts reabsorbed into the TransArabian Caliphate, the
Federation of Imamates, and the Republic of Kurdistan. OutKast's
"B.O.B. (Bombs Over Baghdad)" accompanies key images of the war.
Buildings being blown up. Embedded reporters riding in the back of
military convoys. "B.O.B." is an anachronism, technically, part of the
Stakonia (2000) album, not *Speakerboxxx/The Love Below* (2003). Eliot
was very young when the war happened; most of what he knows about
it comes from movies, video games, and other mediasphere diversions.
Sometimes his father tells stories about encounters he had with per-
nicious antiwar activists, but his father had spent most of the war
stationed in South Korea and had mostly avoided direct contact with
dissidents.

Older celebrities recall their reactions to the Shock and Awe campaign. "That was a dark day," reports Paris Hilton, who does not
seem to be aging well. "And we still don't know where the real Saddam
Hussein went. We may never know." Inevitably, Paris compares the

Iraq war to the subsequent invasions by the Freedom Coalition, under US leadership, of the Bolivarian Federation, Iceland, Benelux, and, most recently, Northern California, after the earthquake. Eliot liked Paris better before she turned to celebrity activism.

The mediaroom's door opens and Sarah comes in wearing her best fashionista getup, a fusion of eras of the near past themselves nostalgic for still more mythical near-past epochs. Subversively challenging hegemonic notions of stylistic originality, she's wearing '00s-era Adidas, green capris, a T-shirt with a Lichtenstein emblazoned on it. The thought balloon above the face of the crying woman on the T-shirt, at about breast height, says "That's the way—It should have begun! But it's hopeless!" A vinyl gym bag with a PEN logo hangs from one of Sarah's shoulders.

Sarah carries two large Greek coffee shop cups, one in each hand.

"I thought you left me, Sarah."

"No, darling. It was you who left me. Twice."

"About last night."

"We aren't going to talk about that now. This is for you."

Eliot kisses Sarah on the cheek and accepts the coffee.

"What I did—"

"We're not talking about that. Let's just be glad you're not being pulled out of a Dumpster in Barcelona."

"It's good to see you, too. Sometimes—I mean, it's funny how you can get into this state of mind and forget what's important. I think I've had an epiphany, an ethical realization."

Eliot feels sentimental all of a sudden. When he leans forward to kiss her, this time on the mouth, she backs her head away and holds open the small olive-skinned palm of her free hand in warning.

"None of that, darling."

"Are we through, then? For good?"

"I'm going, Eliot. I have a Ninjaerobics class before work."

She finishes her coffee, tosses the empty paper cup into the matter defabricator, and leaves Eliot standing there alone with a pounding headache, a puffy body, an empty stomach, and a steaming cup of coffee. He sits down onto a futon and drinks in silence, regretting this decision almost immediately when the coffee starts corroding the inner lining of his empty stomach.

Stop thinking about her, he tells himself.

On the coffee table, he finds a controller and lets himself get lost in a Pentagon-licensed video game called *Operation Icelandic Saga: The Expanded Missions*, a distillation of the Freedom Coalition's invasion of Iceland. Every component of the game, from hardware to tactical trees, has been annotated by military scholars. You can play missions from both stages of the operation, either as the invading Leviathan Force or as the occupying SysAdmin Force. The US and Japan had taken care of the invasion; Norwegian and Swedish firms won the occupation rights.

A buzzer sounds, the front door. Before Eliot can pause the game, Eliot Randolph Vanderthorpe, Sr., steps into the mediaroom, arms held behind his back in a stately manner.

Eliot Sr. wears a tailored suit with a silk scarf draped around his shoulders. He carefully removes his scarf and folds it neatly into eighths and places it on the coffee table. In the game, Eliot is leading a virtual Special Forces team as they secure a bookstore across from Reykjavik Cathedral. Three Icelanders with knives and home-made bombs wait inside. Two civilians huddle in a corner. All are very blond and beautiful. The mission briefing stated that the Special Forces team could only kill armed characters, but Eliot kills everyone. Then Eliot radios orders for a Vulture Drone attack on the cathedral. This is technically not a mission objective, but Eliot wants to watch the stunningly realistic-looking cathedral burn and also wonders how his father will react to this clear deviation from mission.

As an undergrad at Cornell, Eliot Sr. joined ROTC in order to pay for college after Old Man Winston Vanderthorpe lost the family fortune in the '87 stock market crash. Old Man Vanderthorpe was addicted to playing the stock market and, Father liked to say, had a sort of genuine talent at losing money. It wasn't easy to lose as much as consistently as Winston did. During his time at Cornell, Eliot Sr. met, through a mutual friend, Daisy Kimball, a fiercely conservative political science major from Harvard. They carried on a long-distance relationship for several years and, around the time they graduated, decided to marry. A year after finishing Cornell, Eliot Sr. and his now pregnant wife relocated to Kunsan Air Base in South Korea, where, shortly after Eliot was born, they were themselves both born again. Because of his bad eyesight, Eliot Sr. never fulfilled his lifelong dream of becoming a pilot, and so, in the aftermath of the September 11 terrorist attacks, as war consumed Afghanistan and the Middle East, Eliot Sr. pushed paper for the air force.

On the mediawall, the robotic Vulture Drone turns Reykjavik Cathedral into a pile of rubble and the words "Mission Failed" overlay the image of a large column of smoke wafting upward into Iceland's eternal summer day.

"You wouldn't have made it far in the officer corps," Father says.

"I'm much better suited to analyzing Elvis impersonators," Eliot says.

"And causing scandals."

Eliot Sr.'s mouth tightens into something like the hybrid of a smile and a grimace, one of a number of incredibly nuanced facial expressions whose meanings can get lost in the shock of their historical, not to mention statistical, novelty. His forehead must have dozens of very-well-developed muscles devoted to a hair-splittingly precise eyebrow pitch and yaw control.

Eliot turns off the video game and gives his attention to the Li'l El robot doll sitting on the futon. It smiles blankly at him, its large anime-style eyes adorable, creepy. Li'l El wears a black T-shirt that bears the silhouette of a red heifer, the Omni Science mascot. Eliot turns the doll on, places it on the floor, and lets it dance around the mediaroom.

"Well, Dad?" Eliot stands up.

Without answering, Eliot Sr. walks to the opaque window wall and gestures it transparent. He's surveying the city for dramatic effect, tacitly calling on his son to come and stand by his side, to wait for the wise words to come. Eliot Sr. knows how to manage a story situation. He's far more sophisticated at it than Eliot will ever be. Eliot stands beside his father and puts his head down, waiting for it.

"Look out there, son. Out there in that sea of corruption and leftists. They hang on, even now. We broke their grip on the government. We wrestled them away from the media."

"You kicked them out of the universities, too," Eliot says.

Eliot Sr. purses his lips, then his mouth goes into neutral, whatever thought he was nursing gone.

"But they're still out there, ready to pounce. Our victories are, at best, only temporary. Their Marxist theorists and terrorist critics, they're almost certainly, in the final analysis, responsible for the Background Rioting. Have you heard about the Avant-Guardians?"

"I've been kind of out of it, Dad."

"Yes, of course, 'out of it.' These Avant-Guardians: they march around our cities and they carry imitation rocket launchers, bazookas, and AK-47s. When Omni finds proscribed weapons on the Total Terror Surveillance System, and security forces come to arrest them, they claim that they're doing performance art. 'Hacking the system.' Exercising 'free speech.' It's insidious. These godless rebels are everywhere."

"Awful stuff, Dad."

"There was just an incident yesterday where one of these seditious 'performance artists' was shot dead in LA. Now, the so-called artist's homosexual 'life partner' is suing the LAPD."

"Really? Awful. How's the LAPD responding?"

"The officer who owns the footage of the shooting is charging a lot for replay rights. That's cut down on much of the mediasphere's coverage, but that's not my point. I'm trying to talk to you about personal and political responsibility, son. They are, finally, the same thing. Look at the shirt you're wearing." Father points at his Che T-shirt. "Do you even know who Che Guevara is? What he did?"

"Sure, 'Che Guevara' is a Name associated with a conceptual description, which is, under CRAP, owned by the Cuban Republic, part of its 'Communist Chic' line."

Father frowns. "Don't call it 'crap,' son. It's the Cee-Arr-Ay-Pee Act."

"Sorry, sorry. The point remains, every time I appear in a glossy mag with this sucker, or if an Omni movie of me wearing it makes money on the mediasphere, a small part of the royalties that my image generates goes straight to Cuban agricultural relief. So don't get huffy and self-righteous, Dad. I'm doing my part to save the world."

Father bites his lip, then unveils his huge froglike grin and begins laughing. Eliot laughs along, because not to would be too uncomfortable. Father squeezes his shoulder affectionately.

"You thought I would be furious at you, son, didn't you?"

"I guess I did. After what I did to the prime minister's son. And the drugs. And the bad publicity."

"Well, you're correct." Father draws out every word. "I was mad at you. Very mad. But I spoke with Reverend Shining the other night. Your mother and I were worried sick, and I didn't know who else I could talk to. Reverend Shining and I were smoking a cigar after dinner—your mother and his wife, Pam, had retreated to another room to talk among themselves—and the two of us were in his study, and I said, 'I'm so angry at my son, Hart. He's disappointed me so much.' And Reverend Shining, he turned to me, and he said, 'Eliot, have you never disappointed your own father, God rest his soul?' And that gave me pause. It made me think of Grandpa Winston, and I missed him so much, and I was just so happy to know that you were on the Gooney on your way back to Newark. It made me peaceful inside to know I would see you and that you were safe. I realized at that moment that what mattered most wasn't what you had done, but what you would do."

This speech stuns Eliot. His stomach unclenches with relief.

"It's good to see you, too, Dad." Eliot holds his father's forearm.

Father turns to face him, tears in his eyes. His froglike smile, remarkably, extends almost beyond the confines of his cheeks.

"Son, you don't need to say that. I know you're happy to see me. I can see it in your eyes. And I know you're ready to turn things around. A man's Name is the most important thing he has. The only thing he carries with him between life's peaks and valleys."

"I can't go back to grad school, Dad. I just can't."

"Don't worry. You know, I've always told you, that you can have a job as a Junior Concept Analyst at Omni. You're smart, and I'm proud of you, and I won't ask you to go back to grad school if you hate it so much. Your mother will be disappointed—she so wants you to get that PhD—but we both also want what's best for you."

"Thanks. That's amazing. I really didn't expect—I never thought—"

"But while with God's guidance we've both found a way to forgive you for your indiscretions, we do think it's time for you to grow up a bit, to take on the responsibility I was talking about, to manage your Name rationally."

"I can get rid of this T-shirt, if that's—"

"That would be a great start, but I'm talking about finally leaving behind childish pursuits and finding your life's purpose. You must become a man. If you're ready to give up grad school, then I think it's time you show some discipline. I—God knows—do not want to have stewardship of your Name forever; I cannot keep freezing and unfreezing your accounts whenever you cross the line. God's ultimate judgment should be what disciplines us all, but we must also be pragmatic. The discipline you need, son, is the discipline of the market. In the mundane world, it is the market that gives and that takes away. The market cannot bestow heavenly grace, but it determines how we allocate the time and resources we have. It is wiser than any individual, an expression of God's will through the aggregate spontaneous actions that we make as free individuals. Therefore, I came here to tell you that it's time for you to take your Name public."

"You want me to go public?"

"I hope you'll forgive me, son, but I've taken the liberty of scheduling a debut appointment for you at the NYRE. One week from today, your Name goes up on the Reputations Exchange. Karl thinks it could pull in three hundred dollars per share, a good start for any young man's Reputation. Your mother and I are so excited for you."

The New York Reputations Exchange. The room starts spinning. Father is not asking him *if* he wants to take his Name public but rather telling him he *has* to. Eliot releases his father's arm and stabilizes himself by leaning his forehead against the cool windowpane. Visible in the distance, just beyond the Manhattan Island Wall, tall black columns of smoke hover ominously over New Jersey. A pounding sound beside him draws his attention. Li'l El has gotten caught in a loop, it seems, and is slamming itself into the window wall, again and again. Eliot picks up the toy robot and turns it off.

PART II
REPUTATIONS EXCHANGE

THE STORY OF THE OMNI SCIENCE
Corporation—its spectacular birth, its obscenely successful IPO, its transformation of the Internet into what is now more commonly referred to as the mediasphere—is deeply woven into Eliot's memory. He saw it all firsthand. He was, in a sense, responsible. When Eliot was almost ten, the Vanderthorpe Family moved to Silicon Valley from Singapore, where Eliot Sr. had been working as an investment banker and Daisy had been writing a book, her second, about how the free market and traditional family values are inextricably linked. Father had been admitted to the Stanford Graduate School of Business as an MBA student. Mother, on the strength of her first book, a study of conservative popular culture, and her increasingly popular blog, had received a research fellowship at the Hoover Institution.

While attending Stanford, Father met Troy Forester and Stanislaw Hadrian. Troy was a PhD candidate in mathematics, Stan in computer science, with a strong interest in analytic philosophy. Because of his own background as a philosophy-physics double major, Eliot Sr. fit right in with these two. After meeting randomly at an obscure conference on philosophical descriptivism, the three began meeting weekly on campus. Eliot often attended these meetings and listened as the men discussed, over bottomless pitchers of beer, family, pop culture, and interesting problems in analytic philosophy and computer science. He would occasionally pause his video game to observe the men in action; their enthusiastic and intense conversations, though often inscrutably dense with technical jargon, inspired him. Troy had an easygoing Midwestern geniality about him, a sort of dull charisma. You liked him immediately, though you could never figure out why. Stan was a tall lean nondescript man, but his eyes burned with ambition, and he spoke with the air of a brilliant obsessive, someone you didn't necessarily like but knew you had to listen to. Among these minor, if nonetheless brilliant, men, Father seemed to Eliot all the more like a god. His natural grace and precise mind was, even to someone who didn't understand a word he was saying, stunningly apparent. On balance, Stan did most of the talking, Troy most of the drinking, and Father most of the thinking.

"Did you understand anything I just said," Stan once asked Eliot after a particularly long digressive monologue.

"No, sir," Eliot said.

"Do you want to understand?" Stan's eyes glowed intensely from behind horn-rimmed glasses.

"I don't know." Eliot looked to Father for guidance, but Father only smiled cryptically. "I guess so."

"Study hard then, and someday you will." Stan tousled Eliot's hair and, satisfied with his own wise guidance, continued his baffling and incomprehensible monologue.

This was the closest Eliot ever came to contributing directly to their discussions, and yet, as the weeks passed, Eliot increasingly moved to the center of their concern. Daisy, happily occupied at the Hoover Institution, a Utopia of conservative intellectuals and policy wonks, had since the birth of Eliot Jr. and Elijah become fanatical about documenting the lives of her children. She kept, among other pieces of Vanderthorpe Family memorabilia, many hard drives of video and high-resolution images of Eliot Jr., Elijah, Eliot Sr., and members of their church. Memory became for her a physical matter, a way of substantiating, recording, the unfolding flux of life. She loved her children so much, she would say, that she did not want to lose a single moment of their precious lives. And so the gigabytes gathered.

Daisy was obsessed with tagging her massive media archive, with making it searchable. Eliot Jr. and Elijah were celebrities in their own family before they subsequently gained larger audiences. During one of their weekly meetings, Eliot Sr. laid out the technical problem for Troy and Stan. How might one automatically tag the Vanderthorpe Family's archive of photos? How would you search for a specific image—say, all photos of Eliot in his school uniform—using only a baseline image? It was a problem in whose solution Eliot Sr. saw exciting business opportunities.

In a sense, then, the Omni system was developed as a means by which to find pictures of Eliot Jr. and Elijah. The technical questions were fascinating, but the potential to cash in on developing such a system could not be overlooked. Weekly meetings soon became daily, long nights spent not on official work but rather developing a software system that could catalog and search the Vanderthorpe Family's archive with minimal human input. From these humble origins, the legend goes, the Omni Science Corporation sparked a video-search revolution whose consequences may never be fully understood.

Early in their development of a solution to what he and his partners had come to call the "Where's Eliot?" problem, Eliot Sr. persuaded a few angel investors to fund their project. Soon, the three men quit school and moved to Austin, Texas, where Omni Science established its first headquarters. Stan and Troy handled the technology end of the start-up while Eliot steered Omni's business strategy. Omni celebrated its initial round of funding by issuing the rare Li'l

El doll since it was, Father liked to joke, Eliot's baby pictures that had caused Omni to come into being.

The release of the beta version of Omni positioned the Omni Science Corporation as, in the words of the business press, "the new Google." Omni could find footage of any person, place, or thing you wanted to find. Omni's founders had invented a form of multidimensional modal logic they called their Conceptual Descriptive Language (CDL, all rights reserved); any existing videos and pictures could be redescribed in terms of this language. Ordinary users entered text—a person's name, a license plate number, whatever—and Omni correlated that text to an appropriate conceptual description compiled in its database (also known as a Name). In one famous demonstration of this process, Omni associated the word "Red" with the conceptual description—the Name—of a baby red heifer that lived on Eliot Sr.'s cattle ranch. Before a phalanx of reporters and photographers, at the very first Omni World Conference, Eliot Sr. typed the word "Red" in a search field on Omni's mediasphere site and Omni recovered all footage featuring Red from the Vanderthorpe Ranch's video archive.

The US government and various large urban police forces, the company's first and most enthusiastic clients, knew exactly what they wanted to do with the Omni system. Working from baseline photos and videos, Omni could quickly search the rapidly growing archives of Homeland Security's Total Terror Surveillance System for footage of wanted persons. Murderers were apprehended, missing children discovered, stolen cars recovered. The London Metropolitan Police signed on soon after and, drawing on its own extensive CCTV network, captured dozens of high-level Islamic militants. For a time, until criminals and terrorists adapted to the new technology, law enforcement never seemed so easy.

The giddy times at Omni Science didn't last long. The rapacious enthusiasm of various governments for advanced video-search technology began to drive a wedge into the partnership at the core of the corporation. Both vaguely libertarian in temperament, Stan and Troy felt uncomfortable with the ethical implications of helping governments more easily keep tabs on their populations. Eliot Sr., meanwhile, had faith that the market could correct government excesses and missteps.

Despite his partners' resistance, Eliot Sr. negotiated long-term contracts with the Department of Defense worth billions. Mired in the endless and bloody occupation of the Bolivarian Federation (*Operation Democratic Sword*, all rights reserved), the DoD leapt at the promise of the Omni system and, with its help, crushed the Bolivarian insurgency more swiftly than analysts thought possible; the Pentagon pacified left-leaning populations across Latin America and restored capitalist-democratic rule to the region in under a year. In a much-cited *Foreign Affairs* article, the Princeton political science professor Irene Kallas declared that "The Omni video search system has effectively ended the West's Long War with militant Islamism and populist insurgencies. What we once referred to as the Global War on Terror is, in effect, over." Though this opinion proved wrong in a number of crucial ways, it nicely captured the spirit of the times, the Age of Optimism.

After the DoD deal, Omni Science was ready to go public in a big way. Because he had brokered the lucrative Homeland Security and DoD contracts, and because he developed good personal relations with many of those institutional investors who would put up $1,500 per share at the Omni Science IPO, Eliot Sr. was able to seize Omni from his reluctant partners. Stan and Troy were shut out of the company they had helped found.

Eliot remembers when he first learned of his father's coup. The Vanderthorpes still lived in Austin at the time. After Bible study one Sunday, Eliot came home to find Father sitting on the couch in the living room, crying quietly beside Mother, who rubbed her husband's shoulders.

"This is so hard," he was saying, "so hard."

"What?" Eliot asked. "What's so hard?"

Father explained the situation as straightforwardly as possible. Stan and Troy were becoming mad with power. They had the mistaken impression that corporations had some obligation to do good or be moral. Not so.

Fresh from an afternoon learning moral lessons, Eliot admitted that he didn't understand.

The only obligation a corporation has, Eliot Sr. explained, is to maximize profit for its risk-taking investors. Moral agency in a market resides not at the level of the firm but at the level of the market framework itself; only the invisible hand of the market could maximize social utility, set prices correctly, and distribute products efficiently. Stan and Troy, confused by their idealism and naïveté, went on and on about giving away free food in the corporate cafeteria, creating loftlike workspaces, building a hip corporate ethos, giving birth to a so-called ethical capitalism. Total nonsense.

"Maybe we should pray," Eliot suggested, still not fully understanding.

Mother smiled at him. Father perked up a bit. "Yes," he said. "What a lovely idea." They knelt together in front of the coffee table, knees sinking into the rug. Eliot felt terrified. Something about the expression "invisible hand" made him think of ghosts and demons and hell.

Please God, Eliot prayed, Make Dad feel better and bless him and please don't let Stan and Troy get mad and don't let the invisible hand do anything bad to Dad or Mom and, please God, I'll do whatever you want me to do, just make sure these things happen, okay? Eliot peeked at his parents, who he saw were holding hands. Father's lips moved almost imperceptibly. Eliot clasped his eyes shut again and, as it turned out, had his prayers answered. Eliot Sr. took control of Omni Science and steered it in the right direction, away from a too-strict focus on defense and, in perhaps his most visionary move, toward the Promised Land of Celebrity.

Eliot Sr. spent the next five years lobbying for a total reformulation of intellectual property law. The Conceptual Rights and Patent (CRAP) Act, the fruits of his endless labor, redefined all copyrights, trademarks, and patents as descriptions written in Omni Science's proprietary language. Under CRAP, you could only protect intellectual property describable in terms of this language. The technical management of intellectual property had, in effect, been privatized.

Omni provided the only viable means to enforce CRAP. If a criminal wanted to sell unlicensed Elvis T-shirts, for example, his intellectual-property theft would be quickly discovered once Omni picked it up. Corporations could easily do statistical analyses of whether a brand image, as defined under CRAP, was maximizing the efficiency of its profit-yielding potential, and find intellectual-property thieves from behind a computer terminal. Many owners of intellectual property paid small finder's fees to those freelance videographers who discovered CRAP violators, creating an incentive for private citizens to stream massive amounts of video onto the mediasphere. Many people set up cameras in their windows at home, wore video-enabled jewelry during the day, recorded their whole lives and the lives of others. Private citizens, a million Little Brothers and Sisters, voluntarily and in a massively distributed fashion documented their little corner of Planet Earth. After all, you never knew if the video stream you uploaded onto the mediasphere might end up making you money. Omni enabled all of the world's watchers to watch each other watch each other watch each other (etc.).

This new intellectual property regime had another significant and unexpected consequence. Once Omni enabled individuals to easily monitor the use of their Names on the mediasphere, it became obvious that there was a new kind of money to be made from celebrity-watching. Because conceptual descriptions of a person— that person's Name—were clearly definable, they could be bought and sold on the market as easily as anything else. And a Name could be jointly owned.

When the New York Reputations Exchange opened, it became *the* Reputation Exchange. A person, now basically an embodied corporation, could capitalize on his success or hopes for future success by selling shares of his Name. Shareholders gained a voting stake in how the market capitalization—the Reputation—associated with a Name would be invested. You could leverage your Reputation into personal brand image development, thus pushing your Reputation further skyward. Reputation Futures and other derivatives quickly followed.

Under the visionary leadership of Eliot Sr., the Omni Science Corporation had found its most authentic and enduring clients: not Homeland Security, not DoD, not the police, but transnational corporations with intellectual property to protect and celebrities with an interest in maximizing the profitability of their Names. For surely, now that the world had made itself safe from the menace of terrorism and global insurgency, there was hardly anything more important going on than the mediasphere's perpetual interest in itself.

In the years that followed the opening of the NYRE, Eliot Sr. often liked to say that the release of the Omni system made America stranger and more like itself than it had ever been before. On this point, Eliot is very much in agreement with his father.

And the time has come to complete the circle. Eliot must submit himself to the grip of the system his image had hand in helping to create. The New York Reputations Exchange waits for him. At twenty-seven, Li'l El will debut. He will become a man. He's coming out.

Ω

' "Excellence is what happens when you're not trying,' " Karl Vlasic says.

Karl is standing behind the klieg lights, reading from a clipboard. His curious idiolect fuses Old World charm with the cadences of the mediasphere's stereotype of a Hollywood producer, as if a seasoned radio announcer were doing a bad impersonation of someone with a Slovenian accent.

"I don't think so," Eliot says.

"Well, then. How about 'Accidents will happen. Excellence endures'?"

"That's awful. Is that an allusion to Elvis Costello?"

"You tell me, El. You are the world's expert on Elvis."

Eliot hates it when Karl calls him El.

"Look at the mark on your left," says the photographer, Tamara Jones. "Try to look natural," another voice commands. "Keep your mouth open." "Squint your eyes." "Look ferocious." Eliot's gray three-piece suit itches uncomfortably, reminding him how much he'd prefer not to be here. God, these lights are hot. As the day has progressed, Eliot has degenerated to a state of learned helplessness and now willingly accepts whatever these voices that claim to speak on his behalf tell him to do. Only Karl manages to find innovative ways of pissing him off.

"How about," Karl says, "oh, but this one is very terrible."

"Let's hear it. Can we stop with the fucking shoot for one minute?"

Tammy glowers at Eliot. Her willowy frame seems as if it might buckle under the gigantic apparatus of her camera, its spiky knobs and levers sharply at odds with her more streamlined look.

Karl cracks his knuckles. "Take five, Tammy."

Tammy storms off the set. The support staff drop whatever they've been doing and file in an orderly manner to the coffee and donut table, a safe harbor of goodies from Tammy's tempestuous management style.

"That better, El?"

Eliot moves out of range of the intensely hot lights and sits on a four-legged stool beside the green screen. When he reaches for his tie, a makeup girl yells from across the room, "Don't you dare touch that!" Eliot shakes his fist in mock anger. A sharply dressed intern, a girl nineteen or maybe twenty years old, brings him a bottle of water. When Eliot flashes her a smile, she blushes, puts her head down, and shuffles away.

"Keep your mind on business, kid."

Karl waddles up to him. Karl always somehow manages to look slightly ill at ease, drunk, sleep deprived, and apoplectic in equal measures. A nervous person—short and ratlike, round and hairy—Karl loosens and tightens his tie and nervously tugs at the tufts of hair that grow in random patches across his face. As Karl reads his clipboard, his chubby face quivers thoughtfully.

"Let's proceed to the next one."

"I want to hear the one you think is terrible, Karl."

"Okay, you asked for it. 'When excellence finds you, seize it.'"

"Oh, I like it. 'When excellence finds you, seize it.' I like that one a lot. It has an imperial ring to it. Veni, vidi, vici. Carthago delenda est, you know. Carpe diem, anyone?"

"I'm just not lovin' it, El. Studies show that people get tripped up on relative clauses. 'When blah blah, blah blah blah.' Too complex for the middle mind."

"Fine, fine, then, what's next on the list? Give that to me."

"No, I'll keep reading them out loud."

Eliot grabs the list from Karl. "Oh, yes. This one looks good. How about 'Seize excellence'? I didn't think it was possible, but that's even more fascistic."

"Exactly, exactly. Too intimidating."

"How about, 'For only three hundred dollars per share, I'll give you a blow job'?"

"Do you know you're impossible, El? Do you know what I put up with to keep you out of trouble?"

"A seven-figure salary and enough of a commission to pay the mortgage on your mansion in Ljubljana?"

"Ha ha." Karl licks his lips. "Reputation management is serious business. I earn every penny."

"I just can't stand it, Karl. I'm really freaking out about this IPO. How could I let my father talk me into going public? This is even more nightmarish than grad school."

"You'll do just great." Karl moves into motivational speaker mode. "You just have to get this spread of Personal Brand Name ads out. It's a challenge, for sure. We have less than a week to build mediasphere buzz around your IPO. We've got ten ads that are going out in less than forty-eight hours. Top trade journals and glossy magazines, the ones pundits and opinion makers read."

"So what you're saying is one week of this nightmare, then—"

Karl laughs a wheezing, wet laugh. "Then, after you go public—then the nightmare *really* begins. It's all planned out. Two weeks from now, you go to LA to the V-NoCal first anniversary party at the Getty Center. Early next month, you appear with your parents and Elijah Apocalypse at the *Peace in the Mideast Summit Telethon* in Jerusalem. Say good-bye to the 'tweens and hello to Wall Street, El."

"I'm sorry, but did you just say Elijah *Apocalypse*?"

"Your brother is a genius."

"You've got to be kidding."

"He's having his surname legally changed."

"To Apocalypse?"

"The Apocalypse is really big. His timing couldn't be better. Eye for an Eye is taking off."

Eye for an Eye, the Christian punk band that Elijah founded last summer, has been doing spectacularly well, its latest album, *Devil May Care*, having sold millions worldwide.

"Jesus, Karl. This stuff is all too crazy for me. Self-branding just isn't what I'm about. I don't want people to watch a television show about my life."

"Don't get your hopes up. We're still talking to Disney about that one."

"My life and, like, my narrative belong to me. I'm not a corporate guy. I'm just the ordinary son of a multibillionaire. I don't need the Hollywood treatment. If I keep doing drugs and sleeping with women, the value of my Name is gonna stay pretty high. I don't need a listing on the Reputations Exchange or a personal tagline."

"First, it's called a 'values statement,' El. Second, remember what I told you when the Sarah thing happened."

Karl, who has often acted more like a father to Eliot than Eliot Sr., was called in to spin the first breakup with Sarah. Karl often framed his advice in theoretical terms. As a PhD student in Cultural Studies at the New School, he had followed the lead of the critical theorist Slavoj Žižek before metaphorically killing his intellectual father, denouncing stringent Lacanianism in favor of a more eclectic framework. PhD in hand, he joined America's burgeoning Creative Economy, becoming first a Reputation Consultant for multinational corporate brand names and then a Reputation Manager for celebrities and VIPs. After Eliot's first breakup with Sarah, Karl had suggested that Eliot position himself as an "existential player," the marketing archetype that most perfectly harmonized his sexual escapades with his undergraduate philosophy major. At first, Eliot rejected this archetype because it so obviously mischaracterized him, but he finally surrendered and gave a series of interviews to *GQ, Esquire,* and other men's lifestyle magazines in which he had said various things that Karl had scripted for him. Extremely stupid things, in Eliot's view, but the mediasphere had loved every word.

"What did I tell you back then, El?"

"Well—"

"Let me remind you. I told you that the Imaginary storyline you put forward in public has no necessary relationship to the Real, private you. As someone in the limelight, your job is essentially to perform your own life. Any resemblance to the Real Eliot R. Vanderthorpe, Jr., is entirely accidental. So: we are not at this shoot because you enjoy it or because I enjoy it, but because we have to create your narrative. If we do not create it for the mediasphere, the mediasphere will create it for you. And that is the very last thing we want because the mediasphere will, as you would so eloquently put it, 'fuck you up.'"

Eliot had found it hard to argue with Karl's logic back then; it seems equally unassailable now. Karl always knows how to calm him down, no doubt because he has studied sophisticated psychographic software models of Eliot's personality that have told him which rhetorical strategies work best at motivating his client to do what is necessary.

Karl sighs. "And you're especially vulnerable because you come from a successful family. The only acceptable kind of discrimination nowadays is discrimination based on wealth. It's diabolical. If you have even a little bit more money than someone else, you're a target."

"Not to mention if you're a multibillionaire or the son of a multibillionaire."

"Then you might as well come from a caste of Untouchables, as far as your social life is concerned."

"I've led a tragic life," Eliot says.

"It *is* a tragedy because half the population will always earn more than the other half. One percent of the population will always do better than the other ninety-nine percent. It's a statistical law of nature. Iron-clad."

"Your reasoning is flawless, Karl."

Before Eliot can ask whether Karl really believes his own bullshit, Tammy returns.

"Eliot is all ready to go," Karl says.

Karl openly stares at Tammy's ass as he walks over to the refreshments table. Tammy ignores him and sets up her camera. Karl stacks donuts on a paper plate and grabs a soda. "Let's get started, El!" Eliot reluctantly obeys, standing up and going back to his place in front of the green screen. Once he's back in the lights, in a hot blinding whiteness that reminds him of death, the shoot resumes.

Ω

A great basilica of the church of global celebrity capitalism, the New York Reputations Exchange inspires spiritual feelings among those temporal beings lucky enough to cower beneath its vast and vaulted apse. Here in the refurbished bowels of 40 Wall Street, once briefly the world's tallest building, people can have themselves broken up into their constituents and watch as these sundry parts accrue value. The whimsies of speculation will rearrange you, will aggregate and disaggregate your bits, will create of these new composites and syntheses, something you could never have imagined.

BE EXCELLENT.

Dave Lee and Marty Whitebread, a director and videographer under contract with Disney's Bildungsroman Channel, contribute in their small way to the market's balance of caprice by following Eliot and his mother through the NYRE's crowded trading floor, recording clips for the pilot episode of what is tentatively being called *The Eliot Vanderthorpe Show*. Both have a strange preppy-bohemian look about them, as if they choose their mode of self-presentation on the basis of a careful triangulation of the mediasphere's top-ten top ten fashion lists.

BE EXCELLENT.

Eliot has loosed himself from stifling suits and again wears relatively normal clothing: jeans, a white button-down shirt with a strategically preppy checkered pullover sweater, and white tennis shoes. Karl has described this as "a fun and youthful look" and claims that it has tested well in both computer simulations and among live focus groups. Eliot must stand out against the white noise of suited Wall Street types, but not too much. Eliot also wears a video camera necklace—a thin silver chaincam designed to look tastefully masculine—which streams footage wirelessly to Bildungsroman Channel servers, an archive of Eliot POV shots for the pilot.

BE EXCELLENT.

Eliot had finally suggested this slogan, figuring Karl's legal team would discover the phrase, stolen from the classic 1989 film *Bill and Ted's Excellent Adventure*, had already been claimed under CRAP. Quite unexpectedly, it hadn't, so his joke has backfired, and Eliot is now stuck forever with this utterly asinine "values statement." Mother loops her arm through his and gently but firmly leads him toward the small pulpit where the opening bell is located.

BE EXCELLENT.

Dave directs Marty to record mother and son as they make their final approach. "Get their faces," he says.

"Where are Dad and Elijah?" Eliot says.

"Your father got caught up at the office and your brother is rehearsing with Eye for an Eye. Father said he would try to make it to the Waldorf Towers party. As I'm sure you know, he's very proud of you, and is sorry he couldn't be here. We're all proud of you. You've come so far in so short a time."

Daisy Vanderthorpe straightens her already perfect posture for the camera. Her shoulder-length blonde hair shimmers in stage light. Her skirt, jacket, and high-heeled shoes are a shrill shade of lime green. A migratory nation of platinum jewelry has tastefully colonized her body. Her makeup must make her look good on camera: this is the only way to explain why she's made herself up so garishly today. This getup is a legacy of her days as a fully credentialed Southern beauty queen (Miss Arkansas), before she got her political science degree at Harvard, before she wrote her first book, before she met and married Eliot Sr. Much like his father, his mother is a master at controlling her image in the media, an expert at playing to expectation as a means of forestalling serious analysis of her motives and intentions. Unfortunately, the smokescreen of stereotype is always so thick around her that even Eliot is never quite sure what his mother is really thinking, what she really believes.

"You look so handsome in your headshot," she says.

As he climbs the stairs, Eliot has to confront the ten-foot-tall black-and-white press photo erected on the stage, as beastly a deformation of his image as he has ever seen, apart from the Li'l El robots. Karl has layered what might be a corporate boardroom into the background of the image. Actually, Eliot realizes, it's an airport. The blurred word "Arrivals"—cropped by the left edge of the picture to read simply "rivals"—is in the background. Karl no doubt has placed this word off center to invite interpretive controversy among the fan-scholars. Tracing the picture's bottom edge, in a custom-designed font, runs another iteration of Eliot's values statement, BE EXCELLENT.

The Eliot of the press photo has his facial hair cut down to a suggestive, shadowy scruff. He looks off to the right, lost in thought, his eyes focused on something far away. His mouth is slightly open in a way suggesting thoughtfulness. Had he made this face last week, at the photo shoot? Not that he can remember. This close, the pores in his nose seem inhumanly huge. He imagines falling into one of them, finding a quiet place between two monumentally large dead skin cells where he might curl up and hide from the light.

"I always love the sight of so many hardworking men," Mother says. "It's very stirring."

She surveys the brokers at the stations below. The brokers wear blue blazers laden with badges and electronic devices. Amidst this baseline of blue, assistants and technical staff wear a rainbow of blazers: post specialists, analysts, professional gossipers, runners, others. Eliot, his mother, and the Bildungsroman crew have special passes hanging from their necks. Journalists and videographers near the stage wear green blazers. Above this corporate sea flies a flotilla of American flags. They look like sails without ships, full with wind, lost.

"Yeah," Eliot mutters. "It warms the cuckolds—sorry, I mean the cockles—of my heart."

Mother does not turn away from the floor or even so much as arch an eyebrow, yet Eliot distinctly feels the cold breeze of her displeasure. From the trading pits below a thousand men—almost no women—type on touchboards like bunny rabbits hopped up on speed, so fast that fingers and touchboard blur together until they are indistinguishable. Each man wears anti–carpal tunnel braces on his forearms. Their cubicles have as many screens as insect compound eyes have facets. In a few moments, the brokers will begin selling shares of Eliot's Name to the investing public—to individuals, hedge funds, sovereign wealth funds, anyone with idle capital. The invisible hand of the market, really the statistical union of all these typing hands, or of all typing hands everywhere, will take control of his future. His specialist is there, somewhere among them, waiting for the deathly peal of the opening bell.

Eliot has never understood why, in an electronic age, a physical exchange is even necessary. Karl tried to explain the reason once. It's all about the logic of the spectacle, Karl had said, taking on a philosophical tone. People don't like an economy they can't see. At this moment, Eliot would much prefer not to be seeing this part of the economy. The spectacle frankly freaks him out. A clutch of videographers, in their green blazers, makes its way toward Eliot and his mother and his knees suddenly seem like they might give out. Though Eliot has lived under scrutiny all his life, something about the formality of this occasion disturbs him. On many screens in the insect-eyed cubicles below, he can see images of himself and his mother.

"You okay, hon?" Mother asks.

"Fine, Mom. Just a little stage fright. Butterflies."

She smiles, red lipstick framing bright white teeth. She leans in toward his ear and whispers to him, a smile never leaving her face, "Remember, you're being observed and analyzed all the time. Keep it together, dear, if you know what's good for you." Her lips do not move when she whispers, ensuring that observers can't read them.

As she turns her lovely smile back toward the reporters, Eliot can hear the hum of her noise-canceling jewelry, designed to keep clandestine parabolic microphones from catching even her unmouthed whispers. An exchange of severe whispers is the closest Eliot ever comes to having a sincere conversation with his mother, all the better since he'd rather not have too many.

"It's so good to see you, guys," Mother says. "Sure, of course we'll pose for a few pictures. But let's make sure to get the awning in the background, okay, my dears?"

Eliot and his mother position themselves so that the photographers will not miss the awning, which is covered with fractal repetitions of his values statement, BE EXCELLENT. Every photo of today's debut will, per Karl's instructions, stay on message.

"Will Sarah be at the party later?" shouts one reporter.

"Sarah was spotted coming out of the Transcontinental Building a week ago. Have you two started dating again?" asks another.

"Do you stand behind your friend Tom Feldman's decision to join the IDF?" asks a third.

Daisy gives off a subtle aura of fury. Even the most sensitive instruments, the acutest analyst, would be hard pressed to find evidence of any change in her mood, but Eliot can sense the shift. She discreetly presses a panic button on one of her bracelets and private bodyguards almost immediately step in to escort the reporter who asked the political questions off the premises.

"Let's strike that last question from the transcript," Daisy whispers to the Bildungsroman director, then switches to her onstage

Southern accent. This accent is largely a fabrication; like Eliot, she spent most of her formative years in Northeastern prep schools and can speak in a flawlessly standard American accent when she wants to. "We'll answer all the questions you good folks have at the press conference, right after the de-*but* of the social season!"

"Mom, I'm twenty-seven!"

"It's not your fault kids weren't going on the market when you were growing up, sugar."

"That's great banter, guys," the Bildungsroman director says. "Give me more of that."

"How does it feel to see your Name on the Big Board, Eliot?" a reporter asks.

"That'll be all for now," Mother says. Bodyguards herd the press away, except for the Bildungsroman director and videographer, who have their Eliot Vanderthorpe exclusive.

"That was a good question, though," Mother says, her face tilted toward the camera.

"What?" Eliot says.

"How does it feel? Look! You're over there, honey. ERVJ. Eliot Randolph Vanderthorpe, Junior. I'm so proud!"

She rotates her head on its horizontal axis, looking up at the board, a pantomime of pride.

Flanked by American flags on either side, the Big Board, a giant screen hanging on the far wall beyond the trading pit, below the NYRE's apse, is on fire today, a reflection of action on the London markets. Barely legible at this distance Eliot can see his listing, ERVJ. Next to his listing are a number of Xs, which will soon be replaced by his initial public offering price. ERVJ can at best aspire to become a mid-cap stock, Karl has said; sure, he's famous, but not a Hollywood type. Karl maintains that despite the bearish celebrity market Eliot's stock price will get as high as $400 per share by the end of the trading week.

A tall priestlike man with spots of gray peppering his otherwise black hair climbs somberly onto his pulpit and stands behind the podium. This man, the chairman of the NYRE, clears his throat into the microphone and waits for the brokers to stop their typing and chatting. A stately silence descends upon the floor. When the chairman calls for a moment of silent prayer, the brokers obediently put their heads down. Eliot lowers his own head, trying hard to repress a smirk. These guys don't give a shit about God. The prayer ceremony is probably designed to give comfort to those few remaining misguided and gentle souls who might stay up at night worrying that capitalism has no human heart.

Next, the chairman, reading from a pro forma statement, marvels at the miracle of the market and rhetorically genuflects before the sacred glory of this hallowed Exchange. As he continues reading this nonsensical consecration, Eliot and his mother appear on a jumbo television screen beside the Big Board. What looks ridiculous in person about his mother's getup really works quite well on the television. Shrill lime green can, it turns out, look very respectable. Ghoulish makeup hardly registers. Platinum jewelry adds a glamorous sparkle to her image.

Eliot also notices how carefully and successfully his handlers have put him together. Self-consciousness unseats his cool and collected patina. Keep it together, man. Force a smile. Mother taps him firmly on the shoulder, waking him from his trance. The chairman is holding his small gavel as if he's ready to strike Eliot.

"Are you okay, honey," Mother says, displeased.

"What's he saying?"

"He wants you to hit the bell. Three times."

"Why?"

"To open the Exchange, dear."

"Right, of course." This is all part of the script. Eliot accepts the gavel.

All the brokers watch him, cynical-eyed, hungry vultures waiting to feed on his Name. Eliot slams the gavel down, once, twice, three times, as if he were trying to break the back of a brass turtle. A switch flips somewhere and the real, automated open bell begins its sharp, staccato clanging—*dong, dong, dong, dong*—a dull reverberation that echoes in this sacrosanct space like some inhuman incantation. When the mechanical clanging dies down, the New York Reputations Exchange is officially open. There is a moment of silence and stillness, and then the brokers break. Dozens shove their way, shouting, into the narrow space around the cubicle of the specialist selling shares of ERVJ. Meanwhile, in the Futures pit on the periphery of the floor, a contract has already been taken out on his Name. Eliot lays down the gavel and steps away from the podium, shaken.

Ω

The pinkish pâté on the cracker is shaped like a red heifer, an unsubtle reminder of who is paying for this party. Eliot grabs the cracker from the server's silver tray and pops it into his mouth, taking perverse pleasure in crushing the Omni mascot between his molars. The pâté is delicious. Eliot has been downing expensive hors d'œuvres like fast food, the NYRE debut and subsequent publicity events having left him exhausted and famished. The waiter leaves to refill his tray and Pedro returns from the drink table bearing two large glasses of white wine. His clothes always look slightly too large on his skinny frame, but this black tux is an especially poor fit.

"This isn't the place for me," Pedro says. "This woman by the table thought I was a fucking waiter. She asked me to get food for the Chihuahua in her purse."

"I want you here," Eliot says. "You're the only decent human being in the room. Me included."

"Your father finally show up?"

"Why are you asking?"

"Sorry, don't mean to offend."

Eliot blushes. "No, I didn't mean—I wasn't—"

"Forget about it." Pedro hands Eliot one of the wineglasses.

Pedro and Eliot walk among the guests, mostly Mother's Upper East Side socialite friends. None of Eliot's friends are here; the few who even bothered to return his calls made various excuses for why they couldn't show up. The ballroom of the Waldorf is cavernous and intimidating. Crystal chandeliers hover, zeppelin-like, above plush auburn carpets. Dozens of waiters in tailed tuxes, each with a tiny red heifer pinned on his or her lapel, ferry serving trays.

Mother and Karl are chatting across the room by a wall-mounted electric candelabrum. Daisy has changed into a form-fitting black dress and, on three-inch heels, looms over Karl. Simulated candle-light casts shadows across their faces. Karl consults his palmtop and occasionally glances up at Eliot.

"Karl is thinking about something," Eliot says.

"How can you tell?"

"He always scratches his belly like that when he's deep in thought." Karl looks up at him again, then returns to his palmtop.

"What do you think—"

Eliot snaps his fingers. "Of course," he says.

Eliot covers the aperture of his chaincam, testing his theory. Karl is startled. He's been tracking the feed from Eliot's chaincam. What a jerk.

"You know," Eliot says, "did you ever notice he looks a little like a gerbil."

"Karl?" Pedro says.

"That's right." Eliot enunciates every syllable. "Karl Vlasic is a fat, human-sized gerbil."

Karl frowns and slips his palmtop in his jacket pocket.

"You're in a little bit of a state, guy," Pedro says. "Try drinking some more."

Eliot gulps down his wine and recognizes that Pedro is right; he is in a state. Going public has summoned the specter of his shameful summer debauchery and has reminded Eliot, yet again, of his father's disapproval. And how embarrassing, he thinks, to want that approval. Dad isn't even here, too busy with work, as usual, to attend either his debut or the reception.

Pedro stiffens suddenly. The Bildungsroman team is moving toward them, recording footage of Eliot and Pedro for the pilot. Seeing the team's approach, Mother takes Karl by the arm and guides him around the drink table, making small talk with, then deftly parrying, various well-wishers, her eyes unwaveringly fixed on Eliot. Eliot turns off the chaincam, sick of being watched. Karl will get mad, he thinks, but fuck Karl.

"We're free of Big Brother," Eliot says, tapping his chaincam.

"Really?" Pedro says. "Then I can dare you to moon the party without getting fired."

"You really don't want to—"

"Stand on the table over there and do it."

"Man, do you understand that if you ask me—"

"*If* I ask you? It's too late. I already did."

Mother and Karl close in from the left, Dave and Marty from the right. Eliot and Pedro are the target of their coordinated pincer action.

"What do I get if I moon the party?" Eliot says.

"Get, guy?"

"I'm saying, make it worth my while, Pedro."

"My respect for you would not be honor enough?"

That settles the question. Eliot walks away from Pedro, almost strutting, toward the large round table at the center of the ballroom, threading the gap between Karl and Mother and Dave and Marty. Pedro follows, a safe distance behind, hands in his pockets. Eliot removes his jacket and throws it back at Pedro, who catches it and is visibly nervous. Eliot untucks his dress shirt and glimpses a flash of red polka-dot boxer shorts.

It's good that Sarah and Father are not here, Eliot decides. He steps onto a chair, then onto the table. Plates and glasses clatter. The table shakes slightly. Eliot grabs a glass of wine from a passing waiter, drinks it, and strikes the glass with a salad fork until everyone is watching him expectantly. Aging, surgically enhanced Upper East Side faces stare at him. Waiters pause. Pedro shakes his head with disbelief.

Eliot starts: "I am standing here to send a message to the city of New York and to the world. . . ."

Open horror takes hold of Mother's face, a rare event. Eliot feels proud to have provoked an apparently sincere reaction from her. Karl, meanwhile, seems merely disgusted with Eliot, not at all surprised, as if his computer models of Eliot's personality had predicted that this would happen. Dave and Marty, of course, look thrilled. All the videographers in the room converge around Eliot; they smell the red meat, and mediasphere residuals, of a pending celebrity fuck-up.

This sort of stuff—smashing things, getting drunk, shocking the over-thirty set—seemed more funny in Europe than it does now. William had helped, of course, motivate Eliot's summer of insanity; the prime minister's son had a very particular, almost rarified, sense of what counted as a good time. He would have called Pedro a pansy for proposing merely that Eliot moon this audience rather than, say, piss in a punch bowl. Eliot thinks of Sarah, of Father, of the kind of man that they would both, for all their political differences, rather he be. He thinks about showing his red polka-dot boxer shorts to these aging socialites.

"Eliot," Mother says.

Eliot ignores her. "I am standing here on this table—"

"Eliot."

"—to say—"

"Get off the table, Eliot."

"—to say that I'm, like, no longer the sort of person most of you, perhaps justifiably, expected the worst of just now. I'm so sorry, everyone. Sorry, Mom, Karl. I know what an ass I've been, how disappointing I can be. I also know that knowing this about myself doesn't make it better. There's no excusing what I've done, the way I've behaved, but I think today's debut will really be the start of something different for me. I finally have a good feeling about my future."

The crowd doesn't react at first.

Eliot stands dumbly on the table. "Thank you for your attention," he says.

Then, following his mother's lead, the guests tepidly applaud. His ears burn, his chest feels clogged, and his throat is blocked with emotion. Eliot leaps down from the table, recovers his jacket from Pedro—whose face is pasty with horror—and he sulks away, trying to formulate in his mind all the things that he would say to his father, if only he could find words to correctly describe how he is suffering, if only he could invent some technical vocabulary of pain whose inner force Father could not ignore.

$$\Omega$$

As analysts long predicted, Eliot's shareholders have appointed Karl Vlasic as the executor of ERVJ, which means Karl now has power of attorney for his Name and is solely responsible for reinvesting his market capitalization. As the Reputation Manager of the whole Vanderthorpe Family (VATH), Karl has to harmonize Eliot Jr.'s individual branding strategy with that of his family, in anticipation of a big VATH secondary stock offering, scheduled for October. All of this means that Karl, who takes his role as executor very seriously, has become an even bigger fucking asshole than usual. For example, he calls Eliot on his second day as a Junior Conceptual Analyst at Omni Science and says:

"El, go to the location in Central Park I'm sending to your tab."

"I'm at work," Eliot halfheartedly whines, already incredibly bored with his new job. "You can't just pull me out whenever you feel like it."

Eliot has been assigned, no doubt on his father's recommendation, to a small team of Conceptual Analysts who are figuring out how Omni might better distinguish between real and fake weapons. Most of the proposed solutions involve calculating more accurately an object's center of mass from some arbitrary baseline footage, but none promises to solve the fake weapon problem completely. Undoubtedly meant to teach him personal and political responsibility, the tedium and bureaucratic hassle of this assignment is actually teaching him that a serious life, a life of labor, is no fun at all. The prospect of a lifetime of corporate work, of dumbly taking orders from above, of following someone else's agenda, seems odious and unbearable.

"And remember you're contractually obligated to turn on your chaincam when you leave the office."

"That's not the point I'm trying—"

"There's an auto-rickshaw waiting for you downstairs, El. You have thirty minutes."

Karl hangs up. Asshole. Eliot calls his immediate manager, Todd Wilkins. Todd appears on the screen, raccoon-like circles under his eyes.

"Hi Todd," Eliot says.

Todd mumbles in recognition and blinks a few times, then looks away from the camera, typing and subvocalizing commands to the machines that surround him.

"I got a call from my Reputation Manager, Karl Vlasic."

"I know."

"He wants me to——"

"I know."

"Is it okay?"

"Just go."

"O——"

Todd hangs up. Eliot sighs, loosens his tie, and unbuttons the top button of his shirt. Man, does this life sucks. In the last few days, his Reputation has been growing respectably. His Name is selling for $387 per share and, given that he owns a quarter of outstanding shares, this is a good thing. If he weren't already heir to a multibillion-dollar fortune, and if he didn't also now have a nominal income from Omni Science, he could eventually sell his stock and live comfortably off capital gains alone. But the continued performance of his stock—his greatest asset—depends on the marketplace's faith in him. If he fucks up again, Karl insists, ERVJ will lose value. And Father has made it known that, should Jr. misbehave, he would be forced, out of love, to reclaim the Transcontinental penthouse. The Vanderthorpe Family's secondary offering must not be endangered in any way; their family's Reputation must continue to grow.

Eliot grabs his shoulder bag, takes the elevator to the ground floor, and finds the auto-rickshaw Karl has reserved for him waiting at the entrance of the Omni Science Building. Eliot gets on the auto-rickshaw and it joins the great mass of Manhattan traffic. The streets of Manhattan are crowded with bright, happy people. Since the Wall went up a decade ago, Manhattan has become such a lovely place to live. Car traffic has been reduced almost to nothing. Mostly, people use electric bikes, take public transit, hail microtaxis, or travel on miniscooters. Ample public transit—tax dollars reinvested from the formerly public transit systems of the forgotten outer boroughs—makes life here an eco-friendly dream. The Wall has even held back the recent minor rise in sea level.

When the auto-rickshaw drops him off near the Museum of Natural History, Eliot opens Karl's map on his tab. As he walks toward the location marked on the map, Eliot becomes convinced that someone is following him, two someones, in fact, both wearing casual clothing and baseball hats. Manhattan is supposed to be safe territory for celebrities, even those with Reputations far larger than his.

Eliot inserts an earbud and calls Karl. "I'm being followed, man."

"Two guys wearing baseball hats?"

"Yeah, how'd you—"

"Don't worry, El, they're supposed to be following you."

"What?"

"It's Dave and Marty. They're filming for your pilot."

"More Bildungsroman bullshit?"

"That's right."

"I thought I had a day off today."

"We wanted to catch you acting naturally."

"Man, this conversation is being recorded, isn't it? You wanted to tell me you were recording me while you were recording me so you could catch my reaction. You're inventing drama. What's the storyline supposed to be? 'Eliot struggles with the paradoxes of life as a celebrity'? Don't count on me to play along. I've got some dignity. I should go back to work."

"Just remember, your whole family's Reputation depends on your acting reasonably. You know what's at stake. Do not screw this up. And, anyway, El, aren't you curious about what I've set up? I know Sarah would be disappointed if you didn't show up."

Sarah. His throat catches.

Eliot has always kept the women he's dated within arm's reach, on the hunch that he might have missed through sheer blockheadedness how they were in fact perfect for him. The 'tweenage fangirls are basically right: he does have a romantic streak. Because Sarah had cared enough to violently tear out his chest hair, Eliot is increasingly certain that she must be the one he's destined to be with, that she has always been the one, the only one, that if he does not end up with her then he will be alone forever. But, because telling her this would only scare her away, Eliot has decided not to tell her how important she's become to him, which is why he has made a point of *not* calling her since they had sex. Now Karl has gone and screwed up his plan.

Sarah is sitting on a bench near a Disney-sponsored Carousel and is texting on her palmtop. Behind her, kids ride on zany talking horses from the feel-good family animated musical comedy, *The Mongol Hoards*. The Carousel plays music from the movie. Sarah's foot taps in time to the music. Astride the spinning cartoon horses, children scream with glee, singing along, knowing all the lyrics by heart. Eliot sits down beside her; Sarah continues her texting and foot-tapping, acting as if she hasn't seen him. The Bildungsroman team, Dave and Marty, takes a seat on a bench across from them. They open offprints of the *Daily News* and pretend to read, the brims of their baseball hats perched on the edge of the newspapers. Their hats must have cameras and directional mics built into them.

When Eliot begins to remove his earbud, Karl says, "Don't take that out." His hand freezes. "Listen, you've got to invite Sarah to Los Angeles for the Northern California invasion party. V-NoCal Day. The president of the United States is going to be there. Your whole family is going to be there. You need a date, and the only person the focus groups want to see you with is Sarah. Do you understand?"

"Fuck you!" Eliot says.

"What?" Sarah says. Now, in addition to screwing up his romantic machinations, Karl has made him frame this meeting badly. Eliot removes his earbud, shoves it into his bag.

"That wasn't for you. That was for Karl. He's trying to, like, orchestrate my whole life."

"Your whole life may need some orchestration, if Barcelona was any indication."

"It's good to see you, too."

Sarah puts her palmtop to sleep. "Karl told me that you needed to see me and that it was some kind of emergency. I don't have time for more bullshit."

"You're wearing your bracelet."

"Sometimes, at work—"

"Guggenheim busy?" Eliot says.

"Busy? Absolutely crazy. We have a show by a twelve-year-old installation artist from a Riot Zone outside Denver. Stunning stuff. A scathing aesthetic critique of the whole capitalist-warfare establishment. But he's a cranky spoiled brat. Impossible to work with."

"What's his name?"

Sarah considers her answer. "This is not a conversation I have time for. Why am I here?"

"See those guys sitting across from us? The ones with the hats? They're from the Bildungsroman Channel. They're recording us. Karl set this meeting up to create dramatic material for the pilot to my reality bioseries."

"I haven't agreed to appear on a TV show." Sarah grabs her purse, ready to go.

Eliot gently touches her wrist. "Wait, okay, just give me a minute. One minute."

Her mood stabilizer bracelet remains a steady green. She gives him his minute.

"I need to ask you for something. A big favor. There's a party this weekend. At the Getty Center. Celebrating, ah, well, the first anniversary of V-NoCal Day."

"Let me guess." Sarah seems disgusted. "Karl says you need a date for your neo-imperialist party."

"How'd you guess? That's right."

"Charming."

"The focus groups say you're the only one people want to see me with, but don't let that turn you off to the romantic possibilities.

I could use a respectable woman right about now. In fact, I wanted to see you so much that I purposely didn't call you. Karl set up this meeting behind my back. The truth is, I'll be honest, I've screwed my life up badly, but I want to be a new man now."

"Do you? Terrible news. Excuse me while I dump my shares of ERVJ. I was banking my retirement on the promise that you would produce a few more sex tapes for the mediasphere."

"I want to live a normal life, to be a real human being, and I'm coming to realize that I feel most fully human when I'm with you. When we're together."

"So what you're saying, in essence, is that you need me to gratify your desires. This time, it just happens to be your desire to be fully human."

"I understand that you're mad at me."

"No! How could you think such a thing?"

"The party, it's on Friday. I know you're against all this 'neo-imperialist' and 'semifascist capitalist-warfare establishment' stuff, but say yes. Say yes for me."

"Why exactly would I want to come to your neo-imperialist party?"

"Maybe 'cause despite your political beliefs the Getty Center has one of the best art collections in the world and you wouldn't want to miss it?"

"First of all, their new contemporary collection is shit."

Eliot throws up his hands. "I stand corrected. I'm doing my best here."

"Second—Look, Eliot, you have absolutely no perspective. I'm supposed to take a day off work with practically no notice? Just because you've asked me to? I take my work seriously. People count on me. That may come as a surprise to you, the idea of having obligations and following through on those obligations."

"All good points. What you're saying is that I have to sweeten the pot. What if I let you rip off the rest of my chest hair in public? There isn't much left, but it's yours. Or how about this: you'll have, like, an awesome platform from which to denounce capitalism and all its evils. Or whatever it is you're passionate about now. You can tell the POTUS to his face what you think about the invasion."

"The POTUS?"

"The president of the United States."

Sarah rolls her eyes. "I'm sure cursing President Friendly would be very personally gratifying, but I'm not twenty-one anymore."

"What I'm trying to say, Sarah, is that I *need* you. I think I may still be in love with you. Not in the way I thought I loved all those other girls. You're the one I keep coming back to. Again and again, you're always there. Hell, I don't even care that Karl or the focus groups want you at the Getty party. *I* want you there. Now that's gotta mean something."

Sarah takes her purse and stands up. Her mood stabilizer bracelet has subtly changed color. Eliot doesn't stop her from leaving. As she walks away, her short heels click on the pavement in time with the song "Genghis, My Love," playing now on the Carousel, children gleefully singing along. One of the Bildungsroman guys, the director, lowers his offprint and makes a thumbs-up sign to Eliot. He and the videographer high-five, ecstatic over Eliot's splendid and heartrending dramatic performance.

Ω

On the day he's scheduled to leave for LA, Eliot is awakened at an unnaturally early hour by a call that has somehow punched through his system's many blocks and filters. The call must be from someone on his priority list. Eliot gestures on his bedroom mediawall. On the wall appears Tom, his face tanned and weathered. It's late morning in Israel and the room he's sitting in is brightly lit.

"Hey, Eliot? I wake you up?"

"No, man, I'm just, you know, lying here in bed in my boxer shorts. I do that sometimes. Usually nine-ten hours a day, sometimes with my eyes closed."

"Sorry there."

"I'm up now. How's life in the Jewish Homeland treating you?"

"My relatives are all insane. It's just incredible."

"Sucks, man."

"No, that's not what I mean. What I'm saying is I've visited Israel before, once in a while, but when you visit, when you're the American relative staying for a week, everyone gets excited and acts different. They all hate each other and bicker and squabble among themselves, but you can do no wrong because you're a visitor. Their insanity this time, this is how they really live, their real life. It's all so ordinary." His eyes shine at this discovery. "It's so easy to forget that real people live here."

Eliot rubs his eyes. "You aren't, like, fighting to save Israel from destruction?"

"I talked to a recruiter with the Israeli Air Force and petitioned to do helicopter training. I'm waiting for them to process my application and if they accept me to send me to basic, but they're having trouble incorporating new recruits. Thousands of Jews have come from all over the world. It's so frustrating to wait."

"So there hasn't been a war yet? Awful, man! I hope something starts up soon."

"Don't get sarcastic with me," Tom says. "Things are on the edge. Caliph Fred just released a hit single with vague suggestions that the Holocaust might maybe not have happened and, you know, references to the Twelfth Imam and all that radical Islamist end-of-the-world stuff. He *claims* of course that he was going to release the song on his new pop album this fall anyway, and that he's not trying to deny anything, but it's pretty clear that this is part of a broader campaign of subversion. Much worse is that the Caliphate is smuggling evangelicals across the borders from Lebanon and Egypt. A couple riots have broken out in Jerusalem, riots that are happening *outside* the Riot Zone, if you can believe that. These Christian guys, they're going nuts."

"I know," Eliot says. "You know my dad is one of them, right? I mean, he's much respected and he wears a fancy business suit, but he's basically, like, kind of nuts."

Tom frowns. "I know your Father's religious, but he's not like these guys."

Because Tom has always considered Eliot Sr. to be something like a role model, Eliot has hesitated to openly attack his father. But if Tom wants to persist in this ridiculous quest for military glory, Eliot sees no good reason to hold back.

"I'm serious," Eliot says. "When we moved to New York, Dad joined this high-powered Bible study group. Serenity Soon, Richard Dickey, Hart Shining, and Lionel Goodacre were members, and they were all fascinated by the Apocalypse."

"Vice President Goodacre?"

"That's right. Why do you think Omni's mascot is a red heifer? Dad had been breeding red heifers on our Texas ranch, kind of a hobby. He wanted to help produce a kosher, perfectly red heifer, so its descendents could maybe be sacrificed like in biblical prophecy and Jews could reenter the Temple Mount. Even when we moved to New York, he was always flying back to Texas to meet with these Israeli rabbis. They were checking out our livestock. Some of the more promising candidates got shipped to Israel so they could breed."

"I told you in Barcelona. They've got a cow ready—"

"Sometimes, Tom, Dad would let me attend the study group, but I didn't completely understand what they were talking about. They kept talking about things like winepresses and the Valley of Megiddo."

"That's in Northern Israel. A lot of the evangelical types are gathering there."

"Of course they are. That's supposed to be where the antichrist is finally destroyed by the army of the faithful. Jesus ends up killing enough disbelievers to create a sea of blood in the Valley."

Tom laughs halfheartedly. "That's pretty dark."

"Yeah, pretty dark, man." Eliot recalls a passage from Revelation: "'And the winepress was trodden without the city, and blood came out of the winepress, even unto the horse bridles, by the space of a thousand and six hundred furlongs.'"

Tom turns down his green eyes. His jaw seems more square than usual.

"Now, some people in the so-called End Times community, they've calculated how much blood that would be, taking the biblical quotes literally. They did the math. That's a two-hundred-mile river of blood, four and a half feet deep, the blood of, like, two-and-a-half billion people." Li'l El couldn't wrap his mind around so much carnage. Behind the smiling veneer of his family's cheerful brand-name Christianity lurked a longing for a massacre so unthinkable and outrageous that he couldn't stop thinking about this warrior Jesus as a villain. "The way my father talked, I became afraid that I would be left behind, that I wasn't faithful in my heart."

"That's rough," Tom says.

"Don't worry about it, man. I got over all that bullshit a long time ago. Now, I get to sit out the end of the world comfortably in my penthouse. You're the one with the front-row seat."

"Don't throw me any pity parties, Eliot. I *chose* to be here. I'm actually doing something."

"What's that supposed to mean?"

"It means I'm participating, and not whining passively like a little bitch."

"I don't exactly see—"

"Sure, the world sucks. Sure, your father's not a saint. But if you choose not to act, that's your own damn fault. If bad shit happens, we're responsible now. I mean, you're sitting on top of enormous power. The things that you say and do get noticed, Mr. ERVJ."

The alarm clock rings at its preset time. Eliot gestures it off.

"I have to get going, man. I've gotta get to work, then I'm flying out to LA. There's an Omni Science—sponsored party at the Getty tomorrow night. Victory in Northern California, first anniversary." He makes a V-sign with his fingers. "The POTUS will be there, so I'll let him know what you just said about all my power. I'll give you a call when I get back. Promise."

"Sure," Tom says. "We'll talk."

Eliot makes a gesture to end the call and the mediawall goes black.

Ω

Eliot ascends in an invisible elevator to the halo of the Omni Science Building. Father's email summons had said he wanted to reintroduce Eliot to an old family friend. As he enters his father's office, Eliot is, as usual, impressed by its largeness. An antique telescope stands by the window wall, thousands of offprints line heavy wooden bookshelves, and a massive desk carved from a redwood stump sits at the room's center. He's never figured out how the desk got in here.

Father is not around. A tall man is standing in front of the desk, his posture very straight: Retired US Air Force General Richard Dickey. His slate hair is styled in a crew cut. His hawklike nose seems almost patrician. Above his eyes float two startlingly large and tangled eyebrows.

"Why, my goodness." The eyebrow masses rise. "Look at you."

"Sir."

They shake hands.

"Why, I haven't seen you in how long? You were a gangly kid."

"More than ten years, I think," Eliot says.

"You were quite popular, if I remember. Everyone wanted a piece of Li'l El."

Eliot represses a grimace. "Now that I'm being publicly traded, sir, people can literally own a piece of me, or at least my Name."

"That sounds just about right."

"I was talking to a friend of mine about the situation in the Middle East."

"Lots of Apocalypse talk," Dickey says, nodding.

"Is it serious?" Eliot tries not to sound too eager. "I mean—I know you do Foresight stuff, sir, and—"

Dickey winks. "The masters of mankind don't let things go wrong on their watch." Father comes out of the bathroom. "And speak of the devil," Dickey adds. "Eliot, you've got yourself a fine son."

"We all know that," Father says.

Father positions himself between Eliot and Dickey and puts one hand on each of their shoulders. Though shorter than both of them, Eliot Sr. projects a powerful aura, one that gives him license to enter into your personal space without having to ask permission. Whenever father comes this close, Eliot feels mute and stupid.

"Sorry I'm, ah, late," Eliot says, stuttering. "I got caught up with the Bildungsroman people."

"The what people?" Father says.

"You know, my reality show. Karl thought filming me at work would be a good idea, so—"

"I'm sure Karl knows what he's doing," Father says. "Richard and I must get going, son. We have a Leviathan Group board meeting."

Father has been on the board of directors of the Leviathan Group for almost a decade. Financed by the Freedom Coalition's Special Research and Development Fund, the Group is responsible for developing and managing warfare prediction systems. Their flagship product is the Foresight System, which uses real-world warfare data to derive highly accurate battle models for Coalition operations. Their clients are exclusively member nations of the Freedom Coalition or Pentagon-licensed private military contractors.

"You're not coming to LA?" Eliot says.

"Of course I am. I'll be catching the early Gooney, tomorrow."

"What about me?" Eliot says. "I'm supposed to be flying out today."

"Dolly will be back from her lunch break soon. Talk to her."

"Because I haven't heard anything about—"

"Son, we're already late for our meeting."

"Do you mind if I wait here for Dolly?" Eliot says. "The Bildungs-roman people are still at my cube downstairs. We've been filming all day. I need a break."

"Whatever you find convenient." Father grabs his leather brief-case.

"Thanks, Dad."

"A pleasure, young man," Dickey says. "A real pleasure."

Dickey shakes his hand again, then leaves with Father.

Alone now, Eliot paces the room, cagey. He looks through the telescope. Strokes the spines of his father's books. Studies the throne-like chair behind the desk: its frame is an array of silver and black wire coiled together in improbable ways, the product of unimagin-ably precise and expensive nanotechnological manufacturing tech-niques. The organic-metal thing evolves spontaneously when Eliot falls into it, its subtle responsiveness almost human in intelligence. Eliot leans toward the window wall and the chair automatically moves toward it.

The illusion of being two hundred stories above the earth with no physical support is overwhelming. Eliot always loved sitting in Father's expensive chairs. In Austin, Li'l El, once looking out over the city, imagined the devil tempting him with all the kingdoms of the earth. Would he be able to resist? By the time the Omni Science Building was erected, these fantasies had become ironic, almost bitter.

Though he no longer believes in much of anything, Eliot feels some-times as if he hasn't really changed not fundamentally.

Another memory surfaces. When he would visit his father's Austin office, Father enjoyed telling him about the incredible power of the Omni system. America's new Total Terror Surveillance System was constantly feeding tens of millions of hours of raw footage into Homeland Security's Panopticon Database. Anyone who had access to the database could, Father said, use Omni to spy on the secret lives of just about anyone, even the very rich and important. Natu-rally, Eliot Sr. emphasized, such spying was totally unethical. The Panopticon Database was only justified as a tool by means of which one could defend America against its countless enemies, foreign and domestic. But the voyeuristic possibilities had tickled Eliot's young imagination, and he had always secretly wanted to conduct searches on Panopticon.

Eliot turns back toward his father's computer. A classified data-base, the secret life of freedom, open to him. Father never biometri-cally secures his computers. After all, no one has access to where he keeps them. His fingers hover over the touchboard. A thrilling shock of fear runs up his spine. Who might he be able to see? The president of the United States? Director of Homeland Security, the Secretary of Defense? Occupation headquarters in Caracas, Reykjavik, Brussels, Treasure Island? Anywhere in the world, probably, where the Free-dom Coalition has, as Father puts it, enlarged the sphere of liberty.

In the open Omni search window, a whole world at his disposal, Eliot types:

ELIOT R. VANDERTHORPE, JR.

The Omni "working animation" appears on the screen, an image of the cartoon red heifer, Red, munching on grass. Because Omni is searching not only through the totality of mediasphere footage but also through the Panopticon, the search takes longer than usual. Red munches on grass for another couple seconds, then Omni's report opens. Eliot plays the three most recent segments.

Segment 1 (Restricted): Thursday, 23 August: 8:05:12–8:07:45 EST.

Eliot steps into the lobby of the Transcontinental Building and smiles at the doorman. He is wearing dark sunglasses and a baseball hat. This getup doesn't fool Omni, which most likely recognizes him from the signature pattern of his walk or some other subtle algorithm derived from the constantly evolving baseline footage that forms the foundation of Omni's conceptual description of him. Eliot exits the lobby.

Segment 2 (Public): Thursday, 23 August: 8:07:52–8:49:34 EST.

In front of the Transcontinental Building, Eliot finds the Bildungsroman director and videographer waiting for him. They offer to take him to the Omni Science Building in a microtaxi, but Eliot refuses. They follow on foot, recording footage. When he gets to the subway entrance on 95th Street, Eliot pauses. The weather is so nice (Eliot remembers having thought) that he decides to stay above ground today. Eliot goes to a Segway stand and rents a miniscooter. The director and videographer rent a tandem powered tricycle and follow Eliot, who is speeding along at ten miles per hour on a dedicated miniscooter lane, the Bildungsroman tricycle right beside him. Eliot fast-forwards the footage.

Inside the Omni Science Building, the archival record goes blank. The irony is not lost on Eliot. Even the notorious Panopticon Database can't see the inner workings of Omni. If this is the best view a restricted database can give, Eliot is so far not very impressed. There is a third segment, though, whose time signature corresponds to the time that Eliot has been inside this building. It begins to play.

Segment 3 (Restricted): Thursday, 23 August: 11:35:34–11:50:45 EST.

Eliot passes the BART station on Shattuck Avenue, wearing a leather jacket, smoking a cigarette. Hands stuffed into jeans pockets, he passes various military checkpoints. There are no significant breaks in the footage, only jump cuts when he moves out of range of the first camera and into range of the next. Private military contractors with Canadian and Freedom Coalition flags sewn above the hearts of their SysAdmin Force uniforms smoke cigars and play cards near a Bradley Urban Tank parked by what might once have been a car garage, before it was destroyed. Eliot is walking down Telegraph. He finds a small café, the Revolutionary Rebel Coffee House, which is filled with more Canadian soldiers, and he orders a coffee. After finishing his coffee, he—

Eliot pauses the video. This last segment can't be real. First of all, It originates from within the Occupied Zone, in Berkeley, California. Eliot hasn't been to Berkeley since he was fifteen, twelve years before the Big One, thirteen before the invasion and occupation of Northern California (*Operation Win the West*, all rights reserved). Secondly, during the time that this video was taken, Eliot has been sitting right here, behind this computer terminal, in the Omni Science Building. Holy shit is one of the thoughts that cross his mind. What the hell does this mean is another. He resumes the segment, hoping to find some answers.

Eliot is walking up Telegraph away from the UC Berkeley campus and arrives at a comic book shop called Creative Destruction Comics, which he enters. The video ends.

After the specified time interval, even at this clearance level, Omni can't find any unique instances of Eliot's conceptual description in the mediasphere or on the government's databases. He tries searching for himself using slightly different parameters but he either finds the same video segments or nothing at all. His fan sites and media stalkers have been less active in the last two days, so there isn't even much ordinary news and commentary about him in the mediasphere. Eliot breathes more quickly, his palms get sweaty, his hands shake. There's someone who looks like me in Berkeley, he thinks. In the Occupied Zone of Northern California. Who the hell is that in the video?

Papers shuffle outside his father's office. Dolly has come back for something—that's right, for him. Her voice calls from the outside, "Are you still in there, Mr. Vanderthorpe?"

"No, Dolly. It's just me. Eliot."

"We're closing up for the afternoon," she says. "Everyone's heading for their flights."

"I'll be out in a minute."

Eliot steadies his hands. Working efficiently despite his panic, he transfers the third Omni segment to his smartwatch and deletes all traces of his search from Father's computer. When he stumbles into the vaultlike reception area, Eliot finds Dolly waiting, fixing her makeup. A former Ms. New York, she is blonde and tan, poised and pleasant. Mother hates Dolly for being all these things and for being a decade younger than her, though she has of course never said a single negative word about her husband's personal assistant. For as long as they've known each other, Eliot Jr. and Dolly have always enjoyed flirting in an innocent way—Dolly has been married to an Omni Science VP for many years and has three children—but Eliot isn't in the mood right now.

"You okay, hon?"

"Been a long first week."

"Next week will be better."

"I sure hope so."

"You get going, or you'll be late for your Gooney. There's a sedan waiting for you in basement level two."

On unsteady legs, Eliot enters the executive elevator. As the doors shut, and ambient Muzak fills his head, he leans back against the chilly metal wall. The elevator begins its long descent from the halo to the main building. A headache looms darkly on the horizon of his mind, its rumble warning of some dire future. His haggard reflection stares back from mirrored doors with confused and questioning eyes, for which he has no answers. More than answers, Eliot wishes he had a tranquilizer handy.

PART III
ANOTHER WORLD IS POSSIBLE

On Gooney Flight 1177, a some-what more sedate Eliot discovers an article about himself in *Bird*, the in-flight magazine, that features photos of him wearing his three-piece suit in airport-lounge-like places, hand confidently grasping his stubbly chin, eyes gazing longingly at some middle distance *out there*. In addition to this spread, there's a full-page picture of him in his new hipster chic getup walking down some Manhattan street, a cup of coffee in his hand, aviator shades obscuring his eyes. When he boarded the plane, Eliot shaved his face clean and changed from his work clothes into more or less the same costume he's wearing in the photo.

Karl has prescreened all his clothes, has scoured them free of Che. Eliot wears "street-modified" limited-edition Nikes, Air Incredibles. Jeans handcrafted by wear-and-tear specialists from a Shinjuku-based participatory textile collective, Radu Jeans. On top of a T-shirt he wears a tweed jacket with strategically punched holes and rough patches, a jacket that screams "hipster academic," and a guard from the air-conditioned cabin cold. Rani Kim, Eliot's new fashion consultant, calls his look "the '90s–'00s liminal boundary layer by way of today." Rani is herself twenty-one years old, so Eliot wonders what the hell she knows about either the '90s or '00s. Eliot's T-shirt bears his new "Meaning" logo, a collection of abstract shapes with no discernible pattern.

"You're co-branding with a label called 'Meaning,'" Karl had told him.

"What kind of a product is this logo attached to?"

"That's the brilliant thing, El. It's not attached to anything. Not yet."

"Wha?"

"It's a brand without a product. It's pure meaning, so to speak. Meaning is hoping to use licensing deals to grow its Reputation. Then, the Meaning people—really, just a group of graphic designers working out of a loft in Seoul—hope some bigger firm will buy out their Name. They've got a dozen Brand Names growing, evolving, in the mediasphere. It's a great business opportunity and a whole new way of building brands."

"At least I'm not trying to *sell* something," Eliot said.

"Well, El—you're selling the brand identity of a product that might or might not someday exist."

"That makes me feel better." And it *had* made him feel better, somehow.

Eliot is vaguely excited to read the *Bird* interview because his responses are, in fact, not his own, but have been fed to the reporter by his personal assistant. These answers were probably written by Karl, run through various focus groups and simulations, and refined to stay exactly on message by teams of unpaid marketing interns with BAs in Cultural Studies. Which means that Eliot is learning for the first time what he thinks about things he has probably never thought about.

BIRD: What's this new look you're going for? It's not quite '00s. It's more a kind of philosopher-slacker '90s.

ELIOT: Well, slackers aren't only figures from the '90s. The slackers, my father's generation, have had a long afterlife. We're still living with their complex legacy. I'm going for what I would call Late Generation X Naïveté. A pre-9/11 sort of mentality thrust against its will into a world full of ugly knowledge. I want to bring back that feeling of unearned innocence that reigned in the slacker mind during those first nine months of 2001, a womb swelling with terror, ready to give birth to some new recognition of what sort of world we live in, a world of personal and political responsibility. So this is very much a '00s look. Quintessentially '00s, in fact.

BIRD: Were you even born before 9/11?
ELIOT: A few days before.

BIRD: I see.

This exchange kills Eliot's interest in the interview and makes him conscious of the fact that he's flying in a plane. He reassures himself that only three or four major flights are shot down annually inside the territorial US and that those three or four are almost never Gooneys, which fly too high and too fast for personal missile launchers to target and hit. Eliot is more likely to die in a car accident than die on this flight. He puts the magazine away, orders a drink on the cabin's computer, and digs around in his bag for the over-the-counter tranquilizers he bought at Newark Airport. He needs another hit.

The flight attendant brings him his Blood Mary. She's lean and willowy, blonde hair pulled back into a tight bun, sky blue uniform tightly fitted to her body, hugging narrow hips. She lingers in the private cabin for a moment longer than she should.

"I hope you enjoy your drink," she says.

Sexual tension has been building between them over the course of this three-and-a-half-hour flight. She has served him three times. She's interested. He probably has this one last chance to make a move before landing. He steps toward her, and she stays in place, expectant.

When the temptation to kiss her becomes too great, he leans in, and she closes her eyes. Sarah, he thinks. You meant what you said to her. This thought disrupts the smooth movement of his head, and he lightly headbutts her. The flight attendant waits for something more, but there will be no more.

"Thanks there," Eliot says and moves back toward his seat.

Her mouth tenses when she realizes that he has politely rejected her; the let-down flight attendant turns around on flat heels and quietly exits the cabin.

Eliot chases another tranquilizer down with his Bloody Mary and begins reading his newly fabricated copy of Wittgenstein's *Philosophical Investigations*, pen in hand, the habits of a grad student hard to kill. He tries to repress what he knows he'll have to do when he gets to LA; to forget that random wackos shoot down planes on a probabilistically determinate, though random, basis; to care only about what Wittgenstein has to say; to believe that he has become a better person, that this time really is different, that everything will be okay.

$$\Omega$$

Eliot squints and slouches in the LA sun. The shock of left-behind air conditioning strikes him like climatic whiplash. Residue of tomato juice coats his tongue. A lit cigarette, which has materialized in his right hand, docks with his mouth. The noise of the Gooney terminal fades behind him as he walks toward the pickup area. He puts his jacket into his duffel bag and finds his aviator glasses. They cut down the glare, of course, but are also part of today's Eliot R. Vanderthorpe, Jr., brand identity getup, hipster chic, which has at last completely colonized every part of his body. A ticker crawls on his aviator glasses, stock prices marching like army ants in a neat row across the bottom of his field of vision. *ERVJ 387 388 387½ +½* is in the mix. The New York markets must be closed at this hour. He's up one-half. He taps his smartwatch to kill the display.

Eliot takes a drag on his cigarette and taps another command into his smartwatch. His earbuds begin playing "ERVJ," his newly released "theme song": a track on an album Karl purchased from an eighteen-year-old Brazilian "music landscaper" named Evo. "Evo's stuff is very Conceptual," Karl had said. "Very pop, but spiritual too. He takes the terror out of our sublime confrontations with the everydayness of the Real." The song plays like an admixture of a Buddha Box, a Franz Ferdinand impersonator, and a Stephen Hawkins–like computerized voice, as synthesized by Philip Glass. Eliot feels a little less squinty and slouchy now, more hopeful.

Suffering from a buzz born of a few too many Bloody Marys, Eliot makes a game of walking in a straight line along the crease formed between two concrete plates, veers toward the Humvee waiting for him at the curb. Pedro is at the wheel. A native of LA, Pedro came in on an earlier flight with the rest of the Vanderthorpe Family and Omni Science support staff. On the Gooney, Eliot had requested that he be the one to pick him up. Before he can make it to the Humvee, two men overtake him, Dave and Marty. They flew, business class, on the same flight as Eliot. Eliot had hoped to ditch them quietly while they waited at the baggage claim. He had turned off his chaincam and hidden it in his duffel, contractual obligations be damned. But they're too quick. His palmcam out, Marty is already recording him.

"You shaved," Dave says. "And you're drunk!"

"That's right!" Eliot calls back, mocking Dave's eager tone.

"Can you stumble and swagger a little more? Right on, that's perfect."

When Eliot nears the Humvee, Pedro comes around to load his duffel.

Pedro laughs. "What the hell are you wearing?"

"I'm supposed to evolve into some sort of chic hipster. Karl wants me to develop a new look, to 'search for the centerless essence of cool.' Those were his exact words, man. 'Centerless essence of cool.'"

"Good luck with that, guy."

When Pedro slaps his back, Eliot stumbles forward into an awkward half embrace with him. He reduces the volume of the ambient pop coming through his earbuds so he can hear better. He puts his free hand on Pedro's shoulder and leans toward his face. Pedro flares his nostrils with displeasure, backs his head away.

"You *are* drunk."

"Help me get rid of those two," Eliot says. He raises his aviator glasses to look Pedro in the eye. Pedro squints suspiciously and turns toward the Humvee. Dave and Marty have loaded their gear and are already sitting in the backseat. Marty fiddles with his palmcam. These two will not be easy to shake.

"Just tell them to go away," Pedro says.

"I can't. I'm under contract. I have to do something they can't find out about."

"What do you have to do?"

Eliot considers whether to be honest. "I need to get to Berkeley."

"In-the-Occupied-Zone Berkeley?"

"That's the one."

"You nuts, guy? You even know how you gonna get there?"

"No idea."

Pedro looks over his shoulder, then turns back. "Then you're in luck. Here's the part of the movie where it pays off for the spoiled rich white kid to be friendly with the brown extras. We minority types always got us some shady contacts. If you're serious, really serious, you go to Westwood and ask for Tony Mendoza. He's my cousin, couple times removed."

"He can get me there?"

"Ex-marine. He runs a cab service now. Freelance shit."

"I can't just take a taxi to Berkeley."

"When I say a cab service, I mean he transports stuff. People, things. Tony's been in private security for years, ever since he got back from Iceland. A real badass. Last I heard, the border's wide open to him. He does subcontracting work sometimes for the NoCal SysAdmin Force. You tell him Pedro can vouch for you."

"What's his user name," Eliot says.

"Tony doesn't take calls for business. He deals with clients face-to-face only. Listen, go to the Westwood Diner on Westwood Boulevard, ask around. Tony's always holding court there when he's in town. If he's there, he'll take you into the zone."

"And if he's not?"

"I guess you'll have to find another way to get there, guy."

"I don't want to get you in trouble."

"Look, I'm not under contract to take you anywhere you don't want to go. And I'm not obliged to listen to what these reality television guys tell me. I don't work for them. So you say to me, 'Pedro, I'm going to take a cab to the hotel.'"

"Pedro, I'm going to take a cab to my hotel."

Pedro grins a lopsided grin. "Very good, sir."

Before Dave and Marty know what has happened, Pedro gets in the Humvee and accelerates away from the curb. Dave looks back through the rear window, fury on his face, and Marty turns with his palmcam. The Humvee joins a knot of traffic and disappears.

When his smartwatch rings, a call from Dave, Eliot turns off his ringer. He hobbles over to the rental cars parked near a concrete island in the asphalt sea of LAX. He chooses a Toyota Conserva, a one-seat electric buggy. His smartwatch synchs with the car's system, and cash from his checking account transfers automatically to the rental account. A green light on the dashboard indicates the vehicle is under his control. Eliot types "Westwood Diner" into the navigation system, waits for directions to appear on the windshield, but nothing happens.

The car insists that Eliot blow onto a breathalyzer before it allows him to drive manually. Pretty sure he'll fail the test, he sets the car to autopilot. When the buggy pulls onto the northbound 405, a frenzy of speeding steel and plastic, he slaves his playlist into the sound system and closes his eyes. Evo pumps in over the sound system and his inner ear is spinning and, stricken with disequilibrium, Eliot decides that Dave and Pedro are right, he's definitely drunk.

Ω

Though he stands at only five feet ten inches, Tony Mendoza projects a hulking aura. Knotted venous muscles voluminously fill his black T-shirt, spill out of arm and neck holes. He keeps his mustache neatly trimmed. His eyebrows are large and angular. Otherwise, he has no hair on his head. His domed pate shines in the fluorescent lights of the Westwood Diner. Wrinkles have begun to carve his face into plates. He must be in his late thirties, maybe early forties.

"What should I call you? Tony?"

"You call me Mr. Mendoza."

Tony takes a Heinz bottle from next to the booth's tiny tabletop jukebox and begins lavishing his omelet with ketchup. His fingernails are well manicured. An uncommonly beautiful redheaded waitress, an aspiring actress or UCLA undergrad, brings them two cups of coffee and a tuna melt for Eliot. Eliot winks at her, but she seems unimpressed. Is it perhaps his sour breath that turns her off? His far-too-artfully self-conscious taste in clothing? Maybe mid-cap celebrities don't impress these LA girls as easily as they do back East. When the waitress leaves, Tony spikes his coffee with whiskey from a small metal bottle he keeps openly holstered to his belt.

"You want?"

Eliot doesn't refuse.

"So you know Pedro. He's a good kid. He's your driver, you say?"

"Well, he works for my father. He drives me around. We're friends."

"Oh, I'm sure. Let's not mince words. You're very lucky you found me. I'm scheduled to make a run up to San Francisco. I'm leaving as soon as I finish this omelet. So what is it I can do for you?"

"Well, Tony—"

"Show some respect for your elders. It's Mr. Mendoza."

"Right. Sorry, I forgot. Well, Mr. Mendoza, I need to get to Berkeley. Berkeley, California."

"And?"

"I was hoping you could take me there."

"Why do you think I would take you there?"

"I, well. I guess, I thought, Pedro said—"

"Do I look like a cabdriver to you?"

"Pedro said—"

"I asked you a question, Eliot. Look me in the eye when I talk to you, boy. Do I look like a cabdriver to you?"

"No."

"Then let me ask you again. Why do you think I'll take you to Berkeley, California, which is, as I am sure you are fully aware, under the provisional occupation of the Freedom Coalition's SysAdmin Force until such time as a democratically elected government can be installed?"

Eliot gathers his thoughts. What does Tony want him to say? He has to give the right answer if he wants to track down his doppelgänger. The right answer comes out of his mouth before he realizes that his brain has performed the necessary computations.

"Because I'm going to pay you a shitload of money?"

"Now you're talking sense, boy. Pull out your tab."

Eliot complies with the order. While stuffing his face with ketchupy omelet, Tony pulls out his own tab, a weather-beaten military model that could probably emerge from a nuclear fireball unscathed. On both tabs, a contract opens. A Singaporean bank account is the receiving party. There is one number in the contract that Eliot has trouble explicating.

"What's that over there, that five-digit number. Your Zip Code?"

"That's what you're paying me to take you to the Bay Area. Safe passage, up and back."

Eliot rehearses outrage in his mind, imagines haggling strategies that might reduce the price. Father, a natural and ferocious salesman, could probably negotiate Tony into a quivering mass of flesh were he here, but he's not. Eliot can't think of anything to say or do. He has the money, so he signs the contract. He thumbs the biometric reader on his tab and looks into its camera; his main checking account, which carries a six-figure balance, takes a not-insubstantial hit. Eliot's hand shakes as he puts his tab back in his duffel bag.

"When do we go?" he asks.

"Mmm—Soon—hrmf—as—mrmgh—I—finish—urp—eating."

Despite his sudden loss of appetite, Eliot goes to work on his tuna melt. He feels too embarrassed to let it sit there after he went to the trouble of ordering it. Before he gets to work, he chugs the spiked coffee.

Ω

Sarah visited Eliot in Cambridge shortly after the Freedom Coalition invaded Northern California, almost a year ago now. She had taken the Amtrak to Boston from a rally in DC, where she had been one of the million protesters who sought to disrupt *Operation Win the West* in midstream, who had cared enough to do something. But the Leviathan phase of the invasion terminated so quickly—Northern California having no army to speak of—that major combat operations ended almost before the protest properly began. When POTUS Friendly declared victory on television, Sarah told Eliot, no one had the stomach to keep protesting. Sarah should have gotten off the train in New York, should have returned to her responsibilities at the Guggenheim, but she was too emotionally torn up. On a whim, as Canadian and Mexican private military contractors closed in on the Bay Area, Sarah called Eliot, hoping he might make her feel better, might make her laugh, might help her forget that there was an outside world.

His obligatory cheering up of Sarah—with whom Eliot hadn't spoken for a month, after their last fight and near-backslide into sexual relations—had quickly transformed into something more. Eliot's moderate fame had declined sufficiently that the paparazzi didn't chase them down when they kissed, near the Cambridge-Somerville border, where they had wandered together, hand in hand. The mediasphere was much more concerned for a change with political problems, with demonstrating its patriotic support for the war, with documenting the Pentagon's marketing and media strategy for this new geopolitical notch in its belt. Sarah took time off work and, unable to forget the world, spent a week flipping between the Pentagon Channel and C-SPAN InvasionTV.

"Are we, like, back together?" Eliot had asked at one point.

"I don't know how I'm supposed to answer that question."

Eliot looked up from his book. "Yes or no are the available options."

"My mother thinks I'm crazy for being here," Sarah said. "She still hates you."

"Justifiably so, but still—"

"Last night, I saw this Dr. Jane segment on the Feminism Now Channel about why intelligent and successful women so often end up dating terrible boys."

"Am I a terrible boy?"

"One second, honey. I want to hear what that asshole Goodacre has to say." Sarah gestured the volume up.

As this strangely muted first week's reunion approached its end, Sarah became increasingly angry at Eliot, began accusing him of indifference to the plight of the Bay Area (true), a tacit approval of the Freedom Coalition's neo-imperialism (false), and a complicity in hegemonic systems of power and control (he didn't even know what "hegemonic" meant). When Father brokered yet another billion-dollar deal with Homeland Security, this time to help rebuild the Bay Area's node of Total Terror Surveillance System, Sarah nearly broke up with Eliot.

"C'mon, Sarah," Eliot had pleaded. "I'm really sorry about the invasion and everything—it really sucks, yeah, sure—but *I'm* not responsible for or complicit in it. I'm just trying to write a dissertation."

"There's no way not to be responsible." Sarah threw one of his books across the room, nearly striking him. "Inaction is always a form of action. By doing nothing, you're revealing your real priorities."

"I don't think—" He took a long drag on his cigarette, thinking more carefully about the right response, the true response. "I know you're a very passionate person—I love you, truly love you, for your passion—but these things are all so incredibly complicated. I'm sure there are perfectly reasonable arguments on both sides of the debate, but avoiding extremes seems like the important thing. How do you even start to understand how and why geopolitical sorts of things happen? The contexts and history are all so complex. Hell, I've been reading technical philosophical articles on intellectual property for years and I still have no fucking clue what I'm doing. So how am I supposed to condemn the Freedom Coalition? What grounds do I have to say anything? My main priority is not having opinions about shit I don't know anything about."

This response, which Eliot had thought was noble and persuasive, simultaneously well-wrought and unpretentious, only enlarged Sarah's rage.

"If you're not protesting, Eliot, then you're basically assenting. There's no middle ground."

Though he did not press his line of argument any further, brilliant as he thought it was, Eliot couldn't disagree with Sarah more. He has always privately entertained the idea that he lives by something like the celebrity version of the Hippocratic Oath: do no harm, at least not to others. Certainly, he's never suffered from the illusion that his way of life helps improve the world, but he's also always imagined that the Yin of Uselessness came in tandem with a Yang of Not Fucking Things Up Further. But now, a year later, things have changed. For some reason, the motivations of his Berkeley-based impersonator have come to concern him, to utterly and totally obsess him. Eliot has so far been able to work out three logically distinct explanations for who this man is.

* That he is someone who just happens to look like Eliot, someone Omni can't distinguish from Eliot. Eliot knows that the Omni system is more likely to fail to see a family resemblance than to too broadly generalize its descriptive picture of a particular person. Moreover, the man in the video segment bears more than a passing resemblance to Eliot. This guy looks way too much like him for this to be some sort of technical failure on Omni's part.

* That Eliot has some kind of long-lost identical twin brother. Yes, Mother has a long rumored history of infidelity, mostly connected to her work at the Shining Foundation, but Eliot is of course himself legitimate, so he can't imagine any plausible reason why a twin brother of his might have been raised separately from him.

* That a fanatical fan, a dedicated Eliotlover, has surgically sculpted his face to resemble Eliot's, has studied and adopted Eliot's body language, has done everything in his power to mimic Eliot. This is almost certainly the explanation. Some of Eliot's fans are pretty scary people, after all.

The idea that his life has touched someone else's deeply enough to inspire such a disfiguring decision creeps the shit out of him. The amateur fan-scholars and their relentless analyses of the minutiae of his life have always amused him but have always also seemed unreal. This new development, however, makes his celebrity, perhaps for the first time, seem really real. What would Sarah consider to be the correct response to this situation, the responsible choice? Eliot isn't sure, but he wants to follow the lead of his newly cultivated ethical rudder, wants to find his doppelgänger, whoever he is, wants to shake him by the shoulders and say, "What was so wrong with your own life that you wanted to look just like me?"

Ω

By the side of the road, two hitchhikers emerge from the dusty haze, interrupting Eliot's drunken ethical ruminations. This far north on Highway 5, past the mountains, only supply trucks, military convoys, and those vehicles with special dispensations freely reign. Tony's narrowing and suspicious eyes suggest to Eliot that it is rather unusual to encounter two random hitchhiking civilians here. As Tony's massive SUV, a Ford Juggernaut, approaches these two figures, they resolve from the murk: a woman and a man, both in their early thirties.

The woman is petite and somewhat pale, standing akimbo, legs planted firmly on the dusty shoulder of the road. She wears cargo pants, black boots, and a green tank top. The man, who looks Indian or Pakistani, is a picture of black: black pants, black Adidas, and a black T-shirt. Two black cameras hang from his neck, not the palmcams people in the Biz use, but vintage models with lenses, knobs, and switches, possibly even film; taking photos with old-fashioned cameras is getting trendier. The man guards their bags and plays with one of his cameras.

The woman raises her arms and waves at the Ford, a tab in her hand, an offer of payment. His interest in making money overwhelms his more cautious instincts, and Tony pulls over. The passenger-side window rolls down, letting a bolt of August heat into the air-conditioned cabin.

"We need a lift to the Bay Area," the woman shouts over the roar of passing trucks. She has a British accent.

"How the hell did you two get out here?" Tony says.

"We drove in from Nevada, merged with the road north of here but got turned back at the checkpoint up the road. We parked a couple miles off road, that way, and walked over. We're with the press. I'm Janine. This is Samir, my photographer."

"I didn't stop to have a tea party, Janine," Tony says.

"I have an expense account." She waves her tab.

Tony squints, nods, then unlocks the back hatch. "Load your bags in the back," he says.

After they've loaded their bags and touched tabs with Tony, the Juggernaut roars back onto the road, crossing deeper into the heart of the blank Californian landscape. In the back, Janine sits beside Eliot, Samir next to her.

Janine has flat mousy brown hair, an upturned nose, and alert eyes. Still a bit cowed from his encounter with the unfriendly waitress at the Westwood Diner, and still committed to the idea of getting back together with Sarah, Eliot makes a preemptive decision not to flirt with this woman. No need to make things more complicated than they already are. And besides, Eliot thinks as he takes another swig from Tony's whiskey bottle, she's probably with Samir.

No one says anything as they hurtle along. Janine and Samir do work on their tabs and occasionally partake of Tony's whiskey. Traffic gets worse and worse, and soon they're sitting in what looks like a two-lane parking lot of trucks behind the military checkpoint that marks the Occupied Zone's official outer boundary.

A pair of small but lethal-looking Bradley tanks manned by Mexican SysAdmin Force soldiers stands guard on either side of the road, their big guns swiveling periodically. Insectlike microdrones, prehistorically large, patrol the airspace above. Visible a mile away, a redwood-thick bundle of wire mesh arches over I-5, scanning incoming traffic for visas and interdicted weapons. Two automated machine-gun embankments underwrite the seriousness of this first checkpoint, which the Juggernaut eventually passes through, without incident, moving on to the second segment of the checkpoint, the car check.

Vehicles with more than one passenger must stop on the shoulder of the road for inspection by a pair of Mexican private military contractors. Tony stops, rolls down his windows, and one of the checkpoint guards sticks his head in on the driver's side. A second soldier opens the rear passenger-side door, glaring at Eliot, Janine, and Samir. An XM8 is strapped to his shoulder. Eliot is afraid he'll be recognized; he shaved on the plane in order to look less like himself, but a stubble-free face is no guarantee.

"Hola, Señor Mendoza," the first guard says. "Usted lo tiene?"

"Si, está en el tronco del coche."

"Muchas gracias."

Satisfied, the first guard pulls his head out of the window, and the second slams the door shut. With some help from a third guard, they open the back of the Ford and pull out a large metal suitcase, which seems very heavy. Carrying it together, they place it in the back of a supply truck on the side of the road. The first guard opens the suitcase, studying its contents, then nods to the second guard, who waves Tony through the checkpoint.

"Here we are, boys and girl," Tony says. "The Occupied Zone. Traffic looks good today. Maybe another three hours before we're in San Francisco."

"I need to go to Berkeley," Eliot says. "I'm paying you for Berkeley."

"Calm down, boy. I'll take you into Berkeley tomorrow morning."

"Where am I supposed to stay tonight?"

"That is not my problem," Tony says. "Our contract said nothing about lodging."

"We know some people you can stay with," Janine says. "And I think we'll be joining you tomorrow in Berkeley."

Eliot rocks nervously in his seat.

"Hey, you," Samir says. He also has a British accent.

Eliot is startled. "Are you talking to me?"

"I knew I recognized you! You're that Elvis Vanderbilt kid—"

"That's Eliot Vanderthorpe."

"Right, that's what I meant. Eliot Vanderthorpe. You're kind of famous. You just went public."

"Mid-cap IPO," Eliot says.

"A pleasure to meet you, Mr. Mid-cap IPO." Janine shakes his hand, squeezes it. Her eyes lock onto his.

"The pleasure's all mine," Eliot says in his most deadpan voice.

"Why're you going up to Berkeley, pal?" Samir asks.

"Visiting relatives," Eliot says. "You?"

"Putting together a couple photo essays on the occupation," Samir says. "Doing a spread on Freedom Coalition occupation zones, see. I've got a show on Benelux showing now in London. Very good reviews. Never got to see Iceland, unfortunately." Tony turns his head at the mention of Iceland, but says nothing. "If this whole Armageddon business really gets going," Samir says. "I'm hoping the Mideast will open up with some new photographic angles. I can see it already: a big End of the World show, huge."

"Don't listen to him, love." Janine smiles. "I'm the breadwinner in this relationship. Samir's my photographer. I'm on assignment for the London *Activist*."

Tony snorts sarcastically. "Oh, Christ. I shoulda known."

"Don't think I've ever read it," Eliot says.

"It's sort of like the anti-*Economist*," Janine says. "A nonhierarchical participatory workplace with a pretty militant editorial line, but good reporting. We were part of PEN in London, before the Freedom Coalition designated PEN a terrorist organization. We've had to moderate our statements since the crackdown."

"And you're going into the Bay Area why?"

"No one from the press has been allowed in without an official license from the Pentagon."

"And you have a license?"

"Of course not," Janine says. "That's precisely the point."

"Now that we're inside the zone," Samir says, "I'd like to start taking pictures, if everyone allows. You need to sign some press licenses first. I pay standard rates."

Tony considers the offer. "I would need to consult my agent."

"A mercenary with an agent," Janine says. "There goes something new."

"That, honey, is slander. I'm a *freelance military contractor*. I have a Reputation to protect."

"How 'bout you, Elvis?" Samir says.

"Eliot," Janine says.

"Right on. Eliot. You game?"

Samir holds out his tab. Its red light stares at Eliot, an ominous eye. Eliot knows he shouldn't give Samir a press license. Karl will kill him. The prospect of infuriating Karl is finally what convinces Eliot to say yes. When Eliot and Samir touch tabs, the terms of the one-week press license appear. Eliot pages through the agreement without reading it very closely; it seems standard enough, so he biometrically signs it.

"There you go," Eliot says.

"Terrific," Samir says.

"That's a nice design on your shirt," Janine says.

She rubs the "Meaning" logo on his chest, straightens the collar of his tweed jacket. Her hand touches his neck and quickly brushes his shaved cheek. His neck is sweating, with nervousness, not heat. Janine seems unable to look away from him. Oblivious to her open flirtation with Eliot, Samir takes a light reading and begins snapping photos of him. Eliot repeats to himself, as if it were his mantra, Sarah, Sarah, Sarah.

Ω

Lo and behold, the ghostly apparitions of Cool Ages Past cross over to this temporal plane from across sediment layers of lost time. Aging hipsters and over-the-hill bohemians haunt the Mission's cafés and bars, yo-yoing up and down Mission Street with no sense of purpose, driven by autonomic reflexes buried deep in muscle memory. Eliot feels bad for them: fifty-year-old men and women wear orthopedic high-tops and tweedy newsboy caps, play with nose and eyebrow rings in too-large piercing holes, massage heavily tattooed arms that have begun to sag, listen longingly to Franz Ferdinand on vintage iPods (circa the early '00s), wires dun with decay emerging from ears like some strange prosthesis in a dated cyberpunk film. A blight of nostalgia grows moldlike everywhere upon these streets and these people.

Worse are those who, thanks to new miracles in cosmetic microsurgery, have chosen to remold face and body. Their face jobs are usually just expensive enough to pass at first glance as natural but not enough to fool the eye for very long. One meets such people among Manhattan's modestly wealthy hangers-on and learns to ignore their freakishly plasticlike look. In such unpleasant situations, when Mother would force him as a teenager to meet older family friends who had not yet joined the ranks of the superwealthy, Eliot would pretend that he was talking to manikins come alive. This would help, but only for a while.

Once he accustoms himself to these nostalgic apparitions, Eliot begins to notice other curiosities. On windshields and bumpers, stickers shout slogans. PARTICIPATORY ECONOMICS NET-WORK AGAINST ECONOMIC FASCISM or sometimes just PEN. Almost every car parked on Mission Street seems to have one. Other bumper stickers read PEN IS MIGHTIER THAN THE SWORD and ANOTHER WORLD IS POSSIBLE. PEN pennants or upside-down American flags fly from the windows of some storefronts and apartments, flapping in the wind. These flags and stickers abruptly disappear when they cross over from Mission onto Valencia Street.

Here, in the space between the two main car lanes, there is a column of SysAdmin Force vehicles with Mexican and Freedom Coalition flags stenciled on their sides: tanks, trucks, jeeps, military bikes, SUVs with roof-mounted .50-caliber machine guns. Grounded on the trailer of one flatbed truck, a matte-black pole sways thirty feet above street level. A Mexican soldier, sitting in the surveillance bird's nest at the top, has a total overview of this segment of the road.

"That guy must be shitting his pants," Samir says. "In Amsterdam, Islamic militants sniped at the SysAdmin bird's nests all the time."

"The hip geezers hardly notice a few more Mexicans in costume," Tony grunts.

"There's something I'm curious about," Janine says to Eliot. "Let's talk about why a member of one of the wealthiest families in the world is trying to sneak into Berkeley, into the Occupied Zone. I don't buy the whole 'visiting family' thing."

"Let's not talk about that," Eliot says.

"Mexicans in costume?" Samir says. "Are you some kind of self-hating Mexican?"

Tony scowls. Samir snaps a few photos out the window.

"What exactly are you trying to hide, Eliot?"

"First of all, I'm Puerto Rican. Which means, as far as I'm concerned, American."

"You've been photographed wearing Che merchandise. Are you getting ready to renounce your father and his brand of evangelical capitalism?"

"Second of all, if you ever call me self-hating again I will smash my fist into your face."

"I don't even know what evangelical capitalism is. Is that, like, different from ordinary capitalism?"

"Testy, testy, Mr. Mendoza. Slow down for a moment. I want to—perfect. Got the shot."

"Don't think you can hide your secrets from me, love." Janine squeezes Eliot's knee.

Samir continues snapping photographs of Valencia through Tony's SUV's tinted windows, oblivious to Eliot and Janine. They turn from Valencia and approach Dolores Park. Here, the density of aging hipsters becomes unbearable; among Dolores's swaying palm trees walk pet dogs garbed in clothing more fashionable than anything worn by people in most of the rest of the unoccupied United States. Tony pulls over to the curb and brakes. Seat-belt-less, Eliot jerks forward. A Boston terrier wearing a bowler barks furiously at the SUV; its owner drags the yappy dog away.

"I'm not responsible for any injuries. It's in your contract. Read it."

"I'm fine," Eliot says.

Their bags get unloaded in front of a charming but run-down Victorian mansion, near Mission Dolores, three stories tall. Tony does some paperwork on his tab.

"So here's the story. I'm back here tomorrow morning, quarter to seven. Bay Bridge opens to civilian traffic at seven. If you're not here, you're out of luck. I'm not coming back for you. And just so you know, the Provisional Occupation Authority sets the civilian curfew for ten p.m. Pretty serious, that curfew. Try not to get shot, ladies."

Tony leaves Eliot, Janine, and Samir standing on the curb. Three men and a woman come out of the Victorian, and wordlessly take their bags into the mansion.

"What is this place?" Eliot says.

"A former participatory hostel," Janine says. "Used to be an important meeting place for the movement."

"PEN?"

"That's right."

"Is it legal to sleep here? I mean, since the war—"

Janine seems sad. "Workplaces like this were forced to publicly disavow PEN. The smart ones did it if they wanted to survive. So they're not illegal, but hopefully they're still internally democratic."

"I don't know about this. I just want to—"

"Relax, calm down. No one's going to bother us."

Quite worried, Eliot waits beside their bags while Janine talks with the clerk on duty. In a back room, behind the check-in desk, Eliot witnesses through an open door what he takes to be a surreptitious workplace council meeting. Ten people sit in a circle, on couches and in ratty chairs, arguing, it seems, about the mundane details of managing their hostel. There is an undertone of anger and despair in their hushed voices. Eliot goes outside and smokes, watching palm fronds shuffle in the wind, until Janine calls for him.

By the time they're checked in to their filthy rooms, it's almost nine thirty p.m. In his present state of disarray and hyperanxiety, Eliot wants to coil himself up into a ball among the bedbugs and lose consciousness until tomorrow morning. It's precisely for this reason, perhaps, that the gods of bad fortune inspire Janine to say, "I am absolutely famished. We *have* to get something to eat. They say the Mexican's amazing."

"Go with Samir," Eliot says, desperate, tired.

"I've got some photos to take." Samir pulls out a tiny digital camera. "This is my chance at a Murdoch."

"You and your fucking Murdochs," Janine says.

Samir kisses Janine on the mouth. "The Photo of the Year is hidden somewhere in the seamy underbelly of this city. Its calling out to me. 'Find me, Samir,' it's saying. 'Don't let me be lost forever. I need you.' I won't be back tonight."

"What about the curfew?" Eliot says, afraid to be left alone with Janine.

"What about the curfew, mate? I've been roughed up by the German SysAdmin Force in Brussels, beaten nearly to death by the South African Army, tortured by CIA spooks in The Hague. They were the worst: needles under fingernails, barking dogs, burning. Vicious motherfuckers."

Samir grabs his bag and leaves Eliot alone with Janine. Eliot sits on his bed.

"Get up, lazy boy," Janine says.

"The more I think about it, about eating I mean, the more I think—"

"We have to get something out of the way before we eat."

Eliot stands up, curious. Janine puts two pieces of a waferlike substance between her lips and jostles them around her open mouth with her tongue. Almost instantly, they expand into a solid mass of white foam. The white foam builds and builds around the corners of her mouth. She grabs Eliot by the lapels of his jacket. He feels like an antelope that a lion has marked for death. He lifts his head as if to give over his jugular to her foaming mouth. Just kill me now, he thinks. She tilts his head downward, in the direction of her face, and stands on her toes. Her foam-covered tongue pushes its way into his dry mouth. The foamy substance tingles inside his mouth, tasting lemony. The foam is at length distributed evenly between their two mouths. She wipes her mouth and licks his clean.

"Let's get dinner now," she says.

"That foam," Eliot says.

"It's called Xite. Ex, eye, tee, eee. Takes about an hour to kick in."

Janine leads him from their nasty narrow room, her fingers soft. Asking her about the effect of the foam seems like the wrong thing to do right now, and anyway he can pretty well guess. An hour later, after they've eaten, Eliot pulls his mouth away from the swollen nipple of her left breast and asks a question that has been bothering him all night.

"What about Samir?"

"What about him?"

"He kissed you."

"We're in an open relationship," Janine says.

Her panties have cute little hearts with arrows through them. Their clothes lie tangled, involved together, on the floor. Eliot wears only his argyle socks and silver tribal thumb ring. Janine grabs Eliot in a very sensitive place and seems unwilling to let go.

"How open is your relationship?"

This is when the Xite kicks in. His penis takes on the form of some alien organ grafted onto his pelvis. It must know what it's doing. Janine's panties have somehow slipped off.

"Very, very open."

Lost inside a maze of his own bliss, Eliot decides not to protest.

Ω

Early the next morning, Eliot wakes up with a terrible headache and a very sore dick. Sheets and pillows are scattered across the floor. Even in August, San Francisco can get shockingly cold. Through a miraculous force of will, he drags himself into the common shower, stands on his tiptoes to avoid the filthy floor, and endures its freezing cold jet of water. By the time he manages to dress, he's decided he's feeling way too miserable to make it into Berkeley today.

"I think I'm staying here," Eliot says.

"Stop your surly moaning," Janine says.

She's dressed, bundled up in multiple layers, ready to go. A vintage Dolce & Gabbana purse hangs from her arm. Square-framed black glasses betray their computer functionality only from the ghost images that flicker occasionally on them.

"I can't go," Eliot says.

"You're such a whiney brat. Here, I bought these from Tony while you were showering."

Janine drops two small spherical caplets into his hand and gets distracted looking for something in her purse. After about two seconds of careful consideration, Eliot swallows both pills dry, figuring they can't make him feel any worse than he already does. Janine finds a bottle of water, lipstick ringing its mouth, and hands it to Eliot.

"Take one for now," she says. "Keep the other one as a special gift, a thank-you for last night." She kisses his cheek.

"What do you mean by 'take one'? You gave me two. I already swallowed them both."

Janine seems stunned. "Well."

"Am I fucked? Am I going to die?"

"They're Hyperphainein B, a stim that American marines use when they go on special ops. Government-developed, illegal for non-military personnel. You just took a dosage that would be appropriate for an eighteen- or twenty-hour mission. No permanent harm done, love, but you're going to be a bit frantic for a while."

She smiles. Firmly holding his hand—her hand is so soft—she pulls him toward the door. Before they cover the distance to the door, Eliot begins to feel wonderful, just terrific, superattentive and focused.

"Wow," he says.

Eliot grabs his duffel bag and goes out into a beautiful, crisp, clear San Francisco morning. The golden sun casts sharp-edged shadows onto the filthy streets of the Mission. The hipsters are all still sleeping, hungover, drugged out, or perhaps heading to work in civilian duds. Down the street by Dolores Park a Bradley tank is parked on the sidewalk, near which a local mariachi band sings to amuse Mexican SysAdmin Force soldiers. Birds are singing, too. Birds! When was the last time Eliot noticed birds singing? This Hyperphainein B is really something.

Tony rolls down the Juggernaut window. "We ready, girls?"

"Sir, yes, sir," Eliot says, saluting.

"Don't you ever do that again. That salute means something. Got that?"

"Yes, s—Yes. Yes."

As they make their way toward I-80, and the Bay Bridge, Eliot glances occasionally at the map of the city projected on the windshield. He closes his eyes and tries to imagine the layout of San Francisco, to visualize how Market Street fractures the city into two intersecting grids that sit at an angle with respect to each other.

Eliot remembers the San Francisco of his youth, its surprising peacefulness compared to the Northeast, its lame touristy cable cars, its crappy clam chowder in sourdough bread bowls at the Fisherman's Wharf, Union Square. They had turned one of Father's business trips into a family vacation. His father was wearing a Windbreaker, his mother jeans and a sweater, as ordinary an outfit as she ever wore. Her third book, an extensive study of how uncontrolled democracy subverts freedom, had just been released to critical and surprising popular success, and she was in an unusually relaxed mood. Even at eleven, Elijah was a chameleonic terror, a rebel in quest of a cause, an inveterate performer of preteen rage, ready to say anything to anyone to capture a larger market share of adult attention, all prelude to his recent transformation into a Christian punk. In those days, Eliot had still been the pious child, the obedient one, the one longing to do right. Elijah had no interest in religion back then. Only when he entered his freshman year at Princeton did militant evangelical Christianity come to seem like an appropriate form of rebellion. Somewhere along the way, the brothers flipped theological positions. Elijah became respectable, Eliot an agnostic maniac. Almost fifteen years have passed since the Vanderthorpes visited San Francisco.

Now the Freedom Coalition occupies the Bay Area. Despite Sarah's obsession with the invasion, and its pivotal role in getting them back together, Eliot had only vaguely followed *Operation Win the West*. Sarah tried to explain everything to him: after the Big One, FEMA began selling off the Bay Area's assets at fire-sale prices—public utilities and housing, Golden Gate Park, the damaged Bay Bridge—to raise revenue for reconstruction. The local population, though still dazed from the earthquake, eventually revolted against the privatization plan. The Bay Area arm of the Participatory Economics Network had in the last decade expanded to more than ten thousand nonprofit cooperative workplaces with extensive links to PEN-International, to its think tanks, institutes, and consultancies. PEN's International Council held an emergency meeting in London and voted to donate billions in "cooperative capital" to the Bay Area, to showcase the subversive power of its creeping alternate economy. To do her part to rebuild San Francisco, a city she loved, a city she had lived in for the first twelve years of her life, Sarah donated the equivalent of a month's rent to PEN, an amount she certainly couldn't afford to give. In return, she received a PEN bumper sticker, which she still proudly displays on her Volvo, a six month subscription to the London *Activist*, and a grab bag of PEN-sourced gourmet cheeses.

Flush with cash, emboldened, PEN–San Francisco Bay Area seized the Bay Bridge in the name of the public good, which it claimed to represent. Its financial arm gave conditional loans to local building contractors, funding firms that renounced "corporate-capitalist" operating principles, cold-shouldering firms that didn't. Under these desperate circumstances, some companies began internally restructuring themselves. When he learned of PEN's efforts, President Friendly saw the danger immediately: its openly anticapitalist aspirations threatened to undermine the foundational freedoms the Mexican and Canadian SysAdmin Force would later bid on the right to help preserve. Citing its terrorism against private property, the Freedom Coalition charged into the Bay Area to, in the words of an op-ed Eliot's mother wrote for the *Wall Street Journal*, "liberate the (weak-minded tree-hugging Teva-wearing socialist-sympathizing) people from PEN's nefarious bullying grassroots populism." When she read his mother's *WSJ* editorial, Sarah openly discussed the possibility of bludgeoning Eliot to death with her tab; Eliot is pretty sure she was joking. After the successful invasion of the Bay Area, the Mexican and Canadian SysAdmin Force retrofitted PEN's jury-rigged Bay Bridge—which turned out to be a brilliant bit of desperation engineering—into its operational nerve center; the Coalition Provisional Authority set up its headquarters on Treasure Island. This, Sarah insisted, was the most pathetic of ironies: that the occupiers tacitly acknowledged the good work of the Enemy. Eliot called her crazy for giving her money away in the first place and tried to cover her losses. She refused his offer.

From the rebuilt I-80, downtown San Fran looks like Manhattan in the early twentieth century, giant girder edifices rising up into the fog, spiderlike construction robots climbing up and down cable meshes wrapped around and threaded through these new superstructures. Rafters, posts, and struts crisscross in visually astonishing arrays, eerily random-seeming designs born of evolutionary structural engineering. Among the giant billboards that dominate the space between here and downtown there lurks a red heifer: Omni Science, Father's influence, everywhere. Eliot thinks of Sarah, of how he has hurt her, again and again.

"This military-industrial thing is no joke," he says.

"Of course not," Janine says. "The multinational construction corporations building those things are making a killer profit and also get massive taxpayer subsidies."

"You sound like my girlfriend Sarah," Eliot says.

Tony laughs. "I can't believe I got myself a carload of champagne socialists. Poor billionaire Eliot. Poor bourgeois journalists playing rough-and-tumble communists in the least dangerous occupation zone in human history, thanks, in large part, to Omni Science. I always find it fascinating when I meet genuine collectivists. It's like encountering some primitive tribe."

"Don't give me that bullshit 'collectivist' line," Janine says. Though high-pitched and stereotypically feminine, her voice has a pretty dangerous edge to it. Eliot leans back into his soft seat and lets her do the talking, fascinated by her intensity.

"You PEN people never cease to amuse me," Tony says. "Have you ever read anything by Milton Friedman, sweetheart? 'The free market is the only mechanism that has ever been discovered for achieving participatory democracy.' Friedman wrote that in his introduction to Hayek. Do you even know who Hayek is?"

"Do you do any thinking for yourself, Mr. Fascist Pig, or do you just spend all your time quoting your favorite Great Men?"

Listening to Janine argue with Tony, Eliot finds himself loving Sarah unbearably, miserable with guilt, ashamed of his lust, his poor judgment, his inability to take responsibility for himself apparently under any circumstances. His ability to always generate logical caveats and keep in mind complicating factors seems to be breaking down.

"Are you not going to take us to Berkeley, Mr. Mendoza?" Eliot says.

"I may revile you because you hate freedom," Tony says, "but you're also paying customers and I always honor my contracts. That, my dear collectivists, is the spirit of capitalism for you, right there."

The Bay Bridge comes into view, much changed since Eliot last saw it. Gigantic piles of rubble lining the Bay emerge from the fog, five—no six—heaps, each maybe ten stories tall, cracked concrete blocks, crooked steel girders, shattered glass, charred papers, splintered furniture, burnt-out cars, tangled wire, broken pipes, melted plastic, abandoned shoes.

"Earthquake damage," Eliot says.

"Not the earthquake," Janine says. "The Leviathan Force flattened the business district, knocking down three skyscrapers. Two more had to be torn down, they were so damaged. The invasion did more damage than the Big One."

"I never saw footage of the collapse," Eliot says. "My girlfriend and I were watching C-SPAN InvasionTV the whole time."

"Freedom Coalition owns the rights to those videos," Samir says. "But I have an illegal copy on my tab if you want to see it, mate." Samir offers his tab to Eliot. "Horrible stuff."

Eliot pushes the tab away. "I don't want to see it."

"Their own damn fault," Tony says. "The collectivists were hiding in those skyscrapers, using civilian buildings as cover for anti-capitalist terrorism."

"The collectivists *were* the civilians!" Janine says. "And they weren't terrorists. They just seized the local economy!"

"You just proved my point for me," Tony says.

Now the bridge occludes the piles of rubble. On the bridge there are squat automated machine guns, surface-to-air and surface-to-surface missile embankments, and laser weapons. Tony's forged visas get the Juggernaut and its payload of champagne socialists through the checkpoint and out over the icy bay. They're on their way now, pushing through morning fog, passing over Treasure Island. Eliot suddenly comes to feel that his entire life before this trip has been spent asleep and that now, pumped up on drugs and adrenaline, he can see things as they really are. Eliot's commitment problems, Sarah always said, were not only romantic in nature. Sarah desperately wanted Eliot to realize that what they were watching on C-SPAN

InvasionTV was not some transmission from a distant or unreal world. "These events are happening," she had said. "The bodies of the dead are not actors. That rubble, Eliot, don't you understand, it's not part of some movie set. It exists. It's real."

$$\Omega$$

Tony gives them each a forged electronic visa and says he'll meet them again at five, two hours before the Bay Bridge closes for the night to civilian vehicles. "Don't be late or you're on your own," he says. Janine and Samir silently strike off toward the UC Berkeley campus, leaving Eliot alone on Shattuck, paralyzed with indecision. On his aviator glasses is projected a map of Berkeley and his location on that map. The only available mediasphere connection comes from the Provisional Occupation Authority; all other signals are being jammed. Before he can connect, he has to read a message warning that the SysAdmin Force strictly forbids illicit blogging and unlicensed electronic communications within the Occupied Zone.

After repeatedly watching the Panopticon footage, Eliot has determined the exact location of the comics shop into which his impersonator disappeared. Workers are rebuilding the Shattuck BART entrance, destroyed either in the earthquake or the invasion—it's hard to tell which. The sky is a forest of giant cranes building new office complexes and high-rise condos in what Eliot remembers used to be a fairly low-rise kind of place. Red maple leaves adorn the sleeves and breast-pockets of the SysAdmin Force soldiers, European and Asian faces, Canadians. Despite the occupation, university life continues, trendy children and their wealthy parents packing the streets, buying supplies before the semester starts. A few undergrads, seeming vaguely to recognize him, nudge their parents and point at him, but his lukewarm celebrity inspires little more.

Eliot's realization that ten years had passed since he first entered Harvard as an undergrad was what had finally compelled him to leave grad school, that straw breaking some mental camel's back. His doom stared out at him one day, mocking him, from across a seminar table, on the first day of Intermediate Formal Logic, a philosophy department lecture class for which he was teaching a discussion section. The bloodshot eyes of boys and girls, undergrads, puffed up like his own and for the same reasons, more or less, reproved his previous night's debauchery. Their faces seemed frighteningly youthful, much like the faces of these children here in Berkeley. At one corner of the rectangular seminar table sat a familiar-looking girl. Large black Gucci sunglasses covered her eyes. On her neck there was a hickey whose contours bore a more-than-passing resemblance to his own mouth. This discoloration on her neck was in fact a product of his mouth, a mouth that tasted that morning something like what he always imagined cinders must, a mouth that still uttered sincere declarations of love for Sarah. The distance between New York City and Cambridge had begun to strain their relationship. As Sarah's initial passion about the invasion had transformed into the more normal routine of work and the occasional weekend visit to Cambridge, Eliot began to wonder why they were back together at all. His shame-inducing indiscretion with the undergrad in Intermediate Formal Logic turned out to be the means through which Eliot let himself know he wanted to end his second relationship with Sarah.

Eliot ogles college girls in their short-shorts. On the small of one girl's back blinks an animated UC logo tattoo. Down Telegraph come more precocious undergrads, swing dancing on the street, juggling bowling pins, playing mutations of music far beyond Eliot's rapidly dating ken. Vendors man bustling street stalls. The Marxist-Leninist Chamber of Commerce, quite satisfied with the near total destruction of PEN—its strongest competition for the hearts and minds of hip young radicals—is back in business, and business is booming. Dreadlocks, bongs, pierced bodies, tattooed skin, high-tech skateboards, militant scowls, radical books—*How to Grow Marijuana in Your Home*

Hothouse, The At-Home Chemist, Revolutionary Style for Beginners, Sticking It to the Man 101. Television crews from the Revolution Now! Channel and the Neoliberalism Network loiter near a bookstore, guzzling coffee, yelling obscenities at the college girls.

He finally arrives at Creative Destruction Comics, a small storefront, indistinct. Parked in front is a vintage '00s-era Mini Cooper, a British flag painted on its roof. This is his destination, marked on his mediashades. He wants to turn around, go back to LA, get to the Getty Center party on time, forget he ever saw the video of his duplicate. But no, he can't turn back. He may not be able to stop his father from profiting from *Operation Win the West* or change the political condition of the world, as Sarah might like him to, but he can still locally affect the lives of others. He can take a stand against his crazy fans, can preach a gospel of personal empowerment and individual responsibility. That sounds good, really good. He could write a book—like his mother's, only liberal—addressed to his fans. Karl would probably approve. There would be lots of licensing opportunities, his Reputation would grow, and even Sarah might respect him more.

So it's decided. Eliot puts his mediashades into his shoulder bag, then pushes in the door of Creative Destruction Comics. The shop smells sour, like a body-odor bomb has gone off. Eliot slows down his breathing to minimize his intake of funk. Behind the counter is the Source of All Funk, an obese man with short arms and stubby fingers on which there are many rings, with an explosively large stomach, and with very long blue hair. He nods at Eliot.

"I wasn't expecting you this early," he says.

He thinks I'm my impersonator, Eliot thinks. This simple act of recognition has escalated his sense of imminent crisis. Things are no longer just Pretty Weird, but are instead Majorly Fucked Up.

"I, ah, finished up sooner than I thought," he says.

"Right on, comrade."

The fat man studies Eliot's face. "Yo, you've shaved."

"Yeah, I did. Is that a problem?"

"Vanderthorpe shave himself?"

"Yeah," Eliot says. "Of course he did. On the plane from New York. Saw it on Omni."

"You're a sharp one, comrade. I'm glad someone's keeping track of Vanderthorpe."

"Sure."

The man smiles, revealing a mouth full of horrifically underserviced teeth. Not sure what more to say, Eliot goes over to a thin cylindrical wire rack near the register and leafs through new comics featuring men and women in funny costumes beating the shit out of each other. Browsing through these has the effect of calming him down.

"Our orders just came in from Jersey," the man says.

"What do you mean?" Eliot says.

"We replace Vanderthorpe tonight, after the Getty Center party. We think he might be wearing a chaincam for a reality television pilot, but we've figured out a way to make the switch seamless."

Eliot bites his lip. "Cool," he says. "Comrade."

"Calm down, kid. You're going to do a terrific job."

A man wearing blue coveralls comes into the shop. Of medium height, thin but muscular, with a high hairline and very red hair, the man leans back against the wall and crosses his arms. He licks his lips, waiting for recognition.

"Hey, Peter," the comics-shop clerk says.

"Ah, hi, Peter," Eliot says.

Peter speaks in a controlled panic. "It's Vanderthorpe. Omni shows him getting into a Ford Juggernaut with tinted windows and scrambled plates. Then he disappears from the public record. No one knows where he's at."

"What's the worry, comrade?" the man says. "People drop off the

Omni grid all the time, especially celebrity types. They're the best at disappearing."

"Well, it wasn't any Juggernaut. Our tech guys tracked down the owner. It belongs to a mercenary who sometimes does runs into the Bay Area, Tony Mendoza."

"Doesn't mean nothing, comrade."

"Right on, comrade," Eliot says.

Peter glares suspiciously at Eliot's outfit. "You shaved, Al." Eliot doesn't realize he's being addressed. "Something wrong, Al?"

"Al?" Eliot says.

Peter is about to say something more when the real Al (Alfonzo? Aliot?; Eliot settles for the latter name) swaggers into Creative Destruction Comics, shaggy-faced, wearing a Che T-shirt and black Levi's.

Aliot points at Eliot. "Hey!"

"It's you," Eliot says.

"No, it's you," Aliot says.

Aliot speaks not in what Eliot considers to be his own authentic voice, but rather in that simulacrum of his voice available to him only from audio and video recordings, a hateful voice that doesn't sound a damn thing like how he sounds to himself, way too nasal, high pitched. Eliot stares at his mirror image, this replica of his exterior life, sculpted of hair and flesh and fashion.

This isn't second-rate plastic surgery. These guys have done their homework, have gotten every detail right: bone structure, skin texture, build, posture, subtle tics and mannerisms. Aliot is not a fanatical fan but rather, it seems, part of a real-world conspiracy, a conspiracy to replace him. No one will believe this. He doesn't quite believe it himself.

"We're so fucking lucky, comrades," Aliot says. "He just fell into our laps."

"Indeed," says Peter. "Do you have your shotgun behind the counter, Jack?"

The fat man, Jack, rifles around behind the counter, looking for said shotgun.

"Two things," Eliot says. Everyone pauses. "First of all, excellent impersonation, Al. I would definitely use the word 'fucking' as an intensifier. But be careful: I don't think I've ever used the word 'comrade' unironically."

Aliot and Peter nod, taking mental note of this advice. Jack puts his hands flat on top of the counter, pausing from his shotgun search. Aliot looks disaffected and empty-eyed. Eliot doesn't look like that, does he?

"There was a second thing," Peter says.

"Right, this one's for you, Jack." The fat man looks up expectantly. "I think you won't be needing that shotgun."

"Why's that?"

His drug-enhanced senses pull in all the channels of information that they can handle. Eliot kneels, grabs the base of the freestanding cylindrical comic book rack, stands back up, and swings the rack in a half circle, hoping its radius clears the walls. It does. Peter ducks. The rack hits Aliot hard in the chest and knocks him down. The tip of the rack nicks Jack on the nose. Blood violently arcs out of the nick. As Eliot pirouettes on his heel, comics fly out of the wire rack's various pockets at a thirty-degree angle. At a certain point, Eliot lets the wobbly rack go. The rack strikes a glass display case, knocking it backward, throwing from it a dozen or so resin figurines.

"Not the toys!" Jack wails, his face covered with blood, his large hideous mouth open in something like a parody of an Edvard Munch scream. "They're vintage! They're vintage!"

Peter has scrambled to the corner of the room and, crouching, seems poised to attack. Aliot, panting, is also already back up. Resilient bastard, Eliot thinks. Nothing like me. Eliot lopes out the front door of Creative Destruction Comics back onto Telegraph where a number of dreadlocked undergrads are pounding away on improvised drumlike instruments.

Assorted students plus parents part when they register that Eliot is maniacally running toward them, in the direction of the UC campus. He takes a quick look backward. Peter is putting a key into the door of the vintage Mini parked in front of the comics shop. Eliot decides he ought to get out of Peter's line of sight, so he turns, running with long strides down a residential street toward Shattuck. A couple blocks down, parked on the sidewalk in front of a house, a Bradley Urban Tank idles. Two Canadian soldiers sit on lawn chairs beside the tank drinking lemonade, apparently purchased from a lemonade stand from which a young girl in pigtails is selling little plastic cups of lemon-flavored sugar water at, it seems, ridiculously inflated prices. One of the soldiers notices Eliot and puts his empty plastic cup on the ground near his lawn chair.

He stands up, places his hands on his hips, and yells out.

"Excuse me there, could you please stop running for a moment?"

Eliot instinctively wants to obey this nice Canadian man, but just then the Mini comes screeching around the corner, so he keeps running, as fast as he can. The Canadian steps into the middle of the road.

"Ay, there! Stop running! You're not supposed to be doing that."

Looking back, Eliot observes the unfolding scene. The Canadian turns around to find out what is making that unpleasant screeching noise behind him. The source of said screeching is a car, a Mini, barreling toward him. Unable to move out of the way in time, he just stands there, looking shocked, perhaps even slightly angry at the rudeness of the oncoming driver. The driver of the Mini, meanwhile, hits the brake and swerves around the soldier. Its rear wheels lose traction and the car arcs one hundred and eighty degrees around. The price-gouging lemonade salesgirl has just sold a second plastic cup of overpriced sugar water to the other soldier when the Mini smashes backward into her stand, instantly destroying all her capital assets. The Mini slides backwards between the soldier and the girl, then stops. Neither girl nor soldier seems hurt. The girl screams, more angry than scared. Satisfied with this outcome, Eliot can focus on the task at hand: getting the hell away from here.

As he runs, Eliot sticks in an earbud and calls Janine.

"Hey, Janine, where are you and Samir at?"

"Interviewing people near the campus. What's going on?"

"I can't really explain. You could say I'm being chased."

"Could we? Who by?"

"By Canadians. Well, actually, not exactly. Not just by Canadians. It's sort of complicated, this whole chasing thing."

"Where are you, love?"

"I—"

"Send your coordinates to my tab. Samir and I, we'll come and get you."

"Okay."

Eliot sets his smartwatch to transmit his live coordinates.

"Got it, love," Janine says. "We'll be right there."

When he makes it back to Shattuck, he pauses to pant and wheeze, to let his heart slow down. He's so fucking flabby. While on the Harvard heavyweight crew team, almost a decade ago, he was fantastically fit, in the best shape of his life. Tom would laugh to see him now. Eliot stoops in front of an abandoned car dealership, panting, not sure what to do, where to go. The Mini practically leaps from the cross street onto Shattuck, aimed against traffic, oncoming cars barely missing it. Peter is bleeding from his head, a gun is in his hand. The Bradley, following close behind, jerks its main gun around, and the building behind Eliot melts into a rain of debris. A horrible ringing fills his head. Oh, shit. The Bradley has fired its gun.

Eliot steps stupidly away from the debris piled beside him. His body is covered in dust, but, as far as he can tell, he's not hurt. Peter passes him by in the Mini, then stops short; a wall of stopped cars, all honking angrily, has made moving farther against the flow of traffic impossible. Peter begins performing a K-turn so that the Mini can be properly aligned to run Eliot over.

"Hey, dummy!" comes a call from behind Eliot, Janine, on a Harley-Davidson motorcycle with Samir riding astride behind her. Both wear padded helmets. The hog, which is on the sidewalk, has a sidecar with a Hells Angels logo stenciled on it. "Get in!" She points to the sidecar.

"How'd you get the Harley?" Eliot says, shouting over his ringing ears.

"Stole it, mate," Samir says.

"Oh."

The Bradley growls down the street, squat and saurian, moving far faster than Eliot thought a tank could. Its big gun swivels, more precisely this time, taking aim.

"Would the driver of the Mini Cooper please get out of the car, please." A Canadian voice over the loudspeaker. "We would really like to have a serious discussion with you."

The Mini has finished its K-turn. Other cars have turned to flee the scene of this developing battle, an unprecedented event in the Occupied Zone of Northern California.

"We're trying to be reasonable here."

The big gun flashes. Puffs of smoke explode, one, two, three, from its barrel. In front of the Mini, the street erupts into a Vesuvius of asphalt. Eliot's ears are filled with ringing again, more frequencies lost forever. Undergrads scatter, screaming. Their parents seem displeased. This occupation business was never supposed to involve Canadian private military contractors actually *using* weapons on American soil.

"Get *in!*" Janine says. "Now!"

Eliot does not hear her so much as read her lips.

"There's no dignity in a sidecar!" Eliot shouts.

"There's dignity in being run over by Canadians in a tank, love?"

Conceding the point, Eliot hops into the sidecar and Janine takes off, racing. The Harley screams down Haste Street, drawing the attention of a number of other Canadians lounging about on the porches of single-family homes. Samir hands Eliot something that looks like an aviator cap.

"What am I supposed to do with this?" Eliot asks.

"Put it on your head," Samir says.

Eliot puts the cap on his head. When he snaps the chinstrap shut, the cap inflates into a full helmet. Behind them, the Mini Cooper has resumed the chase. Behind the Mini, Canadians follow fast. Eliot wonders what it might feel like to have your body parts scattered spherically away from your center of gravity at the speed of sound. It might, Eliot thinks, as they bank a hard right at San Pablo Avenue, hurt like hell. The Mini crashes through a row of orange cones. Canadians in a convoy have joined the tank in pursuit.

"Ay!" cries the Canadian over the loudspeaker. "You in the Mini, please, really, pull to the side of the road. We don't want to shoot, but if you don't stop we're going to have to fire another warning shot to let you know we're serious."

With its small gun, the tank fires another warning. Tom will shit his pants, Eliot thinks. He'd love this or at least the version of the story Eliot hopes to tell him, assuming the tank or Peter doesn't kill him anytime soon. Tom and Eliot used to love watching shitty action movies together, the worse the better, a major source of rapport. Eliot finds himself missing his friend, regretting their recent quarrel, instinctively asking God to protect Tom in Israel. The Harley bounces hard over a pot hole.

The freeway on-ramp appears very suddenly. The tank fires its big gun once again, and the on-ramp disintegrates just behind the Harley. The Mini rockets through the broken segment and crashes into a mass of rubble below. An instant before the Mini impacts, it fills with crash foam, which turns the vehicle and its passenger payload into a single solid white mass. Before long, Janine gets them through the SysAdmin Force checkpoint, thanks to the forged visas that Tony gave them, and they're crossing the Bay Bridge again, returning to San Francisco.

Ω

Eliot spends a sizable chunk of money buying a 2007 Toyota Corolla with tinted windows and scrambled plates from a shrewd old man who can tell, through some masterful leap of intuition, that his buyer is really desperate to purchase any mode of transportation he can find, as soon as possible, and at any price. They meet the old man only minutes after crossing the Bay Bridge, near an overpass that Janine confidently assures him isn't under observation by the TTSS or Omni. The baldheaded old man claims to be a former worker at a participatory grocery store, reduced to penury after the invasion. The Corolla has a PEN sticker on its back bumper, which the man offers to scrape off for an additional fee. Whatever his political convictions are on matters of political economy, the geezer negotiates like a mean motherfucker.

Janine and Samir refuse to leave Eliot, insisting that they return to LA with him, saying they would be happy to buy the car off him when they get there to defray some of his expenses. After agreeing to pay one-third of the outrageous price he has shelled out for the car, they leave the city: Eliot, still traumatized from the chase, sits sullenly in the shotgun seat, and lets Janine drive. Samir lays in the back, earbuds in, editing photos and videos on his tab. Speeding along at 80 mph down Highway 5, Janine needles him with detailed questions about the man in the Mini, about the Canadians, about what he was really doing in Berkeley in the first place. Eliot has decided to say nothing about his doppelgänger, to shut up about everything; he needs more time to think things through.

As they drive, Eliot tries to pretend that nothing has changed, but he can't stop thinking, over and over: They want to replace me. To distract himself from such troubling thoughts, to put a lid on his body's insistence on hyperventilating uncontrollably, Eliot inserts an earbud, closes his eyes, and listens to his accumulated voice-mail messages. Eleven messages have been recorded since he left LA yesterday afternoon.

» Dave (Thursday, 23 August, 16:15:34): *Eliot! Pick up the line. Tell Pedro to come back around. You're under contract, you ass. We have you five hours today. You're messing with the wrong people, Eliot.*

. . . .

» Karl (Thursday, 23 August, 16:32:56): *El, it's Karl. I just got a call from Dave. He says you've sort of, well, abandoned him. You're violating the terms of your contract. That's a big no-no. Never, ever break your contract. You're imperiling your future, to say nothing of your family's.*

. . . .

» Dave (Thursday, 23 August, 16:44:13): *I hope you realize that if you don't answer your phone within the next half hour you'll have technically violated the terms of your contract. If you violate the terms of your contract, Bildungsroman Productions and the Walt Disney Company are going to pull you, and the Vanderthorpe Family, into civil arbitration.*

. . . .

» Sarah (Thursday, 23 August, 18:01:23): *Ah, hi Eliot. This is Sarah. So I decided to come out to LA. You better not go back on your promise. Your remaining chest hair belongs to me, darling.*

. . . .

» Sarah (Friday, 24 August, 00:17:27): *I'm just, hm, calling again to see if, well, never mind. Karl set me up at a hotel near the 405. I'm going to be getting together with some friends in the area. Call me.*

••

» Sarah (Friday, 24 August, 03:11:59): *I'm feeling a little—I don't know. Where are you, Eliot? I haven't heard from you. I haven't been able to sleep. I'm in the hotel bar with my friend Lauren. And I think I'm drunk. I'm not supposed to drink, you know. Lauren told me I shouldn't make this call, but where are you, Eliot?*

••

» Karl (Friday, 24 August, 07:33:16): *Disney's threatening to bring us into the arbitration system, and we're clearly violating the terms of our contract, so there aren't a lot of ways I can spin this. You don't know what you've done, El. You don't know how bad this will get. Let me tell you, El, in case you don't get it: this will get very, very bad.*

••

» Eliot Sr. (Friday, 24 August, 08:02:41): *Son, I was just interrupted during a meeting by Karl Vlasic. I don't have to explain to you how very serious it is for me to be interrupted during a meeting. Karl says that he's having trouble getting in touch with you. I certainly don't have to remind you that it's in the interest of the family that you have a good working relationship with Karl. I don't have time to talk about this at length, especially to your voice mail, but let me assure you that I expect to see you at the Getty Center party tonight.*

••

» Karl (Friday, 24 August, 9:10:02): *A word to the wise, El, call me, or I'll have to get the FBI involved, tell them you've been kidnapped, something. I Omni'ed you and found video of you getting into a black Ford Juggernaut with a person who, if his Web site is to be believed, seems to be some kind of mercenary. What's this about, El? If you've got some kind of mediasphere strategy in mind you're not telling me about—if you're doing something behind my back—call me now.*

••

» Sarah (Friday, 24 August, 10:23:29): *Where are you, Eliot? Why aren't you returning my calls? Why isn't Karl returning my calls? Where the hell is everyone? I came out here to see you. Where did you run off to? I can't believe I'm so stupid. I can't believe—I'm getting very upset. I refuse to cry on the phone. You bastard. You fucking, fucking bastard. Do you know that my therapist told me not to come out here? But I came out anyway. I said, no, let's give Eliot another chance. He seems sincere this time. Maybe he's finally growing up. He can't stay a childish prick forever, can he? See, now you've done it. I'm crying. I can't believe this. I'm supposed to be this strong, independent woman—everyone tells me I am, and I keep reminding myself of that, but sometimes I find it hard to believe. Look what you've done to me.*

• •

» Elijah (Friday, 24 August, 13:00:34): *Yo, bro. Lij here. Warmin' up with Eye for an Eye, but I talked to Karl and he seems pissed at ya. Everythin' a'ight? I'm here for ya if ya need to talk 'bout somethin'. We're stayin' at th' new Hotel California. In the Celebrity Suite. Word.*

• •

It may be at this point in his journey that Eliot goes completely numb, that he ceases to feel even panic, now witnessing his unfolding life as if it were a dull television drama. Eliot rubs his face. His eye sockets hurt. Janine gives him a kiss on the cheek, right in front of Samir. "You okay?" she asks. No, I am not at all okay, but thanks for asking is what he would like to say. Instead, he finds himself making dry choking noises. Assisted by the Hyperphainein B, which still has a firm grasp on his senses, though their inputs seem dreamy and almost abstract, he has a panic attack.

"Poor dear," Janine says. "You've had a hard day. We're almost in LA. Where shall we drop you off?"

Janine's question lingers. Samir takes photos of Eliot, who continues to make dry choking noises as he reflects on his answer, his heart racing. Sarah hates him, now more than ever. Karl wants to have him arrested. Father and Mother are probably ready to disown him. Tom is many time zones away. Pedro, the only person not to have renounced him completely, is probably working, probably already driving someone to the party. Eliot knows he's not really having a heart attack, that it only feels as if he is. If he were to die, he suspects, the world would be letting him off too easily. His suffering has probably only just begun, but the very thought of anything more going wrong in his life is almost unimaginable. Eliot has no one he can turn to, no one left to call, no one he can trust, no one except, well—

Ω

Here comes Elijah Apocalypse strutting through the lobby of the Hotel California, bandmates following at a respectful distance, all on their way to Eye for an Eye's jalapeño-pepper-red tour bus—the Rapturebus—waiting by the curb. His spiked hair stands tall, a still-under-construction cathedral of red and black and silver dye. Extremely tight tan leather pants hug his thin thighs, leaving little to the imagination. Over his black mesh wifebeater hang diamond-encrusted crucifixes on platinum chains. Densely lined tattoos cover his body with, among other things, representations of the four horsemen of the Apocalypse, numerous somewhat angry seraphim, and (on his chest, visible through the black mesh) the face of an apoplectic man, silver sword jutting from his mouth like a metal tongue. On the backs of either hand are brands, made with a hot iron, shaped like Jesus-fishes. Multiple safety pins, seeming in this context very unsafe, hang from his earlobes. Some mediasphere critics maintain that he wears too much mascara.

Behind him trail his bandmates—bassist Gideon Finch and drummer "Rapture" Rodriguez—decked out in similar getups. But neither holds a candle to Elijah's inner blowtorch. Elijah practically metabolizes limelight. Young women mob around him, hungry for his rapturous energies. He seems not to notice them, though occasionally his eyes flick behind his lightly tinted sunglasses at some of the more ostentatiously slutty ones. Even these glances come fleetingly, hard to make out through the haze of tinted glass and mascara, at least to Eliot, who is presently making his way through this sea of skank.

"Why aren't you with a girl?" shouts some reporter disguised as a teenybopper fan. A volley of camera flashes strafe Elijah, which makes him pause en route to the Rapturebus. A more sober question flies inward: "Is it true what your Web site says, that you've reclaimed your virginity?"

Markets churn. Elijah's star soars. EDV 636 634 634½ +½, according to Eliot's mediashades.

"When I decided, recently, to get closer to God"—radiating like the sun, Elijah projects confidence and self-assurance—"I decided I, like, needed to reclaim my virginity. I had been sinning and I hadn't known real love with a woman, only the pleasures, the corrupt and seethin' pleasures, of the flesh. So I reclaimed my virginity. *Re*claimed. Re-*clai*med." Something like the Holy Ghost manifesting in it, the woman mob mumbles "Amen" under its collective breath. "So there it goes, ladies. *There—it—goes*." Elijah brushes the exposed arm of a girl with red and purple spiked hair. Her arm erupts into a field of gooseflesh. "I recommend that you consider this: your purity is the most precious thing you have. Con-*sider* it, a'ight?"

From behind the partition, Eliot waves at Elijah, but his younger brother keeps talking.

"Me, being a virgin again is really a part of who I am as a Christian, part of my spiritual journey. In my new pure state, I've learned so much about myself. Life has become so much richer. Three things have become more important to me than anythin', fresh and rich and crisp. One, to rock hard with my vintage Fender Stratocaster, real hard, harder than anyone else. Two, to love you, my great fans. Three, and most important, to sing for Jesus, to get *punked* for Jesus, to go fuckin' *cra-zy* for Jesus!"

Elijah finally notices Eliot, his frantic arm gestures.

"Yo, ladies, you've got to excuse me now. My bro needs a moment o' my time."

Disappointed, the girls give Eliot enough room to climb over the barricade. When a teenage girl with a shaved head and piercings all over her face tries to follow, bodyguards move in and beat her back with soft batons.

"You look terrible, bro," Elijah says. "Just terrible."

Elijah is more classically handsome than Eliot, a few inches taller, with a full head of wavy blond hair (when not dyed), and a straighter posture, the product of many hours in the gym. Though his body language screams "Don't fuck with me" in a thousand subtle ways, Eliot knows this is all so much posing. His brother is only being oppositional for Christ.

"I look pretty much the way I feel. You look fine, though."

"Yeah, bro!" So excited, he speaks in sentence fragments. "Big night. First time Eye for an Eye has played for such an important crowd. It's our big shot. We got this new song. Our new single, 'Grapes.' Yo, listen, bro, listen, it goes like this." In a Holy Spirit—possessed voice, some heaven-forged fusion of punk, heavy metal, and hip hop, Elijah sings:

> *The winepress will sma-a-a-a-sh the grapes*
> *The grapes are you, muthafuckas.*
> *Your insides are coming o-u-u-ut.*
> *Jesus is comin' to get you, you muthafucking sinners.*
> *You know who you are.*
> *He's comin' to take you muthafuckas, take you aw-a-a-a-ay, to hell.*

Elijah used to have such a beautiful voice, almost angelic. Eliot remembers how his brother would sing, despite his youthful rebelliousness, in the choir of Shining Ministries. Even back then, he was the most popular boy in his age group and the most talented. While at Princeton, Elijah discovered his love for evangelical Christianity and punk rock at about the same time and saw in their synthesis the most authentic picture of his soul. In his collegial enthusiasm for the Sex Pistols and the Ramones, Elijah began systematically destroying his singing voice, hoping to sound authentically DIY, like some random (Princeton-educated) dude who decided to pick up an electric guitar and say "fuck you" to the Man. Granted, Elijah now wanted to say "fuck you" to the Secular Humanist Man, but the Man's still the Man, whomever he happens to be.

Bandmates jump in to sing the disharmony, and Elijah completes the song with great gusto:

Jesus will blow you up.
He will pop all you muthafuckas like the grapes you are.
He will squash you flat, flat, fla-a-a-a-t in the winepress.
Let him save you now, you sinful muthafuckas.
Let him save you before
You can't be saved no mo-o-o-o-ore.

Elijah smiles with satisfaction, an artist discovering with some surprise his own powers. Eye for an Eye is stoked. Their fans scream, almost rioting with joy.

"Now imagine that with screechin' feedback. A million screamin' girls throwin' their panties at us. Me usin' my guitar at the end to smash an amp. Imagine that!"

"Oh, yeah, Lij, that's great, your best work yet. It has, I don't know what I should call it, integrity. But I'm not up for talking about your artistry right now. I've had a very bad day."

"Yeah, bro, sure looks like it."

"Are you going to the Getty Center party? I need to get there."

"We're boarding the Rapturebus right now."

"Let me come with you. I need to fix myself up."

"Yo, family first, right, bro?" he says, as much for the cameras as for Eliot. "We got a bathroom in the bus, probably even a spare tux for you."

Eliot follows Elijah and his bandmates into the black bowels of the red Rapturebus, practically a house on wheels, grateful for his brother's open heart and easy nature, a decided contrast to his more discordant public face. The Rapturebus disembarks from the pickup area and bullies its way, through a cloud of videographers, onto the open road. Out there, in the mediasphere, the fan-scholars already sense that something strange has happened to Eliot, something bad. Ten thousand furious Omni searches begin. Countless new forum topics open on *Eliot's Den*. Nervous inquiries go out to professional analysts. Many of Eliot's shareholders will have a difficult time sleeping tonight.

$$\Omega$$

By all mediasphere accounts, tonight's first anniversary celebration of Victory in Northern California Day is the party of the year, a mad celebrity fest, attended by more than three thousand Very Important Persons who, counting only the valuation of their Reputations, have a total market capitalization that exceeds the gross domestic product of all of sub-Saharan Africa combined; and yet despite this basic fact, his luck being as bad as it has ever been, the first person Eliot encounters as he approaches the main stairway in the arrival plaza of the Getty is a not-very-famous woman wearing a completely stunning form-fitting red dress, who is sitting on the steps in front of a lead sculpture of a naked woman, none other than Ms. Sarah Glickman.

The sky is reddish, sunset imminent. Sarah seems almost to glow in the light.

She descends upon him, more enraged than he's ever seen her, her newly manicured nails digging into the lapels of the spare tux jacket he found in Elijah's bus, her face inflamed from crying, her hair flying outward behind her as if it were electrified. Eliot can't bear to look her in the eye, so he averts his gaze, and fixates his attention on the statue of the naked woman. Eliot finds the lead sculpture strangely arousing, perhaps a side effect of the Hyperphainein B.

"This is it," Sarah says. "This is the end."

"It's not my fault," Eliot says and takes her hands into his. "Let's not make a scene. Come this way. I meant to be here earlier. I have an explanation for everything. An incredibly good explanation, for once."

Eliot leads Sarah up the stairs, away from the statue. Her heels make a rhythmical clacking noise as the two of them head toward the entrance of the museum. They pass through an open set of doors. The Entrance Hall contains an installation consisting of a matrix of old-style tube screens, a seven-foot-high wall of televisions that diagonally crosses one corner of the gallery. Each television plays a news report or amateur video showing images of violence or warfare in the Middle East, recorded sometime between 1967 and the present day. Rocks are thrown, civilians murdered, airstrikes launched, cluster bombs exploded, convoys ambushed, improvised explosive devices set off, oil fields burnt, hostages beheaded. A computer program coordinates these images so that they form patterns of sound and light. These patterns are almost beautiful. Only at close range do you begin to see and hear the individual explosions, the blood, the gore, the wreckage of shattered lives.

"Who did this one?" Eliot says.

"An artist called Modulus. The piece is called *Middle Eastern Tensions*."

"It's pretty amazing." Eliot hopes he's right.

"It's a piece of shit, Eliot. Pure fucking kitsch."

"But, man, look, it's, like, political. You like political. Speaking of, you won't believe what I've seen."

"Do you know what the professional critics find most impressive about this piece, Eliot? What makes it suitable for a museum as prestigious as the Getty?"

"Why don't you tell me."

"Not its supposed political content—'Boohoo, war is horrible, but we let ourselves forget that by distancing ourselves from it,' as if the metaphor weren't perfectly obvious to any decent person who pays any attention whatsoever to the world—no, that isn't interesting to the critics, but rather the outrageous expense of licensing so many samples of protected video. Every second that this installation plays is costing the Getty Foundation a small fortune."

"Well, that *is* sort of impressive, don't you think?"

"Here's what I don't understand, Eliot." Sarah massages the knots of stress in her forehead. "You invited me to LA. Karl reserved a ticket for me, set me up in a hotel. I came out Thursday night and you're nowhere to be found. And now the party is half over, Eliot, and you come staggering in here like this. Look at you, you're drunk."

Yes, Elijah had offered Eliot a few glasses of champagne in the Rapturebus, and, yes, Eliot had accepted these glasses, but he's not drunk, just a bit tipsy.

"I'm not drunk," Eliot says.

"And you claim you have an explanation. One that'll make sense."

"I had to go to Berkeley. There's a duplicate of me. It's an insidious plot."

"Oh my God, look at your pupils. You're high, too. You said you'd stop with the drugs."

He considers lying, but he knows that at this pivotal moment in their relationship he must be totally honest with Sarah, the woman (he's pretty sure now) he loves.

"Yes, Sarah, I am on drugs, but I also happen to be telling you the truth. This time."

"And—what the fuck—do you have a hickey on your neck?"

"Oh, that's no one. A reporter named Janine, someone I met on my way to Berkeley. She helped me out, saved me from Canadians in a tank and a Mini. She has a boyfriend named Samir."

"Did you have sex with this no one named Janine with a boy-friend named Samir, Eliot?"

"No. I mean, yes. Yes, I did. I have to be honest with you. I'm completely committed to being honest with you, Sarah. I am. And I am, in fact, in love with you. I am, for real. I'm so for real this time, but it's very complicated."

"Fuck you. Fuck your complications. I guess I deserve to be pub-licly humiliated like this for trusting anything you said. Publicly hu-miliated *again*."

"I can't be a whole person without you. You're, like, my moral faculty, my conscience."

"Then I must be doing a pretty awful fucking job, Eliot."

"I saw San Francisco and Berkeley. I saw the Bay Bridge. You were, like, totally right about everything. The whole invasion thing is really fucked up!"

"And you think this realization deserves some kind of prize?"

Other patrons of the arts, an activist celebrity couple and the senior senator from California, have discreetly exited the scene. Vid-eographers just as discreetly start recording their fight. Eliot grabs Sarah by the shoulders and kisses her hard on the mouth. When it comes, the blow to his crotch isn't entirely unexpected. The "Nut Blow," as the mediasphere will shortly dub it, has been recorded from at least seven different angles. Ninjaerobics has made Sarah fiercer and more lethal than ever.

Middle Eastern Tensions, Sarah, the paparazzi, and other high-level celebrities metamorphose into a commotion of glowing screens, humiliating grins, exploding camera flashes, and vast empty stretches of whiteness. Eliot finds himself outside, in the declining summer light, amidst travertine-clad pavilions, beside a shallow ornamental fountain near the West Pavilion. An internationally renowned avant-garde zydeco band plays excitedly by the edge of the fountain. A short tuxedoed man approaches, carrying a silver tray topped with an array of champagne in crystal glasses.

"Uuuuugh," Eliot says and takes a glass.

Eliot drinks it fast, returns it to the serving tray, and takes another.

A dark knot of people moves toward him, its individual members indistinguishable. Heads and bodies, tuxedoes and expensive shoes, surround him. Something lopes and dances inhumanly among them, a bipedal red heifer, someone dressed as Red, the Omni Science corporate mascot. Clapping in time with its dance, the president of the United States—POTUS Jim Friendly, "Liberator of the West," as a recent *Commentary* article has dubbed him—cheers Red on. An affable-looking man, with the easy presence of someone who knows he's the most powerful person who has ever lived, the POTUS is thin, reed-like, a gaunt latter-day Bob Dylan. His tuxedo hangs loosely from a bony body. A gigantic black Stetson caps his thinning curly hair; snakeskin boots add extraordinary height to an otherwise short man; and a very thin mustache does its best to substitute for his almost invisible upper lip. Around him like angry hornets hover Secret Service agents, who aren't at all pleased that the (clearly messed up) Eliot is standing so close to the president, whom they've codenamed "the Horseman." The POTUS ignores his overcautious agents and grins his famous good-natured grin.

"Howdy, Red," says the POTUS to the mascot. "You're sure looking awfully good today."

Red shakes the president's hand and, to Eliot's extreme horror, smiles broadly, revealing large square white cartoon heifer teeth.

"Thank you, Mr. President," Red says in a voice genderless and ageless, both human and not. "You're looking real good there, too!"

"No black or white hairs?" POTUS Friendly inquires.

Red shakes its head in an exaggerated way and says, "No, sir, not a one."

Red smiles directly at Eliot. The head is animatronic, Eliot tells himself. Calm the fuck down.

"Terrific!" shouts the president. "Julia and I own a couple shares of Omni Science stock ourselves. We're hoping it goes up, way, way up, if you know what I mean."

"We're all working very hard to make sure it does, Mr. President," says Eliot Sr., who has appeared suddenly, Mother by his side.

Father refuses to look Eliot in the eye. Her arm locked with Eliot Sr.'s, Mother stares Eliot down, a smile on her face, until he has to look away. Daisy is wearing a very tasteful blue dress. She plays nervously with her wedding band, which Eliot takes as a sign of her undoubtedly violent anger toward him.

Red resumes its jig, shakes its hoof-hands in the air. Watching the creepy creature cavort, Eliot feels suddenly close to death. The Hyperphainein B is wearing off at last, fast.

Eliot drinks his champagne and throws his empty glass at the zydeco band. It misses and smashes into the fountain. The band stops playing. Secret Service move in to protect the Horseman. Everyone eyes Eliot. On a nearby stage, Elijah stops setting up with his bandmates and looks over at his poor bro. The POTUS laughs, unveiling again his famous grin, and waves away the Secret Service.

"Li'l El just drank a bit too much," he says.

Everyone laughs with the POTUS at Li'l El. Only Eliot Sr. looks openly displeased, his froglike mouth having become a hard thin line. Eliot hasn't felt this embarrassed since a time in middle school when a teacher he'd had a crush on caught him doodling pictures of her in his notebook. The zydeco band picks up where it left off. The mascot grabs his hands, and they do a funny dance together, Eliot and Red, rotating around a common axis, facing each other.

"Let's boogie, Li'l El!" Red says, speech synched to heifer lips. "Let's celebrate freedom!"

Red seems demoniacal, a nasty cow clown. The POTUS laughs. His father's face stretches and warps into devilish proportions, not in laughter, but in thinly concealed rage. Everyone else, however, is in good spirits, is willing to laugh at Li'l El. Furious at this humiliation, Eliot releases Red's forward hoofs. Red falls over onto its ass and its cow-head mask pops off, revealing that Red is a she: a young black girl with short-cropped hair dyed blonde and an eyebrow ring. The lips of Red's severed animatronic head contort at first through a range of expressions but then freeze into a monstrous sneer. Eliot stumbles across the shallow pool, knocks over one of the million-dollar conceptual sculptures at its center. The sculptural installation, which had been resonating harmoniously with the zydeco band, changes pitch, becomes discordant, pained.

Eliot stumbles beyond the far boundary of the pool, toward the South Pavilion. He makes it to a parapet overlooking the cactus garden and the city. The day is dying fast. I-405 snakes southward into the distance, a great rushing river of cars. Men and women behind their steering wheels are reduced from this vantage point to imprints of radiance upon a fine crepuscular silkscreen, their cumulative desires and drives, a miracle of coordination, flesh and steel flowing toward the I-5, down eventually to San Diego, twisted statistical knots, more patterns than people.

I could jump, he thinks.

Climbing onto the parapet is remarkably easy. The freeway boils below. Before he can take another step, two Secret Service agents grab his legs. Gasps and screams come from somewhere behind him. How very nice that people are finally concerned. Trying to free himself, Eliot claws at the Secret Service agents. Below, the basin coruscates in twilight.

Eliot feels weak and helpless. Five minutes ago, when the drug was having its full effect, he could probably have fought off these Secret Service guys, taking them down single-handedly, without a weapon, with nothing more than his wits, his fingernails, and his megalomania. But after far too many hours of manic attentiveness, he needs to take a nap, just for a bit. His face is being slammed against the floor. A plastic cord restrains his wrists, tied together behind his back. POTUS Friendly's—the Horseman's—black snakeskin boots are all he can see.

With Sarah gone, he has no one, no one who will care for him, no one who will make any effort to help him. His moral center has split the scene. Even Jesus, with whom he once had a more amicable relationship, is nowhere in sight, lost in the reverberating feedback of Eye for an Eye, which continues to warm up despite the panic and confusion. Though pressed flat on the floor, Eliot struggles against the Secret Service agents, refusing to be put down like an animal. How fucking humiliating, he thinks. There is a crunchy, electrical sound, like a bag of glass shaking. Someone has tasered him. Paralysis overtakes him and things go black.

PART IV
THE RIOT ZONE

THE MARKETS ARE NOT KIND TO Eliot when they reopen. Three factors have conspired to destroy Eliot's Reputation: these factors are the topic of discussion in Karl Vlasic's swanky midtown Manhattan office, a vast space dedicated to glass tables and leather chairs and bearskin rugs, its main media-wall broken up into hundreds of square tiles upon which established channels or nonlinear television feeds play, each ready to expand to a more viewable size should Karl choose to focus on it, but all of which are presently muted so that Karl can carefully and ruthlessly destroy whatever complex molecules of dignity Eliot might be trying to preserve. Three sausagelike fingers, hairy in a creepy way, stand erect, waiting to be ticked off by the squatter and hairier thumb of Karl's other hand. Karl makes hacking and wheezing noises, viscosity coiled within his throat, hidden biological gears and pulleys adjusting themselves in anticipation of the onslaught to follow.

"Try to keep up with me, here, El. First, your little drug-induced romp through the Getty Center—what the tabloids have taken to calling your 'Near Suicide'—and that weirdly aggressive kiss-thing with Sarah and the 'Nut Blow' was broadcast more or less live across the world, and has been viewed—let me get the figure up on my tab—five hundred twelve million times as of right now—by approximately thirty five million people. You've gone viral, El."

Eliot tries to pay attention to what Karl is saying, but a horrible sluggishness still clouds his mind, a lingering consequence of the Hyperphainein B. The days following the Getty Center party come back to him only in fragments, short declarative sentences of memory. The Secret Service processed and released him. Father shipped him back to New York. Karl, the first finally to break communications silence, left a message ordering him here.

"Second, responding to your new infamy, several girls have surfaced in the tabloid press in Spain who claim to have had special relations with you. Several of these are girls who, if you had slept with them here in the US, would be considered underage. No sex videos have surfaced yet, so we're lucky for now. All the more reason to abolish this country's draconian statutory rape laws, you say, and I'm all with you there, believe me, but you have to understand that those age-consent restrictions reflect the values of *the people*, and markets have a way of giving people what they want, and so, this allegations-of-sex-with-sixteen-year-olds thing, you understand, is playing very, very well in heartland communities. And if you're unclear, what I just said, about this playing 'very, very well': that's called irony. It is, in fact, not playing well at all. You are so 'completely fucked' right now, as you might put it, that words escape me."

Karl takes a personal moment to utter a few wet disgusting throat-clearing noises. Behind him, downtown, the Freedom Tower turns on its red, white, and blue floodlights for the evening.

"Now, third, and this is the best part: There is this man named Samir Bhavsar who says he has a one-week press license with your biometric signature on it. This Samir Bhavsar is selling left and right pictures he took of one Eliot Vanderthorpe on his way to, get this, Berkeley, California. These pictures are now all over the mediasphere.

An obvious question has been quickly hit upon and repeatedly asked, not least of all by your family: What was Li'l El doing in Berkeley, California? What kind of crazy drug-induced frenzied kick exactly is this kid on? Even the most hard-core Eliotlovers—God bless them, holding the line against the world's Eliothaters—are under attack, accused of being 'plants' on the electronic discussion boards."

"They *are* plants," Eliot says.

"That is entirely beside the point," Karl says, forehead vein pulsing. "El, you've lost half your market capitalization. The money isn't an issue for anyone but you and anyone foolish enough to have bought into your IPO, but your Reputation affects the Good Name of the Vanderthorpe Family and the Vanderthorpe Family Fortune is in no small way pegged, if only indirectly, and Symbolically, to the Vanderthorpe Family's Good Name. You're bringing your whole family down with you. Look at this!"

Karl points at his mediawall, initiating a montage of clips: Daisy Vanderthorpe standing next to Eliot Sr., mascara flowing down each rosy apple cheek. Eliot Sr. talking about his feeling of "deep disappointment," his fears for the future of his son. President Jim Friendly at a White House press conference somberly saying, "I do hope that that young man gets himself some help." Elijah shaking his head, disavowing the crazy behavior of his brother. Celebrity analysts talking about this shocking blow to the Vanderthorpe Family Name. Fan-scholars contextualizing his behavior, historically and theoretically. "We're all so very disappointed in Eliot" is the consensus.

"Well, at least the mediasphere is paying attention to me," Eliot says. "There's the silver lining for you."

Karl shakes his head. "A Reputation is a delicate thing, El, and not identical to the median price your Name can demand from the mediasphere at any particular moment. Sure, you can temporarily send your market price up. Video of you may sell for a crazy amount of money right now, but that'll burn out the long-term prospects of your Reputation. There are only so many sex scandals you can afford to have, so many hours of bad press, before the media is done with its Eliot Jr. snack. There's nothing more fickle than the gaze of the mediasphere. You've created conditions that make them temporarily interested in you, but you're also using up all your cache of celebrity capital. Making matters worse, you practically gave away the rights to reproduce your image to this Samir person. So here's a novel idea: You don't give out a press license to anyone, never ever, not without my express and written approval, not without long-term licensing agreements already set in place, coordinated, synergized. It's that simple. You might think maximum exposure is good, but you would be wrong. Did you know the one-week press license you gave to Samir was transferrable?"

"Meaning what?"

"Meaning, he sold it to the Spitting Image Agency, which is leasing it to NYC-based photographers and videographers. Dozens of 'exclusive' pics and videos have popped up all over the mediasphere. Your brand, as pathetic as it was, is being diluted. Your situation is actually interesting from a theoretical perspective, as a case study. Your Name is temporarily generating huge revenues, and because you have a percentage of that, you're making money, but your share price is simultaneously plummeting. You've hit something like an inflection point in your earnings potential and your shareholders know it, so they're jumping ship. Deadly stuff."

"What are we going to do?" Eliot asks.

"*We* are not doing anything. When your board meets tomorrow morning, I suspect we'll add a layer of oversight to all your electronic transactions. No more contract signing without my explicit approval. You don't take a shit anymore without my approval. Got that? We should have done that from the beginning, but who knew? Apparently, we can't trust you, El. It breaks my Slovenian heart to say that."

"They can't do that, Karl. I can't live my life under the threat that you'll veto my choices."

"Yes, they can, El, and they probably will. That's what it means to have your Name publicly owned. Now get the hell out of here. I've got to run simulations to figure out how we can leverage this. Don't get me wrong, we're going to make money off these scandals in the short term, a lot of money, but the attention of the mediasphere will go fickle fast. It might take a decade to rebuild your Reputation to anything resembling its former rather modest glory, let alone grow it any further."

"Fickle fast" are the words that stay with Eliot on his way down to the basement-level parking lot. Pedro is waiting for him in a black sedan. The back passenger-side door opens automatically for Eliot, but before he can get in a man with a palmcam and a blue press immunity wristband jumps out from behind a parked car and runs quickly toward him.

"Why did you try to kill yourself?" the man yells.

Eliot punches him hard in the face, knocking the palmcam along an arc, onto the roof of a small electric car. The man sits stunned on the asphalt for a moment, then a big smile spreads across his face. This video will make his career. ELIOT R. VANDERTHORPE JR. GOES BERSERK, the headline will probably read. Eliot grabs the palmcam and gets into the sedan. Breaking the camera is harder than he expects; the hard plastic components don't come apart easily.

"You're wasting your time, guy," Pedro says. "That rig is feeding live to some kind of server. You're just giving the dick more footage."

"Fuck, fuck, fuck, fuck!" Eliot says.

He tosses the palmcam out the window and starts punching the back of the passenger seat.

"Yo, calm down."

"I am such an idiot."

Pedro looks grim. "Yeah, there's no denying that, but you might as well just ride it out. Enjoy the attention."

There was a time, perhaps as recently as a month ago, when he would've enjoyed the attention. But he would also have been concurrently high on so many drugs that shame wouldn't have found any handholds within his psyche to cling to. Now, things are otherwise, and he finds within himself various rocky knobs and handles onto which shames and humiliations, brambly and persistent, may stick forever.

"What got into you in LA?" Pedro says. "I tried talking to Tony, but he isn't returning my calls."

"What got into me? You really want to know?"

"Of course I really want to know," Pedro says. "What is it?"

This is what he wants to say: There is a man in Berkeley who looks exactly like me, a duplicate created to replace me. My impersonator doesn't show up on regular Omni searches because he's hiding behind the search restrictions that the Occupation has put in place. They're out to get me! They probably want to kill me!

"It doesn't matter," Eliot says. "I think I'm going crazy. My whole life is caving in on me. Scramble the license plates before we go outside. I don't want to be followed."

"No problemo," Pedro says.

The black sedan joins an anonymous flow of traffic on one of Manhattan's remaining car-friendly roads. Eliot takes off his smartwatch and looks at it. Almost ten p.m. Though exhausted, he finds the prospect of sleep frightening. Nightmares might visit him, camp out on some futon of the mind. Things might go from ugly to unbearable. His smartwatch rings, a video call from Janine.

"I gotta take this, Pedro."

"Another girlfriend?"

"Sort of."

Eliot closes the soundproof partition between them and pulls out his tab.

Janine appears on the tab. "Hello, love."

"Janine! Samir's pictures of me are all over the mediasphere. I thought he did private shows, you know, ravages of the occupation, horrors of imperialism, shit like that."

"I can see you're not going to like this. Best to get it out of the way. Samir wanted to talk to you about something. I don't approve, but he asked if I would call you."

Janine moves out of range of the camera and Samir comes into view, a half-smoked cigarette hanging from his mouth, his eyes focused on something offscreen.

"Jeez, you just hit a reporter." He faces Eliot. "You certainly waste no time."

"What the fuck do you want?"

"Hey, there, don't curse at me. You understand I'm recording this call, right? I'll play something for you now—another exciting video—and then we can, perhaps, discuss the matter at hand like civilized men."

The image of a nondescript yet familiar space appears, a white-walled filthy room with a bed in one corner. Janine comes into the frame, moving toward the bed. Her shirt, bra, and slacks come off. She lies in bed wearing nothing but panties. Eliot doesn't understand until he sees himself—not his doppelgänger—enter the frame, also nearly naked. At one point in the video, he asks, "What about Samir?" Janine replies, "What about him?" "He kissed you." "We're in an open relationship." The video ends. Samir reappears.

"What do you want?" Eliot says.

"Five million dollars, mate."

"That's blackmail."

"Actually, it's not. I'm offering this video to you at market value. I took that video in a completely legal manner under the terms of our contract. In fact, it was Janine—who is really quite a lovely person, whatever nasty things you must be thinking about her—who suggested I give you the opportunity to get first dibs on it. You can pay for the video or the tabloids can pay for it. From my perspective, it's the same."

"But you would destroy my Reputation if you released the video. I mean, destroy it more than I've already destroyed it."

"Your father's a multibillionaire, so I think you'll do okay. And you've done much worse than have consensual sex with a woman of legal age. It's shocking, really, the things you've done."

"But I'm not financially liquid that way. I can't just go to the bank and withdraw five million dollars. I'd have to get my dad involved."

"Better give your daddy a call, then."

"Give me some time."

"You've got six hours to tab the money to my account. I want to be fair to you, mate, really, but the way things are going, this video is a rapidly devaluing commodity."

"I thought we had something special, Janine. I thought we had a fine time."

Janine comes back into the frame. "Of course, a lovely time. None of this is personal. Since PEN was criminalized, working the anti-imperialist beat just doesn't pay what it used to. We've got to support our work somehow."

Eliot hangs up on her, unable to bear this conversation. His smartwatch immediately rings again. Karl, screaming now: "You punched a reporter in the face, El! You couldn't even wait five minutes to screw up again? What am I supposed to tell your father? That we need to hold another press conference so he can apologize *again* for your stupidity?" Karl starts cursing in Slovenian.

Eliot hangs up on Karl and turns off his ringer. Tears sting his eyes. His shoulders are heavy with despair. He lowers the partition and tells Pedro to stop the sedan someplace safe, off the Omni grid.

"Wha, guy?"

"I need to take a walk, alone."

Pedro pulls onto a side street. Mediasphere sensors can't detect any surveillance cameras nearby, though you never know for sure where private cameras, uncoupled from the mediasphere and Omni, might lurk. Eliot puts on a hooded sweatshirt he always keeps in the trunk of his cars for occasions such as this, for when he wants to hide himself from Omni. A million Little Brothers and Sisters may be watching, but it's easy enough to fool them temporarily if you know how. Adopting an incognito walk, Eliot meanders away from the sedan, moving crosstown, avenues descending, his spirit broken. He contemplates climbing onto the Manhattan Island Wall and diving into the East River, finishing what he attempted at the Getty Center. Behind him, Pedro lingers for a moment, then drives away. The evening air is surprisingly cool.

$$\Omega$$

On the western face of Secretariat Tower, there hangs a giant banner, whipping in raw river wind, bellowing a rallying cry to shoppers: END OF SUMMER SALE. Arrayed majestically before this architectural monument to international cooperation, this palace of world peace, the flags of many global consumer brands flap: Gucci, Samsung, Sony, Gap, a regular United Nations of the marketplace. Service workers, dressed in particolored corporate costumes, exit the building, closed now for the night. Many minibuses wait for them. The workers seem to be members of another sort of United Nations—black, Indonesian, Bangladeshi, Brazilian—on their way home to worker barracks on Roosevelt Island.

Eliot must have been walking quite a while to have gotten this far east, though without his smartwatch he can't tell how long. After the United Nations relocated its headquarters from the US to Bandung, Indonesia, years ago, NYC Mayor Hart redeveloped the eighteen-acre complex. But the Franklin D. Roosevelt Shopping Center has never lived up to the city's fanfare and marketing blitz. Since the erection of the Wall, Manhattan Island had almost completely transformed into a market for luxury brands. The neighborhood around the FDRSC consequently becomes a ghost town after shoppers from Queens and Long Island return home for the night.

Some dive bars and convenience stores remain open, but the throngs of cool kids who might sustain the nightlife of a neighborhood like this stay away. National guardsmen in green and khaki uniforms patrol the FDR Parapet. The Wall goes on forever in either direction, horrible Stalinist architecture out of a dystopian science fiction film. Hundreds and hundreds of animated billboards hem its top. Gleaming camera eyes keep watch. If he's not careful, Omni will pick him out on the basis of his walk or some other identifying feature. Reporters will find him fast.

Eliot would like to stop at a bar for a beer, but he's left his tab with Pedro, so he's on his own, off the mediasphere, in practice penniless, until he can find his way back home. His bladder suggests he should make a pit stop, but bouncers won't let him into bars without some form of ID. Eventually, on the counsel of his bladder, Eliot finds a semiconcealed alley, unzips his fly, and aims his dick at a line of decompiler Dumpsters. Pissing, he glances upward at a set of crossed telecom lines. From them, laced-together Converse All Star high-tops hang, a mark of nostalgia for some more innocent time, nostalgia fabricated into the shape of a pair of shoes. Eliot looks at the shoes and then looks down at the star-shaped tattoo on the inside of his arm, finds himself wondering when it was that he decided to mark his body in this way, what marking his body thusly had meant to him. His mind stalks up on a banal insight: that he himself has become something like a brand, that whatever it is he's made of, it can be reproduced, bought and sold, like anything else.

You've sunk pretty low, the shoes seem to say to him, swaying on their laces.

"You're a pair of shoes," he says. "You've got no right to judge me."

Sure, we're just shoes, the All Stars shoot back. But what makes you any better? You're feeling bad for yourself, and you're wallowing in self-pity, but have you ever asked whether you really deserve Sarah's love?

"Why wouldn't I?" he shouts.

Sarah's not some kind of moral principle. She's a person.

"You think I don't know that?"

You seem to refer all your successes and failings to something outside yourself. You never take responsibility.

"But man, this time, it's not my fault. Okay, maybe some of it is, but this whole conspiracy-to-replace-me thing is, like, totally real. My Berkeley trip was justified."

The All Stars do not respond.

Even if he's only having an imaginary conversation with a pair of sneakers, Eliot is annoyed. He *does* want to take control of his life again. He can show Father and Mother footage of his doppelgänger, prove his innocence, his virtue, his good intentions. Sarah will eventually accept that he was tricked into sleeping with Janine for purposes of blackmail. None of this is his fault. Feeling better, more clearheaded, almost like himself, Eliot zips his fly and turns to leave the alleyway.

There are two guys with full-face animated tattoos blocking his way. In his newly optimistic mood, Eliot concludes that they're probably perfectly friendly body-mod types who need to take a piss in this convenient dark alley. Eliot knows all about this tattoo stuff; it's a hot area of ongoing research in cutting-edge applied philosophy departments: *body écriture*. A biopowered mediasurface, embedded just under the surface of your skin, a newish form of nanotechnology that can run simple graphical programs. Below their ears, invisible unless you know where to look, are tiny nodules that interface with computers. These two wear grim skull faces, trying hard to look gruesome, largely succeeding at this effort. Grinning Death-like, they approach. Eliot tries to slide past them.

One lays a hand on his shoulder. "You got a smoke, buddy?"

A meshwork of metal and precious gems appears in his mouth. A smile.

"Can't help you guys. I'm all out."

"Oh, listen to him, Jeb, he says he can't help us."

"I don't like his attitude, Ted."

Keep calm, he tells himself. Pull off your hood. The Total Terror Surveillance System or private cameras may not cover this alley, but Eliot should make his face visible to Omni, just in case. As casually as possible, he reaches up to pull down his hood, wishing—for the first time ever—that he had his chaincam.

"Oh no you don't," Jeb says.

Both skull faces become red, demoniacal. Jeb seizes his wrists. With two quick gestures, smooth and professional, Ted gags Eliot and pulls a black mask over his face. Then: Sounds of a vehicle. Doors open. Jeb and Ted toss Eliot into a cabin. Doors slam. The vehicle—a van?—begins moving. Voices whisper. A sudden prick pokes Eliot on the neck and paralyzes him. Unable to move, but still conscious, Eliot feels them strip his clothes, his T-shirt, sneakers, jeans, even his socks and underwear, until only the mask remains. There is a rustling of clothing. More voices. The van stops. People get out. Someone gets in. Doors slam. Then the van drives off again.

Ω

When his mask and gag are removed, Eliot finds himself sitting on a narrow metal bench, completely naked, in the front of the van's cabin. The muzzle of a gun that almost looks too sleekly stylish to be deadly points squarely at the center of his chest. Eliot will act as if the gun is actually deadly, in no small part because the person holding it is his mirror image—Aliot—and is wearing the clothes that were stripped from him, Levi's, "Meaning" T-shirt, sweatshirt, argyle socks, Nikes.

Aliot waves his gun at a pile of clothes on the floor between them, underwear, jeans, a black T-shirt, tennis shoes.

"Put those on," Aliot says.

"You're back," Eliot says.

"Put them on. Now."

Aliot looks so much like him, and yet there is this small difference, some absent diacritical mark of self that Omni is not yet capable of describing in terms of its conceptual descriptive language. Aliot lacks Eliot's self-consciousness. With Eliot, there is always, before he sins, a feeling of preparation, of silent submission, of anticipation. Eliot knows he's about to do wrong but does wrong anyway, this knowledge ineffably marking his body. Aliot, in contrast, seems not to suffer from these sorts of doubts, seems to live in the sort of moral universe where certainty is possible. Should his masters order him to pull the trigger, to watch as Eliot's body empties of blood, Aliot will do as he's told without hesitation. Eliot is certain of this, if nothing else, so he puts on the clothes and waits for further instruction. Eliot envies his impersonator's faith.

Aliot tosses a tablet computer to Eliot. A set of documents is open on it.

"Approve them," he says.

"What?"

"Sign and give your biometric approval to the ten contracts on that tab."

"I don't—"

"You have thirty seconds to approve them before I shoot you in the heart," he says, then adds an afterthought: "Capitalist scum."

Eliot pages through legal jargon and technical descriptions written in Omni's proprietary language and, as he approves each of the contracts, comes to realize what he's doing: he's turning over the electronic extensions of his identity to Aliot. If his board had already given Karl oversight, as it will likely do tomorrow, Aliot could not so easily steal Eliot's identity. All his major electronic accounts will become associated with Aliot's biometrics and will, with the sole exception of Homeland Security's genetically validated database, treat Aliot as if he were Eliot. If no one checks the Homeland Security file, Aliot should be able to get away with this ploy. Omni will recognize him as Eliot. Will anyone care enough about Eliot to notice that he's acting a little weird? After all, Eliot is always acting a little weird.

"There," Eliot says. "I did it."

"Very good," Aliot says.

Aliot takes an old-school '00s-era cell phone simulacrum from his pocket and presses the speed-dial button. "Got it," he says into the phone, then listens patiently to the person on the other end. "I understand."

Aliot puts the cell back in his pocket and then shoots Eliot. There is a soft pneumatic noise, like lips popping, and a tiny dart jams into Eliot's chest, its barbs having pierced his shirt, a tranquilizer. The gun wasn't real, Eliot thinks, losing consciousness fast. I should have fought back, he decides. I should have taken a stand.

$$\Omega$$

A nondescript man, slim and tubular, shoulders slumped: Blue jeans with no belt; mock turtleneck; black socks; incredibly worn-out New Balance 991 sneakers. Severely receded grayish hairline, horn-rimmed glasses. Memory somehow fails to hold him firmly in its grasp. Eliot wouldn't be able to pick him out of a lineup of dot-com retirees—all of whom have modeled their personal style of self-presentation on that mythical beast, Steve Jobs—any more than he could remember a long distant dream. And yet this isn't a dream.

Eliot lies on a white leather couch in a small living room. A large flat-screen television hangs on the wall. A controller and touchboard rest on the coffee table beside an offprint of the *Wall Street Journal*. The headline reads PRES. FRIENDLY TO CALIPH FRED: "ALL OP-

TIONS ON THE TABLE." The man sits down gingerly in a white leather armchair orthogonal to the couch. He wears a chunky college ring, Stanford University logo. Eliot and the man blink at each other across empty space.

Eliot figures it out. "You're Stanislaw Hadrian, my father's old business partner."

Stan unveils his straightened and whitened teeth, the end product of too much dental work. This is meant to be a friendly smile.

"I'm sorry Aliot shot you like that. He can be overzealous sometimes."

Eliot looks down at his hands, sees something strange about them. Against a brown and black background of skin crawl active and evolving fractals of silver, a colony of virtual insects unfolding fantastic patterns over a burnt landscape of hands and arms. Eliot tries to shake off these strange patterns, but they are branded onto his flesh. Animated tattoos. His face, similarly tattooed, reflects back at him in the television. There is no control nodule on him, so the tattoo must be hardwired to repeat a preprogrammed pattern indefinitely. His whole body has been tattooed with an animated fractal pattern, his own body heat powering the tattoo. Barring outside intervention, the tattoo will die only when he stops providing it with heat, that is, when he dies.

"Why—" Before he finishes asking, he understands. "To keep me from showing up on Omni."

Stan makes a jaunty gun-shooting motion. "You got it, kiddo."

"None of this makes sense. What do you want with me? Revenge 'cause my father had the board fire you from Omni? Are you still working with Troy Forester?"

"It's complicated," Stan says. From between the horned rims of his glasses his black eyes stare out at Eliot, contemplative.

"You're Horned Goat," Eliot says.

Stan repeats his impression of a smile. "You could say that."

"That biblical reference makes no sense, man. It's not Apocalypse-related at all."

"The focus groups thought it sounded very apocalyptic."

"Maybe, but then the focus groups you organized were pretty fucking ignorant, man."

"We thought. . ." Stan removes his glasses. "How very funny."

"So you're behind the attack. The destruction of the dome."

"Depends what you mean by 'behind,' Eliot. Legally no, I think it was a group of evangelical Christians who attacked the dome, with equipment that we—misguidedly, perhaps—happened to sell them, with no foreknowledge whatsoever of what they were planning to do with that equipment. They told us they were going to go parasail hunting in Central Africa. The contract they signed *did* automatically turn over to us intellectual property rights from any acts of violence or terrorism they might perform using our equipment. Standard clause nowadays. You know the drill. You seem to be referring to the fact that Troy and I registered the dome attack on the CRAP Database. So yes, we do own the rights to the attack."

"You must be raking in huge amounts of money. Every channel is playing clips of that attack."

Stan puts his glasses back on. "That is very true."

"What the hell is going on, then? Why'd you kidnap me?"

"Do you want to know? I mean, do you *really* want to know? I'd love to tell you, so you can let your father know what we've been up to. It's really quite neat."

Some part of Eliot finely tuned to the rhythms and narrative logic of shit-kicker action movies understands that this is his very own personal James Bond Moment, the moment of unveiling, of revelation. This New Balanced villain will explain to him anything he might want to know, no bullshit. But might it be better not to know? Not knowing is probably the safer option, indeed, but Eliot nods yes, tell me.

Stan stands up and cracks his knuckles in preparation. "Great." Stan seems excited. "I've put together a briefing, explaining our position, but I haven't had a chance yet to practice delivering it. So let's start at the beginning. You know about this *Peace in the Mideast Summit Telethon*, of course."

Stan picks up the *WSJ* from the table and points to a smaller headline: AMID SECURITY CONCERNS, SUMMIT TELETHON PREPARATIONS CONTINUE IN JERUSALEM.

"Yeah," Eliot says. "Omni Science is one of its main corporate sponsors. I was supposed to go, you know, grow my Reputation, show I was a serious guy."

"The Telethon worries us, Eliot. We had expected—to be honest, Troy had expected—that the destruction of the dome and the attack on the mosque would be enough."

"Enough for what?"

"We thought the attack would spark a war between Israel and the Caliphate." Stan says this in a long, slow, deliberate way. "And that eventually the Freedom Coalition and the United Nations would be pulled into the conflict. Troy was sure the attack would precipitate the Apocalypse, but it didn't work out that way. Caliph Fred rattled his saber, but didn't do much else. I warned Troy, but he didn't want to believe me. The Arab Street has gotten lazy and decadent these last few decades. They'd rather watch halal music videos and shop at Mideast megamalls than do that whole jihad thing."

"Yeah, sorry the whole blowing-up-the-mosque thing didn't go your way."

"It's an unfortunate statement about the status of disbelief in our time. Even destroying the third most holy place in Islam can't rouse the Muslim masses anymore to call for blood, or, at least, not enough of them."

"Sucks, man, but what can you do?"

"You might think that's a rhetorical question, but, well, I had this thought. I read this press release Karl Vlasic put out, which mentioned that the Vanderthorpes were going to be at the Telethon. And so okay, the peoples of the Mideast apparently care more about their celebrity Caliph than fourteen centuries of tradition, fine. But what if *something bad* were to happen to their celebrity Caliph? That would piss them off. So it turns out, we had to work really fast to set everything up, but you're going to be the one doing that *something bad*, Eliot, live on television. However much of a failure you may be as a human being, no one has any reason to suspect that you would assassinate Caliph Fred. You have no motive."

Assassinate Caliph Fred. Stan smiles as though he's speaking not about murder and the end of the world but rather about a pleasant game of golf.

"What are you guys smoking?" Eliot says. "There's probably going to be more security at the Telethon than at any other televised event in, like, human history. My duplicate isn't going to be able to smuggle in a gun or a bomb or anything."

"We probably could smuggle a weapon in if we really had to, but we're not planning anything so messy. Al happens to be a black belt in judo. He's going to break the Caliph Fred's neck before security can stop him."

"And get killed in the process?"

"Our dear 'comrade' is ready to sacrifice himself."

"But isn't he, like, some kind of Leninist or something? What does he think provoking the Caliphate into fighting Israel will do for his cause?"

"We've told Al one big truth and one small lie." Stan gestures, and a map of the world appears on the TV. "The big truth is that geostrategic computer simulations we've developed suggest that over the last thirty years the world has been setting itself up, slowly and methodically—as if through ineptitude or by design—for this moment. A series of alliances and affiliations are now in place that are somewhat similar to what historical computer models of the period before the First World War look like, except this time the scale is much larger. Do you know what caused World War One, Eliot? The proximate cause, I mean."

"Ah, anarchists killed that archduke Franz Ferdinand guy?"

"That's right." Stan flicks his index finger, and little graphical 1914 people go to war all over Europe. "But isn't that really very weird? One death, committed by a small group of politically marginal people, shouldn't much matter if ten million lives are at stake, should it?"

"The anarchists were in the right place at the right time," Eliot says, doing his best to remember high school history. "The archduke was an important dude, something like that."

"They were. He was. But in a sense, the war was going to happen, no matter what. The archduke's death just set the chain reaction into motion. The political world was at something like a critical state, supersaturated with whatever it is that makes war happen. All it took was a mote of dust to precipitate the system into its more stable state, war. We don't usually think of war as a stable geopolitical state, but it's quite stable and self-sustaining once it gets going, as long as it has its fuel supply of human bodies." Stan gestures away the completed World War One simulation. "Now, here's the interesting part. What we've got today is the following: On one side, the Freedom Coalition." The US, Israel, India, Japan, Central America, part of South America, and part of Southeast Asia turn blue. "On the other side, whatever's left of the United Nations." China, Pakistan, Brazil, Indonesia, Russia, and most of Sub-Saharan Africa turn red. "Whatever their differences and disagreements, the members of the Security Council all have nukes and a common interest in opposing the Freedom Coalition."

"And the Caliphate and Imamate? They're both green on the map."

"The TransArabian Caliphate and Federation of Imamates have always been wildcards in the system. They've been flip-flopping, playing each side against the other, but have more often than not allied themselves with the Freedom Coalition. The prospect of the Caliphate and its clients flipping the other way is a big deal. So these are the dominos that are in place, the two alliances that will duke it out in the next—and, we hope, the last—World War. Really, from a certain point of view, the first and only truly World War." With a gesture, Stan initiates the simulation of this hypothetical World War. Lots of parabolas, presumably representing the pathway of ballistic missiles with nuclear payloads, crisscross the planet. These missiles make cute squeaking sounds when they strike. Cartoon smiley faced mushroom clouds pop up all over the map. "We've been poised on the brink of Armageddon for almost ten years now. If Al succeeds in his mission later this week, he's going to give the system, now on the unstable edge between phases, the kick that'll move it into its next, more stable phase, full global war." When the whole planet is covered with adorable smiling mushrooms, the simulation loops back to the beginning.

"Why would you want to start the Apocalypse? You're not evangelical types. Is this about my father? Are you trying to get revenge or something?"

"Sure, we're still a little pissed at your father for shutting us out of Omni Science, so destroying your family's Reputation would be nice, but, frankly, your father kicked our asses fair and square and, you know something, he was right to do so. Whenever I tell people he's a ruthless bastard, I mean that as a compliment. The fact is, we're businessmen. Terrorist attacks, violent actions, and their first-order consequences are considered works of intellectual property or art protected under CRAP. Sooner or later, the world is going to precipitate into its apocalyptic phase, either by accident or design. If it's by design, well, can you think of a bigger moneymaker than the Apocalypse? As it's unfolding, and we predict it may take years to fully unfold, it'll be a story of interest to every person with a mediasphere connection, everyone in the world. Billions and billions of eyeballs tuning in from dozens to hundreds of times a day, tracking emergency after emergency, will feed royalties straight to us. Our simulations suggest the US will come out okay at the end of the day, with at least half its population intact."

Eliot now notices the lower concentration of cartoon mushrooms in the US. Israel, for its part in this simulation, is border-to-border mushrooms. The rest of the Mideast has done no better. Everyone seems to have taken a shot at blowing up the Holy Land. Jesus, Eliot thinks. Tom was right. Stan gestures the briefing to end, and the TV goes black. Stan sits down, smiling with the satisfaction of someone who has just successfully rolled out a new product line.

"We have this tagline we want to use. 'Whosoever owns the rights to the Apocalypse shall control the future.' What do you think, Eliot? Be honest."

"*That* one I like," Eliot says. "Has that biblical ring to it. But there's this one small thing."

"Do tell."

"Don't you think that, I don't know, maybe there's like something *immoral* about starting a nuclear Apocalypse?"

"I'm glad you asked. Actually, Troy and I have discussed this at great length. We even hired the services of a Moral Philosophy Consultancy, a small firm called Categorical Imperative Limited."

"I know that company," Eliot says. "Wasn't it founded by—"

"Professor Barney Cornelius."

"Isn't he emeritus at the University of Chicago?"

"That's right. He's concluded that we're taking the right path, the only moral path under these circumstances. He's written up the logical proof and is planning to publish his white paper in the aftermath of the assassination."

"I don't want to judge or anything," Eliot says, "and moral philosophy wasn't my strongest subject—I was studying Elvis impersonators—but I just don't see it. How the proof would work."

Stan seems suddenly bored with Eliot. "Well, okay, I don't have a lot of time, but here's the elevator-talk version. Given the current geopolitical situation, the Apocalypse I just outlined to you *will happen*, one way or another. This year, next year, whenever. Take that as a given. If it happens by accident or is initiated by people who do not claim their intellectual property rights, then the world will just get nuked and no one will make a cent off the whole thing. Now, if some person or group figures out that there's money to be made off the destruction of the world, then that person or group will be within reach of an unprecedented business opportunity. Again, given the geopolitics of the matter, this is really low-hanging fruit.

"It is, therefore, immoral *not* to take advantage of this knowledge, because if the end of the world doesn't come about by accident, then some other, more malicious group will take advantage of this knowledge. On behalf of our investors, we're obligated to take every step we can to ensure that we corner the Apocalypse market before anyone else does. And we're prepared to use part of our profit, after dividends are paid out, in a very charitable way. We're not only going to be the most profitable corporation in history but also the greatest philanthropists the world has ever known. As good corporate citizens, we have an obligation to the whole world community. We'll help rebuild things, pick up the pieces of our sad and broken world. Make sure these kinds of unstable geopolitical situations can't happen again."

"Where are you going to rebuild the world from? The bottom of a nuclear bunker?"

"We've bought a small surplus space station from China in geosynchronous orbit. Most of the world's financial networks and major banks run off orbital server farms, so even if—God forbid—Wall Street is vaporized, we can hold on to our fortune. All of which is to say, Troy and I have to get going to the Miami Space Terminal. Our shareholders and families are waiting for us."

"You haven't finished," Eliot says, desperate not to be left alone. "Why's my duplicate helping you? What's the lie you've convinced him of?"

"It's the funniest thing. Al belongs to this crazy 'Creative Destruction' school of Marxist-Leninist thought. They interpret Marx's writings as literal predictions of the future, so they consider it their mission to *help* capitalist markets spread to every corner of the world, because that's the necessary precondition for a truly socialist revolution. They were really upset when the anarchists took over the Bay Area, thought it interfered with the design of history or something. That's actually how we met him. After PEN seized the Bay Bridge, the Marxist-Leninist Chamber of Commerce and the Silicon Valley Society of Entrepreneurs started working together, part of the anti-PEN vanguard. We've convinced Aliot that we're also secretly Creative Destruction Marxists and that we're going to rebuild the postapocalyptic world along what he considers to be egalitarian lines. He's a good kid actually. Very earnest. Don't let that 'capitalist scum' stuff fool you. He cares."

"I take it you're not," Eliot says.

Stan checks his smartwatch. "Not what?"

"Going to rebuild your new world along what he would consider egalitarian lines."

"This is also a question for philosophy. We believe that innovators who develop a successful brand have every right to use their wealth in whatever way they see fit. Free markets and private ownership of capital are the foundation of any just and democratic society, as I'm sure you know." Stan stands up. "Sorry to cut our conversation short, but our space plane is waiting."

"Wait!" Eliot says. "Are you going to, like, kill me now?"

Stan looks annoyed. "Come on, Eliot. Of course not. We're businessmen, not murderers. You'll stay here until Caliph Fred is dead, then we'll let you go and you can tell your father what we've done. No doubt he'll be furious that he missed the business opportunity sitting right there in front of his face."

"I'm sure that's *exactly* what he'll think," Eliot says.

Stan picks up his briefcase and turns to leave. Eliot examines the room more carefully, notices metal bars outside the windows, meant to keep people out, not in. This house is inside an active Riot Zone.

"I'm in New Jersey," Eliot says.

"That's right, kiddo, but don't worry, the Terror Forecast predicts Rioting Levels will be relatively low this week. Calm before the Apocalypse, so to speak. Ha ha. Make yourself at home. There's a bathroom through that door. You're free to use the television and mediasphere connection in passive mode. If you need anything, we have a man on call to make sure you're comfortable. Do you want anything before I go?"

Eliot considers his answer. "Food would be nice. And a coffee. And a pack of cigarettes, if you've got them."

Ω

During its livestream later that night, *That's So Fucked Up* reports that it has obtained exclusive footage of Eliot R. Vanderthorpe, Jr. ("heir to the multibillion-dollar Vanderthorpe Fortune and an odds-on favorite to win the Most Fucked Up Person of the Year Award"), having sex with Janine Lane, a reporter for an anarchist periodical, the London *Activist*. In the version of the footage *TSFU* streams that evening, fuzzy dots cover up all the relevant naughty bits. To view the uncensored footage, you must register with its mediasphere site. The passive mediasphere connection prevents him from registering, but Eliot notes that the uncensored version has already been viewed almost sixteen million times.

"Look at the schlong on that kid," says *TSFU* host Doug "Douche-bag" Baloney.

Cagey, practically out of his mind with unfocused rage, Eliot channel surfs. Even Toothpaste Central, with its endless lineup of programs on orthodontic health and practically avant-garde attitude toward the dental arts, can't stop his mind from racing. A kindly seeming elderly man occasionally brings him takeout. Other than this old man, who checks in on Eliot every couple hours, there seem to be no guards here. Eliot wants to shove the old man to the floor and run screaming through the streets, but he knows better than to try escaping: even if Aliot hadn't stolen his electronic identity, he doesn't want to face the Riot Zone. It would crush him.

As the evening proceeds, Eliot grows increasingly haggard. He can't sleep. His appetite disappears. Political news coverage, when he works up the courage to watch it, triggers panic and despair. The Indonesian president has denounced the Freedom Coalition. As it prepares for the *Peace in the Mideast Summit Telethon*, Israel begins massing troops along the Jordanian and Egyptian borders. With a cheerful smile, POTUS Friendly denies rumors that American satellites are targeting Dubai. UN Security Council Resolution 19247 denounces "the persistent belligerence of the Freedom Coalition." Caliph Fred releases a new single, a big hit on the Muslim mediasphere, in which he makes some sort of threatening references to jihad.

Political coverage makes Eliot want to throw up, but news about himself makes him feel even worse. *Eliot's Den* has had no choice but to shut down its discussion forum indefinitely. Conservative pundits have launched a propaganda war against left-leaning Eliot fan-scholars. Financial analysts, meanwhile, have come to their own consensus: Investor, sell whatever shares of ERVJ you may still be foolish enough to own. You can buy shares of his Name now for less than a dollar. The mediasphere conversation around Eliot has become deeply polarizing, if not downright toxic. His fan base has shattered into a thousand competing and confused factions. Even his most loyal followers no longer love him. Only a handful of the more dedicated amateur fan-scholars remain and then only because they've already unwisely staked their futures to Eliot's.

On the afternoon of his second full day of captivity, running on almost no sleep, Eliot mutes the TV and paces around the living room. The street outside the house is almost devoid of life. House windows are all barred and tinted. People occasionally poke heads from behind steel-reinforced doors. Armored cars, bullet-pocked, speed back and forth. A roving gang passes, shirtless teenagers in baggy cargo shorts. Orange and black tattoos cover their bodies. The word TIGERS is tattooed in huge gothic letters on each of their chests. Prosthetic tiger ears have been surgically affixed to each of their heads. Whiskers sprout from cheeks still slightly chubby with baby fat. They're mods, child gangs of the Riot Zone, surgically modified, bat-shit crazy.

Eliot backs away from the window. The shiny animated fractal on his face stares back at him, in reflection. There is something hideous and yet deeply appealing about the way these patterns of silver swarm across his face. At first he found the animated tattoo revolting, but he has learned to look past the surface of his disfigurement. His real face emerges like the hidden thing in a magic eye picture from amidst swirling galaxies of silver. Omni could pick him out from the visual noise if it could correctly guess the algorithm governing its motion. Unfortunately, there is no general solution for the problem of tattoo masking, especially with tattoos that dynamically modify their underlying rule-set, color, and albedo, that can create the illusion of three-dimensional change on a person's face.

A mediasphere feed he has set up beeps, reporting a new story about him, marked urgent. Eliot turns on the TV and discovers that the Vanderthorpe Family has issued a press release onto the media-sphere.

> *To Our Loyal Friends and Supporters:*
>
> *We are writing to thank you for your hundreds of thousands of very supportive emails and texts and voice messages. We are overwhelmed by your prayers and love.*
>
> *At this time, we would like to express our disappointment that TSFU has shown such poor moral judgment in choosing to expose the personal affairs and failings of our beloved Li'l El.*
>
> *We stand fully behind our son as he tries to resolve the spiritual crisis that he is working presently to overcome. Eliot will address his fans and supporters tomorrow.*
>
> *God bless you,*
> *The Vanderthorpe Family (VATH)*

The letter seems ridiculous to Eliot. Who would believe that his recent stupidity constitutes some sort of spiritual crisis? From what he can tell browsing the feeds, Aliot has effortlessly infiltrated his life. He artfully dodges reporters around Manhattan, repeats "No comment" over and over like a mantra, ducks into black sedans, Pedro at the wheel. One program shows him and Sarah meeting at a Greenwich Village café, and she seems almost interested in what Aliot has to say, attentive, excited even. What the hell's he doing with Sarah? What could he have said to persuade her to see him? Eliot tries not to ask himself the obvious follow-up question, which would only make him feel even shittier than he already does.

Ω

The next afternoon, Aliot appears at a news conference wearing a suit with a tiny silver lapel crucifix positioned directly below American-flag and Freedom Coalition pins. Hundreds and hundreds of flashes explode everywhere around him and Aliot is saying, "Thank you. Thank you all for being here." Father, Mother, Elijah, Karl, Sarah—Sarah!—and a number of other nameless handlers crowd around him, offering silent support. Sarah must be sacrificing a lot to be here, bracketing her dignity to help the person she must think is Eliot, deigning to stand in the presence of Eliot Sr., Mr. Military-Industrial himself, virtually Satan walking the earth to her, given her political convictions, not to mention Daisy, whose books she has on repeated occasions threatened to burn. Her bracelet is blinking madly—she must be in terrible shape.

Tears slide freely down Aliot's cheeks. Father and Mother caringly brush his shoulder. Elijah winks and slaps the back of his faux bro. Sarah hugs Aliot and kisses him lightly—what the fuck?—on the lips.

"I am here today," Aliot says, "to submit myself to the American people's and to God's judgment. I am here today to atone for my sins. I have committed many and will commit many more before the end. But I am here to ask for your help, support, and prayers as I try to move past my mistakes and to renew my life, to accept a personal and sustained relationship with Jesus. To refresh my soul. To these great and worthy goals I pledge myself. I look you in the eye, America, and I admit I've done wrong. I ask you, and the whole world, to give me another chance. Do you have it in your heart to hear what I am asking for? If you do, I will do everything in my power not to disappoint you again."

So it has come to this. Aliot shakes the hand of someone in a Red costume, apologizes to the Omni Science mascot for having shoved it at the party. There is light laughter at this absurd spectacle, at all this self-conscious fun. In the sickening display of humility and prostration before God and Country that follows, Eliot picks out only a few words, too filled with rage to concentrate.

Aliot concludes with a flourish: "I want to reaffirm the supreme value and inextricable interconnection of the three Cs: Christ, the Constitution, and Capitalism. I am happy to unveil, on behalf of my family, for our forthcoming secondary offering of stock in the family Name, our new family values statement: 'Three Cs: Christ, the Constitution, and Capitalism.' All rights reserved."

The motto appears on a patch of mediawall behind Aliot. Cameras flash wildly.

"What comes next for you and your family, Eliot?" a reporter asks.

"Why, we're all going to Israel for the *Peace in the Mideast Summit Telethon*." Aliot smiles and steps away from the podium. "Be sure to watch, tomorrow at three p.m. GMT."

Eliot can't recall ever having felt so decisively angry about anything. When in the future he reflects back on this moment, he suspects he'll probably be most grateful for the purity of the rage that Aliot's speech has given him permission to feel, for the decisiveness of action it has inspired. Eliot exits the mediaroom and walks down the hallway toward the front door. The house seems empty. He knows what he has to do, but before he can try to open the door, it opens on its own. In come two men with XM8 rifles slung over their shoulders, one carrying a tray of coffees and a box full of donuts, the other holding a few pizza boxes. Beyond the door, cars speed on the street.

"Hey, Eliot," says the one with donuts, Jeb, his face tattoo turned off.

"Thinking of going out for a walk?" says the other, Ted.

"As a matter of fact, I was," Eliot says.

"You wouldn't want to do that. The Riot Zone, as you know, is a very dangerous place."

"Yes," Ted adds, "here in the Riot Zone no one would notice another unidentified corpse, riddled with bullets, left to rot under a freeway. We might never find you if you got lost."

"You make a very convincing case," Eliot says, "but I think I'll take my chances."

Ted unfastens the snap of his sidearm holster, while Jeb seems to work at coming up with a witty retort. On the street, visible through the doorway, a blue hatchback with tinted windows pulls up, stops in front of the house, then begins a K-turn, but pauses on the vertical axis of the K, its rear end facing the house. Its hatch opens up. Three masked figures are crouched in the back of the car.

"What is that car doing?" Eliot says. "And who are those masked men in the back?"

"You think you can fool us into looking away from you?" Jeb says.

"We're not *that* stupid," Ted adds.

Eliot raises his hands with exasperation. "No, guys, I'm not nearly that clever. There's really a car, a hatchback, right behind you. The back is open and there are these people wearing masks and it looks like they're holding—"

Deciding they ought to take the risk of trusting Eliot, Jeb and Ted slowly turn around.

"Well, look, he's right. What do you think they're carrying, Ted?"

"An excellent question, Jeb."

The car accelerates backward toward them, fast.

"Those are AK-47s, Jeb."

"Ah," Jeb says.

The sound of shots further clarifies the situation. Shouting and confusion follow. Jeb and Ted scream at each other over gunfire. Pizza boxes go flying. Eliot grabs a coffee cup that Jeb has dropped, then flees to the relative safety of the living room. Other voices, outside, shout orders. Go, go, go. Boots stomp on stairs. Before Eliot can flee into the bathroom adjacent to the mediaroom, three masked men march in, smoking AK-47s in hand. Outside the volleys continue, rapid syncopated reports. The AKs aim in his direction, casual.

The shortest soldier is covered in blood, crazed wingnut eyes visible through mask eyeholes.

"Stay where you are!" the tallest shouts. "Put your hands on your head! Lie down on the floor!"

Which should he do first, put his hands on his head or lie down on the floor? The second tallest lets his AK hang from its strap and tries to pull out his sidearm, but he's having difficulty getting his gun free of its holster. The crazy-eyed soldier whose flack jacket is covered in blood pulls off his mask, revealing that *he* is in fact a *she*, a teenage girl with a mess of brown hair plastered down with plastic barrettes to her head.

"Ohmygod, Justin!" she screams. "You were so right! Ohmygod, put your guns down, guys. This *is* Eliot. The *real* Eliot Vanderthorpe. Not the phony one going to Israel!"

The soldiers commiserate as gunfire continues outside in the hallway.

"Who are you?" Eliot asks.

The leader pulls off his mask. A blond, wholesome-looking kid, no older than sixteen, stares at Eliot with jejune eyes.

"We're the Eliot Vanderthorpe Brigade," he says.

"That is still *such* a stupid name, Justin," says the second tallest. "A brigade has, like, thousands of soldiers in it. We have four! We should be called the Eliot Vanderthorpe Squad, something like that."

"Who's in command here, Major Taylor?" Justin says.

His second snaps to attention. "You are, sir."

"Yeah, Shawn," Jen says. "Justin is, like, our commanding officer."

"That's right, and I say we're the Eliot Vanderthorpe Brigade. Go help Chris—I mean, go help Private Saunders!"

Shawn runs off, AK raised, to help Chris.

"The Eliot Vanderthorpe Brigade?" Eliot says, horrified.

"Ohmygod!" Jen says.

"Calm down, Jen, we're soldiers. We're on a mission."

"But I can't believe it, Justin. I'm meeting the *real* Eliot Vander-thorpe. I've been your biggest fan my whole life. *El-i-o-o-t!*"

"How old are you?" Eliot asks.

"Fourteen, silly. Ohmygod. Your face is all messed up with that tattoo, but I knew it was you from the way you were standing. I'd recognize you no matter what they did to you."

Outside two AK-47s go off in an alternating rhythm. Justin's eyes are alight with some combination of pride and fanaticism. Here is another human example of something Eliot had, before meeting Aliot, largely avoided coming face-to-face with: total, true belief.

"They called me crazy," Justin says. "They called me a conspiracy theorist. But I was right. Sometimes, there are conspiracies in the world and when there are it's up to people like us to discover them, to stop them. Power to the fans! Power to the fans!"

Chanting, Justin raises his AK. Jen raises her own rifle and repeats the mantra.

"Power to the fans! Ohmygod! Power to the fans!"

This embarrassing display of silliness eventually calms down.

"I knew that something was strange when you got back home, three nights ago," Justin says. "None of my friends believed that I had found real footage of you, because you masked yourself from Omni, but I figured it out. You went into this alley by the Franklin D. Roosevelt Shopping Center in Manhattan. Then this van pulled up to the alley and then you didn't come back out. When you resurfaced on Omni, you had something new in your jeans pocket, some kind of bulge. I saw you, well, your duplicate, pull it out and take a call. It was a sim cell phone. But that makes no sense, right? No sense at all! Why would you have a sim cell phone you never had before? There was no record of it anywhere. I made my case, showed my evidence to my so-called friends, but they called me crazy and began defriending me. The admin on *Eliot's Den* started censoring my postings. But look, we here, the true believers, we're victorious. Eliot *was* kidnapped and replaced with a duplicate, just like I said. Look! We've done it! We've really saved you!"

"Oh my God!" This is Eliot, not Jen. "Where did you get the AK-47s? Those costumes. Everything. You're teenagers. Are you crazy, risking your lives like this?"

"We found these guys selling guns and equipment on the media-sphere," Justin says, doing his best to imitate the gruff authority of movie military commanders. "And we borrowed our tactics from *Tom Clancy's Counterinsurgency Online*." A new round of gunfire erupts from outside. "But we have no time for idle chatter. We're fighting to save your life. There's going to be no backup. We're it."

Jen runs up to him and hugs him tightly around his waist, tears staining her face. From a pocket of her cargo pants she pulls out a smelly silver marker and a copy of the *Eliot R. Vanderthorpe, Jr., Unofficial Philosophy Book*, a pamphlet of aphorisms Karl paid a ghostwriter to slap together a few years ago. Eliot signs the pamphlet for her.

Justin and Jen put their ski masks back on and rejoin their compatriots, all citizens bound together by civic mysteries known only to the Nation of Eliot. Standing there, all together at the foot of the stairwell, they shoot their AKs. The smell of burning guns—plastic, metal?—is nauseating. The hatchback door beckons. Should Eliot go with these kids? No serious alternatives come to mind.

"Let's get out of here," Eliot says. "Before the police come."

Jen stops shooting. "Police?" She seems confused.

"Police are people who stop crime," Shawn explains between rounds of gunfire. "They're almost like private security, except they're paid with taxes."

"Oh, okay," Jen says. "I think I understand."

"Is that going to be a problem for us?" Justin says, nervous. "I mean, police or security?"

"No," Shawn says. "Private security firms refuse to service this part of the Riot Zone. The profit margins are too low, I think."

"Let's get out of here," Eliot says.

Once the members of the Eliot Vanderthorpe Brigade resolve among themselves questions related to police and private security, everyone gets into the car. Justin jumps into the shotgun seat and Shawn drives. Chris and Jen and Eliot crowd together in the back. Chris has remained silent this whole time. Together, Eliot and his brigade delve deeper into the Riot Zone, into lawless New Jersey. Shortly, Ted and Jeb's XM8s become just another faction of gunfire amidst a more catholic riot all around them. Eliot doesn't look back at the house, glad to leave it behind.

Ω

Single-family homes whose front lawns are sprinkled with shell casings eventually give way to ugly apartment buildings that pop up like giant concrete fungi along the road. Farther in the distance, behind the apartment buildings, colossal black columns of smoke rise skyward toward a low dark ceiling of boiling storm clouds. The gray apartment buildings blend seamlessly with the clouds, a single solid slate field mottled with occasional red spots of fire. Cars burn on the side of the road, and the smell of smoke and soot fills the blue hatchback.

"It's your destiny," Jen is saying to Eliot. "You've got to go."

Eliot blinks. Jen leans toward him, unalloyed earnestness on her face. In the front, Shawn and Justin are arguing about where they should take Eliot. Chris watches Jen and Eliot argue, too shy to say anything. Eliot should have listened to that part of him that warned against explaining to the brigade why he had been kidnapped and replaced. The brigade proved quite receptive to the idea that Aliot was planning to precipitate a nuclear Apocalypse. Given their paranoid worldview, this development seemed all but a natural extension of their existential purpose as a group and as individuals. Saving Eliot and saving the world were already deeply connected in their minds. For Jen especially, their mission seems now to have taken on well-nigh messianic proportions.

"Don't just sit there," she says. "*Say* something."

"I guess all I can say is that I respectfully disagree. I'm all for taking moral responsibility, but what am I supposed to do about stopping the Apocalypse from happening? The Summit Telethon is going to air in less than twenty-four hours. None of my biometrically validated accounts are accessible to me. I can't even get through to anyone on your phone."

As they sped away from the house, Eliot tried using Jen's palmtop to call Father, Mother, Karl, Sarah, Pedro, anyone who he might convince to pick him up or get word to someone who would know what to do about this Apocalypse business. But the whole Vanderthorpe Family and its support staff have already long departed for Israel, and Jen's username would have no priority in the phone system of anyone who mattered. He got through to Pedro's voice mail, not that Pedro would be able to do anything to help him stop the Apocalypse. For all Eliot knows, Pedro has joined his family in Israel. Without the invisible electronic and human network that has always taken care of things for him, Eliot is completely helpless, a fish flopping on the beach, gills straining for life-giving water. His situation, he is beginning to conclude, is hopeless.

"With all this tattoo stuff on me," he adds, "I don't even come up on Omni anymore."

"Yes, you do." Jen searches for his Name on her tab. "See, you don't come up with normal searches, but you do get sent to the False Positives folder. How do you think we found you? There was a video of you in the False Positives folder, those two guys carrying you from the back of a van into the house and you were already tattooed and everything but you were clearly you if you knew you were you."

"All very nice to know, but you're probably the only people crazy enough to have even thought to look at—"

Justin turns around. "Crazy? We *saved* you, Eliot! We *did* it."

"You said it yourself," Jen says. The *Unofficial Philosophy* book reemerges from her cargo-pants pocket. "Section two, thesis forty-five. 'We all want a purpose or mission in our lives,' you write. 'But only the very bravest of us are willing to recognize our true purpose or mission when it appears before us.'"

"And?" Eliot says.

"And going to Israel is your true mission, Eliot. It's what you were born to do."

Jen shoves the slim book into his hands, her eyes misty. Eliot refuses to accept it.

"But I signed it for you. Please, no, keep it."

"I never thought I'd live to say this, but you need it more than I do. You've forgotten who you really are."

"Oh, God," Eliot says. "Jen, I don't think you understand how very *not me* this book is. If my friends and family are to be believed, I'm a narcissistic, self-obsessed, selfish, sexist, irresponsible deviant of a human being. Frankly, that's a very penetrating description of me. As a matter of fact, I don't want to undermine any long-held illusions you may have, but about this book—"

"You're better than this, Eliot," Jen says. "I've always known you were good in your heart, ever since I was nine. I've always known that you had a special destiny. I believe in you. Take the book."

Eliot, his willpower sapped, accepts the book and puts it in his back pocket. The hatchback gets on the New Jersey Turnpike. Eliot stares out the window as they speed along, past the sound barricades, the late afternoon gray and dysphoric. Shawn has decided to drive to Justin's gated community, the closest of their homes.

"Why is the Turnpike so empty?" Eliot says.

"Guess we're just lucky," Justin says.

Shawn makes a groaning noise. "No, Justin, I don't think we're 'just lucky.'"

"Don't talk to a superior officer that way, Major Taylor. My rank, as you know—"

"Do *you* want to know something, Justin, I'm pretty sick of all this superior officer bullshit and our military ranks and all that stuff." In his anger, Shawn has started swerving the car erratically on the empty road. "Did you check the Terror Forecast before we left?"

"Well. . ."

"Kids, could we maybe drive in a straight line?" Eliot says. "Do you even have a driver's license?"

"I have a permit," Justin says. "I'm letting Major Taylor—"

"I ask about the Terror Forecast," Shawn continues, "because an empty Turnpike is the sort of thing you might expect to find if, I mean . . ."

Jen tries to call up the Terror Forecast on her palmtop, but all wireless signals are being jammed.

"We have a problem," Chris whispers. Chris has been so incredibly quiet and shy this whole time that his assessment that they are having a problem suggests to Eliot that their condition of problem-having must be very serious indeed.

To wit: A pyramid of cars has been constructed on their northbound lane of the Turnpike. All the cars on the pyramid are, for reasons unknown, BMWs. Shawn stops, then puts the car into reverse, but finds his backward path interdicted by about a dozen golf carts that have emerged, somehow, from the gray murk of the movie-set-like environment of the empty Turnpike and have surrounded them, occluding their escape. Each of these golf carts overflows with people, mods. Their leather jackets are emblazoned with their gang's logo, the Sharks. Each Shark has a fin—maybe made of real shark cartilage—grafted onto his shaved skull. Eliot catches a glimpse of serrated teeth, freaky nubs, either filed down or implanted.

"It's the Sharks," Shawn says.

"I can see that," Eliot says.

"Their show on the Gangland Warfare Channel is pretty cool," Justin says.

Accompanying the Sharks is a crew from the Gangland Warfare Channel. The director, who is wearing mediashades, trails behind the golf carts on a Segway scooter. Half a dozen embedded videographers ride along on the golf carts. A few support staff straggle around on foot, carrying handheld lights. More support staff, Eliot sees now, are setting up equipment around the pyramid of cars. There's a media equipment truck parked on the southbound lane.

"They're in a turf war with the Tigers," Shawn explains. "They're trying to capture gangland mediasphere market share from them."

Gangland mediasphere market share. Eliot has never heard these words strung together in a sentence, but he can guess well enough what they might mean.

"How the hell do you know that?" Eliot says.

Shawn seems confused at the question. "I saw it on *That's So Fucked Up.*"

"Of course."

The Sharks-infested golf carts begin circling the blue hatchback. They're making some kind of noise, a monotonous droning. Justin wipes his sweaty hands on his cargo pants. Eliot opens his window, the better to hear.

"Da-dum da-dum da-dum," the Sharks hum in unison, their golf carts closing in.

Jen seems confused. "What are they singing?"

"More menacing, guys," the director shouts from his Segway.

". . . DA-DUM DA-DUM DA-DUM . . ."

"I think it's supposed to be the theme of *Jaws,*" Eliot says.

"Theme of what?" Jen says.

Eliot wonders whether or not they needed to license the rights to use the song.

"Okay, Mr. Commander," Shawn says. "What are we supposed to do? I can't break out of this circle. And even if I could"—shrieking now—"there's that giant pyramid of BMWs blocking our way!"

Shawn pushes Justin, and soon they're tussling together, shouting obscenities, eroding the morale of the rest of the brigade. Chris has started openly bawling like the thirteen-year-old boy Eliot suspects him to be. Jen shakes her leg and hums nervously to herself.

"What kind of car is this?" Eliot says. "The one we're driving in."

The front-seat fighting stops, and the brigade goes silent.

". . . DA-DUM DA-DUM DA-DUM . . ."

"It's a BMW," Chris says between two especially loud snotty sobs.

"Okay, guys," Eliot says. "I'm as big an advocate of nonviolence as you're likely to find on this planet, but in this special case, well, you've got those AKs. Use 'em. The Sharks don't seem to be carrying guns. They won't stand a chance."

"We can't do that," Shawn says.

"Why not? What's the problem?"

Shawn holds up his AK-47. "Well, I know this really *looks like* a gun."

"Very much so. As a gun, I find it very convincing."

". . . DA-DUM DA-DUM DA-DUM . . ."

"There's a problem of its not being a gun, you see. There's, um, this group that goes around carrying fake weapons. They're called—"

"The Avant-Guardians. I know, my father told me about them."

"Yeah, they're really being cracked down on, apparently. Lately, Omni has gotten really good at finding them. So now they're selling their fake weapons and ammo and stuff really cheap on the media-sphere."

"To you?"

"To us," Justin says.

"I did all the logistical work," Shawn says. "Guns, armor, ski masks, everything except checking the Terror Forecast." His voice has escalated again to a screamlike volume. "Our Glorious Leader was supposed to check the fucking Terror Forecast but forgot to do his fucking job."

"That blood on your armor, Jen?" Eliot says.

Jen giggles. "Silly, that's just paint."

". . . DA-DUM DA-DUM DA-DUM . . ."

The golf carts all suddenly stop. The leader of the Sharks—who is carrying a flamethrower kit—is a lumbering hulk of a human being, built like a professional wrestler, who has clearly taken great care to cultivate an image of menace and savagery. Standing on the top of his golf cart's canopy, looking rather menacing and savage indeed, he shouts at the top of his lungs, lisping through serrated teeth.

"Step out of the car. We are in need of a car to burn for our spectacular car pyramid."

"DA-DUM DA-DUM DA-DUM," most of the rest say in support.

When it becomes clear that the brigade will be no help in this situation, Eliot opens his door and gets out in front of the hatchback. "There are lots of other cars around here, guys." Eliot points to a flipped-over car by the side of the road. "Why don't you burn that one over there?"

The Sharks seem confused at this suggestion, slowing the tempo of their "da-dums." The Gangland Warfare Channel director rolls forward on his Segway to explain the situation.

"BMW is our featured sponsor this season," he says. "They've paid us a lot of money so that we'll only burn *their* cars and we need one more to top off our pyramid. It's really quite lucky that you came by. We need to get this week's show in the can."

Baring serrated teeth, a dozen Sharks leap from their golf carts. "DA-DA-DUM!" the pouncing Sharks sing as the rest continue their "da-dum da-dum" chorus. Eliot covers his eyes and waits to be beaten up, but nothing happens. The *Jaws* theme has suddenly ceased. Eliot uncovers his eyes and discovers that the formerly charging Sharks are now slowly backing away from him.

Behind him, wearing their ski masks again, the members of the Eliot Vanderthorpe Brigade have stepped out of the blue hatchback. Justin and Chris step onto the hood of their Beemer, gaining height. Shawn and Jen flank Eliot. The Sharks are not sure what to make of these short masked soldiers with AK-47s.

"We're going to cover you," Shawn says, in command. "I mean, we're going to pretend to cover you. Run as far away from here as you can, Eliot."

"Are you guys serious?"

"Our mission is to protect you," Justin says. "Nothing else matters."

"Please be safe," Chris whispers, almost inaudible through his ski mask.

Jen is in tears. "But don't forget who you are."

"Okay, guys, enough chatter," Shawn says. "Lock and load!"

Eliot wants to live up to the faith that Jen and Shawn and Chris and Justin seem to have in him. He may have been kidnapped, tattooed, and replaced by a duplicate intent on starting a global nuclear Apocalypse, but his spirit remains, as yet, inexplicably, intact, so he won't let the Sharks stop him.

"Power to the fans!" comes the shout from behind him. There is a touch of last-standish mournfulness in this slogan. "Power to the fans!"

Four fake AK-47s fire in unison. The Sharks scatter, creating an opening through which Eliot can run north on the Turnpike, around and beyond the pyramid of gasoline-doused BMWs, toward some approximation of freedom. And so Eliot runs. It seems as if running is all he does now, all he'll ever do.

Ω

Getting off the Turnpike turns out to be harder than Eliot had hoped. The sound barriers on either side of the road keep him fenced in. Off-ramps—all of which seem to be privately owned—have been sealed off until this particular section of road riot dies down. Eliot eventually comes upon two homeless men sitting by the sound barrier. The first has only one arm and is eating dried ramen. The second carries a stainless-steel spatula with which he is scraping something that may once have been an animal off the pavement.

The one-armed man breaks off a clump of instant noodles from the mass and shoves it into his dirty beard where his mouth must be, hydrating it with saliva. Eliot fights his instinctive revulsion and squats down in front of the man. He has an army surplus look about him, probably some traumatized Iraq war vet or something.

The man's blue eyes regard him with caution. "This is my stuff."

"I don't want your food."

"You better not."

"I need help. I'm—is there a way to get past the sound barrier?"

The one with the spatula pauses from his roadside labor. "Well, mister. You could try running real fast."

Both men find this joke hilarious.

Back toward the pyramid of cars, the gunfire stops. Eliot wonders what has happened to the brigade. Did he do the right thing in leaving them to fend for themselves? They're only children, but what else could he have done? It's not too late, though. He can still go back. Maybe he has an obligation to make sure they're safe. Maybe that's the ethical thing to do in this situation. The pyramid of cars suddenly explodes into a finger of flame. A northerly wind blows smoke toward Eliot. Following the explosion, a second sound comes from down the road, a familiar drone—"da-dum da-dum da-dum"—and a pair of approaching golf cart headlights emerges from the smoke.

Eliot decides to resume his running. After all, doesn't he have an obligation to respect the wishes of the brigade, to escape as they would want him to, to honor their noble self-sacrifice? The golf cart—bearing three Sharks and their embedded videographer—cuts him off before he can further develop this line of reasoning. The Sharks leap from the cart and surround him.

"This is your big moment, guys," the videographer says. "Don't blow it."

The tallest Shark presses Eliot against the sound barrier. "Don't mess with the Sharks."

"I certainly would prefer not to," Eliot says. "I wish you all luck winning market share from the Tigers."

"The Tigers?" the second says. "I fucking *hate* the fucking Tigers!"

"How much do you hate them?" asks the videographer.

"I wanna rip the fucking heads off those fucking cocksucking fucking Tigers."

"Bleaaarge," adds the third Shark.

Soon they're all yelping, a show for the camera. The Gangland Warfare Channel, Eliot knows, positions itself in that part of the marketing Venn diagram where fans of professional wrestling and snuff films meet.

The videographer presents his tab to Eliot. "We need you to sign this release form."

"What?"

"If you don't sign the release, we can't use the footage leading up to the Beemer attack."

"I'll only sign if you promise not to hurt me," Eliot says.

"Fine, fine." The videographer checks his smartwatch.

"And the kids. Don't hurt them."

"The kids will be fine," the videographer says.

Eliot will have to accept a verbal agreement. He presses his thumb to the tab's reader and looks into its camera, biometrically signing the release form. Satisfied, the Sharks start moving back toward the golf cart, when the videographer lifts his hand.

"Hey, guys," he says. "I just got word from the director. He says—I'm *so* sorry guys—that we need another shot of you beating someone up."

The Sharks moan.

"I'm so fucking sick of beating people up. When will all this violence end?"

"It used to be fun, then it became just another job."

"I like burning things better."

"Yeah," Eliot says. "Routine kills everything."

But the videographer insists. "We need one more shot, about five minutes' worth, of you beating *someone* up. Doesn't matter who."

The Sharks murmur. The tallest Shark punches Eliot in the stomach. The other two Sharks look at him, puzzled.

"C'mon, don't look at me that way."

"We told him we wouldn't hurt him."

"He already signed the release form. You want to try to find someone else at this point? I wanna get home in time to see *That's So Fucked Up.*"

The rest nod reluctantly, ceding the point, but before the five minutes of ass kicking can commence, an unsettlingly loud horn blares, and draws the Sharks' attention. A black Humvee, its lights off, emerges from the still-thick black smoke, and smashes into the golf cart at what must be more than sixty miles per hour, then screeches to a halt, stopping so abruptly that its rear tires practically lift off the road. The cart flies and bounces off the Turnpike sound barrier, then tumbles front over back until it comes to rest upside down. The Sharks scatter. The videographer, fearless, follows the evolving action with his palmcam.

The Humvee's headlights blaze on. "Eliot!" a familiar voice cries out from behind the lights. "Get up!"

Eliot only half recognizes his own name. A baseball-capped head sticks out of the driver's-side window. Eliot matches the voice and head to a person: it's Pedro.

A second voice suggests: "Turn off the camera, my friend." Tony Mendoza, a shotgun pointed at the face of the videographer, appears from behind the headlights. The videographer falls over backwards onto his ass and drops his palmcam.

"Get in, guy!" Pedro shouts.

"You heard him," Tony says. "You're goddamn lucky you got yourself a sentimental employee."

Eliot crawls toward the Humvee and gets in. The Sharks have disappeared and the videographer sits against the sound barrier, keeping his eye on Tony's shotgun. Tony backs toward the rear passenger-side door and gets in. The videographer closes his eyes and, breathing heavily, rests his head against the sound barrier. Pedro accelerates up the Turnpike, northbound.

"Oh my God, Pedro. Tony—" Eliot says. "Mr. Mendoza, I mean, what are you doing here?"

Tony wipes his shotgun with a cloth. "Taking a little vacation, boy. Your trip west got me all nostalgic. Made me think I should visit the family. Haven't seen Pedro and his brothers in a while."

"No, I mean how did you know? How did you find me?"

"Your duplicate didn't do too good a job impersonating you," Pedro says.

"You know about him?"

"We figured it out. You left your smartwatch in the car when you ran off the other night. Your duplicate, he didn't ask for it, and I forgot to give it back to him. So a few days later I was lurking around the *Eliot's Den* bulletin board system, just before they closed it—"

"You visit *Eliot's Den*? I'm honored, man."

"Don't bust my chops. I got my reasons. Anyway, there were these crazy people who were writing about you being replaced by a duplicate—"

"The Eliot Vanderthorpe Brigade."

"The what?"

"You didn't see them when you passed by the pyramid?"

"The place was cleared out. I'm telling you, you're lucky the Hummer made it through. We fucking had to smash through the flaming debris."

"Never mind."

"So anyway, these guys knew you'd gone walking around outside on your own and the exact time you'd gone and shit. Your duplicate was acting all weird when I drove him to the airport, so I got suspicious, and then I was talking with Tony, and Tony here found a way to access the video in the memory of your watch." Pedro throws the smartwatch at him; Eliot catches it, but it remains dark, no longer responding to his biometrics. Eliot throws the now-worthless smartwatch out the window. "All of which is to say, guy, you shoulda told me."

"I wanted to, man. I *so* almost did tell you. But when I told Sarah at the Getty, she thought I was crazy from drugs. Frankly, I thought I was a little crazy. But I have this tattoo shit on me. How'd you know I was on the Turnpike?"

"You still come up in Omni searches," Tony says. "You just get sent to the False Positives folder."

"Yeah, once we figured out you weren't you, finding the real you was pretty easy."

"Wow, Jen was right."

"Jen?"

"Never mind again."

"Let's get first things out of the way first. Here's the multimillion-dollar question, guy. Why the fuck did someone want to kidnap you, replace you with a duplicate, and send your duplicate with your family to Israel?"

"It's complicated."

Tony snorts. "I bet."

"Let's get you cleaned up, then we'll talk," Pedro says. "I gotta say, no offense or nothing, but you look like shit, Eliot."

Ω

Six-foot-seven Lyle "Little" Andrews points something that looks very much like a gun at Eliot's face. Little has an animated scorpion tattooed on the top of his hand. Its tail strikes out again and again in a looping pattern. A lit cigar sprouts from his beard. His jeans have holes large enough for small rodents or large cockroaches to crawl through. His black T-shirt, beneath a black leather sleeveless vest, bears a Hells Angels logo. Eliot is naked and standing on a podium in the middle of a small smoke-filled room.

"Put your arms out," Little says. "Grab the bars on either side of you. Close your eyes tight." His voice is grizzled from decades of smoking. "This is gonna hurt. A lot. Especially around your pubes."

Eliot grabs the handles on either side of the podium and closes his eyes. The podium begins to rotate. When Little pulls the trigger of his gunlike thing, Eliot's skin begins to burn. Countless tattoo pixels explode under the spray of Little's chemical bath. Little is a tattoo application and removal artist who, according to Pedro, has a reputation for doing good fast work.

Good fast work comes at a price, one not only financial: his body burns, especially his pubes, as promised. Don't scream, he tells himself. That would be undignified. It will take fifteen minutes, Little has said, to completely remove his whole-body animated tattoo. As the procedure continues, Eliot's mind races. There's so little time before the Telethon airs. It's already very early on Saturday in Jerusalem. Pedro's repeated attempts to contact someone who might be able to do something have all been forwarded directly to voice mail and remain unanswered. The Vanderthorpe Family and its attendant support systems have gone into communications blackout until after the Telethon. So there's nothing he can do, Eliot tells himself after a particularly painful series of explosions on the small of his back. Eliot can go to Pedro's apartment in Queens, wait until Aliot does his damage, then explain everything to his family when they come home. At least he's safe.

When the pain stops, Eliot opens his eyes and sees what he fails at first to recognize is his own skin, red and raw. His star tattoo has been cleansed with the rest. Little is now spraying him with a gel that'll help prevent swelling and irritation. The gel feels wet and cool and terrific. After getting hosed down with water, Eliot dries off, puts on a robe, and sits in a recliner in the back of the tattoo parlor. In the front room, Tony and Pedro are talking tensely.

"You're being an idiot. Your loyalty is completely misplaced."

"Man, Tony, we're friends."

"He is *not* your friend. He's not even your employer. He's the jerk-off son of your employer."

"Well then maybe his father will be grateful I saved his son."

"Total bullshit. You live your life by your contractual obligations. Beyond that, these Vanderthorpe people don't exist. You do one thing for free, they'll ask you to do a hundred more."

"You're not going to help me? Tony, I'm family. I just need a little help here."

"You're family. He's not. If I were you, I'd take my advice to heart. Never shit where you eat. Bad news. You owe this jerk-off nothing. But, hey, so you've made your choice, now you pay for what you've done. I usually charge a lot of money for what I've already done for you. Consider it a gift."

"Fucking cold, guy. You're ice cold."

Tony exits the parlor, and Pedro and Little exchange whispers about payment for Little's services. Pedro says, "I'll be back," then heads out. Eliot tries to relax. An hour later, when he begins to feel a little more normal, Eliot prepares to head out. Little gives Eliot a buzz cut to get rid of leftover tattoo traces, though his hair remains a strange color. Looking himself over in a mirror, he finds that he doesn't recognize himself. He's clean-shaven, crew-cut, dark-haired, puffy-faced and puffy-bodied, with hideous circles under his eyes. Even now, Omni would probably regard him as a False Positive of himself.

While waiting for Pedro, Eliot thumbs through the *Unofficial Philosophy* book.

> Section 3, Thesis 9: The mind of man knows only those
> boundaries the heart imposes upon it.

What total clichéd bullshit. The cover of the book features Eliot staring off smugly into the distance, a picture from his early twenties. He's sitting at a café with a giant clay cappuccino cup, foam rising up suggestively from its wide top. The picture brings him back to the Café George Orwell, reminds Eliot of what Tom had said to him when they met in Barcelona. The choice everyone has to make, he had said, was the choice between what is easy and what is right. That's what he'd said.

Pedro and Little enter the room together. Little calculates the bill on his tab, a bulky old machine covered with pornographic stickers. When Pedro sees the amount, his face drains of color. Eliot has no money, of course, so Pedro has to pay.

"Thank you so much, Pedro."

"Don't mention it."

"I mean it. Thank you."

"I said don't talk about it."

"No, really, I can't say thank you enough."

"Shut up, guy. I'm in a really fucking bad mood right now." Pedro settles up.

"I can't help thinking you look sorta familiar," Little says. "I feel as if maybe you were mentioned in a recent Hells Angels bulletin. Very recently. Hm."

Various framed pictures on the wall display Little in full Hells Angels regalia driving his hog. Does he know about the bike Janine and Samir stole in Berkeley? Eliot folds up the *Unofficial Philosophy* book with the picture of him on the cover and puts it in his pocket.

"Who can say," Eliot says. "It's a small world."

A tobacco-stained grin parts Little's bushy beard. "True, little buddy. Very true."

They leave the tattoo parlor, but only when they get back on the private expressway does Eliot calm down. Pedro clamps his hands on the steering wheel, his knuckles white, far less relaxed.

"So what's the plan, man?" Eliot says.

"Check the glove box."

Eliot finds a smartwatch in the compartment, a cheap Casio. It responds to his touch and biometrically imprints itself to him. Eliot is so grateful to have a working smartwatch. All his life, invisible systems have surrounded him, propped him up, pushed him forward, made life possible. Something as simple as a smartwatch can mean the difference between access and invisibility, personhood and noth-ingness. Eliot straps the Casio to his swollen wrist.

"It's got some cheap fake credentials built into it," Pedro says. "Tony got it. We can get you into New York with that, though not through the Island Wall. I won't mention how much that cost me."

"Everything you've paid out, you understand I'll—"

"Man, shut up. I'm in deep shit, guy."

"Pedro."

"Not to mention I gotta return this Humvee pronto, and it's a fucking wreck. How am I supposed to explain the bumper and the scorching on the side?"

The watch display glows dimly in the cabin. The Humvee muffles all external noise, its electric engine inaudible as Pedro tailgates his way along the expressway. A road map with a color-coded representation of the Terror Forecast appears on the windshield, suggesting how to remain maximally safe during their trip into the city. Terror levels have taken a turn for the worse; on the map, New Jersey is lit up all in red. Getting into Queens will take some time, time Pedro doesn't seem to think he has. Pedro almost hits the car in front of them but brakes just in time. One of the many stickers on that car reads, "I Know Where I'll Be When the Rapture Comes—Do You?"

"No," Eliot says.

"What, guy?"

"We're not going back to New York."

Pedro frowns. "And where, if I might so rudely ask, do you think we're gonna go instead?"

"You're going to hate me."

"Where do you think we're going, guy?"

"I understand you're going to interpret this in terms of what Tony said to you back at the parlor. Sorry, I overheard."

"What the fuck, Eliot?"

"Newark, Pedro. We have to go to Newark Airport."

Ω

In the short-term parking lot of Newark Airport, you can see the Gooneys rise rhythmically into the evening sky. These tiny stars of light merge into the overhead dark mass of clouds, shuriken launched into the baleen underbelly of some great gray whale god. Somewhere over the Atlantic, high above layers of cloud, they break the sound barrier and streak off to another terminus in the global network of Gooney facilities.

The terminal is packed tonight. Thousands of the superwealthy, the nearly superwealthy, and the modestly wealthy want to escape this land in riot for joyful weekend jaunts to African, Asian, European, Middle Eastern, and South American hotspots. Eliot still hopes to catch the Gooney from Newark to Tel Aviv, a five-hour trip. His decision to try to personally stop his doppelgänger is coming to seem rather foolish. For a while, he had liked the idea, thought it heroic: given his lack of an official electronic identity, he reasoned, he would need to personally confront Aliot if he hoped to convince anyone that he is in fact himself. However, he now realizes, his very lack of an electronic identity has put him in an awkward position vis-à-vis Pedro.

"You still smoking that crack pipe, guy?"

"I wish."

"I don't have that kind of money coming to me anytime soon."

"I'll pay you back, man. You know I will."

"When?"

"I don't know. After I stop the end of the world? What kind of question is that?"

"And who is gonna pay me back if you *don't* stop the world from ending?"

An inverted tree of lightning explodes in the distance, followed by ominous thunder. When rain begins coming down, they leave the lot and run toward the terminal.

"That won't be a problem, will it?" Eliot says as they run. "That's exactly my point. You've got absolutely nothing to lose here. If I fail to stop the world from ending, you won't really be needing that money anyway. If I do prevent it from ending, I can guarantee you'll get it back with a substantial bonus."

"Lots of things could go wrong here. You could stop the world from ending but die while stopping it and then what? Or the world could end and I'd still be pretty pissed that I don't have money to bribe my way into the nuclear bunker with."

"Dude, what are you talking about? Based on everything I've told you and everything you've seen, do you accept the premise that the world's, like, maybe right on the brink of ending?"

"Sure," Pedro says. "The world is about to end. Fine."

"Quod erat demonstrandum," Eliot says. "Conversation done. Buy me the ticket, Pedro."

"Don't give me that Latin shit. You're not giving me enough credit here. Why does the fact that the world will end imply *I* ought to buy *you* a plane ticket?"

Eliot has been assuming all along that he didn't need to make this logical bridge in his argument explicit. Under a canopy by the terminal's drop-off zone, they dry off. The smartfibers of their clothing eject a torrent of water. Beyond the canopy the sky really unloads itself now, a great rain pouring with building violence upon yellow taxis and a rainbow of umbrellas.

"That's a fair enough question," Eliot says. "I guess you should help me because you want the world *not to end*. I'm assuming that. Continuing to live is a good thing."

A bit drier now, they enter the departure terminal through a doorway sculpted to resemble two giant stainless-steel trees whose delicate branches meet in a natural arch. Beyond the threshold of the trees the airport's ecosystem, built on principles of total ecological design, presents itself: light tinted with a pleasant green, the smell of outdoor air pumped in. Instead of Muzak, the stylized cries of animals that have never lived and a fresh-river-rushing sound create a sense of peace and natural calm. Pedro surveys the terminal space.

"Look at this world, guy. It's one big piece of shit. You got your Riot Zones in New Jersey, full of violence and malnutrition and other horrible shit, and right here plop in the middle of it you've got your Swedish evolutionary designed organic-mechanical Gooney terminals. Like some futuristic sci-fi city. Seems to me, you stop the end of the world, things aren't going to get better where it counts, for people in the Riot Zone. You're just saving the asses of the Swedish-design people. Why should I pay for your trip with my hard-earned money? Why do you deserve rich-boy welfare from my pocket?"

Eliot considers his answer. "Because you'll be famous? You'll be the guy who helped the guy who stopped the end of the world from happening? We could be a team, you know, Pedro and Li'l El, Apocalypse Busters. They'll make movies about us."

Pedro shakes his head with disappointment, wiping water from his hair, says, "Shit. You are crazy. You don't even have a serious answer for why the world's worth saving. You really haven't got any kind of clue at all about the real world, do you? Someone's always bailing you out before you get too deep into trouble. Maybe Tony was right."

Eliot stares up at the terminal's asymmetrical dome, noticing for the first time how natural-seeming the light coming in from many angles through the folds, ridges, and slats in the ceiling seems. They've entered a zone of the terminal filled with well dressed folk sitting at "outdoor" cafés. Animated advertisements for French perfume flash on freestanding holographic billboards, the dimensions of which resemble those monolith-things from *2001*.

"Why are you saying no, Pedro? What's this all about?"

"Why, Eliot? Because you are what they call a bad investment. You have no common sense whatsoever. You're asking me to give you a lot of money, to take a big personal risk. Want to know something? I didn't want to say anything before, but I used my summer bonus to buy shares of ERVJ. I believed in you. Your bullshit shenanigans in California and that sex tape lost me a big chunk of change. Not to mention the money I just laid out for tattoo removal. Now this?"

Eliot finally asks, "Are you going to help me or not?"

"Here's what I'm asking: You really think you going to Tel Aviv will make some kind of real difference? That you're going to do something other than get a serious suntan? Am I just throwing my money away on you again?"

"Maybe, maybe not. I just don't know."

"That's maybe the first genuinely honest thing I've heard come out of your mouth." Pedro considers what to do. "Okay, then. I'll buy you the fucking ticket. But you better get off your ass and do something for once in your sorry life. 'I don't know' isn't good enough anymore. Take some responsibility. You better save the fucking world, guy, or I'll be pissed."

A well-put-together woman in a flowery frock who is checking a stylized palmtop in one hand and rocking a curly haired child in Armani toddlerwear in the other gives them a dirty look, signaling displeasure at Pedro's unsavory language, his rude irruption into the cozy sphere of her total ecological design experience. With vague outrage, she whisks her child away from the scary foulmouthed people. In the Gooney check-in zone, which is saturated with the sound of a faux wind blowing through the summer faux grass, Pedro searches at a workstation and finds a few open seats on Gooney Flight 1135, Newark International Airport to Ben-Gurion International Airport, 8:00 p.m. EST.

"How much are the first-class cabins?" Eliot asks. Despite Pedro's incredulous look—a disbelieving expression that approximates the question *You've got to be kidding?*—Eliot proves that he is in fact not kidding: "What about business class?"

"Business class seats go for forty thousand dollars, guy. I'm not paying forty thousand dollars so you can get your extra leg room and complimentary glass of champagne. Don't even ask how much the first class cabins cost."

"Fine."

Pedro focuses his attention on the check-in terminal. "There, I just put eighty-five hundred dollars on my credit account so you can get a one-way ticket to Tel Aviv. You can figure out getting back on your own. I need you to biometrically sign and then, 'cause you don't have an ID device, you've got to go to the genomic station over there to pick up your boarding pass."

"Get a ticket for yourself, too. I want you to come with me."

"Are you completely crazy?"

"I need your help."

"You *are* completely crazy."

"Please. Pedro. I can't do this alone."

"I just practically maxed out my credit line. I couldn't afford to buy another ticket if I wanted to. Do you know what that means? You want to know what my interest rate is?"

"Oh," Eliot says. "No, that's fine."

Eliot gives his biometric signature and then walks over to the genomic station, manned by a Homeland Security officer, a thin middle-aged East Asian woman. She asks Eliot to place his hand into the genetic scanning machine. The light becomes green, and everything checks out, his biometrics and genes matching those on record with Homeland Security. Thank God for our authoritarian national security surveillance state, he thinks. When the woman gives him a boarding pass offprint, Eliot almost cries with joy. It doesn't even matter to him that he's not in first class or business class, he's so happy. He hugs Pedro.

"Don't go gay on me."

"Thank you so much for doing this. You have no idea what it means to me."

"Actually, Eliot, I think *you* have no idea what this means to *me*."

"I'm trying."

On that note, Eliot waves good-bye and passes through the security checkpoint, an archway that automatically scans those who step under it. Pedro stands behind the checkpoint threshold, shaking his head, arms crossed. Can he trust me? Eliot wonders. When a security guard approaches him and asks for his electronic credentials, Eliot shows his genetically validated boarding pass. The guard asks Eliot to step over to be checked a second time, a standard procedure. The scanner at the security gate blinks yellow several times, then green.

"You can go," the guard says.

"Right on. Thanks."

Eliot finds his gate. Eventually, the gate agent calls his boarding group, checks his boarding pass, and lets him in without incident. Eliot squeezes himself into his cramped economy seat and waits for takeoff. This is really happening, he thinks. Tel Aviv, Jerusalem, and the Western Wall are waiting. Aliot will try to kill Caliph Fred in less than twenty-four hours. Is Pedro right, he wonders, watching from the window as bags get loaded into the side of the plane. Am I a bad investment?

PART V
FINAL JUDGMENT

IMPOSTOR, IMPERSONATOR, DUPLI-cate, doppelgänger, look-alike, clone: these are the words that jostle around in Eliot's tormented and hollow-feeling brainpan and try, desperately seeking escape, to slip from his lips again and again during the five-hour Gooney flight from Newark to Ben-Gurion. Why are there so many words for someone being mistaken for you? Being replaced by someone exactly like you, even in the most metaphorical sense, surely can't be something that happens very often. A jolt of turbulence rocks the plane.

The pilot announces that they'll be landing shortly, and Eliot cranes his neck at an awkward angle to watch through the window. As it descends, the Gooney's wing—a dozen or so jagged pieces held together by almost-invisible wires and narrow struts, a Cubist sculpture of precise aerodynamic control—suddenly changes shape. Eliot almost screams at the sight.

Stay calm. This is perfectly normal. We're landing.

The old woman sitting next to him gives him a suspicious look, clears her throat audibly, and settles finally to mumbling curses in what Eliot takes to be Hebrew. She must think that he's some kind of terrorist or worse. The *Summit Telethon* has roused whispered rumors among the passengers of a possible increase in the frequency of rocket attacks targeting civilian planes.

Such rumors seemed somehow apt on a flight transporting, among others, a congregation of evangelicals loudly engaged in detailed debates about Revelation ("In what language will the name of God be inscribed in our foreheads?") while their children yelled obnoxiously among themselves and played Christian-themed video games on handhelds; a blond family, white almost to albinism, dressed in matching turquoise jumpsuits, whose creepy pale gray eyes fixed onto Eliot as he was standing in line waiting to pee; a group of Hasidic rappers, side-locked, dressed in sandals, smelling vaguely of pot, and breaking out into spontaneous improvisational rap sessions (in English, for some reason) about Israeli Human Rights Violations and the Desperate Plight of Palestine; a planeload of American Jews, anything but pleased with the rappers; and two (completely independent, fully costumed) Elvis impersonators, one an out-and-out rockabilly, coiled with hip-swiveling sexual energy, who was traipsing up and down the tight airplane aisles, curling his lip at anyone whose attention he could catch, the other a '70s-era arena-act Elvis, sloppy, tired, and, judging from the barf bag he was holding tightly in his hand, all shook up by turbulence. This terrifying journey to the economy cabin's rear lavatory had set Eliot's nerves on end, had prepared him for anything.

What is it about Israel? he had wanted to ask.

The Gooney's gear finally thumps down. When the wing folds up, Eliot tries to accept that this landing is the real thing and that no one will be dying anytime soon, at least not in this particular Gooney, not within the next five minutes. Passengers break out into applause. Eliot lets out his bated breath and, shaking now, clapping with the rest, finds his hands and body releasing massive amounts of tension that have springlike been coiling up, tighter and tighter,

within him. As the Gooney taxies to the terminal, he feels desperate
to deplane.

Ω

Everything Eliot knows about the forthcoming *Summit Telethon*—and,
frankly, about Middle Eastern geopolitics in general—he has learned
very recently from *Bird* magazine, the current issue of which is specially
devoted to the intricacies of Apocalypse Fever, which its editor-in-
chief claims in his introduction to this Special Issue has become "the
hottest mediasphere frenzy in a decade and a truly global brand."

CALIPH IN THE HOUSE

Repressive, authoritarian dictator? New hope for a war-torn region? Bird
magazine's RYAN SCALLION *interviews the Mideast's* POST-
MODERN CALIPH *and asks him some tough questions.*

A former host of *Lebanese Pop Sensation* and a Eurovision cham-
pion (on behalf of the Netherlands), the controversial but
always hip and charming Fred al-Baraka became a militant
Islamic activist after his native Amsterdam was leveled by
the invading Leviathan Force of the controversial Freedom
Coalition operation in Benelux (*Operation Muscles in Brussels*, all
rights reserved).

Initially a radical, Fred soon gave up his opposition to
the Freedom Coalition and, under his moderate and visionary
leadership, the Progressive Brotherhood of Islam captured the
hearts and minds of the Arab world and proved itself willing
to recognize the legitimacy of the Freedom Coalition. Fred
has consolidated much of the Mideast and parts of North
Africa under the banner of the TransArabian Caliphate and

has played a vital role in containing the radical Shi'a Federation of Imamates.

Bird magazine caught up with Caliph Fred at his villa outside Beirut. The Caliph is six foot three and on this hot day was wearing a loose-fitting, earth-toned Armani robe. One of his gorgeous wives, Fatima (a former Ms. Lebanon), served us tall glasses of lemonade dappled with droplets of condensation.

BIRD: It's a pleasure to interview you, Your Grace. A few months ago, you made a state visit to the White House. The first ever by a Caliph—since you are, after all, the first Caliph in centuries. What did you think about First Lady Julia Friendly's redecoration of the State Dining Room?

FRED: I have to say, I really did love it. I asked Fatima to take a look at what she'd done with the place. We're considering a possible redecoration of the Grand Skyscraper of the Caliph [located in Dubai]. Something with spring colors, you know. A softer and gentler look and feel.

BIRD: If you could have dinner with anyone, living or dead, who would it be?

FRED: It would have to be, for absolutely sure, Ronald Reagan. He's the guy who made it possible for guys like me to become world leaders. He showed that just 'cause you're popular doesn't mean you're shallow or stupid. And, as we all know, he almost single-handedly and most heroically defeated the Soviet Union and rescued us from menace of global communism. That has got to count for something.

BIRD: Not to get into politics now—

FRED: No, please, go ahead, Ryan.

BIRD: But there was a bit of controversy over your recent decision to nuke the Federation of Imamates. What is your response to these criticisms?

FRED: Well, it was a tough call. Real tough. But the Federation simply didn't recognize the Caliphate's legitimacy. The Shi'a regimes were fundamentally *for* the destruction of the Caliphate and that's just not acceptable to my people. So we conducted a regime change. I'm a big believer in the doctrine of preventive war. We stopped the Imamate terrorist regimes before they could even consider striking us, as they surely would have. Any responsible Caliph would have done the same. That is why one of your intellectual journals called me the "Liberator of the East." And I think it's safe to say, our actions have liberated Shi'a peoples and we're definitely winning the war for hearts and minds, especially since we purchased our new surveillance systems from the Pentagon. The pacification of the East has been largely successful thanks to our good relations with the Freedom Coalition.

BIRD: Are you talking about your contract with the Omni Science Corporation?

FRED: That's it. We've got so many hearts and minds in our corner now, we don't know where to put them! [laughs] The Umma [the universal community of Muslims] is happier today than it's ever been. The line of Abu Bakr [the first Caliph] remains as strong as ever.

BIRD: Speaking of rights to exist, do you recognize Israel's?

FRED: Well, if we're speaking abstractly, I don't know if anyone can recognize anyone's right to exist, if you catch my meaning. I mean, no one has a "right" to exist, right? You just exist one day, and don't the next. What a silly question. Next.

BIRD: Do you believe the Jewish Holocaust happened?

FRED: Well, something happened, sure, but I think the opinion of the expert community is divided about, you know, the details. I am not wise enough to know much about these things. I am not a student of history. That's why, a few weeks ago, on *Ask the Caliphate* [The Caliphate Channel, 17:00:00 GMT], we had an instant mobile-phone poll. Opinion is evenly split among my Caliphate constituency— 54 percent, I think, came out on the Yes side, but who knows? We do believe in global warming though. That's bad news and getting much worse, fast.

BIRD: What are the latest trends in fashion that you see in the Middle East?

FRED: Well, this too is hard to say. The Ministry of Opinion is compiling data for the fall, and it looks like we're moving toward a time of lightness and airiness. Women will begin to wear gossamer cloaks and floral-patterned head scarves. Among men, goatees are on their way out and neatly trimmed full beards have increasingly become the vogue. I hesitate to claim any responsibility for that trend [laughter; strokes his neatly trimmed full beard].

BIRD: After the attacks on the Dome of the Rock and the al-Aqsa Mosque, do you see any chance for peace with Israel and the Freedom Coalition?

FRED: Like I've said, I'm not a wise man. I listen to what my people want. I trust them. So we'll just see what happens at this *Peace in the Mideast Summit Telethon* that's coming up [the Apocalypse Channel, Saturday, 1 Sept., 15:00:00 GMT]. As you may have heard, we're holding a mobile-phone poll at the end of the *Summit Telethon*—live!—to decide what course of action the Caliphate takes. I'll tell you, I find this event extremely exciting. I think the whole world is rightly sitting on the edge of its seat to find out what happens. Be sure to tune in, Ryan!

BIRD: I certainly will. Thank you, Your Grace.
FRED: Don't mention it. Anytime. Salaam, dudes!

The "Salaam, dudes!" tagline, which the Caliph Fred Entertainment Group owns the rights to, appears again, several pages later, in a full-page advertisement suggesting that if you're ever in Dubai, you should come check out the five-star hotels, restaurants, indoor theme parks, malls, plazas, casinos, and world-class boutiques at the Mountain, an arcology that, at almost two miles in height, looks more like a man-made Everest than a building.

In the foreground of the picture of the Mountain stands Caliph Fred, regal and statesmanlike, wearing elaborate layered robes and a big puffy turban that resembles a truffle. He is winking at the camera and making a thumbs-up sign. "Salaam, dudes!" is written in a fancy script, designed to recall Arabic calligraphy. In a similarly ornate, but larger typeface there is a slogan that reads, "THE MOUNTAIN can't come to you, but if you're in Dubai you should come to THE MOUNTAIN!" Eliot groaned when he read this, then he flipped through the rest of the magazine, trying hard to avoid looking at advertisements for food and drink, which he could not afford to buy; he took his complimentary mixed nuts, ate them slowly so they would last, and sat in silence, rolling an almond on his tongue, his hunger growing.

Ω

Even though he has not qualified as a believer for more than a decade, Eliot thanks God for Tom Feldman. When Eliot made a collect call from the Gooney, Tom not only accepted the charges but also agreed without qualification to meet him at the airport. Finally getting through to Tom had seemed unreal, something out of a dream. "Where the hell are you, Eliot?" Tom asked. "What's happened to your face? It's all swollen." "I'm on a flight coming into Tel Aviv." "I thought you were already here with your parents. I was wondering why you hadn't called—thought you were maybe mad at me." "I didn't call because that's not me." "What?" Eliot had looked at the snoring old woman in the seat next to his, fearful she might hear some of what he was saying. "I'm on Flight eleven thirty-five, Tom. Please, just meet me at the airport. I can explain everything."

Getting through Israeli customs and security turns into a huge hassle. Cruel and pimply IDF conscripts question him for almost two hours; gratuitously strip-search him; and give him a lengthy lecture about the necessity of bringing proper electronic identification into the country. Eliot is finally allowed to go when his genes and biometrics are matched, yet again, to his official record in the US Homeland Security database. Eliot fears Tom will have left the airport after this huge delay, but here he is, coming over now, hair still crew cut, skin transformed from olive to deep brown. Eliot and Tom hug.

"Thank God you're still here, Tom. Security was impossible to deal with."

"I know how they are. They even give Jews a hard time."

"It's so good to see you. I was afraid you'd be in boot camp or unavailable."

"I wish. The IAF is taking forever processing my application. I've been stuck playing video games and babysitting my cousins. I could've been enjoying the summer at Martha's Vineyard. I'm starting to think you were right."

"No, *you* were right, Tom. The Apocalypse *is* coming. The End of the World isn't just a successful global brand. It's, like, *really nigh!*"

"You okay, Eliot? I thought all that stuff you said on TV about capitalism, Christ, and the Constitution was just some kind of marketing stunt Karl set up for your family's secondary offering. Have you really gone over the edge?"

"Dude, I'm being serious. The End of the World is coming."

Tom laughs. "You really waiting for the Rapture and the conversion of the Jews? I've got to warn you, this Jew isn't converting. I'd rather spend an eternity in hell than one second in heaven with these evangelical types."

Whatever calm Eliot has thus far been able to feign disappears.

"No, no, no," Eliot says. "I'm still as secular and cynical as ever. Look at me, Tom. Look at me. I'm not joking. My hair is shaved. My body is swollen. The person who said those things about Christianity and capitalism and the Constitution didn't look anything like me. My father's former business partners at Omni Science, Stanislaw Hadrian and Troy Forester, they've created a duplicate of me. They kidnapped me, forced me at gunpoint to sign over my electronic identity to the duplicate. They——"

"Would you please *calm the fuck down down*," Tom says, using his trademark leadership voice. "You're cracking up. What's really going on, Eliot?"

Eliot whispers. "I'm *telling you* what's really going on. I'm scheduled to be at the Summit Telethon tonight. Except it's not me that's going to be there. You thought I was already in Jerusalem, didn't you? See, I'm right. That's not me. It's my duplicate, Aliot."

"Aliot?"

"Stan and Troy, they've instructed Aliot to kill Caliph Fred live on TV. They want to precipitate a World War. Just like you said. Israel versus the Caliphate. Freedom Coalition versus the United Nations. Everyone nukes everyone else. Adorable smiling mushrooms all over the world."

"Adorable smiling mushrooms? Look, why would anyone want to—"

"They own the rights to the Dome of the Rock attack. They're Horned Goat. He told me everything, like some kind of James Bond villain. They ran these simulations showing what would happen if they kill the Caliph. They want to make lots of money, then rebuild the world. They're crazy! The whole world has gone crazy!"

Tom drops the leadership voice. "You're shitting me, Eliot."

"I can prove it to you right now. Use Omni to search for my Name."

Tom does the search and, sure enough, Omni reports that "Eliot" is presently lounging with Sarah by the pool of the five-star Ariel Sharon International Hotel in West Jerusalem. The Eliot to whom Tom now speaks, meanwhile, ends up in Omni's False Positives folder.

"You're not shitting me," Tom says.

"You know I'd never shit you. You're, like, family."

"Eliot, this is not a joke."

"That's what I'm saying."

The elder Elvis impersonator from the Gooney rolls his suitcase past them. Silently and side by side, Tom and Eliot follow the ersatz King of Rock 'n' Roll into a ferocious Israeli heat that seems intent on boiling off Eliot's thin white skin. The heat itself would be almost bearable, but Tel Aviv's humidity makes him wobble on weak legs. Aviva, Tom's aunt, waits for them in her tiny Nissan Electrica by the curb.

Aviva hops out of the car and meets them. She's maybe five-feet three, in her late forties or early fifties with a shock of curly black hair, a dark complexion a few shades darker even than Tom's, striking hazel eyes, and a fine array of lines around her mouth that would illustrate the entry for "Nurture" in any dictionary of wrinkles. Despite never having met him, she gives Eliot a big warm hug.

"So you're Tom's famous friend Eliot. He's told us all about you. You'll be staying with us, in our guest room. We have cats. Are you allergic to cats? No? Good. My God, look at you. You're so pale and skinny! It's criminal. We have to feed you right away. You poor dear. Get in the car."

When Tom opens the front passenger-side door, Aviva scolds him in Hebrew. Eliot delights to hear his friend responding in his own stuttering Hebrew. They seem to be arguing about whether Tom should offer the shotgun seat to Eliot. Apparently losing the argument, Tom surrenders the seat.

"It's okay," Eliot says.

"Get in the front seat," Aviva says. "You're our guest. Don't you worry about anything. We'll take you home, clean you up. But it's half an hour to the house. Do you want us to stop at a drive-thru? We could maybe get you a hamburger. We have hamburgers here that are just as good as in America. You want to go to a McDonald's?"

"I—"

"No, of course you don't want to go to a McDonald's. You could get that in America. What am I thinking? I know just the place. They make the best falafel. Have you ever had falafel?"

"Of course Eliot has had falafel, Auntie!" Tom says, embarrassed on her behalf. "Where do you think he lives, Outer Mongolia?"

"Well, he hasn't had falafel like this."

They leave the airport. A terrible driver, Aviva frequently stops short, accelerates severely, veers a little too close to cars in adjacent lanes. Angry horns honk all around them. After a series of near-death experiences, the Nissan pulls suddenly and sharply toward a Falafel Shack in an outdoor shopping complex near the on-ramp to the highway.

"Eliot, I recommend the Super Falafel. Do you want a drink with that? I'll get you a cup of iced coffee. You look tired. A bit of coffee will do you good. And a bottle of water. You have to be careful here. It gets very hot. Tel Aviv is humid, but once we get away from the water it'll get dry. Make sure to stay hydrated while you're in Israel."

Eliot is almost delirious with pleasure at the promise of food. The only thing that could make this moment more satisfying would be a cigarette, but this is definitely not the car of a smoker. A Hello Kitty doll hangs from the rearview mirror, wholesome and sweet. If he asked her for a pack of cigarettes, Aviva would probably begin lecturing him on the many dangers of nicotine addiction. Aviva rolls down the driver's-side window and a wave of heat fills the air-conditioned car. The computer terminal at the entrance to the Falafel Shack Drive-Thru automatically detects Aviva's electronic identity and speaks to her in Hebrew.

The electronic voice occasionally utters words like "Aviva" and "Falafel Shack," the latter spoken in an idiomatically (and probably proprietary) American accent. Aviva negotiates loudly with the machine, seeming to wrestle with the talking box over arcane and technical details of fast-food falafel. At the end of this dispute, the screen registers her order, in Hebrew. The Nissan lurches forward in fits and starts toward the food pickup window. Before long the window opens and a tongue automatically extends, a bag of food on it.

Aviva passes the bag over to Eliot. It quivers in his hands like a living thing, a sacred relic resplendent with its own godhead, a thing almost impressed with itself, smug in its power over him. Super Falafel, indeed! Eliot slowly and methodically tears away the bag, the paper wrapper, the layer of metal foil, all exterior shells of a *matryoshka* doll, the warm falafel its innermost essence, something like its soul. Before he knows what has happened, the falafel is gone. Yogurt sauce stains his fingers and mouth. His stomach rumbles uncertainly at this deposit of food, slightly nauseated.

"My, you were hungry," Aviva says, a genuine look of concern on her face, more nurture lines creasing her forehead. "My, my."

Eliot represses a burp of gratitude and, embarrassed by but also always obedient to his own animal drives, gets to work on the iced coffee. Focusing on his coffee helps distract him from the fact that Aviva has pulled onto Highway I, the main road linking Tel Aviv and Jerusalem. It would be rude to duck his head or cover his eyes every time Aviva almost hits another car. Electronic signs passing overhead list traffic information in Hebrew, Arabic, and English. Spare shrubs border the road on either side, a blur of green and brown. Aviva cuts off a growling truck, and its air horn howls. She seems not to notice. How funny would that be, Eliot thinks. To have made it all the way to Israel only to die in a traffic accident.

Not very.

$$\Omega$$

Aunt Aviva and Uncle Danny live in Pardes Perez, a newly built gated suburb balanced almost exactly between Tel Aviv and Jerusalem, a city of thirty thousand people, near Highway I. Daniel Cohn, Tom's mother's brother, grew up in Stamford, Connecticut, where he attended various private schools before earning a political science degree at Columbia University. For a few years following college, he roamed the Northeast Corridor, a partying nomad, paying for his Amtrak tickets by working as a nightclub promoter and professional party planner. This lifestyle came to seem unbearable to him after the terrorist attacks in New York. Several of his schoolmates died in the attack. Though he wasn't personally close to any of the dead, a malaise of ambiguous and largely unfocused depression took hold of his life for a while, but a complimentary Birthright Tour of Israel turned things around for him. On this tour, Daniel met the half-Spanish, half-Algerian Aviva Savorman: a stunning beauty, and Jewish, too! Though they met in Israel, Aviva was living at the time in Somerville,

Massachusetts, on an H-IB visa, a web designer who had survived the dot-com bust.

"It's kind of hard to believe my uncle and Auntie were ever so hip," Tom says. Aviva makes a clicking noise with her tongue, gently rebuking Tom's accusation of unhipness.

Danny and Aviva married a few years later and eventually had three children together. The happy Cohn family moved to Israel after the successful conclusion of the Twenty-Four-Day Israel-Lebanon-Syria War (*Operation Gentle Fist*, all rights reserved), not to be confused, Aviva explains, with the Eight-Day Israel-Lebanon-Syria-Egypt War (*Operation Righteous Jews*, all rights reserved) of a few years later. After living in Tel Aviv for a few years, the Cohns moved to Pardes Perez, their new suburban paradise, the avant-garde of risk-free planned community life in the Holy Land. During his time in Israel, Daniel had become a well-known journalist and political analyst, Aviva a full-time mother. Pardes Perez, so close to both Tel Aviv and Jerusalem, suited their needs perfectly. As the years passed and their children grew, the hipness of the Cohn parents was slowly and methodically chipped away, a tragic loss of cool, although Eliot marvels at how fulfilling an uneventful suburban life seems to him right now, how very lovely it would be to live in some community walled away from the troubles of the world. Perhaps, he muses, his values have been changing, well below any threshold or tolerance discernible to his conscious mind.

As they drive past the Pardes Perez bomb shelter, built beneath machine-gun-topped town walls, Eliot reconsiders his risk assessment. Then again, other than shelters and machine guns, this might as well be some suburban subdivision of Southern California. Ivy crisscrosses the rustic city walls. Luscious palms line the major streets. Spacious adobe homes, each customized but obviously part of a single brand family, stand at polite distances from each other. Backyards have pools and clubhouses, gardens and canopies. Children bicycle and tricycle on dedicated lanes, safely away from drivers like Aviva.

A studied sort of dullsville, Pardes Perez wears its promises of community and security prominently on its figurative sleeve. There is one odd bit, though. Gigantic ornamental sculptural masses emerge from the center of the roundabouts that Aviva has been speeding through, artificial trees of plastic, glass, and steel, their transparent pneumatic branching tubes rising up fifty feet like the exposed ends of huge fiber-optic cables. As the Nissan sharply turns from Benny Morris Way onto Martin Luther King Drive, one of these trees makes a rapid thumping noise and its plastic simulacra fronds shake gently, as if moved by a breeze. In the sky, forty-five degrees above the very flat-seeming horizon, there are a few smallish explosions.

"What's that?" Eliot asks.

"Those are amazing," Tom says.

"Noted. But, like, what is it?"

"They're part of the city's 'Arrow Five' Antimissile Defense System. They've got the most sophisticated object tracking and targeting capabilities in the world. They could shoot down a bird a mile in the sky."

"Did someone just try to shoot a missile at this town?" Eliot says.

"Yeah, but don't worry," Tom says. "You're more likely to be struck by lightning than by the improvised missiles the Arabs occasionally shoot at us. People are very rarely hit. You get used to it."

"I hope so."

"The missiles are not nearly as bad as the cyberlocusts," Aviva says.

"Cyberlocusts?"

"Don't ask," Tom says.

Aviva lurches from Martin Luther King Drive onto Theodor Herzl Street. Eliot's fantasies of suburban bliss have turned nightmarish. Arab missile attacks, bomb shelters, machine guns, cyber-locusts, and—coming soon—the Apocalypse. Something about the antimissile tree in particular still nags at him.

"Hey, Tom," Eliot says. "If Israel has these antimissile trees, how did that evangelical guy get so close to the al-Aqsa Mosque?"

"I think the system wasn't set up to defend the mosque."

Asking more pointed questions in front of Aviva might be rude, Eliot decides, so he holds back, but a hundred questions come to mind. Something in the air here is making him tense. Apocalypse Fever has infected him, at last. Nothing else matters anymore. Agitation pressurizes his chest. His ears burn.

"Actually," Tom adds, "I'm sure you'd be glad to know, Arrow Five uses software designed by Omni Science."

"Oh, yes, I'm very glad to hear that, man."

"An Omni Science subsidiary, actually, called Target Science."

"Original name."

"Your father personally names all his companies."

"Really?"

"How do you not know that? He mentioned that in his memoir, *The Science of Omni.*"

"Didn't get around to reading that."

Tom rolls his eyes in mock horror at Eliot's ignorance. Aviva brakes hard, and everyone in the car jerks forward. The Nissan has almost collided with the Cohn residence, a ranch-style home whose indisputable loveliness does nothing at all to excise Eliot's sense of waking nightmare.

As the garage door lifts, a vision of the earth presents itself to Eliot, a preview of things to come. If the Apocalypse were condensed into a movie trailer, it would look something like this: Ballistic missiles leave behind parabolic contrails. Satellites drop down deadly payloads. Bright flashes mark the places where humans live. Mushroom clouds sprout in pretty patterns; he can't help imagining them as they appeared in Stan's simulation, as cartoon mushrooms with big smiley faces. From a safe vantage point in space, it would all look very beautiful.

$$\Omega$$

A very skinny twentysomething man sits at a kitchen table typing rapidly in the air on what must be a virtual touchboard. His square glasses perhaps do something to correct his vision but their main purpose is relatively clear. These glasses open a window into the mediasphere. Occasionally, he scratches his head and neck. His dark hair would be raucously curly if it were not so closely crew cut. He wears camouflage army pants, a black sleeveless shirt, and a fern-green IDF beret at a slanting angle on his head. A silver fleur-de-lis is pinned to the front of the beret. His arms are amazingly skinny, his hands large but nimble.

"Ari," Aviva says, "why are you wearing that uniform around the house?"

Ari indicates a portion of the mediawall tuned in to the Apocalypse Channel. "We're at war, Mom."

"Not yet we're not," Aviva says.

"You never know when it'll start."

"You don't even need to wear that uniform. You're a programmer."

"I'm in the Intelligence Corps! I program for Israel."

"Ari, we have a guest. So stop playing with your computer and say hello."

Ari does not stop typing or say hello. Tom once mentioned in an email that his cousin almost never takes off his mediaglasses, except to sleep and for occasional hardware upgrades. Eliot mentally matches Ari to a familiar pigeonhole. Ari is the sort of obsessive who finds a natural home in codes, numbers, patterns, and equations. These paint for him the most touching and personal portrait of his soul. They give him comfort and support. Such lovers of abstraction haunt applied philosophy departments everywhere, and Eliot can peg them instantly.

Eliot stands beside a refrigerator trying to keep his hands from shaking visibly. The fridge is covered with shopping lists, Post-it notes, animal-shaped magnets, and animated photos of children in various stages of physical development. This is a fridge in use, a center of active family life. A normal family, Eliot thinks. Tom was right. Real people live here, and they're so different from the Vanderthorpes.

On the Apocalypse Channel, J-Riv—the amazing Japanese Joan Rivers drag impersonator—holds court at the Lions' Gate, hosting the all-day Telethon preshow. At the bottom of the screen a countdown clock indicates that a little less than five hours remain before the Telethon officially starts. Celebrities walk the red carpet, entering the Old City under an elaborate security archway that scans them for weapons and explosives. Aliot and Sarah walk arm in arm toward J-Riv. Tom and Eliot trade horrified looks. Ari and Aviva seem too occupied with work to notice.

"Is it true what all the nasty gossips are saying?" J-Riv says.

Aliot smiles. "What do the nasty gossips say?"

"That, inspired by Elijah Apocalypse, you've reclaimed your virginity. That you and Sarah are dating—I can hardly believe I'm saying this!—without having sex."

"I don't kiss and tell, Joan." Aliot winks. "For that matter, I don't *not kiss* and tell either, but it's definitely true that, sometimes, you can learn something from a younger sibling."

A thousand cameras flash. Sarah blushes, and her mood stabilizer bracelet blinks more rapidly, but she doesn't seem surprised or unhappy about what Aliot has just said. Aliot squeezes Sarah's hand affectionately, and she smiles.

J-Riv shoves the mic toward Sarah. "Is that true, honey, what Eli—"

Tom gestures the mediawall off before J-Riv can finish asking her question. Aviva turns from the kitchen counter, her brow wrinkled. "Why did you turn that off, Tom? I want to watch the Telethon preshow. So many celebrities!" She gestures the Apocalypse Channel back on. Aliot and Sarah have passed through the Lions' Gate and have been replaced on the red carpet by the aging, stern-faced Paris Hilton.

As Aviva prepares lunch, a boy, about twelve, comes marching through the kitchen, his nose buried in a thousand-page book. This must be Aaron, the youngest Cohn child. Relying almost purely on muscle memory, hardly looking up as he walks, Aaron pulls out a can of juice from the fridge.

"We have a guest, Aaron," Aviva says. "Say hello to our guest."

Without looking away from his novel, Aaron says, "Hello to our guest."

"I'm making lunch. Do you want anything?"

"I ate already," he says and then leaves the kitchen as efficiently as he entered it.

"Why are you standing around, Eliot?" Aviva says. "Sit." Eliot sits.

Aviva continues to prepare food, enough to feed ten people. A gray shorthair cat sulks into the kitchen and performs a series of acrobatic leaps, settling finally on top of the fridge. Eliot taps his fingers on the tablecloth, checkered red and white. He desperately wants to talk with Tom, to spill his guts in great detail, but his hunger keeps him grounded here. Tom sits uncomfortably in his chair, rocking on its back legs. The cat releases a long purr. Though still largely in his world of numbers, Ari occasionally glances across the table at Eliot.

A voice from the mediawall. "The Apocalypse is by far the hottest brand I've seen in thirty years as a Reputation Manager. Not since the iPod has—"

J-Riv has cornered Karl Vlasic and his latest girlfriend, the Slovenian supermodel Kaja. Kaja stands a full head taller than Karl. Her face glows with an unreal sheen, almost sculptural, classical in its perfection. When he finishes his answer, Karl lets J-Riv talk to Kaja. Kaja mostly smiles and nods blankly at J-Riv's questions.

"That Kaja is so beautiful," Aviva says. "If I were a man, I would definitely want to have sex with her."

Tom shifts uncomfortably in his seat. Karl and Kaja pass beneath the gate.

"Karl is a lucky man," Tom says.

"She's one of the dumbest people I've ever met," Eliot says.

Aviva seems excited. "You've met her?"

Eliot nods.

Ari turns to Eliot. "What about you, Eliot? Are you smart or are you dumb?"

"Ari!" Aviva says. "Eliot is our guest, a friend of Tom's."

"It's good to be up front about these things," Ari says. "Even Tom maybe has a few stupid friends."

There is a moment during which only the buzzing mediawall and whirring refrigerator are audible. Now J-Riv assails none other than William Pearson, who is entering the Lions' Gate with his mother's coterie, his eyes puffy, pupils dilated, obviously high. The prime minister, Loretta Pearson, hovers behind him, her face twisted, as usual, in its eternal sneer. William is undoubtedly attending the *Summit Telethon* for the same reason that Eliot was supposed to: to grow a respectable Reputation.

"That's okay," Eliot says. "If you'd asked me a month ago, Ari, I would have said smart, much smarter than everyone around me, dazzlingly smart. At this point, 'dumb' seems much closer to the truth."

Ari nods, satisfied, then gets back to work. Aviva composes a plate of cheeses. Across the table, Tom and Eliot try to communicate by means of meaningful blinks. Eliot can no longer keep his hands from shaking. He wants to turn screaming into a vocation, to become one of those people perpetually warning of the pending doom of the human race, standing on a corner, placard in hand. Tom mouths calming words to Eliot.

Calm down, he's saying. Trust me.

Fuck, Eliot mouths back. Fuck fuck fuck.

Tom points to Ari. Ari, he says.

Ari?

Ari. Trust me.

Trusting Tom seems like a wonderful idea, a reason to give himself permission to calm down, so Eliot tries. Sixteen-year-old Edith comes in, wearing a pair of shorts and a bikini top, carrying a palmtop on which she is instant-messaging with friends. Eliot makes a concerted effort to look away from her well-developed breasts and stares instead at a bowl of black olives on the table. He grabs one and bites into its flesh. Its pit is hard and ribbed.

"Put a shirt on right now, young lady!" Aviva says.

"I was sunbathing on the roof, Mom." Exactly like an American teenager.

"You're indoors now. Dress like a civilized person."

Edith leaves the room in a huff and comes back shortly wearing a practically transparent T-shirt that covers little more of her body than the bikini top had. She pushes her brown hair away from her eyes and notices Eliot. Eliot gnaws stupidly at the olive pit, then spits it out. She's Tom's cousin, he thinks. His cousin. Eliot finally looks over and gets his eyes caught up with hers.

"You're Eliot, Tom's famous friend," Edith says.

"Yep," he says.

"I saw that video of you on *That's So Fucked Up*."

"Watch your language, young lady," Aviva says.

"*That's the name of the show*, Mom. I didn't make it up."

"You still don't have to repeat it here, in decent company."

"That video with you and Janine was really sexy," Edith whispers, leaning in, her lips practically touching Eliot's ear. "What kind of drug did she give you?"

Edith lets her arm brush up against his. Eliot jumps back.

"I was looking at your friends list. Like, practically everyone has defriended you. Tom's almost the only one left. It's so unfair. You seem like a pretty cool guy. I could friend you."

"Now there goes an idea," Eliot says.

Edith cries with delight. Immediately, she navigates to her social networking app and friends him. Given that Eliot has no functional electronic identity, his response will have to wait. Eliot lays his face in his hands. He wants to cry. Ari regards Eliot with suspicion, then refocuses on his mediaglasses. The cat, bored with these people, jumps off the fridge and leaves the kitchen.

"So, Eliot," Ari says. "Weren't you supposed to be at the *Summit Telethon?*"

Tom almost falls back in his chair. Eliot buries his face more deeply in his hands. Maybe if he closes his eyes, this insane, abusive nightmare will end.

"I ask because I just did an Omni search on your Name and—"

"Cut it out, Ari!" Tom says. "Eliot has had a stressful couple days."

"Leave the poor boy alone," Aviva says.

"But, all I'm saying is that I did this Omni search and—"

"You can talk about computers with Eliot later, Ari. He works for a computer company, too. Isn't that right Tom?"

"Yeah, Auntie. Eliot works as a Junior Conceptual Analyst for the Omni Science Corporation. He was also getting his PhD at Harvard in applied philosophy for a while."

"A PhD! Harvard!" Aviva says. "Wonderful, just wonderful. You're a philosopher. I didn't know that. Can you read Aristotle in Greek?"

"Unfortunately not," Eliot says.

Ari scans his mediashades. "Oh my. No, Eliot doesn't study Aristotle. He's writing his dissertation on *Elvis impersonators.*"

"I *love* Elvis Presley," Aviva says. "He was so sexy before he became fat. I didn't realize he wrote philosophy."

"Neither did I," Ari says. "Now, it says here you study the philosophy of mathematical modeling of intellectual property and conceptual descriptions. That's kid's stuff. I got my PhD in computer science when I was twenty-three, then I helped design the architecture of the Aman electronic security system, Military Intelligence. Most secure system in the world. I should also mention, you look different from your official photo on Harvard's applied philosophy Web site. A little puffier, swollen. I feel obliged to ask the obvious question—"

"Knock it off, Ari," Tom says.

"Yeah, stop being such an asshole!" Edith adds.

"Watch your language," Aviva says.

Ari holds up his hands, feigning innocence. "Just saying."

"It's complicated," Eliot says. "It's all very complicated."

Before Eliot can explain these complications, Tom's uncle Daniel strides into the kitchen wearing a blue and white gym outfit, his confident presence silencing everyone. Though not particularly tall, he's in good shape for a man who must be in his early fifties. Sweat on his bald head gleams under the kitchen lights. His ears and eyebrows show former piercings, traces of an earlier incarnation. An offprint of the *Tel Aviv Telegraph* is tucked under his arm. Daniel kisses Aviva on the mouth, sits down at the table, and nods at Eliot. Aviva begins the multistage project of laying out food on the kitchen table: salad, lox, cream cheese, hummus, pita, pasta salad. It keeps coming and coming. Despite his anxiety, Eliot stuffs his face. Daniel decides to make friendly conversation.

"You know I'm *the* Daniel Cohn."

"Didn't know that," Eliot says. Eliot has never heard of *a* let alone *the* Daniel Cohn.

"The left-wing political columnist for the *Tel Aviv Telegraph*."

Tel Aviv Telegraph? Maybe Daniel has connections to politicians. Maybe he knows someone who can help Eliot stop his duplicate from assassinating Caliph Fred. Maybe coming to Israel was the right decision after all.

Daniel gestures the television mute. "I'm working on a new column, Eliot. Let me try the argument out on you. It'll be good to get an American perspective."

"Sure, Mr. Cohn," Eliot says, hopeful.

"The problems we face today—by 'we,' I mean Israel, but the same arguments apply to any member nation of the Freedom Coalition— the reason we've been either fighting wars or poised on the brink of war with the Muslims for decades with no decisive resolution, is that liberal democracy has made us all too nice. We don't fight wars like we used to, back in the good old days of the twentieth century. If we did what we had to do, what we ought to do, we might have to get our hands dirty. It's the same with food. I want to develop a food meta-phor in the column, you see. You get your hamburger, you delight in eating it, but you don't want to see how it's made anymore. If you saw how it was made, you'd become a vegetarian."

"There's nothing wrong with being a vegetarian, Daddy!" Edith says.

"Are you a vegetarian?" Eliot asks.

"Of course I am. Are you?"

"No."

Edith seems disappointed in Eliot.

"Look," Daniel says. "That's our problem. That's what I'm saying. With Omni and the mediasphere being what it is—that is, being everywhere—we are forced to *see how our hamburgers are being made.* And we don't like it because we are weak and coddled, way too comfortable. We want our hamburgers, but do a half-assed job processing them. Then we complain when our hamburgers come out undercooked or packed with E. coli or whatever. I haven't perfected the metaphor, but you get my meaning. See where this all leads?"

"I don't want hamburgers, Daddy."

"Should we all become vegetarians?" Eliot says. "What would that be? Pacifists?"

"We shouldn't *become* anything," Daniel says. "We are what we are. We want what we want. What I'm saying is that if we had fought proper wars, then everything would be fine for everyone right now. Smarter Jews would have put the Arabs into the meat grinder sixty years ago when we had the opportunity—and I mean *all* of them, their military, their civilians, their pets. If we had done that, we and the current generation of Arabs would be happier today."

Edith throws her plate hard against the ground. It breaks into five roughly equal pieces. She shrieks "I hate you, Daddy!" and storms out of the kitchen. This outburst distracts Ari only slightly from his work. Daniel seems not to understand why his daughter has gotten so angry.

"Daniel used to be a real charmer." Aviva comes up behind her husband and grabs him by the scruff of his neck. "Before he became rich and lazy and got all those book deals, he used to be a committed leftist. He had principles. His father and mother lived in a kibbutz, for God's sake, before they moved to Connecticut."

"Who says I'm not a leftist, Viv? Leftists don't have to be pacifists. I completely supported PEN. The invasion of Northern California was a great crime! And I'm not saying we should grind up the Arabs *in peacetime*. That would be impossible given the state of the mediasphere and counterproductive, too. But if we had done what needed to be done sixty years ago—hey, stop that, you're hurting my neck, darling. I'm making a point about the paradoxes of liberal democracy!"

Paradoxes of liberal democracy, Eliot thinks. Tom clenches his jaw with embarrassment. His face turns visibly red beneath his tan. Ari continues working, oblivious to his father's performance, probably deep inside layers of code, a kind of Utopian sanctuary from the outside world. Aviva places a pink coffee pitcher on the table. Hello Kitty stares out from its side, adorable.

"You'll have to excuse my uncle," Tom says. "He has a somewhat funny sense of humor. Part of being a pundit. He gets paid to shock."

"What's so shocking, Tom?" Daniel protests. "Don't think I'm

244 / POP APOCALYPSE

anti-Arab. I've met some very nice Arabs. But if we're fighting them, then they're the enemy. And if they're the enemy, then we can't afford to show them any mercy, for our sake and for theirs. Give them a hundred Hiroshimas, a thousand Dresdens. I like the Japanese, too, but nuking them was right given the circumstances. The Germans, I don't like. They're still anti-Semites. Anyway, my thesis is simple. If there's a hot war between the Freedom Coalition and the Caliphate, we should just keep all of this in mind. Someone needs to remind the people what real war means. If we want to kill each other, I say let's *really* kill each other."

Ω

Time is short and the end is near. The Russians, Chinese, Indonesians, Brazilians, and Pakistanis—the nuclear-armed, permanent members of the UN Security Council—have put their respective militaries and navies at a heightened state of alert in anticipation of the *Summit Telethon*. The Freedom Coalition has repositioned its surveillance satellites and robot drones to watch and target the Middle East, with a special focus on the Caliphate, the region's most powerful actor, after Israel. The *Clinton* Carrier Group, armed for any contingency, is moving toward the Gulf.

The Freedom Coalition does not anticipate any problems with the United Nations. POTUS Friendly has every reason to believe that when the facts shortly present themselves, the TransArabian Caliphate and its client, the Federation of Imamates, will back away from their inflammatory rhetoric and recognize their own geostrategic interests. "With the possible exceptions of Indonesia and Pakistan," Irene Kallas has opined in the *Wall Street Journal*, "the rest of the UN doesn't have a dog in this fight so long as the region's oil keeps pumping." The Caliphate and Imamates will get over the al-Aqsa attack and the pending construction of the Third Temple. Their public postures of rage will almost certainly dissipate.

The Freedom Coalition is prepared for the contingency, however unlikely, of simultaneous war against the Caliphate and Imamates. The first phase of this hypothetical war would marshal the military might of a combined American, British, Israeli, and Indian Leviathan Force; the Pentagon has even preemptively registered this operation (*Operation Dispensation*, all rights reserved) on the CRAP Database and has already begun planning the equally hypothetical occupation by scheduling the SysAdmin Force occupation rights auction for early next week. Pentagon lawyers have drafted hundreds of contracts, each targeting a different aspect of the prospective aftermath. An editorial in the *Pentagon Post* has speculated that, in the very improbable event of war, Turkish, Indian, and South African private military contractors would probably have the strongest occupation portfolios. But none of these preparations will be necessary, the editorial concludes, since war is so very unlikely.

Ω

They sit in a media privacy booth at a Café Hillel franchise in the Har HaBayit Shopping Center, just outside the suburb walls. Ari has set up a media scrambler on the table, a black box the size of a palmtop computer, beside his beret and tab. On the café's far media-wall, rendered hugely, Eye for an Eye—Elijah Apocalypse, Gideon Finch, and "Rapture" Rodriguez—explode into a new mix of their hit single, "Punked for Jesus." From the bottom of his soul, with a voice that gives shape to his aesthetic vows of poverty and his opposition to all that is phony in the world, Elijah Apocalypse screeches the Good News into his mic:

> *They shoved nails through your [bleeping] h-a-a-a-nds.*
> *They [bleeping] speared your [bleeping] s-i-i-i-de.*
> *And what the [bleep] do they expect, man?*
> *[Bleeping] [bleep] those [bleeping] [bleeps].*
> *Yea-h-h-h-h-h.*

[Bleeping] [bleep] those [bleeping] [bleeps].
That's what I-I-I-I'm sayin'.
[Bleeping] [bleep] those [bleeping] [bleeps].
Oooooh, yea-h-h-h-h-h-h.

Whoops of applause arise both from the *Summit Telethon* audience and inside the café, even among Jews, an object lesson in why pop music has been among the most effective evangelizing tool yet hit upon by the Christ-fearing world. Millions of impressionable folk have converted to the true path after discovering the soul-moving power of deafening feedback and studying with great care Eye for an Eye's profanity-laden, Christ-loving lyrics. Karl is right: Elijah may be some kind of a genius.

"Simply unbelievable!" shouts the *Summit Telethon*'s host, *That's So Fucked Up*'s Doug "Douchebag" Baloney.

A little more than three hours remain before the Telethon properly begins. Following lunch, Tom and Eliot dragged Ari away from the Cohn home, part of their jury-rigged plan to save the world. Ari's cooperation will be absolutely crucial to their success, Tom insisted. Tom overcame his cousin's paranoia and irritability only by promising to reveal everything to Ari about what he called "the Eliot Situation." Ari, a lover of secrets, gave in to his curiosity. Now that Eye for an Eye's performance is over, Ari waits, wanting to know.

Tom turns on the booth's sound-dampening field so that they can talk privately. Eliot rehearses everything that has happened to him, the whole absurd story: how he discovered the existence of Aliot, tracked him down in Berkeley, and learned of the plot to replace him; how Aliot plans to kill Caliph Fred with the aim of catalyzing a World War; how Horned Goat hopes to profit from intellectual property associated with the Apocalypse; and how Tom and he have come up with a plan that might avert total catastrophe. Really, he insists, all of this is entirely true. Ari takes off his mediaglasses and rubs his eyes and laughs. Without his glasses, his resemblance to Aviva becomes much more obvious. His convulsive laughter eventually dies down.

"I knew Omni was a piece of crap," he says.

Tom turns on his leadership voice. "You've got to help us, Ari."

"We need you to break into the Aman security system," Eliot says. "You said you designed it."

"Why should I put my neck on the line to help you?"

"It's the end of the world, Ari!" Eliot's voice carries past the sound-dampening field. Latte-sipping evangelicals at a nearby table turn toward Eliot and nod with approval. Eliot continues more cautiously. "Weren't you listening to anything I just said?"

"We'll win, you know," Ari says.

"Win what?" Eliot says.

"The end of the world. We'll come out on top. The Freedom Coalition has the guns and the intelligence. I know exactly what we've got planned for the *Summit Telethon*. Our strategy is fairly straightforward and foolproof. We can't lose."

Tom and Eliot blink desperately at each other. This conversation is not proceeding as it's supposed to. Even while not wearing his glasses, Ari seems distant, safely protected by whatever mental filters he uses to keep the world away. Eliot wonders how he would argue with a member of his applied philosophy cohort. Logically, he thinks. Viciously. You break down your opponent: anatomizing arguments, disemboweling propositions, deboning assumptions. Eliot used to be good at this, masterful even.

"Let's be clear about first principles here," Eliot says. "Can we agree that, like, the world being destroyed is essentially a bad thing. Arguably, the worst thing that could happen."

"Okay," Ari says. "I'll concede that."

"And a corollary: the world not ending is a good that supersedes other kinds of moral and legal codes. For instance, because the whole End of the World thing is so bad, it would be moral to break the law, even to commit treason, in order to prevent the world from ending."

"No argument there," Ari says. "If you have to commit treason to prevent the end of the world, you should."

Eliot twists the final logical screw. "So you agree then that helping us try to stop the end of the world is a worthwhile pursuit. And not only that, but that you're pretty much obligated to help us if you're a moral person. What you're really saying," Eliot says, "is that you're afraid of getting caught."

"I never said that."

"But that's what you must be saying, isn't it? You've already conceded the point that you're morally obligated to help us. You haven't contested the fact that Aliot plans to kill Fred. So you're either an immoral person by your own definition or you're afraid and your fear is causing you to act irrationally. You're afraid of being tried for treason if you help us."

"That seems rather unlikely," Ari says. "Given my knowledge and abilities."

"Bullshit, man. You're probably just one of a thousand military programmers, working on your little code module. I know how big corporate bureaucracies work. I worked at Omni Science for, well, for three and a half days. Everyone there is replaceable, even the very smartest people. You're also replaceable, Ari. We're wasting our time, Tom. Let's get out of here."

Eliot stands up as if to leave. The nearby evangelicals laugh at something.

Ari puts his mediashades back on. "Obviously, I didn't design Aman alone, but I do have backdoor access. I can show you *Summit Telethon* spoilers: for example, the proposed options of the mobile-phone poll. After the results of the Foresight System Simulation are presented to the Caliphate and the Imamates, a Freedom Coalition representative will open the phone lines and offer the Caliphate and Imamates an ultimatum. A peace proposal that the Arabs and Persians can ratify via mobile phone." Ari opens up the spoiler text on his tab; Tom and Eliot read over his shoulder.

Given the strategic interests of the Freedom Coalition, and the total certainty of the Foresight System's battle scenario analysis and forecast, we have concluded that you, the peoples of the TransArabian Caliphate and the Federation of Imamates, have two objective choices in this geopolitical situation. Please select one of the following two options.

If you would like the Dome of the Rock to be fully bulldozed and the Third Temple built in its place, please phone: +234343 3432 09232.

If you would like your civilization destroyed and the radioactive moonscape of your remaining lands occupied by an army of infidel invaders, please phone: +234343 3432 09233.

Tom waves his hand, unmoved. Eliot shrugs his shoulders as if what Ari has shown them is so much nonsense. In fact these options terrify Eliot, especially the "radioactive moonscape" bit. How might that phrase be translated into Arabic and Persian?

"Oh, impressive," Eliot says with ambiguous sarcasm. "But all the spoilers in the world aren't going to be worth a damn if you can't help us, Ari. You did an Omni search on my Name. You saw what comes up. That guy at the Ariel Sharon Hotel—that's not me. I'm not making any of this shit up. He's going to kill Caliph Fred in two or three hours if you don't help us out. He kills Fred, the Caliphate's gonna, like, select the Option Two and rain fire down on Israel first. Then the Freedom Coalition will retaliate and vaporize the Caliphate. Then the Federation of Imamates will declare war on the Freedom Coalition. Then the Freedom Coalition vaporizes them, too. Then, maybe China, Indonesia, and Russia—the whole fucking UN—angry that their oil supply has just been nuked into oblivion, will get involved. Then, well, by then you're going to have to pull your radioactive PhD off the wall to use as toilet paper in whatever postapocalyptic wasteland will be left over. How does that sound? Do you think you're smart enough to survive the end of the world from behind the lenses of your mediaglasses? Are you *that* smart?"

Ari says nothing. No one in the café, not even the group of evangelicals, has noticed Eliot's outburst. Eliot thinks he can see the inverted image of his impersonator floating in a tiny screen in the lower left-hand corner of each of the panes of Ari's mediashades, the results of another Omni search. Ari's eyes flick back and forth rapidly between his mediashades and Eliot's face, his mouth working with thought.

"If you're so smart, Eliot, how do you plan to stop the end of the world from happening?"

Eliot resists the urge to strangle Ari, who is right now the only narrow thread from which all hope for a better or at least less terrible future hangs, a rapidly fraying thread, held together by nearly invisible strands. Eliot fakes a cocky smile. Tom sighs with relief.

"We have two things in mind," Eliot says. "If you're as good as you claim, you could do both before we leave this café."

Ω

Tom parks in the Cohn garage, then leaves with Ari while Eliot, trying hard not to lose his mind, stays behind in the Nissan. Visions of mass death loop in his mind. The passing minutes become increasingly unbearable. Tom returns, dressed in an ill-fitting IDF uniform he's borrowed from Ari, an electronic identity pass hanging from his neck. Ari has hacked his own identity pass: Tom's face appears in the photo, but the name still reads "Ari Cohn."

"You okay, Eliot?" Tom says. His leadership voice has given way to what Eliot likes to think is his authentic voice, a kinder voice, the voice of someone who behind all his intensity and drive genuinely cares.

"I'd like to say I'm okay, man, but you know."

"I know."

Ari returns holding something that looks like a silver plastic comforter, high-tech camouflage that he surreptitiously borrowed from the military for use in home lab experiments. His previous cocksureness has phase-changed into agitated anxiety, nervous pacing around the square cage of the garage space. Tom and Eliot empty the Nissan's trunk of its quotidian contents, tennis rackets, sneakers, a bike rack, and loose bottles of water. Tom lays the camo flat on the bottom of the now-empty trunk, lays a crowbar flat beside it, and says, resuming with his leadership voice, "Let's roll." When Eliot gets in the trunk, Tom wraps him up like a human burrito, the camo a sort of silver tortilla.

"This is going to work, right?" Eliot asks.

"Give me your smartwatch, Eliot," Tom says.

"My smartwatch?"

"We've got to make sure there are no signals coming out of this car."

Eliot surrenders his smartwatch.

Tom covers Eliot's head, turns on the camo, and shuts the trunk. For an excruciating length of time the car sits idly and then, with no warning, backs up. They're moving. Every bump along the way asserts itself forcefully. Eliot holds together the seam of his camo covering. Time seems to pass in strange ways. This may be the first time in his life that circumstances have conspired to keep him totally disconnected from the mediasphere, even if this disconnection is only temporary. His previous bouts of mediasphere fasting were voluntary, part of situations always circumscribed by the possibility of logging on.

His time alone spawns sundry thoughts. He becomes convinced that he's going to die horribly, that Tom will be arrested or deported, that Ari will stand trial on charges of treason, and for what? Maybe he should let the assassination happen and only subsequently reveal himself to his family, just as Stan suggested. That would, of course, be the safest path, and no one would blame him for taking it. And, in fact, the situation could very well play out the way the Freedom Coalition analysts project it will. After all, the Coalition uses the most advanced available computer models to forecast the outcomes of war. It must know what will happen in the event of a war with the Caliphate, what dire consequences would follow. But because he's choosing to risk his life, because he is in the trunk of this car, some part of him must believe in the plausibility of Horned Goat's prediction. But his being here also entails the unpalatable proposition that the ruling elites of the Freedom Coalition would, against their interest in self-preservation, push the world toward mass destruction. The ruling elite, Eliot realizes, isn't some sort of abstraction. It's Dad. Is his father the sort of person who would, perhaps inadvertently, risk destroying the world?

Eliot feels ashamed that he is asking himself this question, ashamed for his family, for his fellow humans, for all their mundane savagery. This nightmare of shame started back at the hotel suite in Barcelona, back when he saw the dazed face of that drugged girl, her sleeping innocence, back when the irreversibility of what William Pearson was about to do to her had dawned on him. Like some inoperable cancerous *thing* inside his brain, a new mental organ had awakened, insistently and without mercy pushing him forward, punishing him with guilt, compelling him to feel things and want things that can't be argued for or against on the basis of logical reasoning, analytical skill, rational self-interest, sexual desire, or anything of that familiar sort. This, Eliot decides, sucks; it sucks, sucks, sucks. Fuck this moral feeling. He wants, more than anything, not to think in this way anymore. He wants not to feel shame for his family, for himself, for the actions of people he will never meet and for whom by any reasonable criteria he has no direct responsibility.

"Wake up." Tom is shaking him from his half sleep. They're in a dark place, in an empty parking lot beneath the shade of a giant hangar building, presumably at their destination, the Benjamin Netanyahu Israeli Air Force Base. "Pull yourself together. Get out. And don't forget the crowbar."

Eliot follows Tom through corridors into a building beside the hangar. In a locker room, Tom pries open two lockers containing flight suits that will, according to Ari, fit them. With help from Tom, Eliot puts on his suit. Tom puts on his own, and they exit together, like jaunty fighter pilots in some sort of terrible action movie.

"The base seems completely empty," Eliot says.

"Everyone's probably watching the *Summit Telethon*," Tom says.

"Really?"

"You really have no idea how interested people are in the outcome of the *Summit Telethon*."

Mention of the Telethon makes Eliot's stomach tighten.

In front of the hangar they find, as promised, a solitary Sikorsky UH-60N Rumsfeld helicopter. Ari has done what he promised, has proved that he's as good as his boasts imply. The automated prep system has pushed the chopper from inside the hangar to its launch platform. Thanks to Ari's intervention, this chopper is now officially listed as part of tonight's active fleet, assigned to patrol the airspace above the *Summit Telethon*, near the Western Wall.

Tom climbs into the chopper, checks its dashboard, and puts on his helmet. With his visor down, he looks nothing like the Tom Feldman that Eliot knew back at Harvard. What sort of a Tom is this? Eliot thinks. Eliot puts on his own helmet and adjusts his chin strap. He can see his distorted reflection in the side of the Rummy. He looks even less like himself than Tom.

In the twilight, the Rummy looks not like what it is—the Freedom Coalition's most advanced multipurpose aerial fighting platform—but rather like an antediluvian beast risen from a marsh, one of the giants whose bones were buried below layers of strata after the flood. The chopper's thwack-thwack-thwacking growl gets under Eliot's skin and into his own skeleton. Tom gives Eliot a thumbs-up sign, signaling that he should get on board, but Eliot hesitates.

"Tom!" he shouts through the communications rig of his helmet.

"Not so loud, man," Tom says, his voice right beside Eliot's ear, intimate. "What is it?"

"Does the helicopter have a bathroom?"

"Are you going to throw up or something?"

"I've got to pee."

"For God's sake, Eliot. It's the end of the world out there. Can't you hold it?"

"I don't want to pee my pants in front of the whole world. I really have to go."

"Hurry up then."

Eliot pees against the wall of the hangar, then boards the Rummy.

"Sorry about that, Tom. Coffee is a diuretic, you know."

"If we don't stop your evil duplicate from assassinating the Caliph because you had to take a fucking piss, I promise you I'm going to personally kill you before the world ends."

"I wonder if he's evil," Eliot says.

"What?"

"I said, I wonder if my duplicate is really such a bad guy."

Tom shakes his head.

The Rummy lifts off.

The end is nigh.

Ω

At 15:00 GMT, 3.2 billion inhabitants of Planet Earth and several hundred people in orbit tune in to the Apocalypse Channel to watch the *Peace in the Mideast Summit Telethon*. They watch on mediawalls from luxury penthouse suites; on primitive tube-based televisions connected to satellite and cable feeds; on mediashades and -glasses, palmtops, tablet computers; on foot-pedal-powered laptops that pipe in wireless feeds; on televisions embedded in the underside of bunks in corporate dormitories for armies of service workers. On Copacabana Beach near Buenos Aires stand three hundred thousand people who watch the *Summit Telethon* on a twenty-story projection screen; this is the largest gathering here since the Stones played back in January of '06. In Jakarta's Freedom Square, hundreds of thousands of Indonesian citizens stand watching four screens set up around the Monas Monument, not far from Istiqlal Mosque, Southeast Asia's largest. In Tiananmen Square ten screens have been set up for a million Chinese.

Wherever they are, every viewer is paying, directly or via the feeds they pay service providers for, royalties to the Apocalypse Group, owner of the Apocalypse Channel. The Apocalypse Group is in turn redirecting some fraction of its money to Horned Goat. In addition to the pay-per-view fees flowing in, advertisers have paid huge sums of money to slot ads in thirty seconds before the official livestream begins. Other companies have pursued the path of product placement. POTUS Jim Friendly is wearing Nike Basketball Leadership Line Sneakers, Air Powers, sneakers improbably shaped to resemble cowboy boots. Secretary-General Chang Yin-Xiong, here as an observer for the UN, is wearing decorative earbuds and matching mediashades, round and highly stylized, by LV. Caliphate and Israeli heads of state are wearing Puma- and Adidas-branded merchandise respectively, for obvious reasons. After all, Rudolph Dassler, the founder of Puma, was a more devoted Nazi party member than his brother Adolf, who founded Adidas; some rumors maintain that they split their sneaker company in two for political reasons.

Eliot is watching the *Summit Telethon* on the head-up display of the visor of his helmet. The local time is now exactly 5:00 p.m. On his visor a dancing animated red heifer begins singing about the virtues of universal surveillance. "The *Peace in the Mideast Summit Telethon* is brought to you by Omni Science!" the goofy cartoonish cow announces.

The *Summit Telethon* begins. Tonight's event is being held on a stage set up in front of the Western Wall, which has long been a sort of outdoor temple. About one thousand dignitaries, their heads all respectfully covered with kippahs, sit on the stage, five thousand VIPs below, in the audience. On television the stage looks gigantic, majestic. In person, some elite bloggers snarkily comment, it's somewhat less impressive. Other bloggers note that members of the Vanderthorpe Family are part of the POTUS's coterie, which includes, along with ranking members of the Friendly administration, Retired General Richard Dickey (partner at and official representative of the Leviathan Group), Media Mogul Roger Murphy (a board member at the Apocalypse Group and CEO of the Nonlinear Television Corporation), and various evangelical leaders.

"Eliot R. Vanderthorpe, Jr.," one blogger comments, "is especially noteworthy of attention, given the recent disasters that have befallen him." In only a matter of days, he has made a near-miraculous mediasphere comeback. The change is evident in his posture, in his choice of words, in his whole more-professional attitude toward the mediasphere. This new and improved Eliot—Aliot—is wearing an exclusively tailored Josephus Marty suit with a very white tie on which the faintest trace of a crucifix pattern is discernible. Smiling, behaving in a perfectly civilized manner, he shakes hands with the many dignitaries. The young man says something that makes POTUS Friendly laugh. Amateur lip readers all over the world are already trying to reconstruct what the Vanderthorpe kid has just said. The POTUS's coterie hasn't yet begun to mingle with the Caliph's. This will be a major part of the forthcoming formal introduction ceremony and is eagerly anticipated by the viewing world. From across the stage, Caliph Fred catches the young man's eye and smiles. Aliot smiles slyly, as if he's remembered some sort of private joke. Sarah comes up beside him and kisses him on the cheek. They seem so happy together, so very much in love.

Ω

Tom once, years ago, convinced a reluctant Eliot to go skydiving with him in Orange, Massachusetts. Eliot had gone tandem with Tom, harnessed to his friend's parachute system. Free fall was less scary than he had expected. Like floating in a dream, air pressing against his suit, Tom in control. The opening of their ram-air chute was a cold shock, like waking up from that dream, a sudden reorientation. What does it feel like to die? he had wondered the whole time. Though the landing had gone well enough, without incident, this feeling of proximity to death had convinced him to never go skydiving again, much to Tom's disappointment. As he watches Jerusalem's streets, the uneven jigsaw of lattices far below, Eliot wishes he had given skydiving more of a chance, and paid more attention to what Tom had tried to teach him.

"Has the end of the world started yet?" Tom asks Eliot.

"Not as far as I can tell, man. How long till we get there?"

"Soon. I'm trying to lift up as high as I can so that we'll be at a safer altitude. I'm going to be feeding some important information into your visor."

A satellite map replaces the video feed of the *Summit Telethon* on Eliot's visor. Their helicopter is very rapidly approaching the Old City. On the right-hand side of the display there's a live feed of the stage, an aerial shot, not from the official broadcast. From this viewpoint, individuals look much like ants. Near the center of the stage, a strange red oblong blob is moving.

"Is it coming through, Eliot?"

"Got it."

"I'm going to switch on the overlay for the stage. That's the most important thing. When you jump, the image of the stage will become centered on your HUD. Focus your eyes where you want to land." Data overlays the aerial shot, transforming blurry individuals into sharp green dots. Eliot's targets, marked on the display as "Aliot" and "Fred," appear in a darker shade of green.

"Do you have your parachute on?" Tom says.

"Yeah," Eliot says.

"This isn't like what we did in Orange. This system's automatic. There are some manual controls and an override button on the suit's chest. But you don't need to do anything. Just let the computer take care of everything—remember, look at the spot on the stage where you want to land—and don't resist what the chute does. It's smarter than you are."

"I have no doubt about that, man."

Wanting to look out onto reality for a moment, Eliot lifts up his visor. The Old City's narrow streets snake in all directions around them. The damaged Dome of the Rock is brightly lit from below. In front of the Western Wall, the stage is set. *Why am I doing this?* he wonders. *Why is the world worth saving?* Before he can think of an answer, all at once, everything that Eliot has been preparing for happens.

A smoke screen explodes around the Rummy to block snipers'

lines of sight. Eliot pulls down his visor, and the actual image of the scene below disappears behind the HUD data. The chopper door flies open. His fingers grasp the handholds above the door. White smoke is everywhere. The ground appears only as a representation on his visor, all in green. The wind is terrific, unbelievable. The air is hot. Hanging out the side of the chopper, terrified, Eliot hesitates.

"Maybe killing everyone on that stage is the most ethical path," Eliot says. "I would miss my family, but maybe dropping a bomb down there is the decisive action we need to take."

"This isn't a fucking video game," Tom says. "Jump. I have to pull the helicopter away. IAF frequencies are going crazy. They think some kind of rocket hit us."

"Okay, already," Eliot says.

Eliot drops from the side of the Rummy into pure whiteness. Everyone on the stage seems to be looking up, except for the strange unmarked red oblong blob, which stays in place, flanked by two guards. In the confusion below, Aliot seems to be heading in the direction of Caliph Fred. Eliot isn't sure if he will reach the stage in time, but there's nothing he can do about that now.

$$\Omega$$

To officially kick off the *Summit Telethon*, Caliph Fred sings an introspective solo cover—a heartbreaking rendition, really—of Frank Sinatra's "My Way," licensed at great expense from the Michael Jackson Music Corporation, a sign among others of the Caliph's tremendous personal wealth. Some of the lyrics have remained the same. Some have been changed.

> For what's an Imam, what has he got?
> If not Al-lah, then he has naught.

The song goes on this way. At the end of the performance—which mournfully but also somehow triumphantly reaffirms that the Caliph, in the end, did do it his way—sniffling and sobbing becomes audible from the crowd. Even the POTUS seems genuinely moved, removing his big black cowboy hat and placing it carefully beside his chair, standing up, the first to clap, the first contributor to Caliph Fred's standing ovation.

"What class!" Douchebag says. "What style!"

Caliph Fred goes down the line of standing clapping dignitaries shaking hands and smiling broadly with a glow of triumph, taking his time as he approaches the American coterie. While waiting for the Caliph to make his way over, the POTUS whispers something to his pal, Omni Science CEO Eliot R. Vanderthorpe, Sr. The CEO's beautiful and charming wife, Daisy Vanderthorpe, and his son, the newly born-again Eliot Jr., join in on the conversation. They all laugh. Lip readers can't quite make out what they're saying, but they sure do seem amused.

Just as Caliph Fred extends his hand, and POTUS Friendly reciprocates, a loud mooing comes from one corner of the stage. Heads turn and joyful applause rises up from certain segments of the audience. The Caliph seems displeased. An instant later, a patrolling Israeli helicopter—a Rummy—explodes just above the stage. "An attack," someone shouts. Cheers become first grunts and gasps of worry, then shrieks and screams of terror. Security guards run. Everyone scrambles. Eliot Jr. pushes through the crowd, moving purposefully toward Caliph Fred.

$$\Omega$$

Free fall exhilarates Eliot. The timer in the corner of his visor's field of vision indicates that his parachute will deploy in ten seconds. If he wants to, he can stop the parachute from deploying by pressing a red override button on his suit's chest control panel. He considers what it might feel like not to allow the chute to open, to strike the stage. Before he can consider these options further, his chute deploys. Eliot snaps into a new orientation, feet pointed down now. He keeps his eyes focused on the green dot labeled "Fred." Nothing else matters. Eliot emerges from the Rummy's huge smoke screen to find that he's very close to the stage. He prepares to hit the ground. In his peripheral vision, however, he notices the red oblong blob again.

What is that thing?

Unable to resist temptation, Eliot very briefly looks at the blob, and the parachute, sensing the change in his line of sight, reorients itself. Before he can refocus on the Caliph, an instant before he lands, the chute retracts into its casing. Eliot strikes the stage and rolls. Something hard arrests his motion: an actual, flesh-and-blood red heifer, the strange blob in his display, ready for live televised sacrifice. Eliot has missed his intended target; meters away, on the other side of the heifer, he sees Aliot and Caliph Fred, close to each other.

"We seem to have a new guest!" Douchebag says into his mic.

"Protect the Horseman!" shout Secret Service agents among themselves.

Secret Service and Caliphate security form a circle around Eliot and point rifles at his head. Eliot finds that the guns don't bother him as much as he might have guessed. They seem fake, part of this strange stage performance. Eliot removes his helmet and holds it away from his head. His arms are spread in a gesture meant to communicate that he poses no threat to anybody. A videographer approaches. Eliot looks directly into the camera and points at Aliot.

"I am the real Eliot Vanderthorpe and that man is an impostor! He is trying to assassinate Caliph Fred and start World War Three—or Four—or, maybe Five. Depends how you count these things."

Everyone turns to Aliot. Aliot, who has over the last few minutes closed in on Fred, pauses to process the situation, then grabs for the Caliph. Caliphate security agents push their way through the panicked crowd, shouting orders in Arabic. They won't get to the Caliph in time, Eliot realizes. Eliot can't do anything from behind this damned heifer. His knees fucking hurt. His mission is a failure. If only he hadn't looked away from the Caliph at the last moment.

A young woman in a tasteful black dress, a stylish head shawl, and three-inch heels has somehow gotten between Aliot and Caliph Fred. It's Sarah. With a single quick gesture, Sarah demonstrates that Ninjaerobics will do much more for you than merely give you killer abs. Before anyone can register her intervention, Sarah has tripped Aliot, twisted his arm behind his back, and jammed her knee into his back. She repeatedly slams his face into the stage.

"I knew it! I knew it! Date without having sex, you bastard? How could I possibly think you were Eliot?"

Sarah displays a kind of strength in anger that Eliot has never seen in her before. Her voice is quite hoarse by the time the Caliphate security agents pull her away. Aliot rolls on the stage and moans in pain. Sarah's Ninjaerobics assault has left him dazed, though not quite unconscious. Under the careful supervision of Secret Service gun muzzles, Eliot pulls off his parachute and flight suit.

"Should my snipers kill them?" asks Israeli PM Silverman.

POTUS Friendly hesitates.

"One of these two young men is probably my son," Eliot Sr. says.

Another pause.

"That means," Eliot Sr. elaborates, "Mr. President, Mr. Prime Minister, with the utmost respect, sirs, that I humbly suggest we hold off on sniping for the moment. We're livestreaming to the whole world, after all."

"And," Daisy adds, looking at the active camera, putting her arm around Eliot Sr., "despite the fact that he has often made many unwise choices, we do love our son very much, whichever of these two young men he happens to be."

"Sounds good to me," the POTUS says. "We all love our families."

"No problemo," PM Silverman adds. He says something Hebrew into his lapel, probably suggesting that his snipers maybe ought to stand down for now. An Apocalypse Group intern runs from the wings of the stage and hands Eliot a kippah bearing an advertisement for Falafel Hut. Eliot dons the yarmulke.

"So what do we do?" the POTUS asks.

"Well," says Retired General Richard Dickey, stepping forward, his arms politely clasped behind his back, always keen to the exigencies of live and televised geopolitical drama. "Mr. President, Mr. Prime Minister, perhaps we should do some kind of genetic scan to see which of these two young men is the *real* Eliot Vanderthorpe. So the world knows."

"That's a swell idea." The POTUS smiles. "Anyone have a genetic scanner handy?"

"Well," Dickey says, "I'm not sure."

It takes a few minutes of whispering for the masters of mankind to figure out that no one has a genetic scanner handy. People aren't sure what to make of this. The audience seems positively pensive.

"We don't need a genetic scanner to sort this out," Eliot says. "This guy probably doesn't know shit about applied philosophy. You could give us a test to prove it, but here's another idea. Look up footage from my private apartment suite at the Transcontinental Building from about a month ago, the night I got back from Barcelona. See if you can find video of my bared chest. I got a tattoo in Barcelona. The commentators and fan-scholars haven't noticed it yet. I'm guessing this guy doesn't have one on his chest. The tattoo, it's shaped like a fish, and it says 'Jesus Saves!' Well, just look at this."

Eliot pulls up his T-shirt and exposes his chest. Everyone looks blankly at him. His chest is empty. "Oh, hold on there," he says. He taps on his chest, waiting for the tattoo to turn on. It doesn't. "Oh, yeah, I think, ah, the tattoo was removed. Right. Sorry about that. I forgot. I was captured and Horned Goat, they, like, put this weird black and silver fractal tattoo shit on my face and body and then I had it washed off in a chemical bath, which is why my body is so swollen and puffy, but I really did have a fish tattoo on my chest that said 'Jesus Saves!' You'll find it in the video if you look in the archive. Promise."

A sovereign silence reigns over the crowd, viewers the world over slightly embarrassed at his failure to produce the tattoo. Sarah comes forward from the crowd.

"That is the real Eliot Vanderthorpe," she says, pointing—*thank God*—at the real Eliot.

"How do you know it's him, dear?" Daisy says.

"Only Eliot could be this stupid," Sarah says.

Tears well up in her eyes. Daisy hands her a handkerchief. Sarah's sad eyes lock onto Aliot, and she steps toward the Caliphate security agents that surround him; no one tries to stop her. She reaches out to brush his arm and then sinks back into the crowd without attempting further violence. A consensus instantly forms. Caliphate security agents shuffle closer to Aliot.

"It's the one who parachuted in!" Douchebag says. "He's the real Eliot! He's the real Eliot!"

"Mazel tov!" PM Silverman says and pats Eliot on the back.

Not to be upstaged before the world by his Israeli rival, Caliph Fred raises up his majestic thumb in Eliot's honor. "Salaam, dude!" he says. "You saved my life!"

"Okay, then," POTUS Friendly adds. "Let that poor stupid kid go!"

"You fucking rock," comes a shout from the British delegation. "That was awesome." It's William—he's whooping and pumping his fist. His mother, her mouth flat, seems displeased. Taking a cue from William, the audience goes wild. When the Secret Service agents finally back away from Eliot and lower their rifles, the Home Applause Index goes almost off the scale, all the way up to 0.95, which means that of the 3.2 billion viewers watching the *Summit Telethon* approximately 95 percent are responding favorably to this turn of events. Wherever he is, Karl Vlasic must be a very happy man right now.

Caliphate security agents lead Aliot away.

"What have you got to say for yourself, son?" POTUS Friendly asks Aliot.

Douchebag brings his mic over, but Aliot says nothing, betraying no emotion. Sarah looks at him longingly as they take him away. Professional lip readers will later claim that she mouthed something that looked a lot like "I love you."

For his part, Eliot feels ecstatic, not only because Sarah's pronouncement has persuaded everyone that he's really who he says he is (this is nice enough) but, more important, because Sarah has recognized him. Yes, she recognized him by means of his stupidity, but she was still able, through some near-mystical leap of recognition, to see an inner piece of Eliot that can't so easily be reduced to a conceptual map; that no surgeon's scalpel can reproduce; that is visible, finally, only to those who truly know him. Sarah was able to recognize Eliot for who he really is and, though she will probably never forgive him or love him (precisely for being who he really is), this momentary communion between them has set his stupid heart free.

$$\Omega$$

Acting on behalf of the Leviathan Group and the Freedom Coalition, Retired General Richard Dickey gives a twenty-slide briefing to the global viewership of the *Summit Telethon*. This briefing presents the Foresight System's predictions about the outcome of a hypothetical war between the Freedom Coalition, on one side, and the TransArabian Ca-

liphate and the Imamates, on the other. The briefing makes no mention
of the UN. Foresight's projections indicate that should the Caliphate
and Imamates unwisely choose to fight the Freedom Coalition, approximately 28.5 million of their peoples (plus or minus 3 million) would
perish in the subsequent skirmish. The Freedom Coalition would, for
its part, lose only 372 soldiers (plus or minus 2).

These results, Dickey says, are practically certain.

A call for the Caliphate's and Federation's immediate uncondi-
tional surrender follows. The Coalition demands that all remaining
elements of the al-Aqsa Mosque be bulldozed flat and that the Israeli
nonprofit firm, Temple Builders, Ltd., be allowed to erect the Third
Temple on the same location. The Apocalypse Channel would have
the exclusive right to televise the whole process. The Nonlinear Television Corporation CEO, Roger Murphy, has generously offered to
donate 10 percent of the Apocalypse Group's profits to Caliphate and
Imamate charities.

To help the peoples of the Middle East vote on their destiny, the
Leviathan Group, ever dedicated to the irreversible worldwide spread
of democracy-like institutions, has conveniently set up a service so
that mobile-phone-owning citizens of the affected countries can vote
on their leaders' policies. Results will be tabulated five minutes after
phone polls close. Dickey taps through his tab and the choices of
the phone poll appear in huge letters on a jumbo screen behind him.
Dickey turns to look at the display, squints his eyes to read the text.

Douchebag reads from a teleprompter.

"Given the strategic interests of the Freedom Coalition," Douchebag intones, "and the total certainty of the Foresight System's battle
scenario analysis and forecast, we have concluded that you, the peoples
of the TransArabian Caliphate and the Federation of Imamates, have
four choices in this geopolitical situation. Please select one of the following options:

"If you would like the Dome of the Rock to be fully bulldozed and the Third Temple built in its place, please phone: +234343 3432 09232.

"If you would like your civilization (and our civilization, too, frankly) destroyed and the radioactive moonscape of your remaining lands occupied by more or less nobody—'cause everyone'll be dead anyway—please phone: +234343 3432 09233.

"If you would like not to go to war and live in peace and say that Jews are okay and recognize okay so the Holocaust did actually happen and maybe they can sort of build part of a Third Temple in a little corner off to the side and if they want to kill the red cow and let a few Jews into the rebuilt parts of the mosque or temple or whatever, sure, why not, and wouldn't it be nice if we all lived in peace and didn't blow each other up? Wouldn't it? Please, for the love of God or Allah or any other supreme deity you happen to worship, please please please phone +234343 3432 09234.

"If you think all these options suck, please phone +234343 3432 09235."

Interpreters translate the content of this ultimatum in real time and type up translated versions for different geolinguistic zones. The POTUS, Eliot Sr., and PM Silverman look at each other in shock and horror. Caliph Fred and the Imams look merely confused.

Eliot Sr. leans over to Jr. and says, "What have you done, son?"

Eliot shrugs. "Nothing particular."

"Do you realize that, based on preliminary agreements we signed with the Caliphate and Imamates, we are contractually obligated to honor the results of this phone poll?"

"Didn't know that. But the whole legality thing. That's not going to be too hard to get around. No one pushes the Freedom Coalition around, right?"

Eliot Sr. shakes his head. "The legalities are beside the point, son. There is, or was, a framework of legitimacy at stake. It was important for the civil populations of these Arab and Persian states to agree to our terms. This was supposed to be an object lesson in participatory democracy by means of mobile-phone voting, but now you've gone and done a very stupid thing."

Eliot can't help but ask, "Do you think framing the choices the previous way was fair? I mean, I'm still not a believer or anything, but Jesus Christ was, like, a fucking socialist carpenter, not some kind of bloodthirsty warmonger."

Eliot means this to be understood as a biting insult, but Father acts as if he hasn't heard him. His froglike mouth expands across his face, forming a grimace.

"We didn't frame anything, son. These were just the two objective available geopolitical choices, the only coherent and logical and serious choices. We just reported them."

"But what if the voters had chosen the second option? Destruction and occupation."

"They wouldn't have. We ran simulations. We knew they would choose the first option. No one doubts Foresight's ability to predict the outcome of conflicts anymore. They would have chosen to allow the construction of the Third Temple, which we already knew from a careful reading of biblical prophecy. You've muddled up the field with your childish prank. Now, frankly, none of this much matters from God's perspective. The Third Temple *will* be built. My greatest fear is that when the end comes, you won't have already embraced Christ. Your mother, your brother, and I pray every day that you'll be born again before the end. That you'll hear the Good News before it's too late."

Eliot feels incredibly bewildered.

Father continues: "But I'm an optimist at heart. Yes, you've set our plan back by a few years, maybe a decade, but we're tireless warriors. We'll never stop doing God's work. Nothing can stop us. We may not achieve our lofty goals within my lifetime, but we know we're on the winning team. God will not be neutral in the coming war."

Eliot sighs. Douchebag announces that the phone polls are closed, that the results have been tabulated. Live and electronic audiences are silent, expectant. Millions and millions have dialed in, from every region in the Caliphate—the Nile to the Euphrates—as well as from the hundreds of Shi'a Imamates in the Federation. The jumbo screen displays the phone poll results:

OPTION 1: SUBMISSION: 3%
OPTION 2: TOTAL DESTRUCTION: 33%
OPTION 3: RECONCILIATION AND PEACE: 35%
OPTION 4: NONE OF THE ABOVE: 29%

"Looks like 'Reconciliation and Peace' is the winner by a narrow margin," Douchebag says.

"The people have spoken," Caliph Fred says. "Looks like we're at peace, guys."

Fred claps his hands above his head. Applause rises all around and pumps in from all around the world. World leaders shake hands with, hug, and high-five one another. They pat each other ceremoniously on the back. Caliph Fred smiles, gives his thumbs-up sign, and shouts again, "Salaam, dudes! Salaam!" Eliot can't believe how very willingly the Caliph accepts the results of the vote. It's as if nothing could possibly dent his optimistic mood, as if he was serious when he said in the *Bird* interview that he has modeled himself on Ronald Reagan.

$$\Omega$$

At Elijah's suggestion, Eye for an Eye celebrates today's sudden miraculous outbreak of peace by changing its name to Turn the Other Cheek. The newly christened band plays a punk medley of great American songs: "Somewhere Over the Rainbow," "My Funny Valentine," "Heartbreak Hotel," "Like a Rolling Stone," "Satisfaction,"

"Smells Like Teen Spirit," and so on, all with a punk 'tude and creatively inserted profanity. Turn the Other Cheek finishes off its set by playing the hell out of an extended version of its popular "Next-to-Last Temptation of Christ."

Not in the mood to listen to this musical extravaganza, Eliot strolls over to the side of the stage, away from all the cameras and the noise, hoping he might find Sarah. Instead he runs into Karl talking into his palmtop. When Eliot gets close enough, Karl gives him a fierce bear hug and kisses his cheeks.

"You are amazing!" Karl says. "Brilliant. You're a genius!"

Eliot lets Karl get back to his call and approaches the Holy of Holies. Almost two decades ago, when he last visited the Holy Land, Eliot couldn't look at the Western Wall directly, he had been so terrified of it. Crowds of Jewish men, their heads covered, were bowing and praying, filled with spirit. Now, the magic spell is broken, and this place seems merely desolate, almost ordinary. Shrubs grow in cracks in the wall. Handwritten prayers grout the space between its stones. By his feet, he finds a folded piece of paper, a fallen prayer. "Please God," it reads. "I am asking You for a new car, which I need sincerely." Feeling guilty for having intercepted someone's personal communication with God, Eliot jams the paper back into a crack.

Richard Dickey leans against an unused amp, smoking a cigar, bearing himself with iconic poise. Near the amp, over the red rump of the heifer, a pair of rabbis argue. The live televised execution of the heifer has been postponed until the political situation sorts itself out. Their argument escalates into a shouting match. The heifer moos, and both rabbis storm off with rage. The animal looks at Eliot with stupid cow eyes, poor creature. Eliot picks up a large brush by its feet and begins grooming it, moving his hand in long and careful strokes.

When he stops brushing, Dickey offers him a cigar. They smoke together in silence. The cigar has a dry complexity, with an aftertaste of apricots.

"You seem calm," Eliot says.

"I'm always calm," Dickey says.

"But aren't you angry at me?"

"Angry? Why, certainly not. You did good, Eliot."

"What about the Third Temple? The red heifer? Christ, the Constitution, and capitalism?"

Sanguine, Dickey shrugs. "Don't take your father too seriously. Forget all that. Strategic dominance and control are the only things that will keep us safe from the terrorists and the totalitarians and the collectivists. Energy, guns, and markets. We won a victory today, in no small part because of you."

"A victory?"

"Of course. Couldn't have turned out better if we planned it ourselves. Whatever the choices were, the Arabs and the Persians voted within *our* mobile-phone framework. Caliph Fred and his Imam backup singers accepted the result of the poll as legitimate. It's fantastic, really, a huge accomplishment."

"The Caliphate might have, like, voted for war within 'our' framework."

"We planned for that contingency. If Foresight had been wrong, and they'd voted to destroy themselves, we would've won anyway. Rods From God and lasers were already in their proper orbits, nukes ready to rain on those bastards. Even before the poll results would've been presented to the TV audience, we would've begun preemptively pounding the Caliphate and Federation back into the Paleolithic era where, frankly, I sometimes think they belong."

"But your forecasting models are full of shit," Eliot says. "What good are they if they couldn't anticipate the Fred assassination attempt. And the UN, they would've come in. Horned Goat's simulations were predicting a full World War."

"The shitbags at the UN wouldn't have done anything." Dickey puffs on his cigar and then blows smoke. "But you're right about one thing. Your father and I had no idea that your duplicate had gone and replaced you. Crazy business. We had no idea he had anything to do with this. We thought he was just a fanatical fan of yours."

Eliot drops his cigar. "What? You *knew* about him and you didn't say anything to me? Did you know I searched the Panopticon Database?"

"Of course we did. You think your father doesn't monitor his own computer?"

"All the decisions I made: The narrow miss with the Canadians in Berkeley. Getting kidnapped, tied up, and threatened with death. Parachuting in minutes before my duplicate could kill Caliph Fred. Did you know about any of that? Did you predict it?"

Dickey smiles. "Look, we're not omniscient or anything, kid. We knew about your database search, yes, but that's about it. What a terrific plan those Horned Goat guys had. Just stunning."

"You knew about Aliot, but you didn't warn me. You didn't say anything."

Dickey looks confused. "Don't take it so personally. Your father and I thought your duplicate was harmless enough, and we were busy. To be blunt, we had more important matters to attend to. In our line of work, we sometimes have to sacrifice our family life. It's tragic."

General Dickey winks and releases a perfectly formed smoke ring from his mouth. A dry breeze blows past the stage, carrying the ring into this late summer evening's fading light. Too stunned to respond, Eliot stumbles zombielike away from the retired general and the red heifer, past a throng of rabbis and interns, toward the full rapturous atonal frenzy of musiclike noise onstage. In the wings, his parents hold hands, smiling as their beloved youngest performs the final song of what will undoubtedly be the most important set of his career. Eliot exchanges glances with his father. Father puts an arm around him and squeezes his shoulder affectionately, all forgiven. Eliot blinks with impotent rage. In his most brilliant impersonation of an amateur vocalist, Elijah sings:

I'm enticed to do sin all the goddamn t-i-i-i-me, muthafuckas.
I wanna fuck, I wanna rob, I wanna kill all y'all muthafuckas;
But I'm not gonna, no I'm not gonna.
I'm not going to fuck, rob, kill all y'all!

Fuck you, you sinful fuckers you!
Fuck you, Sodom and Gomorra bitches,
All y'all dumb-shit brimstone-stinkin' Satanic mothafuckas, you!
That's a'ight, you shitbags, Jesus Christ has sa-a-a-ved my soul!

EPILOGUE
THE BOOK OF LIFE

HARVARD SQUARE CAN BE ALMOST
pleasant in mid-September. Though class is in session, the undergraduate swarms and spectacled professors who choke up Mass Avenue
are relatively relaxed and collected, alive with energy. The unbearable
summer heat, meanwhile, has loosened its deadly grip on the northeast. Eliot knows that most of Cambridge is owned and operated by
the Harvard Brand Management Group, but his knowledge that the
whole city is little more than a stage-managed redbrick playland for
the intellectually gifted children of the world's plutocrats no longer
bothers him. He hadn't realized he would miss Cambridge. This
place, more than any other, feels like his true and natural home.

Eliot wonders whether he still counts as a child. Last week, he
turned twenty-eight. He celebrated his birthday by hiking—for him,
it was more like limping—with Tom in the White Mountains. The
IAF had quietly discarded Tom's application after his theft of the
Rummy, and so he's back on track to B-School. Because Wharton
forced him to defer for the year, Tom has reluctantly had to accept a
six-figure job at Goldman Sachs as a Reputation Analyst.

On his birthday, Eliot gave himself the gift of not thinking about his future for a day. Eliot had quit his job at Omni Science and was still deciding whether or not he should return to grad school. It would be the easy thing to do, the familiar path. In the week following his birthday, he decided he should return: there was little nobility in the choice, but he could think about more wholesome futures while doing what came naturally. Grad school will have to do, for now. Harvard's applied philosophy department was quick to readmit him. And yet indecision still haunts him. He knows that this will not last long, that something will have to change, for real this time, and soon. His parachuting stunt at the *Summit Telethon*, which feels as if it happened a lifetime ago, to some different Eliot, has rocketed the value of ERVJ skyward. Karl is already drafting plans to split his stock. The frenzy around his growing Reputation ensures that he will never have to work a day in his life.

Eliot's stunt has also inadvertently changed the lives of many others. ERVJ turned out to be the best investment Pedro ever made. Using his capital gains, Pedro purchased a seat on the NYRE and has become a floor trader. He is taking classes at night and hopes someday to fulfill his lifelong dream of managing hedge funds. Many Eliotlovers and fan-scholars have also struck it rich. Some have even themselves become minor celebrities, lucky ticks on the back of his overswollen Reputation. The amateur fan-scholar Dominick McWillis, for instance, is now so sought after for his dialectical-materialist analyses of Eliot that he's able to generate a livable wage from speaking fees and book deals alone, not to mention the money he has made from investing in ERVJ. The first dedicated Eliot Jr. academic conference—a *professional* conference—will be held this spring right here in Cambridge at Harvard's Rupert Murdoch Institute for the Study of Celebrity Name Branding.

As he passes the Coop, his smartwatch rings. It's Karl. Eliot has financially freed himself from Father, but not from Karl. Father can no longer threaten him with disinheritance, can never freeze his accounts, but Karl still manages his Reputation, and, though he would never want to admit it, Eliot can't think of a person he'd prefer to have fighting for his interests.

"Karl, man."

"Greetings from the freeways of LA, El. You're on speakerphone. I'm with your brother."

"Hi, Lij."

"Hey, bro," Elijah says.

Turn the Other Cheek (né Eye for an Eye) has just released a new single, which has topped the worldwide music charts, called "Apocalypse, Not Right Now." In a rather dramatic break with the rest of the evangelical Christian punk community, Elijah has decided to agitate on behalf of *not* destroying human life and civilization and has even reverted to his Vanderthorpe surname, dropping Apocalypse. Many critics decry the negativity of Turn the Other Cheek's peacemongering, but it's a brilliant move from a marketing perspective, the only perspective that counts for Karl.

"How's the anti-Apocalypse trade, Lij?"

"The Man ain't into our new direction, bro, so we're going to have to show all those Establishment bitches the righteous way with this new mediasphere distribution deal we're workin' on. And hey, guess what, I've written this new song, bro. Wanna hear? Yeah, 'course you do. It goes something like this—"

"Lij—Lij, I have complete faith in you. You too, Karl."

"Don't you worry, El," Karl adds. "Turn the Other Cheek will make out very well in this deal. I have it all mapped out. It's our peace dividend. We're riding this new Love of Life megatrend. I've never seen anything quite like it. Big stuff. But that's not why I called. We're talking one-on-one now. El, you have another thirty interview requests."

"I saw those on email. And said no to all of them."

"Yes, but I think you should reconsider the *Esquire* one. Kaja knows the reporter they've assigned to the story and says she's fabulous. Kaja kind of wants to set the two of you up."

"I'm not doing interviews or photo shoots. And I'm not going on blind dates, Karl."

"Think about it. That's all I'm saying. Kaja will be sending you an email with more information. But the real reason I called, El, is to talk to you about this Bildungsroman Channel business. So, they're willing to drop the civil arbitration proceedings, but they want you to work with them. They want to exercise their option on your reality bioseries."

"How many times do I have to say no? I'll pay whatever I owe them. I have the money."

"I think I've found a solution that might please all parties."

"I very much doubt that, Karl."

"Disney has offered to drop the suit and shelve the bioseries in return for the exclusive right to develop a movie about your life. *Fictionalized.*"

"I—"

"You wouldn't be involved in any way."

"Karl—"

"They're thinking of casting Moses as you. I ran into him in Beverley Hills. He's *really* into the idea."

"You serious? He's so fragile and willowy. He looks nothing like me—"

"Let them buy the film option and they'll drop the arbitration suit—blank slate. Think about it, El. They'll never make the movie, so we're talking a genuine win-win here."

"They won't make the movie why exactly?"

"They think they want this now, but securing the relevant rights will get so nightmarishly complicated that they'll eventually lose interest. They'll have to get the Pentagon, the Caliph Fred Entertainment Group, Horned Goat, the Participatory Economics Network,

The Book of Life \ 281

just about everyone to sign on. And all parties will want the right to approve the final screenplay. No way in hell does this see daylight. Have I ever been wrong about this sort of thing?"

"I'll think about it, Karl, but I'll probably still say no."

"I'm meeting with the Disney people for lunch later today. I'll try to hold them off a little longer. But okay, since I have you on the phone, we should discuss the actual real reason I called, which is—"

"Karl—"

"—the Vanderthorpe Family secondary stock offering—"

"—I also have a very important meeting I'm already late for, so I'll have to call you later today, and we can talk then."

"Okay, El, but it's important we talk about this sooner rather than later."

Karl hangs up.

Eliot wants nothing to do with the secondary offering, which looks as if it will be nothing short of a world-historical event, just the sort of spectacle the NYRE likes. Every time Karl has mentioned the secondary offering during the last few weeks, Eliot has found creative new ways of changing the subject. Eliot refuses to talk to Father and is maintaining only limited contact with Mother, who is busy writing a new book about the proper way to raise Christian children. Against all his most ingrained instincts, Eliot has decided to go into therapy. His daddy issues need to be resolved, his therapist says, and he could probably stand to improve his relationship with his mother too, but Eliot wonders whether any amount of analysis will ever unknot this tangled mass of mental rope. He may someday learn to hate his father a little less than he does, or may better understand why his mother acts the way she does, but that day hasn't yet arrived, nor will it anytime soon.

Ω

Sarah looks emotionally calmer and more beautiful than ever when Eliot meets her in front of the Tangiers Café, the site of their first official date after The Kiss, a decade ago. She wears a starched white button-down shirt, a sleekly elegant gray skirt, black stockings, and flat black shoes. Her hair, straightened, sweeps backward with a clean line. She is not wearing her bracelet. Her easy smile surprises him. He hasn't seen her smile so calmly in a long time, for years maybe.

She kisses him on the cheek. "How are you?"

"A complete basket case," Eliot says. "I think I'm going to be in analysis for about a decade."

"Are you joking? I sometimes can't tell."

"I am joking. But I've also actually hired myself a shrink."

Sarah shakes her head. "You always thought my being in therapy was a big joke."

"Rest assured, I still do. But, man, a big joke sounds like a wonderful thing right now."

A tattooed waitress seats them at a corner table. The café is almost empty. Eliot orders a double espresso, Sarah a pot of jasmine tea. The nervousness that had haunted Eliot on his way here transforms into a comfortable, nostalgic love.

"I have to say, Sarah, seeing you makes me feel—I can't believe it. You're talking to me."

"I asked to meet with you. I came up from New York. What's so hard to believe?"

"Well, gee, where do I start? You disappeared after the Telethon, didn't return my calls. I just imagined that, well, that you must really hate me, hate everything I've done to you, all my lies and betrayals and deceit and stuff."

"I've never hated you," Sarah says. "Hate is such a powerfully negative emotion. I've always loved you. I've also been furiously angry with you, again and again."

Eliot blinks with bafflement.

"But this time, I had no idea," Sarah continues, "no idea about anything, the difficult circumstances you faced. I think you really meant it when you said you wanted to fix your life and become a better person. And that you wanted to be with me."

"Does that mean—" Eliot gets misty-eyed. "Do you want to get back together with me? Is that why you've asked to see me?"

Sarah's warmth subtly withdraws. "I think, well, darling, my experience with Al has helped me realize that you and I were never right for each other. I've spent almost a decade of my life loving and, for long stretches, being with, well, the wrong person."

"The wrong person. That would be me."

"Don't feel bad. I think we were both fooled. You spent the same decade in exactly the same bad situation, not counting the dozens of other women you slept with, of course. And I'm so sorry about that—that you were deceived, not about the other women—sorry that we were both so mistaken about our relationship. I do love you, but I'm not *in love* with you."

Eliot waits for her to continue, sensing that she has something more to say.

"Eliot, this is hard for me to say, but, the truth is, I'm *in love* with someone else. With Al. He's so—"

"In love with Al? You can't be in love with him."

"He's a lot like you, but he's also nothing like you. He's more tender, more passionate about life, politically committed, and. . . Look, I'm so sorry, darling. I think Al is destined to do great things. And I'm going to be there with him when he does those things."

"Sarah, he's in the Marxist-Leninist Chamber of Commerce. They *opposed* PEN."

"His politics are very complicated," Sarah says.

Last Eliot heard, Stan and Troy have, despite the failure of the assassination attempt, made billions of dollars from their ownership of the al-Aqsa attack under CRAP. In return for their pledge to help rebuild a market-based economy and eliminate the last vestiges of the Participatory Economics Network in the Bay Area, POTUS Jim

Friendly has pardoned them for any crimes they might (inadvertently) have committed. At their request, the POTUS also pardoned Aliot.

"He wanted to kill Caliph Fred, Sarah. You're in love with an *almost murderer?*"

This claim visibly upsets her. "It wasn't like that, Eliot. I don't want to go into it now, but the reasons for what he wanted to do, everything was so complicated. To be so black and white about these things—"

"Sarah! He shot me in the chest with a dart gun."

"He never meant to hurt you."

"What do you see in him?"

"His political convictions are very powerful. It's hard to explain, but he's incredibly confident and he has convinced me that the road to ending the reign of capitalism isn't to build nonhierarchical economic alternatives in the present but rather, paradoxically, to embrace Total Capitalism. Objectively, that's what *has* to happen, the only way. I had never looked at things like that before. It's one of those startling realizations, it just gives you chills. So, Al is starting a financial services firm in San Francisco, working with Stanislaw Hadrian and Troy Forester to rebuild the Bay Area's market. I'm so excited. Oh, Eliot! I'm moving back to San Francisco!"

Sarah smiles, at peace. Some cognitive curse has finally been lifted from her. Eliot recognizes this equanimity for what it must be, the by-product of newfound faith. Aliot's God of Total Capitalism has given Sarah a foundation of belief upon which to steady herself. And who could hate her happiness? Eliot knows Sarah will never need her bracelet again and so is happy for her, though he can't help feeling as if her peacefulness has come at the expense of other parts of her that he always also deeply loved, her sense of justice, her powerful and sexy discontent.

"And you asked me here, you came all the way up here, why?"

"To tell you. To tell you in person that I forgive you. Al suggested I do this. I feel so much better now. I also came to give you this."

Sarah hands a pink envelope to Eliot. The envelope is bulky, expensive-looking, calligraphy-covered. He sticks his index finger under the flap and tears it open. Inside, there is an off-white card made of heavy-stock paper. "We Invite You" is written on the front in a fancy script. An elaborate lattice of trees, flowers, and humming-birds lines the outside border. He opens the card, reads it, and drops it in shock onto the table.

Mr. and Mrs. Jerry Glickman and Mr. and Mrs. Tobias Smith
invite you to share in the joy of the marriage that shall unite their children,
Sarah and Albert.

Details about the ceremony and reception follow.

They're getting married. In San Francisco. Inside the envelope, Eliot also finds a loose picture of Sarah and Albert hugging each other. His name is Albert. Albert fucking Smith!

"We want you to come. It's not for another year, but it would mean a lot to me if you did, if you would say yes. Say yes. Say yes for me."

Eliot's breathing becomes labored, his eyes increasingly moist. His heart races. His shrink has suggested that Eliot breathe more slowly and imagine himself lounging on a peaceful beach whenever these panicky feelings invade his mind. Eliot gives this a try and what might have become a full-fledged anxiety attack passes.

"Of course, Sarah. You know I will. Anything for you."

Sarah wipes tears from her eyes with a paper napkin. They sit quietly while she sips her tea. Their waitress cleans the table behind them, plates clacking together. Eliot has no desire to touch his coffee. Laughter emerges from the kitchen. Sarah finishes her pot of tea.

"I have to go, darling."

"You just got here, Sarah. Can't you—"

"This is a bit too much for me, too emotional. But thank you so much again. I'll see you in a year."

Sarah stands up, grabs her purse, and gives Eliot a final kiss on the cheek. Then she's gone.

Eliot studies the wedding invitation. Once rereading it again and again becomes too unbearable, he closes it, puts it back into its envelope, and stuffs the envelope into his bag. He discovers that he is laughing, that he suddenly finds this development not tragic but rather somewhat hilarious. For the first time in a long time, his life feels substantial, as if it belongs to him, as if the choices he will make matter, as if these choices will influence the path of his one real life, leaving a trail of existential breadcrumbs that future generations of (equally real) people might choose to follow. That feeling of reality startles him.

His smartwatch rings, Karl again. Eliot turns off the ringer.

Eliot pays the bill and heads down Massachusetts Avenue, toward his newly purchased condo near Central Square. He wants Sarah's pending marriage to count as a happy ending, but some part of him can't accept this conclusion; his initial ethical revelation in Barcelona still haunts him, foreclosing contentment. Whatever else has happened to him, the moral thing that erupted into his mind hasn't gone into remission. If anything, it has only metastasized, secretly colonizing, under the cover of this last month's madness, more and more of his sense of self. He sometimes would call this thing Sarah, would love and resent her through it as if she were a moral principle, but she has gone and undermined his ability to treat her as anything other than the human being she is. And such a conceptual misrecognition, he speculates, would insult not only *her* but *it*. It demands a new name for itself.

So sure, Eliot's still-nameless moral thing lectures him, the near future looks comparatively less terrible for you, but how does the future look for residents of the world's many Riot Zones; for the refugees and war victims; for anyone who is even remotely aware that the threat of global annihilation has only in fact been temporarily postponed? Hold on, Moral Thing, says an older, less empathetic part of him. Life is hard. What're we supposed to do? Care for your own interests. Others will care for theirs. Everything will sort itself out, in the end.

Eliot has to decide which of these voices to take seriously. A heavy sadness, perhaps whatever it was that once hexed Sarah, now afflicts his mind. Eliot has no idea what he's supposed to do, but he thinks he wants to find out, to make himself slightly less stupid, to assault his father's cultivated brand of insanity with heavier intellectual ammunition than he has on hand, and—most of all—to be worthy of the love that Sarah will never be able to give him. Even if it is his destiny, as he suspects it is, to go through life fundamentally alone, he might in time learn to love or at least respect himself. This will not be easy. There is no quick fix, no simple solution.

A ringing bell, not his smartwatch, causes him to pause. The sound comes from a spacious bookstore on Mass Ave. Hundreds of offprints, the work of years condensed into little paper bricks, are visible through the window stacked on tables and shelves and in display cases. Browsers comb bookshelves upon which many lifetimes of reading sit. A breeze cools his face as he watches the people read. On a rack near the entrance, from the fold-out cover of a glossy New York lifestyle magazine, the Eliot Vanderthorpe Brigade smiles at him. Overcoming an instant of hesitation, Eliot pushes the door open and its bell chimes with what sounds to him like an acceptable simulacrum of grace.

FOR I TESTIFY UNTO EVERY MAN THAT HEARETH THE WORDS
OF THE PROPHECY OF THIS BOOK, IF ANY MAN SHALL ADD UNTO
THESE THINGS, GOD SHALL ADD UNTO HIM THE PLAGUES THAT
ARE WRITTEN IN THIS BOOK:

AND IF ANY MAN SHALL TAKE AWAY FROM THE WORDS OF THE
BOOK OF THIS PROPHECY, GOD SHALL TAKE AWAY HIS PART OUT
OF THE BOOK OF LIFE, AND OUT OF THE HOLY CITY, AND FROM
THE THINGS WHICH ARE WRITTEN IN THIS BOOK.

REVELATION 22:18–19

ACKNOWLEDGMENTS

Many people have made *Pop Apocalypse* possible, far more than I can thank in this space.

My immediate family—Dad, Mom, Sabrina—has always unwaveringly supported my passions, hobbies, and aspirations.

John Mullervy read several drafts of this book and gave me detailed feedback. He has more generally been—both in person and via IM—an invaluable sounding board for my many crazy ideas since 1992.

Ian Bagley, Claire Bowen, Katherine Boyd, Parween Ebrahim, Ed "Rummy" Finn, Rebecca Hanovice, Mina Hochberg, Jenna Lay, Aaron Lowenkron, Saikat Majumdar, Mark McGurl, Jon Peck, Matt Pyle, Kate Racculia, Sarah Richardson, Lisa Schwartz, Navin Sivanandam, Stephanie Smith, and Jonah Willihnganz—among others—read early and late drafts of this book. They were all incredibly encouraging and sharp-eyed readers.

I thank Barron Bixler for offering me his expert services. Check out his Web site, darkstarphotography.com.

Heather Green (née Farkas) was the missing—and crucial—link.

Ginny Smith, my fabulous editor, knew what to keep and what to cut. She helped turn my manuscript into a book.

Bonnie Nadell arrived just in the nick of time.

Julie Prieto, meanwhile, has courageously and lovingly acted as something like a human control rod to my occasional radioactive bursts of mania. Thank you so much—for Ninjaerobics, for telling me my original title sucked (it did), and for always being on the other side of the table in the café.

Insights,
Interviews
& More …

About the author

Meet Lee Konstantinou

LEE KONSTANTINOU was born in 1978 in New York City to Greek immigrant parents.

He went to college at Cornell, where he majored in English and psychology and wrote his thesis on Art Spiegelman's Holocaust graphic memoir, *Maus*.

After graduation, Lee escaped the snow and cold of Ithaca by moving to the Bay Area to work as a technical writer for Oracle. This was maybe not the best idea he ever had.

After spending two years exploring the strange and terrifying world of corporate America, Lee started a doctoral program in the English department at Stanford. This proved a better idea, overall. Lee is writing his dissertation on contemporary postironic literature and hopes maybe someday to get a real job.

Lee holds nothing against irony.

Lee lives in San Francisco where he haunts the cafés and bars of the Mission district and is working on a second novel.

Pop Apocalypse is his first novel.

A Conversation with Lee Konstantinou

So, Lee, who would you say are your biggest literary influences? Your biggest comedic influences?

Oh, yeah, start with a simple question, why don't you? My list of favorite writers is so long and varied that I literally don't know where to start.

Let's try chronological order. When I was in high school, I read an ungodly number of science fiction and fantasy novels and loved superhero comics. Neal Stephenson and Dan Simmons emerged as my favorite writers from that epoch of my life, and they're still favorites. When I first read *Snow Crash*, I had that "top of the head coming off" feeling you sometimes get when you're a geeky sixteen-year-old boy and you read something genuinely new. Readers of *Snow Crash* will realize how shameless a literary thief I am.

In college, I became all serious and avant-garde. I went through a modernist phase, where I came to pay my proper respects to the giants: Joyce, Woolf, Conrad, Faulkner, and so on. Joyce remains an especially inspiring and powerful example for me.

But postwar fiction has had more of a direct practical impact on me, in terms of my sentences and plots. Here is a partial list of writers who have most shaped my sensibility and style, presented here in no particular order: Ralph Ellison, Thomas Pynchon, Ishmael Reed, Kurt Vonnegut, Philip Roth, David Foster Wallace, and Jonathan Lethem.

Lately, I've learned to appreciate William Gibson in a way I never did when I was younger. I've also been on a Cormac McCarthy kick.

I should also say that comics and video games and television and movies are all very directly "literary" influences, in a million direct and indirect ways.

Chris Ware's *Jimmy Corrigan*, Art Spiegelman's *Maus*, and Alan Moore and Dave Gibbons's *Watchmen* are favorites.

Charlie Kaufman's movies have consistently impressed me, and I enjoy Wes Anderson's ▶

movies now and then. *The Life Aquatic with Steve Zissou* was really underrated. Fellini and Truffaut are awesome. And you probably shouldn't get me started on Woody Allen. People complain about his recent films—I admit that they're not his best—but you have to respect his hyperproductivity. He's released a movie per year for a few decades now, and most have not sucked. And his best are absolutely stunningly brilliant.

What else? I bow, as I must, before the greatness of *The Wire*, *Arrested Development*, and the new *Battlestar Galactica*. My respect also goes out to the producers and editors of those amazing reality television shows on VH1. *Flavor of Love* and *I Love New York* are either advanced works of avant-garde subversion or just ordinary trashy fun. Either way, I'm a fan.

Which young authors do you admire?

Depends how you define young. Being under forty can get you called a young writer, which is a comfort. I can continue calling myself young for another decade. I'll stick to the under-forty set.

I've been following the McSweeney's people for a number of years. Heidi Julavits's novel *The Effect of Living Backwards* is incredibly bizarre, in a good way. Mark Z. Danielewski and Junot Díaz are a couple other authors I'm reading who might be said to be in their aesthetic orbit. There are some interesting novels coming out of their pirate headquarters in the Mission in San Francisco. I recently read Salvador Plascencia's *People of Paper*, which is a lot of fun, and wall-to-wall beautiful sentences. Stephen Elliott's *Happy Baby*, also originally published by McSweeney's books, is incredibly moving and sad.

I've also been following the minor proliferation of Young Intellectual Liberal Urban Men Dealing with the Difficulties of Life novels. Benjamin Kunkel's *Indecision* is interesting, as is Keith Gessen's *All the Sad Young Literary Men*, as is the whole *n+1* hub generally, though reading about one's own involuted problems in caricature can get to be a bit depressing after a while.

I tend to prefer transformed fictional realities and more indirect meditations on what's happening now. Cory Doctorow is doing terrific stuff with what you could call post-post-cyberpunk; anyone who has read *Down and Out in the Magic Kingdom* will immediately recognize how much I've swiped from him. Max Barry's *Jennifer Government* is morbidly funny, at times hilarious. As a comic book geek, I really enjoyed Austin Grossman's *Soon I Will Be Invincible*. Colson Whitehead is a phenomenal and hilarious writer.

Alex Shakar and Chris Bachelder are also people I've been tracking. They never had a proper chance to "go public," as it were, because their debut novels were published shortly before September 11, 2001. Shakar's *Savage Girl* is a funny and fascinating critique of marketing culture, and an inspiration for my interest in branding theory, and Bachelder's second novel, *U.S.!*, is extremely awesome and strange, about the continual resurrection and assassination of Upton Sinclair.

What inspired you to write the book?

Way back in '05, I was writing my dissertation proposal on postirony in American literature, and I was contemplating the years I would be spending in the library, and I said to myself, "I'm on the wrong side of twenty-five and I haven't yet completed a novel. What is *wrong* with me? How could this have happened?"

That, and I had recently read William Gibson's *Pattern Recognition*, a novel I found exciting. Gibson does something very brilliant with branding that I had never seen done in a novel before. I experienced something like professional envy and felt the urge to strike him down—by writing my own novel about branding. Take that, William Gibson!

Anyway, that impulse, which I'm maybe exaggerating a bit for effect, plugged into an idea I had been playing with since the late '90s for a very hardcore cyberpunk novel about a dystopian future where everyone lives in big skyscrapers and most of the planet is a wasteland covered in gray goo and young men and women of the new aristocratic class "go public" on a reputation market when they come of age. It was very derivative, cyberpunk cliché. Lots of explosions and ponderous technical exposition. I found when I combined that original idea with my newer obsession with branding theory, it all sort of, well, popped into place. I realized I could strip away the science-fictional trappings almost completely and achieve a far stronger effect if I set the novel as close to the present as I plausibly could.

Once that basic framework was in place, the characters and plot and everything else just sort of downloaded into my brain from wherever it is that novels come from. Eliot started jabbering and complaining in my head and he hasn't gone away since.

Have you ever stopped a coming apocalypse?

Funny you should ask. Just last week I stopped the Bog People of Berkeley from conquering the planet. Before that, I diverted an asteroid that was on a collision course with the planet. Next week, I have an even more spectacular mission, but I'm not allowed to disclose the details for reasons related to national security.

Unfortunately, unlike Eliot, I tend to prevent very poorly publicized apocalypses. I'm one of those guys who is constantly saving the world but never getting any recognition for my good deeds. Not that I'm complaining. I'm modest and selfless that way.

Who should play Eliot in the movie version?

If the casting director doesn't think I'd fit the bill, then someone who can be persuasively scruffy but who can also clean up good. Someone who can do cowed and confident—since he will also have to play Aliot. I've been told by those who would know better than me that Jake Gyllenhaal would be a good choice. ▶

A Conversation with Lee Konstantinou (*continued*)

Since we're on the subject, let me offer a few additional suggestions. Philip Seymour Hoffman would make a terrific Eliot Sr. And Daisy? Think Nicole Kidman. Some have suggested Natalie Portman would make an effective Sarah, but I'm not entirely convinced of that one yet.

Elijah might be hard. Part of the point of Elijah is that he's the golden child Eliot can never fully be: taller, better looking, more professionally successful. When he's sober, Eliot is just too self-consciously wracked with doubt and guilt and irony.

The most important casting challenge will undoubtedly be finding a red heifer that can act.

Is there another Konstantinou novel in the works?

Two, actually, both set in the same warped near-future world of this book—but with completely different characters and almost wholly unrelated plots.

The first project, *Hamsterstan*, is very much in progress. The book will prominently feature a giant intelligent talking hamster, a character with a lot more moral integrity and insight into how the world works than Eliot. I should have a draft finished by the time *Pop Apocalypse* is published, if all goes as planned.

The second project is a satire about the hideously destructive effects of climate change. I'm not ready to talk about that one yet, but it's all planned out in my head, and I think it'll be pretty funny when it's done.

Did Elvis impersonators play a big role in your dissertation?

Sadly, no. Then again, I'm a sucker for stories about doubles and duplicates and impersonators: Joseph Conrad's *The Secret Sharer*, Philip Roth's *Operation Shylock*, Charles Johnson's *Dreamer*. Charlie Kaufman's *Adaptation* is a personal favorite of mine. I like it even better than *Being John Malkovich*, which I also love.

Does Stanford offer a course in Intermediate Formal Logic?

Man, I wish. That would be *so* useful. Mostly English departments teach you how to do "close readings" of novels. Fortunately or unfortunately, little formal logic is required to do this, let alone formal logic of an intermediate caliber!

Which is harder, writing your dissertation or writing funny?

I write funny much faster. The problem with dissertation writing, I find, is that you need to do all this reading and research. Ugh! I much prefer making stuff up.

The thing that makes funny fun to write is that you're always your own first audience. If you can't make yourself laugh, then you're pretty clearly doing something wrong.

Is the end of the world nigh?

Basically, yes. We're fucked. Weapons of mass destruction are growing more numerous by the day. The leaders of most countries on the planet, including those in the "free world," are crazy lunatics. We're going to run out of oil pretty soon and kill each other and maybe go all cannibal on each other (read Cormac McCarthy's *The Road* if you don't believe me). And if *that* doesn't happen, our climate system may go haywire and all our ecosystems will be irreversibly broken and our planet will eventually resemble Venus. Then we'll be nostalgic for days when our problems were at least nominally under our own control.

There is no hope. We are all going to die, soon. Unless . . . unless every person on the planet buys *Pop Apocalypse* and reads it and internalizes my message of love and hope and redemption and transformation and democratic participation. If that happens, and only then, will there be hope for us.

That, I would like to add, would be my ultimate selfless act of world-saving.

Will the Eliot Vanderthorpe Brigade ever get their own animated show?

My people have been in talks with their people, but their people are holding out for a better deal. Bastards!

I do hear, however, that they're in talks to produce their very own combat simulation video game.

Does Eliot learn anything from his adventures?

I hope so—I really do—but I'm afraid I'm pessimistic. Things are not going to be so easy for Eliot for a long time to come. It's one thing to have a massive head-rush of a revelation that your life needs to be fixed, maybe just as much as the world needs to be fixed, but quite another to overcome the complex conditions that have put you (and the world) in that position in the first place.

If Eliot has learned anything, it's that he's a pretty ignorant guy. He knows that he doesn't know much of anything. That's not a bad place to start from, if you're trying to figure things out, but it's also insufficient.

So let's keep our fingers crossed.

How far away are we from the world of Omni and the TTSS, in your estimation?

The honest answer is: I have no idea. The pseudoconfident futurist answer is: Closer than you think!

London is already covered in a semi-Orwellian grid of CCTV cameras, to say nothing of the big cities in China. The US won't be far behind. Fortunately, at the moment, all these cameras capture lots and lots of unwatchable video. There just aren't enough people out there to see everything that is being recorded and computers are far too dumb to make sense of all that data. That's why the US government is spending billions of tax dollars to finance a vast privatized ▶

network of homeland security firms dedicated to making that footage useful. Many of these firms are working on making computers smarter at data mining and at finding patterns in an endless, bottomless sea of information, including video. We already have facial recognition software, which still sucks but is getting better with every passing year. None of this is a conspiracy, by the way. It's all out in the open. For software engineers, I'm told, a truly general video search engine would be something like the holy grail, the ultimate killer app, Google on crack. So lots of people, the greatest and best-financed minds of our generation, are working on solving this problem. If it can be solved, it will be. The only questions are: When will it be done and who will control the new technology?

What's scary about Omni—more so than the TTSS—is that it's not a system of centralized command and control, though it's also that when it's in the hands of the government. More disturbingly, Omni is at the end of a lot of trend lines that are driven entirely by a market logic. You don't just have Big Brother in the world of *Pop Apocalypse* but also, more menacingly, a lot of Little Brothers and Sisters, each of them pushed by various incentives to videoblog the entirety of their lives, to share that content with networks of friends, and to make much of that content publicly searchable. What Eliot's father realizes is that given the right incentives many of us will *voluntarily* provide the content that these high-tech, state-financed surveillance systems will subsequently mine. We kind of inadvertently build our own prison, one brick at a time.

The resulting surveillance state has all the effects of total surveillance but leaves a very small footprint behind. It's the macro-scale effects of these seemingly innocuous individual choices that become destructive and subversive. Of course, it doesn't have to be that way. We have a lot more control over our own lives and the future we collectively build than we usually let ourselves recognize. We can arrest those trend lines if we choose to. So okay, no, the end need not be nigh.

What was the most surprising part about getting your novel published for the first time?

Actually, working on the book with my editor turned out to be surprisingly rewarding. She's the one who made this whole publication thing happen for me. She helped me cut the fat from a flabby manuscript. It's so gratifying to take something you've spent years writing and to send it to someone you've never met, someone who has no particular incentive to like or dislike what you've done, and to have that person engage your work.

That's the other side of writing funny. You laugh at your own jokes, sure, and your parents and friends are sort of obligated to laugh, but what about a stranger? When that person laughs, and laughs at the *right jokes* for what you think are the *right reasons*, that's a genuine and rare and powerful moment of mutual recognition. ∿

From the *New York Times* Vows Section
Albert Smith and Sarah Glickman

SARAH GLICKMAN, a daughter of Liza Glickman and Jerry Glickman of Middlebury, VT, was married on Saturday evening to Albert Smith, the son of Mary Smith and Tobias Smith, of Eugene, Oregon. Berkeley-based Rabbi Sadie Rosenblatt officiated at Grace Church at the Presidio in San Francisco.

The bride, 28, will keep her name. She is a senior art curator for the Black Swan Culture Association, a nonprofit organization that tries to preserve art for future generations. She graduated from Harvard summa cum laude with a degree in art history.

Her father is a professor of history at Middlebury College. Her mother is a freelance journalist.

The bridegroom, 26, is an associate management consultant at Black Swan Industries (formerly Horned Goat), a Bay Area–based engineering and financial services company. He is a member of the Marxist-Leninist Chamber of Commerce and is dedicated to overthrowing capitalism by spreading its reach globally. He graduated from Yale with a degree in English.

His father is a city planner. His mother is a retired language arts teacher.

Attending the festivities without a date was the notorious celebrity playboy Eliot R. Vanderthorpe, Jr. (ERVJ), an heir to the multibillion-dollar Omni Science fortune. Asked to comment on the pending release of *Oh No You Didn't! Apocalypse*, a Hollywood thriller loosely based on the events surrounding last year's *Peace in the Mideast Summit Telethon*, Mr. Vanderthorpe scowled and replied, "No comment."

At the reception, held at Zen Chow at the newly reopened Fort Mason Center, Mr. Vanderthorpe, visibly drunk, and the bridegroom had a violent scuffle. A large punchbowl was knocked to the floor and shattered. No one was hurt. ▶

From the *New York Times* Vows Section
(continued)

Speaking through tears, the bride later said, "That's just like Eliot. That's just who he is. He can't help himself. But even *he* couldn't ruin this day. Other than the fight, this has been the most wonderful day of my life."

Ms. Glickman and Mr. Smith first met last summer when Mr. Smith kidnapped and replaced Mr. Vanderthorpe—then Ms. Glickman's boyfriend—as part of a conspiracy to initiate the Apocalypse. The conspiracy was not successful, but Ms. Glickman and Mr. Smith "found true love," according to Mr. Smith. ∾

An Abstract of *Sorting Problems with Young vs. Old Elvis Impersonators*

by Eliot Randolph Vanderthorpe, Jr., Ph.D.,
Harvard University, 162 pages

Abstract (Summary)

UNDER THE CRAP ACT, persons can own the rights
to conceptual descriptions that correlate to an
unbounded array of phenomena, including
objects, actions, and other persons. Though
almost universally hailed as a long-needed
rationalization of the previously confusing
patchwork intellectual property regime, some
unsolved problems remain for the new system,
the most challenging of which is the persistence
of what Ludwig Wittgenstein famously called
"family resemblances." In an effort to contribute
to the emerging field of Family Resemblance
Studies, this dissertation investigates the
philosophical and practical problems posed
by Elvis impersonation. Specifically, I focus on
the problem of Elvis impersonators who fuse
elements of Old and Young Elvis brand identities
in ways technically outside Elvis Presley
Enterprises' intellectual property suite.
    My first chapter reviews the dominant
theoretical accounts of how the CRAP Database
represents persons as conceptual descriptions
and investigates the Elvis conceptual description
suite owned by Elvis Presley Enterprises. My
second chapter ties this descriptive model to
the seminal legal case, Elvis Presley Enterprises
vs. So Lonesome I Could Kry Productions, and
shows how holes in the conceptual descriptions
owned by the Elvis Presley Enterprises led the
Supreme Court to rule in favor of SLICK
Productions. My final two chapters articulate
proposed changes to the CRAP regime that would
clarify certain aspects of the Family Resemblance
Problem. I redescribe Elvis as a polythetic class ▶

An Abstract of *Sorting Out the Problems with Young vs. Old Elvis Impersonators* (*continued*)

and, drawing on new advances in Prototype Theory, describe a hypothetical "Family Resemblance Indexical Extradiagetic Network Database" (FRIEND), derived from already existing and owned conceptual descriptions, which might settle once and for all the issue of temporally nonspecific Elvis impersonation. ෴

From the *Annual Report to Shareholders on ERVJ*

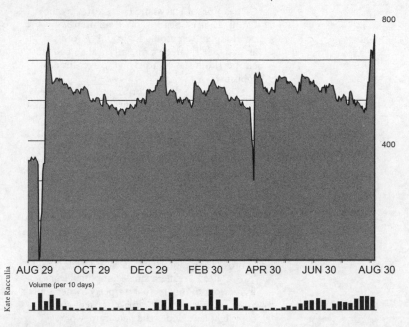

Kate Racculia

800

400

AUG 29   OCT 29   DEC 29   FEB 30   APR 30   JUN 30   AUG 30

Volume (per 10 days)

Summary

ELIOT R. VANDERTHORPE, JR. (Eliot), is a globally recognized celebrity brand. Eliot is largely famous for being famous, for his sexual escapades, and for helping to prevent the annihilation of the planet last year. Eliot is equally popular with boys and girls, mostly between the ages of nine and twelve years of age. Eliot has written a *New York Times* bestselling book of "casual philosophy"; he is the subject of the forthcoming film *Oh No You Didn't! Apocalypse*, which has received lukewarm reviews but is expected to do well at the box office. In the year since he saved the world, revenues associated with his Name have been growing and his Name is expected to continue its strong growth for the foreseeable future. Most analysts see a bright future for ERVJ. Recommendation: Buy. ∿

Glossary

Conceptual Descriptive Language (CDL)

CDL is a proprietary language created by the Omni Science Corporation. Built on new developments in modal logic and conceptual analysis, CDL can describe physical and abstract entities, both static and evolving over time, in robust ways.

The Omni Science Corporation has created bots that systematically transform all describable objects (image, text, video, music) on the mediasphere into CDL code, then caches it on the company's servers. These descriptions are also known as Names. The Omni Science Corporation makes its database of CDL codes searchable to the public for free, via the Omni Web site.

Conceptual Rights and Patents Act (CRAP)

Approved by the US Congress and eventually approved as an international standard by the WTO, CRAP creates a single simplified legal framework of intellectual property ownership and management that replaced patent and copyright law. Under the new framework, all intellectual property must be describable in the terms of CDL.

Foresight System

Foresight is a geostrategic software system, developed by the Freedom Coalition, which builds mathematical models of battlefield situations in order to help manage geopolitical strife and global counterinsurgency. Foresight has absorbed statistics on every war that has ever kept records and is continuously feasting on real-time data from the mediasphere and the Pentagon's military databases.

Freedom Coalition

A coalition of nations led by the United States whose mission is to spread free markets around the world and to crush terrorist and anticapitalist insurgencies wherever they might rear their ugly heads. It divides its strategic operations into two parts: an initial Leviathan Force, which destroys an enemy's military capabilities, and a subsequent SysAdmin Force, which manages the occupation and reconstruction of the defeated foe. The Freedom Coalition leadership council consists of the United States, the United Kingdom, Germany, Japan, India, Israel, and Singapore.

Leviathan Group

A corporation and think tank that developed the Foresight warfare simulation software system and that manages various geostrategic futures exchanges.

Mediasphere

A generic term that refers to the whole universe or ecosystem of networked digital media. This includes (what used to be called) the Internet, cable television, nonlinear television, the Total Terror Surveillance System, among other media inputs.

Name

A Name is a conceptual description, associated with a person, action, or thing. In the case of a person, the owner of a particular Name need not correspond to the person associated with that Name. All Names can be jointly owned. Owners of a Name have no formal control over (and no liability for) the actions of the person or persons comprising the Name, but they do have an interest in making sure the person's Name performs well. Name shareholders express their preferences through a board of directors and Reputation Manager.

Nonlinear Television (NTV)

NTV is a proprietary digital television system that comprises more than eight thousand established (thematically specialized and general interest) channels. Additionally, numerous ad hoc channels coalesce and dissolve per viewer and sponsor interest.

Omni

A software system that allows users to search for content in video and images based on conceptual descriptions.

Omni Science Corporation

A publicly traded corporation that created the Omni software system.

Participatory Economics Network (PEN)

PEN is a globally distributed populist anticapitalist movement that rejects corporate-capitalist, market-oriented, and centrally planned economic models. ▶

Glossary *(continued)*

Its decentralized network of producers and consumers is united by shared radical values and political objectives. The network aims to create a nonprofit cooperative economy modeled around public control of capital assets, negotiated coordination between producer and consumer councils, "balanced" divisions of labor within and across firms, remuneration proportionate to intensity and duration of effort, and worker autonomy.

Members of the network form collective bargaining blocs and provide IT services, preferential loans, and other forms of "cooperative capital" to member producers; they also provide informational resources, complimentary social services, and special rewards programs for consumers who patronize PEN-approved firms. PEN was crippled in North America after *Operation Win the West* destroyed the Bay Area branch of PEN and PEN-International was labeled a terrorist organization.

Reputation (Rep)

A Name's total market capitalization on the NYRE and other reputation exchanges. Often described in terms of the price a share of a Name can fetch on a reputations exchange.

Total Terror Surveillance System (TTSS)

A Homeland Security–built and –operated network and database that links together the CCTV systems of every state in the union and all shared video on the mediasphere.

United Nations (UN)

A formerly global collective security organization, the UN has become a more circumscribed group of nations dedicated to protecting the interests of a handful of remaining members after the United States, Japan, much of Western Europe, and other nations withdrew from it. Presently, the UN Security Council consists of China, Russia, Indonesia, Pakistan, and Brazil. United Nations HQ is based in Bandung, Indonesia. ∾

Don't miss the next book by your favorite author.

Sign up now for AuthorTracker by visiting www.AuthorTracker.com.